THE CLEANSWEEP CONSPIRACY

THE CLEANSWEEP CONSPIRACY

Chuck Waldron

The CleanSweep Conspiracy
© 2018 Chuck Waldron

Distributed by Bublish, Inc.
bublish.com
ISBN-10: 1-946229-01-6
ISBN-13: 978-1-946229-01-4

Also by Chuck Waldron
Tears in the Dust
Remington and the Mysterious Fedora
Served Cold

As with all my novels, this is dedicated to Suzanne first, last and always. You have made this wonderful writing journey possible. Your support is invaluable, your encouragement priceless, and your unconditional love is beyond measure.

CHAPTER 1

UNEXPECTED EVENTS

Matt Tremain saw all he could stomach. In shock at the destruction of his city, he turned off the television, wiping wet tears. All he could think was, *I warned them.*

...

"What the hell?"

"What's going on?"

"Mama, what are they doing? Does that man have a gun? They're scaring me!"

"Gun!" someone nearby screamed.

As Toronto's Subway #312 pulled into Osgoode Station packed with passengers, those in car number three were the first to know something horrible was about to happen.

All around them, fellow commuters began to transform, stripping away their coats to reveal militia-style uniforms. They began waving police batons, lead pipes, and machetes as the subway car approached the station. With a long shriek and hiss, the train came to a stop in front of the platform, and complete chaos ensued. Sounds of the train were instantly replaced with screams and moans as a growing militia of men and women exited from other subway cars and began their vicious assault on their fellow passengers. Over one thousand people charged toward the exit stairways and escalators, pummeling and slashing everyone in their way.

Shrill screams echoed in the underground station as shocked commuters—a growing number of them bleeding or clutching broken bones or crushed skulls—continued to scream, cry, and run toward whatever shelter they could find. The large subway platform's cream tile was quickly coated in bright crimson.

The militia had quickly dispatched the two police officers responding. Both lay dead in a pooling fusion of blood and coffee—a single bullet hole in each of their heads.

As quickly as the subway carnage began, it ended. The rogue militia raced to the exit leading to the city square above. Silent during their killing spree, several could be heard shouting, "Nathan Phillip's Square. Take up your assigned places..."

They speared their way through thousands of spectators gathered in the early morning for a chance to see celebrities and heads of state gathering for the Global Summit for Peace.

"Step it up," a militia leader shouted. "The bombs will blow any second." He held his right hand, looked at his watch, and gave a signal. "Now!"

The crowd, hearing a massive explosion in the distance, began to surge in all directions. Strangers pushed each other in panic.

A police officer watched, helpless, as the throng surged, first one way and then the other. He held up his hands to stop them from trampling those who had fallen.

● ● ●

"I was disappointed," a young man said, a phone to his ear. A waiter was on his way to work. "I hope the tips are better tonight. I'm going to take that job at the Mill Stree—"

He dropped his phone at the sound of the first explosion. He looked at the walls of a brick building, a former factory, seeing them belch outward as the shock waves heaved away from the point of detonation.

Then, the walls buckled inward as the trailing vacuum sucked them back. The waiter put his hands to the side of his head as the overpressure created an ear-splitting sonic boom.

The heat of the explosion released a thermal wave as newly exposed combustible material incinerated in microseconds. Fragments of bricks, plumbing pipes, window frames, and furniture spread out as small shards were expelled at super-hypersonic speed.

He was lucky. Death came mercifully fast. Overpressure ravaged his internal organs as shrapnel shredded his body tissue. A massive fireball immolated whatever was left.

• • •

Police radio traffic increased over the next seven minutes as five separate regions of the Greater Toronto Area were targeted. "What's happening? Report. I repeat, what's going on?"

At an intersection, men crowded around listening as one contacted their commander. "We can't get there, sir. The roads are all blocked."

To the east, firetrucks tried to respond as shockwaves from bombings leveled entire blocks. "Has anyone heard from unit..." the words fading.

The psychological shockwaves were about to begin.

"Authorize terror protocol," the chief said. "I want all nine divisional offices and eight area field commands on a war footing."

Off-duty uniformed officers scanned text messages. Detectives and commanding officers, along with all support personnel, were mobilized, each to a predetermined assignment.

The first clash between police and Free Eagle Militia forces ended with injuries on both sides. The militia carried away their injured, no trace left behind.

A division commander almost screamed. "They're storming a hospital on the east side." He ordered officers onto busses. At other locations, police officers listened in vain to radio traffic describing skirmishes with rioters and raided clinics, as people were beaten and left for dead.

"What can we do?" a first responder said, watching helplessly as buildings collapsed. Many could be seen kneeling, head on hands, weeping at the destruction.

Emergency medical technicians raced their ambulances through thick smoke, dodging bomb-scattered debris. "I can't hear you, say again." It was a familiar expression as the radio communications faded out and back in.

"Fifteen minutes!" a voice on Free Eagle Militia radios growled an order, "Implement exit strategy."

With that, 4,320 militia-style men and women began their withdrawal, fading like ghosts into shadows as stunned emergency responders stood quietly, hearing a soundtrack of breaking wood and hissing embers. With a sigh, more buildings collapsed. They listened to a haunting sound of screams, human screams that no longer had a human sound.

• • •

"This is Roger Naft, reporting for Action 21 News," the newsman said.

Behind him, images of destruction showed the enormity of the rioting. "The famous entertainment district has been destroyed," he added. "The market area's been leveled."

Video of burned out synagogues and medical clinics flashed on the screen. One video showed a woman in tears, the destruction of the Phipps Conservatory and Gardens in the background.

"The numbers are staggering," Naft said. "Thousands have been treated for severe wounds, and there are 737 confirmed deaths. Authorities are still trying to tabulate the number of missing."

He turned from one camera to another to with a look intended to show this was indeed serious news.

"While police won't confirm terrorism, the violence appears to be coordinated, with specific groups targeted," according to a police services spokeswoman. "Hospitals and clinics were stormed. We have witnesses who claim they saw a homeless woman beaten and dragged into a van."

Witnesses describe armed men and woman in camouflage-style uniforms, chanting anti-gay slogans and making derogatory remarks about refugees."

"What have you learned, David?" Naft said.

"Roger, I asked witnesses," the field reporter said before allowing them to speak.

"I saw it clear as day," one stated. "It said Free Eagle Militia. I'd never heard of such a thing."

Another witness said, "I watched them torching a Jewish church, what do you call it? A synagogue. It was like something out an old newsreel."

In the studio, Naft turned to camera one. "The clash between the police and the uniformed mobs ended as the order was restored by special agents from a new program called Operation CleanSweep. Militia type thugs left behind a city shrouded in smoke, its citizens dazed. Curiously, no militia member has been arrested. This is Roger Naft reporting for Action 21 News."

• • •

For Matthew Tremain, it should've been an ordinary day. It was a Thursday morning, his least favorite day of the week as he walked into Le Rôti Français, a popular coffeehouse in Yorkville.

When he came in, Tremain saw a woman watching him. He imagined she was staring at his slight limp. He was self-conscious about the limp. Evident, but not prominent, it was a result of a speed bump in his DNA's double helix, causing one leg to be a bit shorter than the other. It was like that the day he was born and the same thirty-two years later. He tried to pretend it didn't bother him as he glanced at the woman's sympathetic look. *I should be used to pity like that*, he thought. Still, it bothered him. A lot. He pushed anger aside and walked to the counter, looking at a caffeine menu filling an entire wall.

He tried to ignore the TV mounted on the wall. Since the riots, there'd been continuous coverage of the destruction. Action 21 News, the only station back on the air, had been airing commercial-free, nonstop updates. Matt felt anesthetized by the recurrent stories and images.

Running late, this morning, of all mornings! Fidgeting, he asked himself, *Why did I have to end up standing behind these two?*

CleanSweep! The word came, uninvited. *When did I first learn about CleanSweep? Tanner's e-mail! Was it really only a few weeks ago now?*

He brushed the thoughts away, listening to the discussion ahead of him.

"I'm going to have a latte," a woman said, sounding hesitant.

"Are you sure?" her friend asked. "You were going to try a cappuccino. If not, try an expresso?"

Matt wanted to scream, *There's no x in espresso.*

CleanSweep! The word clawed at his memory again.

"I do want something different," the first woman insisted. "I just can't make up my mind," she pouted. Finally, after what seemed like an interminable wait, she pointed vaguely. "What does a masha...machia..."

"Macchiato?" the clerk barked.

Matt gave the clerk an extra-wide smile when she handed him his order.

Walking toward an empty table, his phone started to vibrate. Struggling to get the phone out of his jeans pocket, he swiped at the screen.

His life-defining moment was time-stamped at 9:56 a.m.

Reading the warning he'd hoped he would never need, an emotional trapdoor opened under him.

Matt dropped his coffee cup. It cartwheeled to the floor, a woman screaming as the hot liquid splashed her

Looking at the text message, Matt felt like he'd been sucker punched.

Matt Tremain wasn't brave. Certainly not one of those superheroes full of steely resolve facing danger. Short and walking with a limp, he'd grown up with a bulls-eye on his back. In school, he'd been picked on nearly every day until he finally took a stand and faced down two large bullies. He didn't decide to stand up to them; it was more a lack of alternatives. He went at them like a pit bull, tenacious and unrelenting. The fight over, and the pain subsided, his reputation had been reshaped. Even though he lost, everyone openly admired his tenacity.

It didn't hurt to have a big brain, either.

Now, he'd need both attributes again.

Matt gripped the phone, his breath and heart rate fast-tracking. His eyes widened as a silent primal scream welled up deep inside. He stared at the screen, not wanting to believe what he was seeing.

"ST2MORO@7. GY6. 7FF. 14AA41."

He translated the text in his mind.

ST2MORO@7. "Same time tomorrow, at seven."

GY6. "Got your six."

7FF. "Seven friends forever."

14AA41, the last. "One for all and all for one."

The true message, however, was a numerical code, each number following a number two. He scanned the message. The first was a seven, the next a six, the third another seven. 767 stood for "SOS" on a telephone keypad.

Matt was in grave danger.

How long do I have? He thought.

The simple code wasn't intended to be unbreakable—merely enough to frustrate anyone skimming through e-mails, texts, and chats.

Will it be enough now? Do I have time to run?

A voice in his head urged him to run. He'd been told that'd be the worst thing he could do. Instead, he walked out, ignoring the woman screaming at him about the spilled coffee.

He thumb-clicked two letters in response.

CX, canceled and going offline.

His team knew he'd understood the warning; he would contact them when it was safe.

Will I ever be safe again? He wondered.

Matt's *CX* message triggered a program erasing his computer history. It began eliminating all documents, contacts, search history, and communications related to the investigation. Everything was gone, except for the secret files he'd hidden in a dark cloud on the darknet.

He touched his chest, making sure media cards were hanging on a lanyard under his shirt. *If I'm caught, everything's on these cards*, he thought.

Standing outside the coffeehouse, Matt paused and looked around. He pried open his phone, removing the battery, and tossing it into a trash bin. He pried out the SIM card, dropping it between the slots of a sewer grate. Cyberia, his online friend warned Matt that his movements could be tracked by the SIM card.

Is someone watching me now? How will I know? Matt realized he should've thought about that already. *I must be more careful.*

Glancing around to see if anyone was looking, he let the phone drop. He stomped on it until the plastic case shattered and kicked the shards into the street. He winced at a ticklish feeling, cold sweat droplets forming on his cheek and tracing a slow path to his chin.

Matt walked east on Bloor Street. When he saw the sign for the subway entrance, it took immense self-control not to run. Cyberia warned him teams of watchers looked for that type of panic. "Don't let them see you sweat," he'd told Matt. What Matt knew about the tradecraft of spies and undercover techniques was limited to what he'd read in books and seen in movies.

This isn't fiction, he thought. *Will my clumsy effort at tradecraft be enough? Will it keep me alive? Oh, man.*

He'd been looking over his shoulder like this ever since Operation CleanSweep put a price on his head.

He tried to imitate an oyster closing its shell for protection, to conceal his fear as shoppers and commuters rushed past him like a river's current flowing around a rock.

"Morning, buddy."

Matt's head snapped up. *Why haven't I been paying attention?*

"Filthy weather, isn't it?" A man in a soiled army-surplus jacket stood at a newspaper kiosk, clapping his gloved hands, his breath steaming. "Especially with all this smoke," he said, starting to cough. Coughing soon turned to spasms, causing the man to hold a stained handkerchief to his lips.

"Morning..." Matt managed to mutter. He tried to ignore the man's dirty clothes, turning instead to examine newspapers on display. He started to ask the news vendor why he allowed the homeless man to hang around like that, but was quickly embarrassed by his lack of compassion. *If CleanSweep had its way, the homeless would be first*, he thought. *It must be all the...stress.*

Matt forced himself to act like a man choosing a newspaper to buy. He used the opportunity to glance away from the display racks, on the alert for anything out of the ordinary: a head-turning away too quickly, or someone abruptly stepping back into the shadows.

Didn't I read about doing something like that in a spy novel—to spot someone tailing you?

He reached for a newspaper, choosing one at random. Starting to sort through coins, he noticed a man across the street. *Is he looking directly at me? Yes, straight to me!* he thought. Matt froze as the man lifted his right sleeve to his mouth.

Oh no—he's whispering into a microphone!

Instead, Matt watched the man cough into the elbow of his coat sleeve, then turn and wave to a passing taxi. Matt let out a long, slow breath.

It's nothing, he thought.

He exhaled, maintaining a puzzled look to appear curious, a man with no purpose in mind. He used a store display window as a mirror, nothing suspicious. He started walking again.

If I can only get to the subway, I'll blend in. It's rush hour.

Matt pulled his collar to the falling temperature. He shivered, knowing it was more from fear than weather. The first droplets of cold rain splattered his face.

Then he saw them.

A sharp pang of fear gripped him like a lion was raking him with a claw. Two large men walked toward him. This time, the danger was real. They wore suits like detectives, with plain black shoes. Both men had dark circles under his eyes, badges of sleeplessness and too much coffee. They were the guys Matt knew would come for him. It took all his self-control to look calm and not run.

He was cornered. He almost felt relieved as they drew near. The taller one pulled a hand from his coat pocket. He held something and began swinging his arm in a menacing arc. They flashed counterfeit smiles, recognition in their eyes. Matt flinched, prepared.

They almost knocked him to the ground as they shouldered past him.

Matt turned to see them shake hands with another man walking to meet them.

"We have a reservation," he heard one say in a voice that hinted at annoyance. "I was trying to reach you on my cell just now."

Matt left the rest of their words trailing behind. Intense relief spread over his face as a short, older woman carrying a shopping bag gave him a puzzled look.

He pulled his jacket tight as ice pellets now stabbed his face.

Am I shaking from the cold or that near miss? He thought. Matt wanted to laugh, realizing panic and paranoia were making him act strangely.

Daggers of ice assaulted him as he fast-walked to the subway entrance. He fished his metro pass from his jeans pocket, pushing through the turnstile. Directional arrows pointed toward train platforms, where he met a perfume of steamy clothes, garlic, and tightly packed commuters. Standing on the northbound platform, a gush of wind signaled the approaching train. The grinding wheels sang a harsh song of metal on metal, like the gnashing of a steel giant's teeth. He waited for it to stop, standing aside for disembarking passengers.

He dodged a young woman with a backpack as she exited, then darted in, lunging for an empty seat. The doors *whooshed* shut, and the train began to pick up speed, the scream of the wheels making an ear-piercing racket as the train lurched around a curve.

He started to relax.

I'm going to make it.

He looked up anxiously at the electronic, flat-screen advertising panels. They all ran the same continuous, looping picture. Across the bottom, a scrolling message urged riders to call 711 if they saw the man pictured. The number was for the new hotline established by Operation CleanSweep.

Matt realized it was a picture of himself, his own face staring back at him in high-definition video.

Why didn't Cyberia disable—

Suddenly, the video images scrambled to snowy static—visual white noise—before going blank. Grabbing the back of a seat, he pulled himself up as the subway train braked to a stop, and the doors began to open.

CHAPTER 2

THE NEXT STOP

The train braked to a stop at Summerhill station. When the door opened, Matt jumped to his feet, pushing a man to the side.

"What the—? Of all the rude…"

Matt didn't wait for the man to finish. He needed to get far away from the train. He heard pounding on the door closing behind him. Someone recognized him. He ran the length of the platform, intent on reaching the stairway as quickly as possible. It felt like he was running with lead weights strapped around his ankles. Stopping at the bottom of the stairs, hands on his knees, he struggled for breath. He imagined all the passengers trying to dial the 711 number at the same time.

Whatever…happened…to my…New Year's…resolution…a fitness class? he thought, catching his breath. He rushed the stairs, two at a time.

Matt stepped out of the station into an ambush of wet snowflakes the size of postage stamps. He drew his too-thin jacket tight to his body. The weather wasn't his enemy. It was fear. He had to control his escalating panic.

He tried to reassure himself most passengers on the crowded subway were focused on hurrying home from work, inured to the bombardment of news bulletins following the riots. *Maybe they'd ignored the warnings flashed on the screens*, he thought. He wanted to believe that, but the pounding on the subway door told him otherwise.

Pausing to catch his breath, Matt spotted two uniformed police offi-cers. He knew panic would only draw attention. He watched them standing with feigned boredom, but Matt wasn't deceived. They kept close watch through dull-looking eyes, peering through mist rising in spirals from their coffee cups. They didn't seem to take notice of him, but Matt remained alert.

*Did Cyberia disable their communications before my photo was broadcast? I need to contact him and make sure. If I can't talk to him, get some advice...*the thought trailed off. *Man, I'm clearly out of my depth now.*

The two cops would surely get a good look when he walked by them. *Surely, there must be surveillance cameras at subway stations,* he thought. He saw them; they were installed to sweep the exterior. *The cameras aren't moving.* Maybe they've been immobilized by Cyberia, after all.

Am I safe? Matt needed to be sure. He stared at the cameras pointing away from him. They didn't move. He had to take a chance.

He walked past the police officers, his face down and collar up. A plan formed as he reached the bus shelter. The SOS warning message had to be from Cyberia. He had to contact the Russian. Matt needed to get to his computer.

● ● ●

In one of their few phone conversations, Matt told Cyberia, "I have an encoded program I can use to reach you in an emergency. It can be broken with some effort. I will only use it if circumstances are dire."

"You're right to be careful," Cyberia responded in his thick accent. "We have to always stay alert and assume we're being overheard. Our enemies use the latest software programs, trolling through all formats of electronic communications."

"Will we ever meet?" he'd asked Cyberia.

"Who knows?"

Cyberia was a master of vague and ambiguous. Matt visualized him shrugging while answering in Russian-accented English. The two had a general idea of the other's location, but only within a fifty-mile radius. That left a lot of space to hide. They were never so impolite as to ask for any personal information. Keeping secrets might one day mean the difference between life and death.

Matt was vigilant about governments and authority by nature, inherited from parents who called themselves children of the sixties, who still said things like "sticking it to the man."

Matt felt drawn to Cyberia when they met in a chat room, a site for blogger/journalists. The connection grew to the point Matt felt he trusted Cyberia. Although they'd never met, they had a strong online affiliation. Matt stopped questioning why that was long ago.

Today, Cyberia was the only person who knew why Matt was in such danger, why he was in the crosshairs of CleanSweep.

He'd instructed Matt about their online security measures. "We must always be at least five pings apart. They use a super fast program, but we should be OK."

Should? Doubt cast by that one word always hovered in the back of Matt's mind.

Now, he needed the one clean personal laptop remaining which he'd use to reach Cyberia. He needed some faint trace of hope. He had several laptops; he used them like drug dealers used burner cell phones. He'd pick one at random, hoping it wasn't being monitored. It was an expensive security protocol—but necessary under the current circumstances. Matt didn't even trust those computers. The one he needed was still in the package, stored in a cabinet.

Matt stood in the bus shelter, shivering. The wet snow was mixed with rain, but he knew he was shaking from near panic. *I need to calm down,* he thought, but it didn't help.

He needed to get to his hidey-hole, his emergency backup place. He'd designed it for a time just like this. He touched his media cards again. One held the emergency communication codes.

Do I have what it takes? How can I do this? Matt had no ready answer.

The lingering stench of smoke wasn't as noticeable in this part of the city. Matt hugged himself, trying to warm up as the snow finally gave way to wet drizzle.

He dropped his arms to appear calm when he spotted the two cops he'd seen earlier. They turned a corner and stopped, stamping their feet to ward off the cold. After a short interval, one turned his head away; the taller one, however, looked directly at him. Matt saw recognition in her eyes. His reaction was to run, but there was nowhere to go. He stood, frozen in fear.

Then something curious happened. The two officers exchanged looks. Matt was certain the officer knew who he was but didn't move. She stood with snowflakes landing on the shoulders of her uniform, absorbed by the fabric as quickly as they landed. The officer kept her hand poised on her radio, making no effort to use it. Then she turned suddenly, said something to her partner, and they walked away.

Why didn't they call for backup or arrest me?

Matt sucked in a deep breath, trying to think about all he'd learned about CleanSweep in past weeks, mentally reviewing notes from his interviews. He looked around for any cameras at the bus stop. He wondered whether the high-tech camera surveillance system extended to buses and bus kiosks. He hoped not.

If they did, would Cyberia have disabled them as well?

A bus stopped, interrupting Matt's thoughts. He glanced at the route number; it was the one he was waiting for. It pulled to a stop with a *whoosh* of air brakes. He held the fare card in trembling fingers as the door opened. The driver barely glanced in his direction. Matt walked down the aisle, grasping the back of a nearby seat for support. The driver accelerated as if in a furious race to the next stop. Matt stumbled into a seat as the bus lurched past a parked car.

Unlike the subway, these passengers headed to the night shift, unskilled workers lucky to still have jobs after the riots. These riders minded their own business, rarely looking past their own noses.

Matt watched a young woman staring out the window at some vacant dream, or so he imagined. A man in front of him nodded to ear candy only he could hear, an earbud draping a thin cord alongside his collar. Matt looked around at other men and women. *Are they gazing at the nothingness of their lives?* he wondered.

These are the ones who didn't see it coming, the peril of Clean-Sweep. The word came uninvited to Matt again. He tried to think back. *When did I first realize what Operation CleanSweep really was? When did I find out what it stood for, the enormous significance it held for everyone?*

Claussen! That man and his cronies followed a well-used playbook. First, disrupt the social order. Secondly, offer to replace the chaos with order. Better yet, offer a program with algorithms capable of deciding who lives and who dies. Out of chaos and anarchy comes a perfect world.

Claussen found out I was on to him, Matt thought. *I saw through him. He's the one carrying a cross wrapped in a flag, and that saying describes a fascist.*

Matt wondered why he turned that investigative rock over. All he'd done was reveal deceitful men behind the scrim, skittering from sunlight like roaches. *Why did I have to be the one to blog about their dirty secret?* Matt wondered, not for the first time.

• • •

Jerked out of the thought, the driver slammed on the brakes, then bullied ahead of other cars. Matt risked exposure getting off at his designated intersection. There was no option; he'd have to transfer to his streetcar.

We're going to pass right by the new CleanSweep headquarters soon—a dangerous part of the bus ride.

Matt leaned his head against the window. Recognizing them was easy. They stood at each intersection. They were the new CleanSweep agents; some stood alone, others in teams of two. Their conspicuous suits might as well be uniforms. Matt watched one glance at a paper he held, trying to monitor the streets while remaining subtle. Their identical black leather coats gave them away. It would have been laughable if the circumstances weren't so grim.

Pedestrians did their best to avoid them.

Matt was shocked. They each held a photo of him, Matthew Tremain.

The driver braked suddenly. Matt had to grab the seat in front of him to keep from pitching forward. The bus was stuck in traffic; the driver honking at the snarl of cars ahead.

They were stopped between bus stops. On impulse, Matt jumped and forced the rear door open. He ignored the driver's warning shout as he dove from the bus, darting between the stranded cars.

Matt chanced a look at the surveillance cameras. *They aren't moving. Maybe Cyberia is still blocking them*, he hoped. Matt stood for a moment, then dashed into a narrow alley to his left, dodging dumpsters and boxes of trash.

Matt almost forgot to limp as he ran to safety. With a quick look, no one seemed to be following him; they were too focused on bus stops and street intersections to notice a man jump off a bus mid-block.

Matt reached the end of the alleyway, pausing, hands on knees, trying to regain control of his breathing.

He used back streets and shortcuts to avoid detection. He couldn't shake the feeling that everyone he passed recognized him. He was sure panic made him stand out like a flashing neon sign.

As he made his way east, he looked for signs the surveillance cameras were back in operation. So far, he'd avoided detection, but knew it couldn't last.

With relief, he realized people he met acted as cautious and guarded as he did.

Nearing his neighborhood, he spotted a chain-link fence. It'd been hastily erected around this part of the city, one of seven areas destroyed in the rioting. He looked at checkpoints to his left and right. The miserable weather suddenly seemed like a blessing. Poor visibility made it almost impossible for the inspection teams to see him at this distance.

Matt needed to get through this undetected. *But how?* he wondered. So far, luck seemed to be holding, but he was losing faith in luck.

He peered at the lighted inspection kiosks in the distance. He saw individuals handing over papers for examination before being allowed to pass. Shards of light reflected off the wet pavement, creating a high-contrast, black-and-white, film noir effect. The weather was keeping people off the streets. *How do I get past this?* he wondered.

Turning slightly, Matt noticed something odd. *Is that an opening in a section of the fence, offering an invitation? So, I'm not the only one who needed to get through without being noticed.* He fought his urge to run to the opening.

Looking in both directions, Matt walked slowly and pulled back the separated fencing. Once through, he passed still-smoldering buildings, structures with broken windows, a mute testimony to the rioting days earlier.

Looking for a way to cross the Don River, the Lower Don Recreational Trail provided the answer.

• • •

Matt leaned into a driving, cold wind as he finally reached his a red-brick apartment building. Built in 1937, the art deco design should have made the building trendy and cool, like its neighbors, but it failed to meet the challenge. The brickwork sorely needed tuck-pointing. It boasted unpainted window frames. Trash leaning against the side of the front steps was the final affront.

Inside, Matt recoiled to a dank odor. He should have been used to it, but it still reminded him of years of neglect and mold. In the lobby, panels of wallpaper seemed hanging on for dear life. Taped-up signs with washed-out names scrawled with a magic marker decorated the recessed bank of mailboxes. Only one mailbox retained an original etched-brass plate for Mrs. Simmons, apartment 403. It was rumored that Mrs. Simmons moved in when the building was brand-new. No one ever recalled seeing Mrs. Simmons, but her mailbox never overflowed.

Matt walked past the mailboxes on threadbare carpeting. Reaching the end of the dim hallway, he unlocked the door to the basement. He glanced over his shoulder. No one was watching. Snapping on the light switch, he started down, locking the door behind him. He walked toward another doorway, ducking under heating vents as he went, brushing ghostly cobwebs aside.

He unlocked the door and stepped into a small room he had decorated like a stage. Boxes and used furniture made it look like a storage area. A single bulb dangled on a braided wire. It looked like a place that had been neglected for a long, long time.

In exchange for a monthly sum, Matt was the only resident with access to the basement. He doubted the super passed any of the monthly payment along to the property management company. That was fine with him; Matt wanted privacy, and the super's duplicity was insurance.

He pushed a dresser aside, revealing yet another door.

Matt always left a "tell" at the door to this door when he left—something small to let him know if the super or anyone else intruded. This time, it was a simple piece of Scotch tape near the floor, stuck across the edge of the door and the jamb. It was intact, the way he'd left it.

I made it, Matt thought as he entered his hidey-hole.

It was like stepping through a time warp, leaving 1937 art deco behind. This room was air-conditioned to a very precise temperature and dehumidified to keep moisture from his expansive array of computers and equipment.

"Here's my suggestion," Cyberia said. He gave Matt precise instructions about equipment and security. "Once you turned over the rock and exposed CleanSweep, you were in danger."

Matt followed the suggestions, creating this electronic operations center, vital to his investigation of Operation CleanSweep and Charles Claussen. He checked other telltale traps, finally convinced there'd been no visitors.

Matt unlocked a storage cabinet and removed a laptop, still in original packaging. He placed it in front of his primary monitor, shoulders slumped forward, relaxed for the first time since receiving the SOS message. He leaned back and stretched out. His chin dropped to his chest. When he opened his eyes and looked around, the clock winked 11:13.

Can that much time have passed?

He adjusted a lamp and typed a few words. Matt was patient. He knew his message bounced through at least three locations before arriving at the intended targets. What seemed to Matt to be an agonizing eternity took less than thirty seconds. His teammates would be awake and signed on, despite the variety of time zones.

Matt and Cyberia cautiously recruited their online team, like-minded members from around the world. Over time, they became intimates. Connected by words, each pledged allegiance to the truth, though nobody ever thought to give the group a name.

Добрый вечер мой друг, good evening, my friend. The first person signed in. It was Gennady, the Russian, screen name of Cyberia.

Ubari logged on from somewhere in Africa. Lake Devil joined from her undisclosed location in Florida. The last was Chin, connecting from Chengdu, the capital of Sichuan province in southwest China. Questions about precise addresses were never asked. They were best-kept secret for the safety of all.

Except for Cyberia, the others knew Matt only by his alias: Veritas.

Despite the dehumidifier working at maximum effort, Matt felt a trickle of sweat under his arms. His nerves felt raw and exposed.

"They're on to you," Cyberia typed. "It's the same here. It won't be long until I hear footsteps at my own door. It's the ghost of Stalin rising from the grave." His words were stripped bare of his usual humor.

"It is worse than we thought," Ubari added.

Lake Devil and Chin remained silent, no need in restating the obvious.

"I don't know what to do," Matt typed. With those words, he succumbed to shock and started to shake as tears formed and rolled down his cheeks.

"Five minutes, darlings. Hang in there, dude. We'll talk later." Lake Devil reminded everyone they had reached the maximum limit of the five minutes of connectivity set as a safeguard that they hoped would foil anyone tracing their communications.

As Matt watched, his screen went dark, his friends disappearing; he never felt so alone or afraid.

He walked to wood panels lining one wall. If anyone looked, they would see one stood out from the rest. It was subtle—a slight curl at the upper left corner. Matt pulled the corner. It covered a crude door to a long-forgotten coal chute, now home to coal dust and spiders. Matt remembered what Cyberia said. "Always have a backup, an escape option." *If I ever have to escape through there; it'll mean I'm in dire trouble.*

Matt paid the super to keep him from snooping around.

Did I pay him enough? He wondered.

CHAPTER 3

CLEANSWEEP

Charles Claussen—never Chuck—walked through the lobby, his stacked-leather heels *click-clicking* on the marble floor, his posture military straight. He didn't just walk; he marched like a man with a purpose. He was deeply troubled, however. He'd spent all his political capital and considerable financial resources developing CleanSweep, his top-secret project.

"Imagine a world with streets swept clean, no crime and no criminals," one of his PowerPoint slides boasted.

Now his project was at risk. Security precautions he'd so meticulously designed had somehow been bypassed. The project's internal computer security was compromised. Something wasn't right. He thought he knew what the problem was—better yet, *who* the problem was.

Not given to cursing, he made an exception as he muttered under his breath, "That damn blogger."

Clenched jaw muscles gave away his anxiety as he paraded with his entourage through the lobby toward a waiting elevator. Two uniformed men behind the security counter jumped to attention, the guard on the right tugging his jacket down.

"Good morning, Mr. Claussen," they shouted in unison, creating a stereophonic effect. Claussen raised his right arm in passing, a not-quite-casual wave. Later, they would both recall the great Mr. Claussen acknowledging them in passing.

The guard named Fred spent most of his free time watching the History Channel. The gesture looked familiar—a sort of salute. He couldn't be sure.

• • •

Claussen learned the gesture as a young boy, sitting in a darkened room with an old man. "Show me one of your movies, *Grossvater*," he would often say to his grandfather, Otto. The two spent many hours during Claussen's childhood watching grainy home films.

"*Geheime Filme*," the old man would mutter, lapsing into his native language. "They are old films. Old like me. And they're a secret, just between the two of us, eh?"

When he was older, Charles understood why the old man called them *geheime*, secret, films. They were from the old man's private library, home movies made during his time as a young officer. Young Charles admired the German military uniforms, *Grossvater* strutting with groups of other men, each trying to outdo the other in form and frenzy, flaunting their importance before the camera.

They demonstrated tailored ceremonial poses, posturing in garish uniforms, mimicking high-ranking party officials—especially the Nazi leader familiar to viewers of the history channel and old newsreels.

His grandfather patiently explained the rigid protocol for offering the official Nazi salute. "The right arm is to be extended to at least eye level or higher," he said, insisting the little boy practice until it was perfect. Watching his grandfather's films, however, Charles detected something different when the salute was used by top party leaders. They casually raised their right arm, almost like a wave, the arm bent at the elbow and the palm facing outward.

Like many men and women addicted to power, Claussen felt a need to create a signature move to set him apart. He adopted that old salute as his personal salute, arrogantly, as a mere casual, tossed-off wave. He believed it did indeed set him apart from subordinates. In fact, he considered nearly everyone to be subordinate, inferior. Claussen's salute, walking through the lobby that morning, was his private homage to his heroes—the men in those secret films.

Charles Claussen, at forty-nine years of age, was a man of considerable power and influence.

"He's at the top of his game," someone said with a suggestion of envy.

"He's a force to be reckoned with," a national news magazine reported.

• • •

As Claussen entered the lobby that morning, a member of his security team raced ahead, making sure the elevator would be waiting. A young woman held the door open with a glare that warned away uninvited persons thinking they could take the opportunity to share a ride with the boss. She'd remain on station in the lobby until Claussen headed out at the end of the day.

The security team followed him into the elevator, hovering like swarming insects.

In the elevator, Claussen faced the door, hands clasped behind his back. Claussen understood the importance of posture and body language. Behind him, two men stood precisely two steps back. He wouldn't have approved, knowing one of them secretly longed for a cigarette. A harsh reprimand awaited any team member who left his or her post—it could compromise the safety of Mr. Claussen.

One small detail didn't escape notice, however. In the reflection of the polished elevator door, he saw the two guards look at each other and roll their eyes. It was a sign of impudence—close to insolence. Charles made a mental note to call his head of security, Angela Vaughn. She'd make sure two new men shared the elevator ride at the end of the day.

The elevator slowed gently to a stop, doors opening onto a small foyer. There was no receptionist as this wasn't a waiting room. This top-secret floor wasn't listed in the lobby directory.

Electronic technology determined a passenger's eligibility to enter the elevator. Unique biometrics were matched to a database profile comprising measurements of facial features, height, and weight—even identifiable body scent. If any unauthorized person happened onto the elevator, it would simply wait with the door open, chirping a simple warning message, "vacate." The message repeated until the unauthorized person complied by stepping out.

Optical recognition software scanned both irises of everyone entering and exiting the elevator. A special infrared digital camera focused on both eyes, scanning the structure of each iris in high resolution, noticing the subtle differences between the two. It was much more accurate than a simple retinal scan. All details of each iris were required to match the records of their intricate elements stored in the database before the door would open on the top-secret floor. Charles knew all this. He'd personally designed the technology.

The door opened, and Charles Claussen strode across the small vestibule to a door. He placed his palm on a glass panel, his final security measure. A gentle chirp signaled access was granted.

Inside, he started down a wide corridor.

A young woman waving a paper blocked his path. She tried to avoid looking hesitant, a trait she knew her boss detested.

"He's been spotted, sir."

Claussen bellowed in a cold voice, "Boots on the ground!"

Everyone knew what it meant. Claussen glanced at the paper handed to him, making a face as if offended by a foul odor.

"I want the bastard in handcuffs before my coffee gets cold," he said, stomping into his private office and closing the door. He would slam a door closed, giving away his anger. Meanwhile, workers outside scurried to their desks in a state of red alert. They didn't have to be told that Claussen was talking about Matt Tremain.

CHAPTER 4

TANNER

"When did I first learn about CleanSweep?" Matt said, echoing Bryon's question. He was having a beer with Bryan, a friend since high school. "It started with an email," Matt said, signaling for a refill. The bartender placed a beer mug on the counter. Matt picked it up, taking a long swallow, his face set in a frown. "You have to promise me you won't tell a soul."

Bryan nodded and drew his hand past his lips in a zipping gesture.

"Tanner Woodson told me about it," Matt said.

Matt turned back to his companion after glancing around. "Before I met Tanner, I'd heard about some hush-hush program backed by the feds. It was a new, highly classified method designed to troll e-mails, instant messages, and voice conversations. I'd heard rumors before I met Tanner, but they were like mere whispers, voices talking just out of hearing range."

"When did it become more than a rumor?" Bryan said, leaning forward.

Matt shivered. "I thought I was paranoid. After all, terrorism's our new preoccupation. Charles Claussen's fan base is like a moth to a flame, Islamophobia on steroids. Add anti-Semitism and race-baiting, and you have a potent cocktail. Those fears are used to justify probing our private lives, the equivalent of a body-cavity search. How many stories are written about our obsession with security? Look at the jump in the number of people buying guns." After a pause, Matt continued. "Claussen thinks

CleanSweep is powerful enough to troll everyone's electronic life. Tanner showed me the protocol. He called it a data scrub."

Matt looked around again.

"Who do you think is watching you?" Bryan asked. "That's the fourth time you've looked around like that."

Matt continued. "A scrub is a program sifting through data, looking for information, personal information. Tanner said CleanSweep goes beyond that, matching that information with algorithms, providing step-by-step decision maps identifying so-called genetic errors. Claussen wants to scrub *people*. Doesn't that sound familiar?"

"Are you sure *you* aren't the one obsessed? What you're describing sounds way over the top," Bryan said.

For a moment, the two sat in silence, sipping their beers.

Finally, Bryan shook his head. "C'mon. It can't be as bad as all that, Matt. If people aren't doing anything wrong, what's the harm?"

"What's the harm? You can't be serious," Matt said, slapping the bar with the palm of his hand. "I had breakfast with a source recently. Before we talked, he took the battery out of his phone and told me to do the same. I remember the nervous way he glanced around the room as he spoke. He said they likely knew what the two of us were eating. At the time, I was incredulous, like you. I laughed, telling him he sounded paranoid. He told me that sometimes paranoia is justified."

"You didn't take him seriously, did you?"

"Not at the time, Bryan. When I started asking around, I began to put parts of the puzzle together. Nobody had all the details, but each had some. Rumor had it a new initiative was like PROFUNC, a nasty, malignant holdover from the Cold War. Another source said it wasn't Commies and pinkos targeted this time. The scope was much wider than we could ever imagine. She told me a net would be cast for all who disagree with the government—foreign and domestic."

"Wasn't a story like that reported in the paper a while back?" Bryan asked. "I didn't think it had much substance. It sounded more like crazy conspiracy theorists on ecstasy. Perhaps some people want the rumor to be true."

Matt frowned. "I thought so at the time until I overheard another conversation. I was in an elevator in Government Plaza. One said something worse than terrorism was coming. Terrorism? I heard the other ask. I thought Claussen's project is supposed to take care of that. That and more. The man claimed to have seen the CleanSweep algorithms, then stopped, realizing I was listening." Matt rubbed his left shoulder with his right hand, massaging a muscle as he talked to Bryan. "I remember wondering what could be worse than terrorism."

"And now you think whatever happens will be *worse* than terrorist attacks on our soil?" Bryan said, a sarcastic undertone lacing the question. "I think you need to take some time off, Matt."

Matt wouldn't be put off. "I've heard enough rumors to believe we're being warned about terrorists coming from the outside. I'm convinced the real attack is coming from *within*."

"I can tell you're emotional about it," Bryan said, hiding his feelings behind his mug.

"I began to commit my blog I Publish as Verité to the story. I posted a story saying as a society, we're running out of groups to marginalize. Demagogues are bullies. They always need a scapegoat to create fear and panic. They want support for safety and security programs, money for bigger and more lethal weapons systems. What if Claussen's revising an old handbook, redesigning it to include new classes of people to eliminate? Old targets continue to be demonized and marginalized, and if we needed to invent new ones, we would. That blog generated a lot of responses, let me tell you."

Matt could tell Bryan was still skeptical. "Tanner showed me a list of people Claussen considered misfits, a drain on society," Matt said.

Matt took a final swallow and placed the empty mug on the bar. He nodded to the bartender for another. He could tell Bryan still wasn't buying it. Matt made one final appeal to his friend.

"Since recorded history, tribes indoctrinated the young about the dangers of assimilating with other tribes. Elders told stories about the evils of other tribes, it's us versus them.

"In the early nineteenth century, anarchists had bulls-eyes painted on their backs, the target of propagandists. The truth was on holiday. They were demonized, used to create fear and panic. Newspapers declared that anarchists were out to destroy our way of life. People began to see anarchists lurking behind every tree. Then, socialism and communism were declared evil. The excesses of Stalin and Nazism turned everything upside down. The I-know-best has been used to justify fascist dictatorships since."

Matt saw the melancholy on his face when he looked at the mirror behind the bar. "I tried to keep my writing simple and to the point. People wrote saying as they read my blogs, they began to question what was going on with CleanSweep. Some people, anyway."

The bartender delivered another drink, but Matt ignored it. He kept staring at his image in the mirror. *I'm talking to myself. Bryan is a silent, disbelieving audience, refusing to acknowledge the truth.*

"Today, many support the idea of erecting walls around the country, hoping we'll somehow keep dangerous terrorists out. Who worries about domestic terrorists walking among us?"

Bryan sneered. "I want to agree with you, but..."

• • •

Matt wondered if he made headway with his friend, but didn't really think so. While Bryan stepped outside to make a call, Matt had time to think.

Who are the new devils now? I asked one of my government sources who was considered worse than terrorists. She shrugged and said they're all around us. That's cryptic if you ask me, but it got my attention.

I sat down to write a counterargument to the arrogance of hate. Should I have expressed the opinion, we're all being brainwashed, targeting imaginary groups. That wasn't a popular opinion, I soon found out.

I concluded truth was on an extended holiday, that civil discourse was also on vacation. 'Who are the real targets now?' I wrote. 'Ordinary people?' That brought out the crazies.

"Where were we? Bryan asked when he returned.

Matt was losing his audience but plunged on. "A guy wrote saying it would be OK to give up some of our liberties to make us safe. Another reader wondered what was wrong with surveillance programs. 'The government wouldn't do something like that without good reason.' The idiot even said we should always trust the government."

"I agree with them," Bryan said. "If you aren't doing anything wrong, you don't have anything to hide."

Matt shook his head, gobsmacked, realizing he'd misjudged Bryan completely. He tinkered with his mug, turning it around and around. He felt the tension between them. Matt searched for anything that might push Bryan to recognize the danger ahead.

"I wrote what I thought was a witty blog. It was a bunch of bull at first. I wasn't entirely serious when I started writing. I came up with a lame, sarcastic metaphor, writing we're all sailing on the *SS Morality*. I compared it to the *Titanic*, hurtling full speed ahead, despite icebergs ahead. After all, our boat's unsinkable, eh?"

Talking with his friend didn't help Matt escape his demons. Booze only added to his depression.

"That's when I heard from Tanner. He said the *SS Morality* was, indeed, on collision course with an iceberg. 'Can you handle the truth?' he asked me. He told me Operation CleanSweep was the gigantic iceberg in our nation's course. 'You've only seen the top part, a mere tenth of the story,' he said. He said the damage from the CleanSweep iceberg will make the story of the *Titanic* seem uplifting." Matt swallowed the dregs. "When Tanner asked me if I could handle the truth, I didn't have a ready answer. That was my first encounter with Tanner, his challenging me with the truth."

Matt opened his wallet, putting enough money to pay for the beers on the table, adding a generous tip. He nodded goodbye and turned toward the door, walking sure and steady, completely different from the way he felt.

CHAPTER 5

ICEBERG AHEAD

Matt sat in his car, thinking about Tanner. *I didn't trust him at first. Why would he tell me these secrets? How did he get access to them? When did I decide to believe?*

Tanner established a protocol for communicating, a combination of texts and email. He told Matt how to set up a spoof email. "Get a throwaway phone for texting," he said in the second message.

His third message had PROFUNC in the subject line.

"Operation CleanSweep is roughly based on it. Sounding pretty calling it CleanSweep, it's really a bundle of dirty little secrets," Tanner's message said.

Matt sent a text back. "What can you tell me about it? I looked it up. PROFUNC was a secret program from the fifties, a dinosaur, a program to round up Communists."

"That's what makes it insidious," Tanner wrote back. "No one takes it seriously because it doesn't sound threatening—like a cosmic joke. Citing a failed program from the past hid the truth. This new version, I can assure you, is no joke."

With each email, Matt absorbed the weight of what Tanner was saying. He needed to convince Tanner they needed to meet. Matt judged his sources eye to eye, evaluating truthfulness. Tanner was reluctant, but his conviction burned white-hot through the words. "I'm not avoiding you," he said. "I'm terrified of being caught. You should be outraged and terrified as well."

Matt finally made a direct plea: I need proof CleanSweep is as dangerous as you say.

If Tanner's correct, if this program is as evil as claimed, I must decide if I have the backbone. I'll have to start posting about it, regardless of the danger. Do I have what it takes? Some people call my style 'trash journalism.' That's when I know I've touched a raw nerve. While I may not have a journalism degree, I verify sources before going public.

Tanner grudgingly agreed to meet but demanded secrecy. "There's no room for discussion. If you want to meet, drive to an abandoned parking deck three blocks from the lakefront, on Cherry Street. You will know it—the one slated for demolition. You'll see the sign. They're trying to convert the site into upscale condos. Park on the third floor."

As Matt approached, darkness filled the neighborhood's nooks and crannies. He circled the block three times, checking out the garage, disquieted by the surroundings. There were few operating streetlights in the district of warehouses and abandoned factories. There were signs promising offices, condominiums, and upscale shopping in washed-out paint, a sad reflection of faded dreams.

Alarm bells sounded. *What if it's a setup?* He wondered.

Matt shared the evolving story in e-mails to Cyberia.

His Russian online friend wrote back. "Look over your shoulder, Matt. Take nothing for granted. Always assume you are being watched, that someone is recording your every move, listening to every word."

Cyberia's suspicions got to Matt. He brushed the warning to the side as he turned into the abandoned parking garage.

The arm of the ticket dispenser at the entrance was out of order, hanging at a right angle like a broken arm. He maneuvered past the barrier, his headlights scanning an abandoned vehicle that looked like it had taken up permanent residence.

Continuing to the next level, he saw derelict vehicles parked haphazardly.

In for a penny, he thought, driving to the third level.

He parked next to a pickup with an inch-thick layer of dust.

His doubts floated to the surface. His heartbeat and shallow breathing sounded like the beat of edgy, discordant modern jazz. *What do I have for protection,* he wondered. Matt felt the pen in his pocket. It provided scant comfort.

The truth may be a powerful weapon...until you're in a real fight.

Except for the truck, the third level was deserted. Matt was close to convincing himself to turn around and leave. His wild-goose-chase feeling was strong, growing stronger by the second. He was tempted to put aside the story behind CleanSweep. *I can go back to blissful ignorance,* he thought. Instead, he shifted into park, and rolled the window down, keeping the motor running...in case. The only sounds were the quiet purr of his own engine, along with an odd pinging sound coming from under the hood. It was a sound he'd never noticed before. The noise distracted him.

A sudden movement to his left caused Matt to stop breathing, unable to speak or shout for help. He felt paralyzed, his legs useless. He suppressed an urge to piss.

A man stepped out of the shadows, arms down at his sides to show the absence of threat. As the man walked closer, Matt could make out his face, a look of panic and paranoia—a look mirroring his own. Making a fateful decision, Matt turned off the motor and stepped out. The dome light sparked like a camera flash, blinking obscenely bright. He quickly closed the door, making as little noise as possible. Despite his attempt, the door latch sounded like a pistol shot in the stillness.

Matt's paranoia meter had gone viral, *ALERT, LEVEL RED!*

"Are you...the blogger...Wordster?"

Matt heard his username, the other man's voice just above a whisper. Nodding yes, Matt extended his hand.

The other man didn't take it. After a pause, he leaned forward. "I'm Tanner," he whispered.

"Matt, call me Matt," he said, matching Tanner's hushed voice.

Tanner stood quietly so long, Matt watched Tanner's head swivel, scanning every direction. Satisfied Matt wasn't followed, Tanner put a finger to his lips to signal silence and motioned Matt to follow him.

Matt didn't know why, but he locked his car before taking a moleskin notebook from his pocket. As he followed, their footsteps echoed as they walked toward the exit sign, promising an elevator. Matt stiffened as Tanner opened the rust-covered door. Expecting it to whine in protest, the door opened without a sound. Tanner pointed a flashlight at a can of spray lubricant. "I checked it out yesterday; the door was almost rusted shut."

Safely out of sight in the stairwell, Tanner unbuttoned his shirt to retrieve a file folder wedged down the front. He handed it to Matt, pointing the small flashlight so Matt could read the thirty-four pages of text and diagrams.

As Matt turned each page, a knot in his stomach tightened. "Is this true? How can it be?" he said.

"I told you before you'd only seen the tip of the iceberg," Tanner said.

Matt felt Tanner's gaze as he absorbed the substance. "It's happening right in front of us, in the public eye. Is everyone suddenly a willing collaborator?" he asked.

"Remember, the protocol is still in the beta stage. They're testing it now. Look around. How many street people do you see?" Tanner whispered. "They were everywhere, sleeping on heating grates, or pushing carts down alleys. They were identified using CleanSweep's algorithms, people he deemed unsuitable...." Tanner didn't finish.

Matt didn't have an immediate response.

• • •

"Have you seen any baggy pants lately?" Tanner asked. "Do you see any kids dressed gangsta style? They're the tip of the iceberg. Claussen's targets are below the waterline."

Matt thought about Tanner's questions as he read. Finishing the last page, he felt numb. While leafing through the file, a black hole, a hole inside of him filled with unanswered questions.

This can't be, Matt thought. He said it out loud. "This can't—" he stopped. "Who's behind it?"

"Charles Claussen. It's Claussen's idea," Tanner spat the words, making a face that looked like he'd just swallowed vinegar.

"Charles Claussen? You're kidding, right? What does he have to do with this?" Matt waved the papers. "What's your angle? Charles Claussen is a great—"

Tanner held up his hand, cutting off Matt's words. "Everyone thinks he's an outstanding civic leader, the paradigm this country stands for."

• • •

Matt wanted to go straight home and feed his notes into the shredder. He drove, wishing he'd never heard of Tanner or the truth behind Operation CleanSweep. Thinking about what he read in the stairwell of the parking deck that night, he knew it was too late to turn back. He'd never be able to put this toothpaste back in the tube.

CHAPTER 6

TANNER'S STORY

anner chose other unconnected locations for future meetings. Matt was pleased none were like that abandoned parking garage on Cherry Street. One meeting took place on a subway platform, Tanner using the noise from passing trains to mask his words. He whispered new chapters of the story. Once, the two of them strolled on nearly deserted sidewalks, alert for anyone following. Their final meeting was at dusk, walking along the lakefront near Matt's apartment.

The wind snarled like some enraged creature, blowing cold mist from the lake. *Is that an omen?* Matt wondered.

Matt's distress swelled as Tanner fleshed out details he'd learned about CleanSweep. "Now you know the rudiments of CleanSweep. See how dangerous it is...?" Tanner's voice faded into the dark.

They sat on a bench on the boardwalk, halfway between two lampposts. In half-light, Matt strained to read the latest batch of papers but gave up. Without enough light, it was impossible to read the small print. "I'll read these later," he'd said, folding the papers together and stuffing them in a leather case.

He thought Tanner said something and turned.

Tanner was crying, unashamed. "I don't know if I'm relieved, depressed, or both," he finally said. "I wasn't sure it was the right thing to do, deciding to talk...to tell you."

Matt waited for him to finish, but Tanner stared out at the lake. Matt wondered what he saw in that darkness.

"We both know how important this is," Matt said, knowing the words, intended to be comforting, sounded rather lame. "How did it happen? CleanSweep, I mean? How did it get to this point without...? I'm searching for the right word. I guess *scrutiny* comes close. There must have been government oversight. Why didn't the police or mainstream media pick apart the details—"

Tanner held his hand to stop Matt. "I can't talk about it anymore now," Tanner said, the words bitter. "I've signed my death warrant disclosing this to you. I thought about contacting the Attorney General, or talking to a real reporter."

The "real reporter" reference hurt Matt more than he cared to admit.

"CleanSweep's reach is so pervasive, as soon as I made inquiries, I met a stone wall," Tanner said. "The Attorney General's office closed the door as soon as I mentioned CleanSweep. The police were the same, local or federal. I reached out to print and electronic media. The first mention of CleanSweep ended any approach. I don't need to explain, do I? You're my Woodward and Bernstein. It's in your hands now."

Matt was at a loss for words at first. "I know the story's dangerous. An alarm needs to be sounded. He was interrupted by a flash of lightning and felt the first gust of wind. While he sat, he wondered if it was too late to sound the alarm.

The two sat quietly, and Matt started to write the story in his head, weaving the various parts into the fabric.

It'll take nerve, courage I may not have, he thought. *No. I do have what it takes. I went toe-to-toe with those bullies in school. I won't back down now.*

Matt didn't realize he was already in the eye of hurricane CleanSweep, a category five storm.

Conversation over, Tanner stunned Matt when he stepped forward, embracing the blogger. Matt was self-conscious, ill at ease with the intimacy. He'd tried to hide his awkwardness, aware the embrace was a gift. *Tanner knows I need reassurance and courage going ahead.*

"I believe you, Tanner. I won't let fear stop me. I'll tell the truth about Claussen and CleanSweep."

As they embraced, Tanner whispered, "This won't end well for me. I won't celebrate another anniversary with my wife. My children's—" He choked off the words, unable to continue.

"That's nonsense—"

Tanner clutched him tighter, preventing Matt from finishing.

"Cali and McHale are young; they will soon forget what their father looks like. If you thought I did this for myself, you were wrong," he said. His words boiled with rage. "I'm doing this for my wife and two precious children. I want them to live in a world free from the cancer of Clean-Sweep."

I've never known anyone as brave as Tanner, Matt thought.

Tanner stepped back. "There's no further need for secrecy. Total secrecy was necessary until I could give you the whole story. I admit I wasn't sure I could trust you at first."

That stung Matt some more.

"Now, go public and sound the alarm, spread the word. It won't take Claussen long to determine I was your source for information about CleanSweep. They'll come after me—hard," Tanner said. "Then, they'll come for you as well. Be ready."

"This calls for something—certainly not a celebration. My apartment's nearby," Matt said. "I happen to have some single-malt whiskey, maybe a clean glass or two."

Tanner nodded acceptance. By the time they'd walked to Matt's building, Tanner wrapped his motives and feeling in a shroud, invisible to further scrutiny. When Matt opened the door to his flat, Tanner sounded almost cheerful.

"Nice place."

Matt laughed. He knew Tanner was only being polite. It was a small flat. The front door opened to a large room with a small bedroom off to the right. The kitchenette didn't have room for two people at the same time. It did have a window, however. The kitchen window faced a brick wall six feet away. Matt moved in twelve years ago, and never once opened that window. To him, the apartment was a place to sleep and eat. Housekeeping wasn't Matt's strong point—nor priority.

With a shrug, he pushed magazines, newspapers, and an assortment of junk mail to the end of the sofa, offering Tanner a place to sit.

He was pleased that Tanner looked enough at home to kick off his loafers. Matt smiled at the hole in Tanner's sock when he put his feet on the coffee table. As Tanner leaned back and closed his eyes, Matt wondered if he was falling asleep—until Tanner's head jerked suddenly. "You said you have some scotch. I'm ready to talk about stuff around the edge of the story."

Matt walked to the kitchenette. Opening a cupboard, he pulled out a bottle of Glen Garioch. It was nearly "chockablock," as his father might say. Somehow, he found two glasses, wiping them with his shirttail. He poured the whiskey. It seemed perfect for a time like this.

"Cheers," Tanner said after Matt handed a glass. Like saying "nice place," it was mere habit. There was little to cheer about.

"Cheers," Matt replied, not wanting to be impolite.

Tanner started talking as if he didn't have enough time. It bothered Matt.

"Claussen's a genius," Tanner said. "I give him that. He saw a need and came up with a response. Can we have some music, please? Jazz, if you've got it."

Tanner's request caught Matt off guard. He didn't ask what kind, picking Miles Davis, Matt's favorite. It was Miles's groundbreaking album, *Birth of the Cool*. Set to play at random, the first track was "Deception." Matt savored the irony.

They listened in silence, neither looking at the other, appreciating the intimacy of the moment.

The song finished, Tanner spoke. "I said Claussen's a genius. I should've added *evil* genius. He's the worst kind of evil because he seems normal. So normal, that if he knocked on your door, you would open it wide, waving him in with a grand welcome."

He stared at his glass, finally taking a long, slow sip. "I created notes about his background, especially the grandfather." He reached into his pocket, tossing a flash drive to Matt, who caught it in midair. Tanner continued, "It's all there. You can read it later."

Matt held the flash drive in one hand, his glass in the other, eyes fixed on Tanner. Tempted to sip his own whiskey, he waited for Tanner to continue.

It sounded like an explosion. The glass slipped from Tanner's hand. Shards of glass splintered on the floor, a pool of scotch spreading in an irregular pattern. It reminded Matt of crime scene photo, a blood pool at a murder scene. Matt stared, fascinated and immobile, until he heard Tanner's mournful cry of heartbreak, anguish, and despair. It was a sound Matt never wanted to hear again.

Tanner gazed down at the shards, Matt's cherished Glen Garioch seeping through the cracks of the hardwood floorboards. Tanner seemed puzzled like he didn't know what to do next.

"I should...do you have something to clean—"

Waving his hand to stay seated, Matt pulled himself up. He walked to a closet, coming back with a broom and dustpan. He swept up most of the glass shards.

"Not a very clean sweep," Tanner said. "Pun intended!" If Tanner meant it as funny, it came out humorless.

Matt emptied the contents into a trash can, leaning the dustpan and broom against the wall. He didn't bother with something to wipe the liquid. "I guess we'd best keep our shoes on," he said, walking into the kitchenette.

He found another tumbler, not quite as clean as the first, and filled it anyway.

Tanner's hand trembled, reaching to take it. "I'm so sorry," he said, rubbing tears away with a sleeve. "I don't know what got into me. Actually, I do. That makes it worse."

Matt, unable to help or provide compassion, remained quiet as the music changed. It was the minor blues strains of "Israel" playing in the background. "I like the John Carisi composition. I'm glad Miles included it." He realized Tanner wasn't listening when he saw the man's thousand-yard stare.

Sounding disembodied, Tanner picked up on the CleanSweep story again. "Claussen thought he knew me. I really pulled one over on him, though." Tanner chuckled as he sipped, his hand steady. "Claussen recruited me when I was working on my doctorate, almost ready to graduate. One of his talent scouts sidled up to me, saying he was from Ensûrtech, Claussen's holding company. *Slithered* was more like it, not *sidled*. In truth, he was a snake."

Tanner looked at his glass as if surprised it was empty. Matt refilled it.

"He assured me I would be fast-tracked at Enseûrtech. Except it turned out more like a fast treadmill. I was soon running so hard I never thought about what I was doing.

"I'd been pursued by all the big-league players. They lined up at my door: Google, Apple, Microsoft. I turned them down, choosing Enseûrtech. Poor choice, if you ask me now. What's fate or destiny? Either way, it's mine to live with. And not just *mine*. Fate's followed me to my family. Now to you. I fear for my family." Tanner stopped talking.

"Tell me how you were recruited?" Matt asked.

"What's the guy's name? Oh yeah, Hammond, Don Hammond. No, it was Dan. Hell, it doesn't matter, Don or Dan. He had a corporate jet waiting with engines purring, whisking me off to Pittsburgh. We flew from there to Houston and back here, to Claussen Towers, Enseûrtech headquarters. It's an impressive building, all glass, intended to overwhelm visitors. I was awed—maybe incredulous would be more accurate. Hammond thought they had me back at the first mention of a private jet, truth be told. I told him I was ready to sign, hell I was salivating at the offer even as the wheels were touching down at a corporate airport on the outskirts of Atlanta. The ink wasn't even dry when I got off the plane, reeling from the champagne."

Tanner had a funny look. "I let them believe that," he said. "They weren't the only ones playing a game."

"What was your field of study...you know, in school?" Matt asked as if he were conducting an interview. In a way he was, but he was simply curious at that point.

"For me, it's always been about computers," Tanner said. "Ever since I was a kid, I've had a love affair with computer technology. I was finishing my doctorate in computer science." Tanner took a few moments for himself, smiling about memories of a happier time, perhaps.

"Where was I? Oh yeah. I started working the devil, my Faustian contract. Toward the end of my third month working at Enseûrtech, an e-mail popped up. It was from Claussen's PA, the man's personal assistant. The e-mail was a demand disguised as an invitation. I was expected to give my kneel-before-the-king performance before the almighty Charles Claussen the next afternoon. Declining was not an option." Tanner smiled, remembering something about the story. "The subway wasn't crowded, and I got to Claussen Towers early. The guard at the security desk called me by name. 'You're expected, Mr. Woodson. Carson will escort you.' A uniformed officer appeared as he said that. I was flattered, I admit."

Matt watched Tanner take a long swallow, brushing a hand back through his hair. It didn't help. Spikes of unruly hair refused to get in line. "The elevator stopped on the penthouse floor. Sitting behind the foyer's single desk was the most beautiful woman I've ever seen. She spoke my name in a deep voice—a slight accent that was utterly beguiling."

Tanner laughed. "She also gave off a vibe that could freeze hell over." Tanner laughed at the memory, and Matt laughed along to be polite.

"You want my first impression?"

Matt nodded.

"He wasn't behind a desk, as I expected. There wasn't a desk to be seen. His office suite was furnished like a museum, elegant Victorian furniture. I guessed they weren't reproductions. Two full walls and part of a third were nothing but floor-to-ceiling glass. The effect gave the impression we jutted out over the lake. The view from the top of the world is awe-inspiring, and I wanted to appear dutifully awed and inspired that day.

"Charles Claussen was impeccably dressed, and for some reason, I noticed his shoes. He was wearing loafers. I've no idea why his shoes seemed important at the time. They looked Italian or some exclusive European brand. I found out later they cost more than two months' mortgage on my new condo. I wondered if he was amused when he caught me staring at his shoes.

"When I first entered the office, he didn't seem to acknowledge I was there. He sat on a sofa. Eventually, he stood, as if he'd just noticed someone new in the room. He offered his hand in one fluid motion, a manner suggesting friendship. He didn't beat around the bush. He asked me if I was the one, the one helping him take Enseûrtech to the next level. There was no question in my mind that I was being interrogated. Sure, Claussen made it seem casual. His hail-fellow-well-met manner didn't fool me. He asked questions and listened to my answers, nodding whenever it was called for. Abruptly, he stood and led me to the door. My audience with the wizard was over. He'd tired of my presence. He told me to meet with the head of security, a woman named Angela Vaughn. We shook hands—

all very formal—and suddenly I was standing in the reception area, listening to the door close behind me.

"I was puzzled by the interview. I wondered why it was so lacking in detail. I finally decided he'd merely wanted to see for himself. He knew I was in his pocket. He never knew I was a master pickpocket. The art of picking someone's pocket is in deception, like the title of that Miles Davis song."

"What do you mean, pickpocket?" Matt asked.

Tanner started to chortle. "They thought I was dazzled by a private jet and expensive champagne. Claussen must have thought my kneel-before-the-king performance was real. He gave me the key to a job, but I'd already picked the master key from his pocket, front side, right." Tanner laughed one of the most unpleasant laughs Matt ever heard.

"I took one last look at the receptionist," Tanner said. "I saw her looking at me with a glare. Her job was gatekeeper to the remarkable Charles Claussen. She was indifferent to mere mortals—like me."

Tanner and Matt agreed to set the story aside for a time. Talking about Miles Davis, Tanner asked if Matt had *Sketches of Spain*. Matt nodded yes. They finished the last of the single malt, the trumpet of Miles Davis seducing them with thoughts of Spanish dancers, the music transporting them to a sunny place—a far better place, they both agreed.

"You know the movie *The Wizard of Oz*?" Tanner asked. "That's what I kept thinking about on the way home from that interview. Claussen sat behind a screen, hoping he wouldn't be exposed. Just like the wizard was in that old movie I watch every year with my kids."

He brushed a tear as he mentioned his children. "The bastard didn't know I would be the one pulling back the scrim. I was going to let the world see him for what he really is.

"At times it's easy to trick a genius. They assume you can't play their games. He didn't see through my masquerade. I was a cosmic joke, a mole who would bore into the core for the truth. I'm a card-carrying closet communist, Matt. I wormed my way into that man's most closely guarded secret.

"With a handshake in one hand, I had the other on Claussen's key to CleanSweep. My new job allowed me to discover how devious his plan really was. That's why I've told you all this. History shows dictators are most vulnerable at the beginning, but people are afraid to take action to stop them. You have to promise to *stop* him, Matt!"

• • •

Tanner got up and walked to the door with a slight wobble—hardly noticeable. "Where's my jacket?"

"It's on the kitchen table," Matt said. He handed it to him and watched Tanner leave without another word, not even a goodbye. Tanner walked out with shoulders back, head high, as if proud to play his small role in history.

Matt watched Tanner's back as he walked to the elevator. For some reason, it reminded Matt of the scene in *To Kill a Mockingbird* when Reverend Sykes says, 'Miss Jean Louise, stand up. Your father's passin'.'

Matt straightened up, his show of respect to the Tanner passing by—perhaps aware he would never see Tanner again.

• • •

Two days later, Matt was watching the news when he learned about Tanner's accident. The reporter said police there was no evidence of braking before Tanner's car plunged off the Glen Road bridge. The report was replaced by a video interview with the grieving widow. "I have no idea why he would be there, no explanation," she said, breaking into sobs.

Matt knew it wasn't a coincidence.

When he needed courage, Matt only had to remember Tanner—the way he looked walking out that last night together. Matt could play that image in his mind like a recorded video, honoring the man who pointed out this dangerous journey.

Tanner was proof of CleanSweep's evil.

CHAPTER 7

NOSE FOR THE NEWS

"**S**he's on the way and fuming!" someone shouted.

Nobody had to ask who or why. Interns and reporters scrambled, trying to find a good reason to be somewhere else. It didn't matter where if they escaped her wrath.

Camera crews, the audio man, and the floor director all headed for corners—out of sight.

Her cameraman followed, knowing why she was in a foul mood. Susan Payne generally stomped around, warning people out of her way. Today, however, was different. She stormed into the newsroom with exceptional fury. Remy, her cameraman, watched her grab a run-sheet, staring as if it emitted a nasty odor. Rolling the sheet in a ball, she threw it against a backdrop and marched into her office.

Thriving as the center of attention, she knew her coworkers called her Hurricane Sue behind her back. She secretly enjoyed the nickname. Her ratings were consistently over the top, and viewers loved her. Even her competitors admitted she was the best in the business. Her office held an assortment trophies and awards. Photographs lined two walls, Susan Payne posing with entertainment celebrities, sports heroes, and politicians.

When there was a breaking news story, viewers tuned to Sue wearing a serious expression like a uniform. Looking at the close-up camera, her solemn voice reassured viewers they got the latest, most accurate news.

Seven years ago, when Remy, Carl Remington, joined Action 21, the news director took him aside. "You're going to be Susan Payne's cameraman. I should warn you," he said with a chuckle. "The most dangerous job in the world is to get between Susan Payne's way and a scoop." He paused. "She asked—no, *demanded*—we assign you."

Today, Remy watched two interns trying to avoid her fierce look, enjoying their discomfort. Remy wasn't afraid of her, not anymore. They'd been a team for almost eight years now. He recognized her moods with one look. No, Remy wasn't afraid of her. Not at all.

A cameraman once told Remy he didn't like Hurricane Sue very much. "How do you work with someone like that?"

"Besides smart and knowing a good story when she sees it, she's the best I've ever worked with. Payne's the best there is. I respect her," Remy answered.

He liked to think respect was mutual, but he also suspected the only person Susan Payne admired was Susan Payne. Personal feelings didn't matter to them. They rarely let petty emotions get in the way. Remy knew Susan valued having a pro looking at her through the camera's eyepiece.

The news director, on another occasion said, "You're the finest cameraman around and she knows it."

• • •

Remy knew why Hurricane Sue was going category five. He'd read the run-sheet, attached to an email. Susan was angry, worse than usual. The Susan-Remy team were scooped by a kid, an intern working for the competition. Remy cringed when he saw the video. It was good.

With Susan Payne in her office, the newsroom returned to go live with the evening news. The newsroom clock's a cruel master, the seconds counting down on digital display. The lead story, an accident involving a school bus, didn't have video coverage. The Action 21 News team scrambled without any raw video to edit.

They needed something as a backdrop. This time, the producer resorted to B-roll video from the vault. The scriptwriter typed furiously, but Susan Payne would open the show with a file copy video showing a school bus with happy children waving from the window as it drove by. Worse, it was tired-looking, six-year-old B-roll.

Award-winning Susan Payne missed the story.

Karen, the director, shouted obscenities, and the graphics team and floor crew clawed at their headphone volume control as the director vented her anger.

"What we *don't* have," Karen shouted through their earpiece, "is actual friggin' footage of the story!" She ripped her headset off, hurling it across the control room. "Where the hell was Susan when that story happened?"

• • •

A young man became an instant media hero. A car collided with a school bus. He ran out of a nearby dry-cleaning store and pried open the emergency door of the overturned. Flames and smoke filled the burning school bus. He'd rescued the children and driver. A camera caught it all. Remy knew the money shot was magnificent.

The video showed the hero carrying the last child from the bus, smoldering and tattered clothes, as he cradled a young girl. They were both crying. As the camera moved in for a close-up of the tears, the bus erupted into an enormous fireball behind them, followed by a terrific explosion. It was a video destined for an award.

He watched it several times. It was already posted on the competing station's website. He paused it, looking at the freeze-frame. He laughed reading the credits. The camera operator was Marcia Cameron, a student intern. She'd been in the same dry cleaners when the accident happened. She pulled out her camera and captured the scene flawlessly. She even provided her own breathless voice-over.

Lucky bitch! He wanted to be jealous, but he admired her impressive work.

The Susan-Remy team were miles away, assigned to covering an awards ceremony honoring a retiring court clerk.

Yawn.

• • •

He watched Susan pick up a stapler, throwing it at the wall. It wasn't the first time. Several holes in the dry wall had been patched over because of that stapler. Next, she booted her wastebasket through the doorway. Remy watched it tumble through the newsroom—papers scattering. It was a kick worthy of an NFL place kicker.

He smiled. Despite the display of anger, her perfectly arranged hairdo was in place.

The eye of a hurricane, always ready for the camera, he thought.

Remy also knew Susan Payne was worried about something else. She was probing rumors, whispers about a program called CleanSweep. The more she probed and pleaded with her informants, the more dangerous it sounded. Remy had never seen Susan Frightened. She was now.

• • •

Remy left the newsroom and walked to the storage room used by camera crews. Opening his locker, he lifted a case, placing it on a counter. The case held his two soul-catchers. He'd read that primitive peoples believed a camera could capture their souls. "Now I do it in high definition," he'd once quipped to Susan. He'd once confided to her he would lay down his life to save his cameras.

He placed a camera alongside the case. Pulling a cloth from his pocket, he began cleaning the already spotless camera, a ritual he performed without fail. His primary camera was an expensive investment he never regretted. A compartment inside the case held blank media cards. He could use cards to transfer images, using Final Cut Pro software on a handheld editor. The camera and equipment cost a small fortune. The station offered to pay for it, but Remy wanted ownership. Editing in the field, Remy uploaded files to the station's FTP site using Internet or satellite links.

His footage often went on air live, the video polished. The director trusted his close-cut field editing.

He fit the camera to the case and picked up the mic. Remy preferred a sensitive wireless lavalier mic for audio, attaching it to the person being interviewed. Susan used a handheld microphone, wielding it like a scepter, shoving it into the face of interviewees. Susan was adamant about using a hand-held. "The viewers don't trust it if they don't see a microphone," she'd once told him.

His camera had the latest audio features, able to pick up background sound in high fidelity.

Sometimes he skipped editing, sending raw footage live, using the camera's built-in satellite transmitter. Susan believed that edgy look implied uncensored authenticity to a story.

Remy pretended he didn't care about Susan's idiosyncrasies. She was an award winner and a pro, and he admired her professionalism. He was miffed she received her awards without acknowledging her cameraman, but was aware those egocentric characteristics were important, especially for a woman reporter. She was oblivious—perhaps indifferent—about the power she wielded.

Remy knew he could use the camera for good or otherwise. The shot could make or break a talking head like Susan.

A small movement of his thumb, and the shot would be slightly out of focus. He knew the trick of creating unflattering camera angles. He knew colleagues who sabotaged reporters they didn't like. Remy was a pro. He'd never do such things, especially to Susan.

Camera and equipment repacked, he was ready to follow news, wherever that led. As he locked the case, Remy heard banging doors and raised voices. The news was coming to him.

He raced back to the newsroom.

• • •

"What the—" someone yelled.

"Who the hell are you?" Karen said, alarm in her tone.

"We have a warrant. Stand aside," a man issued the command.

"I don't appreciate your—" Karen started to say.

"Shut up and get out of our way." The man didn't raise his voice, making the threat more ominous.

Karen demanded to see the warrant. Remy watched her face turn crimson. "I'm calling our lawyer!"

Remy realized his camera was back in the storage room. *Who knew I needed it in the studio,* he thought. This was the newsroom after all, a place to report news, not make it.

The newsroom was in disorder and pandemonium. Without his camera, Remy did the next best thing. He raised his smartphone, starting to record the scene—until a man grabbed it. Seven or eight men in dark suits fanned out in the newsroom. Maybe more. Remy stopped counting. These were men nobody argued with; each had shaved heads. Whoever they were, they looked like men who spent serious time in gyms.

Some wore dark glasses, allowing them to avoid the bright studio lighting. None looked friendly as they spread out and began entering the private offices in pairs.

A woman marched in, waving a paper. "Here's the warrant. Everyone, stand aside. Nobody touches anything: papers, flash drives, computer discs, media cards, or electronic equipment. Is that clear?"

"No, it's not at all clear," Karen said, but her voice sounded hesitant. She looked at the woman, clearly in charge. "We have rights. This is a newsroom."

"I don't need to explain. This," she said, holding another paper, "grants search-and-seizure power to CleanSweep agents. These powers allow us to seize anything deemed a threat to national security. I have my finger on speed dial, a number to one of the new CleanSweep appointed judges. Go ahead, call your lawyer. He can't do a damn thing about it."

"You can't do this!" someone yelled.

"This isn't right!" another person said.

Anger and self-righteous tones slowly faded. Newsroom egos realized these people were truly frightening.

• • •

Remy, sensing danger, edged back. He saw the agents look away. He slipped out, softly closing the door. He raced to the storeroom. He reached into a side compartment of his camera case and removed three media cards. Spotting duct tape on the counter and kneeling quickly, taped them to the underside of the table. He stood, putting the tape away when the door opened, banging against a chair.

"What the hell are you doing?" a man demanded. "Phillips saw you leave the newsroom. You had orders to stay put."

Remy stood quietly, shrugging his shoulders. Three more men followed to search the room, rummaging in cupboards, drawers, and closets, without regard to damage. He sensed they knew what they were looking for. He watched one of the men take all the media cards from his camera case. They looked closely at the ones with labels, placing them in a plastic bag. Remy recognized it for what it was: an evidence bag.

They won't find anything on those cards. Please, please don't look under the table.

Finished, he was escorted back to the studio.

He caught Susan's eye, giving a quick up-chin nod; the cards were safe. She almost smiled.

• • •

The woman in charge gave an order, and they left, leaving something unheard of in a newsroom: silence. The beast that devours news was rendered senseless, even worse, speechless.

Karen, the director, waved her hand like it was a magician's wand.

"Live in five, four, three, two, one," the floor director said, pointing at the news desk. On schedule, like every Monday through Friday.

Moments before the newsroom turned on its ear by looking men, Mark the newsreader realized he was holding his breath. The music faded, Mark looking toward camera one. "Fourteen children owe their life to the hero who rescued them from a burning bus..."

Remy thought Mark deserved an award for that performance.

Someone, Remy thought it was the intern, let out a loud sigh, the sound made from holding one's breath, exhaling slowly no longer optional. It broke the thick tension in the newsroom.

"What the heck was that all about?" someone said, the question on everyone's mind finally voiced.

With a roar, the newsroom beast came back to life.

"You've all heard it," Karen said. The show must go on.'" Karen's voice had a noticeable tremble. "Move your asses. Let's get this bitch on air!" Karen whipped her crew into action, screaming over the uproar of staff, cast, and technicians.

"Has anyone seen my weather segment," a man said.

Remy was holding his breath, escaping air hissing. He saw Susan standing in the doorway of her office. The uncertainty on her face was a look he rarely saw. More than hesitancy, it was fear.

He nodded his chin over his left shoulder, toward the storage room. He thought she missed it, ready to repeat it, but she pushed away from the doorframe to follow him.

"What the hell was that?" she asked in a hushed voice, brushing her hair back. Remy knew she did that when she was tense, a gesture hidden from everyone except Remy.

How many times have I noticed her doing that through the eyepiece? He wondered.

She paid a high emotional price to the best in the business, a relentless need to be perfect.

"Did they find them?"

He knew what she was asking. He knelt on one knee, reaching under the table, the media cards still securely in place.

"They knew what they were looking for. They put my blank media cards in evidence bags."

"This is getting serious." She looked up at the ceiling, trying to think of something more to say. "That damn blogger, Matt Tremain, is right," she said, teeth clenched. "It won't stop with this search, will it? They know we know."

Remy flinched. "They didn't find the cards," he said. "I taped the Claussen interview cards to the underside of the table just before they came in. It won't take long to realize they don't have what they're looking for. They'll be back."

"What are we going to do?"

"I need to find a safe place. They're all the interviews we have on CleanSweep, especially your interviews with Mattie and Clifford. That's damning evidence. When you match it with the stuff the blogger has..."

He paused. "What if they know already, and they're waiting outside? They'll search us?" He chewed at his lip in frustration. "Hand me my old camera—that one," he said, pointing to a high shelf. "I have an idea."

Susan did something unprecedented: obeyed without question.

He looked at the vintage camera. "I haven't used this in over seven years. It's a dinosaur," he said, laughing. A compartment opened on the side. Remy saw a video cassette. "Look, it still has footage. I wonder what's on it?" He ejected the plastic case, the size of a small brick. He opened through a tool drawer, sorting until he found the one he was looking for. It was a specially designed screwdriver for unlocking the casing, revealing the tape. He showed Susan how it passed over the recording head, winding from reel to reel.

"As if I don't know who it works," she said, snapping the words like a whip.

"Get the cards taped up under the table," he whispered. He watched Susan kneel, noting vaguely it was an immodest pose. She straightened, handing the cards to Remy.

"I've got the equivalent of more than two hundred and fifty of these old cassettes on just one media card. Technology."

Remy held a card between thumb and finger as he reached for a pair of tweezers. He gently inserted a media card under one of the reels, repeating until the three were well hidden inside an old cartridge.

"There," he said, looking satisfied. He replaced the cover of the cassette, reinserting into the camera slot. "That's the best I can do," he said. "Now I need to remember where I put the old camera bag. He reached into another cabinet and pulled it out, rubbing the dust away. "This brings back memories," he murmured wistfully. He nestled the camera into the case as gently as if it were a baby swaddled in soft blankets.

"You carry it," he said to Susan. "I hope that doesn't offend your on-air talent sensibilities, or get me in trouble with the union. They'll be taking mine apart. Maybe that will be a distraction."

She didn't argue, taking the case, hitching the strap over her shoulder.

He turned back to the workbench and his working camera. "They can look through this all they want," he said. "They won't find what they're after. It'll be painful to watch them taking the camera and case apart."

• • •

Susan and Remy returned to the newsroom, the control center operating in full form: absolute chaos, barely under control. "Make our movements look like we're going on assignment," Remy said. He led through screaming interns and technicians, trying to make their voices heard. Everyone was doing their best piecing together of what remained of the on-air production, the clock approaching the thirty-minute mark, halfway through the broadcast. No one noticed Susan follow Remy out of the newsroom. They closed the door behind and headed down the hallway to a door. It opened to a short set of stairs to the parking garage.

They walked toward their parking space when a woman's voice echoed in the silence: "Stop! Now!" Her tone was dark and rough.

"Drop the cases," a man said, much softer and way more feminine than the woman's. "Put them on the ground," he ordered.

Remy looked at Susan and shrugged. "It works, or it doesn't," he said.

Two men appeared with tripods, attaching lamps—bright light police use at crime scenes. Another man assembled a folding table. *The cameras cases look naked in this light*, Remy thought.

Men began tearing the cases apart, cutting away the lining to see if anything was hidden. A man began taking the cameras apart, causing Remy to flinch.

"Keep your hands visible," an agent told Remy and Susan. Two agents did an expert pat down, leaving nothing to chance. Remy detected her tension, moving so he touched her arm lightly. It was a simple touch, but he felt her tension ease.

Remy smiled, realizing this was an odd time for him to discover he might be in love with her.

The agents examined both cameras and cases. Remy's legs went rubbery when they inspected his old camera.

Did I hide the cards well enough?

He watched a man take the old camera case and camera apart. The man seemed to know his way around cameras. When the agent pulled the cassette tape out of its slot, he stared at it for a long time, finally tossing it on the hood of an adjacent parked car, discarded as no great shakes. He turned to the woman in charge, "Nothing, boss. I'm sorry, I mean...and—"

"You said your informant was reliable," she cut him off with a harsh wave, her voice like fingernails on a blackboard. "Take everything. When you get back to headquarters, I want you going over everything with a microscope. I want your report in two hours." She turned and strode to a waiting car, not bothering to listen for a response.

Remy touched Susan's arm as they watched the two cameras, cases, and accessories loaded into the open door of a minivan, a Nissan Quest. The automatic door closed. The van and chase car sped down the ramp of the parking deck. He pointed to the discarded cassette tape, still on the hood of a car. Forgotten.

• • •

"Are they gone?" Susan whispered.

Remy was surprised at the calm in her voice. He shrugged an answer and looked at the plastic cassette. "It's this story, CleanSweep. I think we've stepped in a big pile of shit." It was all he could think to say. He picked up the cassette, holding it like a stick of dynamite with a burning fuse—a very short burning fuse.

Remy smiled. The subtle change in their relationship felt seismic. Susan followed his lead. Self-assured with inner strength, she often seemed fearless, rarely allowing any display of affection. It was like she flipped a switch, deciding to surrender power, giving him the leadership role. *No*, he thought. *It's different. There's a spark between us.*

Susan, realizing it also, put it into words. "This time we need to rely on your expertise," she said, no doubt in her voice. "I'm a damn good journalist, but this is bigger. It'll take both of us to work it, especially your street skills and contacts." She paused. "I've always known we're a team. I would never get where I am without you."

Remy felt his face redden. He turned his attention to the cassette. "We need to hurry and contact Tremain." He scrolled through contacts on his throwaway phone.

He turned to Susan. "We need to meet with him. The three of us have turned over a rock, and some very nasty bugs are crawling into the daylight."

He looked up from the phone. Susan nodded, waiting for Remy to tell her what to do next.

"If the stories are true, they can even track this," he said, holding the phone up. "It has a SIM card they can track with GPS technology." He pulled an old flip phone from another pocket. "You haven't seen one like *this* in years. Let them try to track it. I've had it since 1989." He laughed. "We like to think new and improved is best, but sometimes old school has an advantage. Someone might be able to eavesdrop, but they won't be able to pinpoint our location."

"Leave it to you to have a relic like that," she said, chuckling. "But speaking of old school, I'm glad you had that old camera. You saved our butts. It was like watching a game of three-card-monte. They never saw the hidden-card."

"We can't go home." Remy looked around, suddenly alert. "Where the hell did they all go? Why aren't they keeping us under surveillance?" Then he held his hand for silence, pointing to a doorway. "It leads to stairs to the alleyway between the building and garage."

At the foot of the stairs, he held up his hand again, listening for footsteps, voices, other signs someone might be near. Satisfied, he dialed. After a moment Remy talked, keeping his voice low.

"It's me. We need to meet. You remember the place we first met?"

He waited, listening. "Yeah, that's the place." He looked at Susan while he paused. "Ask for Susie's room at the desk."

"We're meeting Matt," Remy said. "It's arranged. Now we walk. It's a long walk. Are you up to it?" He knew she was, but he said it to challenge her, to jolt her with energy, keeping shock and fear from creeping from her thoughts. It worked.

Susan's withering look of disdain caused him to relax, she was returning to her old self, for better or worse. He slammed the cassette against the wall to break it apart. He picked out the media cards, shoving them into his pocket. He opened the exit door, and the two of them stepped into the night.

CHAPTER 8

BAD NEWS TRAVELS FAST

Angela Vaughn stood at the door, an office without a nameplate. Everyone knew it belonged to Charles Claussen. Not much terrified Vaughn, but the man in this office did. Instead of knocking, she walked to the restroom, always a good delaying tactic. She knew it was pointless to avoid her report.

She had to face Claussen with the truth. Looking in the mirror, she checked her eyes. *Do they show any sign of weakness?* she wondered. Cupping her hands, she splashed cold water on her face. She didn't have to worry about spoiling her makeup; she never wore any. Angela Vaughn was careful about her hair, however. She used a brush to smooth errant strands.

"I might as well get it over with," she said aloud.

Satisfied with her tailored, dark-blue suit chosen to compliment her physique, she turned toward the door. Angela Vaughn, at forty-two, followed a rigorous workout regimen, a routine since the police academy. Walking back to Claussen's office, her hand reached for her police shield, one she no longer wore.

Angela would still be a cop, if not for a seduction orchestrated by Charles Claussen. For Claussen, seduction wasn't about sex. He seduced with offers of financial rewards and power, like the serpent in the Garden of Eden. "Head up my security team—a specialty security team. You will have power beyond imagination." Angela Vaughn thought that sounded too good to be true.

With a final pause, she rapped softly on the door.

"Enter." The word filtered through the door in a rich baritone voice.

• • •

Angela closed the door behind her, feeling like she was standing over a trapdoor. One false move, it would spring open. Falling through, her name erased from history. She waited.

Charles Claussen played his role with an actor's precision, knowing how long to hold a pause for the right dramatic effect. His eyes gave nothing away.

Angela crossed her arms, as if the gesture would offer protection from his gaze. Angela, unaware of her nervous tendency, didn't know Claussen recognized it, as he continued waiting without speaking.

He held a paper and looked at it before letting it fall from his grip, fluttering like a poorly made paper airplane. "I'm not going to like what you're about to say, am I?"

Angela knew direct to the point was best. "We searched, went through everything," she said. "We tore the Action 21 newsroom apart. Nothing! We took Carl Remington's camera and case apart, zilch. We dismantled his backup camera, looking for hidden media cards or flash drives. I have men specializing in pat-down searches, nothing. My source said they recorded their interviews on three media cards. We just—"

Claussen cut her words short. "I'm not interested in what you *didn't* find," he said, letting the words hang in the air. "Skip the history lesson. Where are you going from here? Tell me your next step to find those cards. I want to know *when* you are going to find them. What's next?"

The soft words made his anger seem ominous.

Angela felt a bead of moisture forming on her upper lip, resisting the urge to wipe it away. "I have a team at Payne's condo right now," she said. "They're tearing it apart. If the cards are there, they'll be found. The cameraman's apartment is too obvious. He wouldn't hide them there, but I have a team taking it apart, in case. I have my best people on this," she said, gaining confidence.

What am I missing? she wondered, shifting slightly from one foot to the other.

"We've also checked safe deposit boxes. Don't ask me how we got into them," she added.

"I am asking," he snapped.

She started to cross her arms again, catching herself. "A special agent, trained in covert investigation, broke into the files of Susan Payne's attorney. A spare safe deposit box key was in the file. It was a simple matter: duplicate the key." Angela gathered her thoughts. "We went through the box, her computer files, e-mail accounts, wireless phone records, nada. Not a damn thing," she said, careful not to shrug.

His eyes sparked when she cursed. She knew he hated swearing. She braced herself to report more bad news.

"It's my fault," she admitted. "We had them. We lost them. We surprised them in the parking deck as they were leaving the studio. There was a moment they weren't under surveillance." She watched Claussen, waiting for a reaction. When there was none, she went on. "I take full responsibility. We were focusing on inspecting the equipment when Susan and her cameraman just disappeared. I didn't check for that back exit."

Angela saw anger in the eyes of the man behind the desk. "We don't know where they went—yet. But there's more," she hesitated. "Matthew Tremain has also dropped out of sight. We had a team—"

"Stop." Claussen pounded the top of his desk. It was uncharacteristic. "I've heard enough!"

The room filled with quiet. Soundproofing kept conversations private, but it also kept outside noise from intruding. The only sound Angela heard was ticking, the expensive watch her boss was wearing. She felt the veins of her neck pulsing as her heart raced. She began to lose track of time. When Claussen finally spoke, his voice was colder than before.

"Ça va," he said with a shrug, "so it goes."

Angela couldn't believe the sudden shift in tone, the nonchalant shrug, and seeming indifference.

"They have to be stopped," he went on. "You know why better than anyone. I hired you to protect CleanSweep, to keep it hidden from view." She heard a hint of anxiety tiptoeing behind his words. "If they go public, everything I have worked for will be ruined. You will *not* let these amateurs do that."

Claussen stood, walking calmly until he was so close she bent back to avoid contact. Minty breath brushed her cheeks like a feather.

"You have forty-eight hours." He didn't need to add threats or warnings. Angela Vaughn knew what awaited her if she failed. She'd read files of those who had disappointed Claussen. Reputations—and worse. She'd been party to worse; Tanner Woodson's blood stained her hands.

He opened the door and motioned with a nod. The grilling was over. As Angela walked out, the door closed softly behind her. Claussen, master of self-control, would never slam a door in anger.

Angela felt as if the floor was flowing like water as she walked down the corridor, intent on surviving.

At least I didn't fall through that trapdoor...yet, she thought.

CHAPTER 9

WHAT JUST HAPPENED?

Susan was the first to speak. "What happened? How did we get away like that?"

"They were distracted, intent on finding the cards. They took their eye off the ball, thinking they had us blocked in. I hoped they didn't have the back stairs covered. Nobody uses them, and they don't attract attention. But I admit, I'm surprised we got away with it."

"What now?" Susan asked.

"We walk."

"At least I have the shoes for it."

"Yeah, the ugliest shoes I've ever seen," Remy said, laughing.

She ignored him.

Electric blue, a vivid neon color, others envied her choice when they found themselves standing in mud, slush, or snow for long periods.

"Sensible shoes are an asset today," he said. They started walking.

"Where are we going again?" she asked. "We've been walking over an hour."

"It's not far," he said, panting for breath, clear evidence he was a former smoker.

"That's what you said fifteen minutes ago," she grumbled. "How does Tremain know where to meet us? I heard you tell him the same place we met before, but we're going in the opposite direction." Susan was insistent. "Where are we going, Remy?" How does he know where to meet us?"

"The first place we met him was that no-tell-motel on Lakeshore."
She nodded.

"I'm guessing the agents know about that meeting place. I'll bet they have a team of watchers there already. Imagine them counting bedbugs and roaches. The only way to ever sanitize that place would be to burn it down. Ah, the romance of renting a room like that by the hour, let alone an entire night. I wonder if the agents got any ideas to look at the mirrors on the ceiling...." He knew it wasn't that funny, but couldn't stop his nervous laughter. "Anyway," he continued, "Matt and I met somewhere else the first time. We're heading there—the Europa," he said, watching her eyebrows lift in surprise.

"That place...." She searched for words. "That's where that horrific double murder was not long ago. What a dump. And you thought the place on Lakeshore was shabby!"

• • •

They walked, planting one step in front of another, east on Cherry to Commissioners, toward the Martin Goodman Trail. They were careful to turn away from headlights and curious looks. They followed the trail to Eastern Avenue. As they turned, a cyclist raced toward them. Susan gasped as Remy put a hand on her shoulder, urging her to the side. The rider sped past without slowing. They watched until the man was out of view and stepped into a lighted street.

"What about surveillance cameras?" Susan asked, as they walked past a streetlight. They saw a camera pointing a bit to the side.

Remy removed a small electronic instrument from his pocket.

"I was preparing the camera up for a shot and discovered this by accident." He showed her. "When I pushed this button, it screwed up the cameras, causing them to go wonky. It interrupts the frequency used to send streaming video back to computers. Tonight, I've been doing that as we pass those damn surveillance cameras," he said, pointing it. "If it doesn't work, well...." He didn't need to finish.

Leaving the walking trail, they looked over their shoulders whenever a car approached.

Remy sensed a difference about one approaching. He pushed Susan into the shadow of a store doorway, clutching her in an embrace. The car slowed, almost paused, accelerated, and moved on. He held her in a hug as the lights swept past them.

Hugging her, he felt a strong desire to kiss the woman he'd been watching through the camera eyepiece. Struggling with his feelings for months, he knew he was in love with Hurricane Sue.

The moment for the kiss passed.

"Don't get any ideas," she said, pushing distance between them. He sensed she was teasing. They stood silently, afraid to talk about the new chemistry between them. They began walking again. She slipped her hand into his. "Just playing my part in this drama," she said.

But then again... He smiled at that thought.

• • •

"When you were talking to Matt earlier, you never mentioned the name of motel," she said. "How can you be sure he'll know?"

"*Susie* was our code word for it. You hate being called that." He smiled as she flinched. "When he heard that name, he knew." Remy explained as they walked. "This job has often taken us to the edge of safety and danger. You and I both feed on risk. But this story is different, isn't it? We both know it. We were always careful. We walked to the edge of danger, but always knew when to step back. I'm don't know if we can step back this time, Sue."

"Remy, you're really starting to scare me."

"Welcome to reality," he snapped, smoothing the tone in his voice. "He knew if I mentioned Susie in a message it meant the Europa; I met him there the first time. I never told you about that meeting."

He saw hurt in her eyes.

"Matt contacted me and wanted my assurance you were a stand-up reporter. He seemed to trust me when I said you are."

If Susan was annoyed, she chose not to show it. "I could use a sit-down," she said. A small park bench sat in a small courtyard safely hidden in the shadows between two stores.

"Damn, it feels good to sit," he admitted. He looked at his watch and massaged the back of his right leg. "We've been walking for almost two hours. Matt won't be there yet. We can rest here for a while."

"I didn't believe Tremain at first. I know now I was wrong." Her voice echoed from nearby walls, wistful and pensive. "The pieces didn't add up for me at first. It seemed incomprehensible that in *our country*—" She stopped. "I mean, locking someone up because they're homeless... Stuff like that makes me uncomfortable. It's preposterous."

Remy looked at her. "I believed him. I sensed it happening around us. People disappeared, the kind we would barely miss. Maybe we subconsciously felt glad they weren't around anymore. Look where we're sitting now," he said. "Six months ago, this courtyard was a nighttime home to derelicts, the detritus of our society. There was a rusted shopping cart over there. I know; I was here. I filmed it."

"I can't believe Charles Claussen is behind it all. That's hard to swallow," she said.

"It's all here," he said, patting his pocket. "I've got your entire interview series with Matt. The two of you interviewing each other was like watching a battle, no quarter given. But did you notice how frightened he was that last time? He appeared more worried each time the two of you talked. When you got on your professional high horse, it got tense. I thought he was going to lose it when you challenged him about his sources."

"Yeah, but you heard Tremain," she said. "He's young and doesn't have much experience, but he had his sources nailed down tight. I didn't expect that from an amateur blogger. And those pictures he has. They're proof it's even worse than locking people away. That video he has looks like it was recorded with a smartphone."

Remy stretched his legs. "We have to get moving," he said without getting up. "I've been thinking about that raid on the newsroom. They pretended to search randomly, but you and I both know they focused on your office and my camera cases. I recognized that woman. She's head of security for Claussen's company. Her name's Angela Vaughn. Besides other documentation, they're after your interviews with Matt Tremain. They knew exactly what they were looking for." He patted his photographer's vest. "They're desperate to get their hands on the cards, desperate enough to stop at nothing—even torture or murder. These, and the evidence Matt has, can bring Claussen down. We've been lucky, but...."

A decrepit, twenty-year-old Saab bounced over a pothole, belching clouds of black exhaust. He relaxed.

"I don't know why they dropped their guard back in the parking deck, but I'm not going to overanalyze it. I'm just thankful we could take advantage of it."

He stopped talking when he saw the crack in her defenses.

Tears began to fill her eyes as she asked, "They aren't going to stop, are they?"

Remy shook his head, no. "I've something else. Matt gave me a copy of a flash drive when we had coffee last week. He left it folded in a newspaper as left, like we were in a spy novel.

"Claussen's agents are after this and think both you and Matt have them. They're tearing our homes apart now—you can bank on it. I left a fake back in my apartment. They'll know it's bogus soon enough, but I have the real-deal here. I made another copy and hid. Four or five years ago, I rented a mailbox under an alias. Last week, I mailed the copy to that box. It's still there. I checked yesterday. I wanted you to know about it, just in case—"

"Did you see what's on the file? Can they find anything on your computer?"

"Not unless they know which computer I used at the central reference library. I never use a computer at home for anything I wanted to keep secret. And yes, I looked at it."

"And?" She left the question hanging.

"The file contains Claussen's family tree. At least the first file does. His grandfather was an engineer in the German army. The old man was one of the first to join the Nazi Party in the 1920s. I uncovered a file with his party number, a number so low he was eligible for a distinctive badge, the Golden Medal of the Nazi Party, *Goldenes Ehrenzeichen der NSDAP*," he said, wrinkling his nose in disgust.

"He was ordered to designed and supervise construction of the wall around Warsaw Ghetto, keeping Jews trapped inside. The grandfather oversaw every detail of the construction, intending it as a template for other cities. Matt found copies of photographs, blueprints, identification cards, and other documents to back up the story. There's one photo of the old man striking a petulant pose in front of the ghetto wall, hand on hip, flashing a wicked smile for the camera. He's still alive, living with Claussen, dressing that old evil in modern words."

Susan trembled at the parallels to contemporary political rhetoric now, building walls now to keep people out.

Remy started pacing. "We have to get moving. I don't like it on the street like this."

Susan, on an impulse, embraced him. Remy pushed her back gently, placing his finger under her chin. They looked at each other, he realizing what she already knew, they were in love.

Susan cried softly as they walked, arm in arm, lovers out for an evening stroll. The mood didn't last long.

Susan stopped abruptly. "All right. How do I look? We need to meet with Tremain and figure out a way to stop Claussen." She smoothed her hair back, putting on her reporter look.

The large sign for the Europa Motel drew them like moths.

"Left, right, left, right," Susan ordered, trying to imitate a drill sergeant.

They'd been walking for over two hours. Remy's pace slowed considerably. "A blister," he said. "I have to warn you. The only good sign about the Europa," he said, gesturing, "is the one we're looking at. Website rating motels these days don't have rating low enough for a dump like this. It's a tie with the one on Lakeside."

"If I can sit and kick these shoes off, I don't care if it has fleas or bedbugs," she said—a comment she would later regret.

"If you can find a clean place to sit, be my guest."

CHAPTER 10

EUROPA MOTEL

The clerk behind the registration desk looked well past retirement age, lacking a decent pension plan. Graham, according to his name tag, quickly stubbed out a cigarette when Susan and Remy opened the door. The motel used a low-tech bell that jangled when the door opened. The clerk coughed, waving smoke away, a thick haze obscuring the no-smoking sign.

Remy peered over the counter at a half-finished crossword puzzle.

His cough lessening, the clerk said, "Eight-five for the night, Fifty by the hour. There're clean sheets and—"

Remy slapped a hundred-dollar bill on the counter to cut off any further explanation. He added a fifty-dollar bill, the clerks' eyes looked widening. "Keep the change," he said, with a sharp tone. "When a man named Kyle gets here, he'll ask for Susie's room. Send him to our room. If anyone else asks," he said, taking his hand off the fifty-dollar bill, "you've never seen us."

"At my age, I don't see much of anything," the clerk said. He made the money vanish like a magician and pushed a registration card toward Remy.

He picked up the key, looking quizzical. "What room?" he asked.

"Room 131," the clerk said. "Around back, ground floor. Do you need want a wake-up call?" He looked at the registration, "Mr. Churchill... Winston?"

"Intrinsicate," Remy said.

"Huh," the clerk said.

"Your puzzle. 23 down. Aspire to loosen this knot. Intrinsicate," Remy said.

A rheumy cough followed them out the door.

• • •

"Hurry, I need to pee," Susan said.

Remy opened the door and once inside, "It's not as bad as I remembered. Still, a reach to claim a one-star rating," he said. As he looked around, Susan hurried into the bathroom. He smiled as she tried closing the door for privacy. The wood was warped, and she gave up trying to shut it completely.

He closed the drapes, turning on a table lamp. He switched off the overhead light, hearing water running in the bathroom sink.

Sitting on the edge of the bed, he held the clock-radio from the nightstand. He adjusted the dial until there was a hint of music. Unable to tune out static, he frowned in annoyance. "What the hell?"

"What?" Susan asked, standing in the bathroom.

"It's nothing. We need noise. These walls are paper-thin. I'm trying to find background music to cover what we're saying. At least they won't be hearing—" he started, leaving the comment unfinished, watching Susan blush.

She inspected the bedding, looking disgusted. "Necessity's the mother of all mothers," she said. She sat on the other edge of the bed, removing her shoes. She fell back, stretching her arms behind her head, staring at the ceiling.

"Damn, this *is* a dump. It's worse than I expected. Your description didn't do it justice. How can it get any worse?"

They both knew she wasn't talking about the room.

Without warning, they were startled by three quick raps, followed by three slower knocks. After a pause, three short raps.

"It's Morse code for SOS. That's Matt." Remy jumped up.

The pasty-faced man in the doorway looked close to collapse. He looked left and right, before stepping into the room.

"My God, man. You look like a train wreck." It was the only thing Remy said.

Matt Tremain wore fear like a suit and radiated a fetid, sweaty odor of tension. His jacket was soaked. His shirt and slacks looked slept in for days. He stepped in, closing the deadbolt and fastened the security chain.

"As if that will do any good," he muttered, tossing his jacket on the chair. He clutched a leather shoulder bag as if he were afraid to let it go.

Remy slipped a media card into his camera, ready to record the meeting.

"I have it," Matt said with a slight shudder. He sat in the chair. Looking like he'd run a marathon. Reaching into the bag, he showed two flash drives to Susan. "Let's watch this first."

Matt opened a laptop and inserted the drive.

Waiting for it to boot up, Remy plugged in the power cord to his video. "Making sure it's fully charged," he said.

"Here it is," Matt said. It was a video of Matt and another man. "That's Tanner. He agreed to go on video record," he mumbled, embarrassed by the unexpected wave of emotion he felt. "He's—was—a hero. In my book, anyway."

Remy turned off the lamp, light filtering through the bathroom door and from the laptop screen. They watched as the video played, listening intently to Tanner.

"Claussen tripped over his own ego," Tanner said. "He wanted a biographer to document Operation CleanSweep, to reveal his significant contribution to the world."

Susan and Remy watched Tanner. Matt was turned away, tears blurring his vision.

Tanner Woodson suddenly became real to them. Matt Tremain told them about Tanner, but seeing made it more powerful. They watched the mole in Claussen's operation putting the dirty laundry on view.

"He's sure of himself?" Matt had asked.

"More than that, even. He expects the highest honors. In one email, he said he would relinquish his citizenship for a knighthood." Tanner explained how he got the information. "Security didn't pay much attention to me. I was hand-picked by the great man, after all. They assumed I was OK," he said, snickering.

"With a mouse click, I could crawl down the rabbit hall. I didn't find any anthropomorphic creatures. What I found was real, and far worse. I found the real Charles Claussen."

Matt handed him a glass of water.

"Thanks, Tanner said. "I had access to all things electronic. I read every word, sneaking into places they thought secure." He started to laugh. "Well, what could they hide from the person who built the security system? When I comprehended the real scope of the plan, I had no choice. It had been my intention to destroy Claussen, but I didn't have a clue about his CleanSweep madness." Tanner sipped water. "That raised the stakes. With CleanSweep in play, our own version of mass genocide will begin. It'll be Claussen deciding who goes to the left, who goes to the right."

Tanner's sad face turned to the camera as he continued. "His plan for CleanSweep echoes *Mein Kampf.* That book outlined the author's intention. People preferred to ignore the tricky bits. Now, Claussen's buried his tricky bits of evil behind his own words. We'll ignore his, I'm afraid. We will do so at our own peril."

The back of Matt's head was visible as he occasionally lifted a glass to drink. "Keep talking my friend; I'll listen."

"It didn't come out, you know, the truth pouring out all at once. I gleaned it in bits and pieces. But this is how it ends." He handed over a paper. "You can cross-check it with the other stuff I gave you. Look at one e-mail. Claussen said he could manipulate the voting to make sure the right party came to power. His empire was built on gathering marketing and financial data. With no regulations to stop him, he legally amassed a database that could be used to influence voting. He knew how to push fear buttons; immigration, refugees, minorities, lifestyle, you name it, he put it into play. He could use voter's fear and greed to influence government decisions.

"Thinking his email server was unbreakable, he wrote about a powerful contact burrowed deep in the heart of the government. He'd bankrolled the candidate perfect to carry out his plan. Claussen used his own considerable wealth, filtering it through private funders, organizations, and decoy donors. Who'd know it was coming from him? Claussen has money in so many offshore accounts, it would look like a huge, tangled spiderweb to anyone trying to trace it back to him. Claussen's not concerned about legality. He spent and spent until he had the government in his pocket.

"He assured his government sources all electronic correspondence were through a secure server, they were private communications." Tanner smiled as he riffled through a pile of papers and held one up for the camera. "Phone calls recorded, text messages downloaded, emails saved. It *would* have been private and secure, except they didn't know about me. Everything went through the system I designed."

"Wouldn't a computer genius like Claussen know you had access?" Matt asked.

"Hubris," Tanner said. "Claussen scanned my program for something like that. I hid the code in the upper-case C in his last name." Tanner's self-satisfaction was evident in his expression. "Every time he scanned my program, it passed over the code to my back door."

Tanner handed Matt another page.

"Claussen writes about needing a straw man to stir up trouble, scare everyone—causing people to look the other way when he used his magician's sleight-of-hand behind their backs.

"In another e-mail, he described secretly financing a group of neo-Nazi skinheads. I have a leader needed to create havoc. Claussen described a man uncanny speaking ability, attractive to the ultra-right fringe element. I can't remember his name." Tanners said, looking thoughtful. "Wait, it was something like Brunner. Yes, that's it: Brunner. Claussen paid Brunner to move to fertile ground; to grow goose-stepping, swastika-wearing fanatics. He called it Brunner's Battalion. Before long, Brunner used Claussen's money to build a mock army camp and a sizable following. They strutted, taunting blacks, gays, Jews, anybody they considered undesirable. Now, they've added Muslims, even *looking* Muslim, to their twisted minds."

Tanner's distaste showed on his face. "Claussen never recruited Brunner in person. He orchestrated it using a cutoff to avoid detection. They shared common ground. After it was arranged, I remember Claussen explaining ethnic cleansing to Brunner. He suggested—no, ordered— Brunner read about holy wars, crusades, and jihads. Claussen told Brunner. The two of them talked about a superior class of people. Of course, they were included in that class."

"Anti-Mexican, anti-Semitism, anti-Muslim, anti-everyone-not-white and Evangelical Christian," Matt said.

Tanner nodded. "Claussen told Brunner racism wasn't new, pointing out it was the excuse for the westward expansion of the United States, the white man's destiny. The government orchestrated propaganda to demonize people of Mexican heritage—misinformation influencing today's attitudes," Tanner said.

"Claussen knew how to use those feelings to build a base of support," Tanner continued. "He told Brunner about our country's systematic eradication of the cultures of Native Americans, Blacks, and Mexicans. He bragged to Brunner about attending a Klan rally in the Florida Panhandle. The speaker ranted, as Claussen put it, 'We're against Niggers, Jews, and Catholics—and not necessarily in that order.'"

Tanner stopped, and the anguish over his own role in the matter was plainly visible in his body language. "I'm sorry I used the *N*-word." He rubbed his shoulder. "In another e-mail he wrote about ethnic cleansing in Bosnia. While he admired the numbers of Muslims they eradicated or forced to move, he said it would have been more if they'd been systematic, having a thought-out plan."

The video camera captured anguish on Tanner's face. He paused. The hint of a tear bled from one eye, a bead of moisture he quickly wiped away.

"Claussen told Brunner he helped disrupt a global symposium. He saw what happened in the 2010 international conference in Toronto, drawing energetic and violent protests. He said rioting needs to be targeted. In 2010 it was random. He used thugs to spread violence in the latter symposium, judging it to be effective."

Tanner kept talking about Claussen's e-mail. "'We need to be ready for the next one. The new international conference would be a better target,' he wrote. 'We will create a perfect storm.' He told Brunner to prepare his militia to cause massive rioting, violence, and destruction. It would create an atmosphere of fear. They will beg me to implement CleanSweep.

"Brunner's had his marching orders, an army created to ensure as much destruction as possible—suggested bodily harm might be in order. Claussen sent a map of the city, indicating areas to target. The center, especially the civic center, was to be left undamaged. Violence would have people crying out for protection—the protection CleanSweep would deliver, willing to pay his price, no matter how high."

Tanner sighed. "They have no idea how much it'll cost them. Claussen used his influence, making sure another global conference would be hosted in Toronto. There was significant backlash. Why subject Toronto to the expense and potential violence?" Some world leaders wanted to avoid a repeat of 2010. They recommended a low-profile location, their arguments ignored. Claussen spent years developing his influence. He had the government eating from his hand," Tanner said, but he had more. "He used Brunner to beta test his plan. One was a White Supremacy demonstration on a college campus, sure to draw a large crowd.

"He had Brunner's Battalion infiltrate crowds celebrating their team winning a championship. The two men used video conferencing to review videos of their efforts the way coaches review game videos of games. Claussen flew Brunner around North America to rant his hateful message at rallies, whispering discontent to lure fanatics to engage in small-scale rioting; Claussen suggested targeting Planned Parenthood, LBGTQIAs, any group or organization considered unsuitable. With rehearsal riots in full stride, legitimate protesters were shoved aside by stiff-armed salutes, beatings, and worse."

"You look tired" Matt said. "Do you want to continue tomorrow?"

Tanner nodded, yes, and the screen went dark.

• • •

Matt used fast-forward, and Tanner's image reappeared. "This was the next day," Matt explained to Susan and Remy. They saw he'd changed clothes, but still showed fear.

"They learned from the experiments, practicing until they could follow Claussen's plan to a *t*," Tanner said. "I saw the playbook," he said.

"Rioting would target five designated sections of the city. They had lists of smaller synagogues that couldn't afford costly security, called them soft targets. Clubs frequented by gays and lesbians were to be torched.

"While that was taking place, teams had a list of people to be dragged away, interrogated and beaten. The lists included people never to be seen again. Homeless men, women and families would disappear, ending as corpses in back alleys.

"One email raised the hair on the back of my neck. Claussen hinted abandoned mine shafts were safe places to dispose of bodies. I know I'm rambling, but there's so much, and I don't have time.

"Claussen wanted the riots to be highly noticeable so the riots would be remembered. The playbook called for smoke from many fires filling the air, the constant sound of police sirens a constant fear that needed protecting."

Tanner took a deep breath and rushed to finish. "He promised his government cronies that when the time was right, he would deliver a federally-endorsed security forces and put all the untidiness back into proper order.

"The government chaps not only agreed to his offer, they gave him billions more than he'd asked for. Is Claussen doing it for the money? He was addicted to power. The thought of having his hand on the throttle of unchecked power activated the pleasure centers of his brain the way cocaine does to a cokehead."

Matt, Remy, and Susan sat looking at the screen, Tanner's testimony over.

Matt turned off the video. "Is that enough? Have you seen enough?" Matt pleaded with Remy and Susan, not wanting to have to witness it all again. "I can't bear to watch more."

Susan gave a long glance at Remy.

He nodded silently.

"I've seen enough for now, she said."

CHAPTER 11

ROOTS

ngela Vaughn recognized the signal: a double-click code. It blended in with static. She looked around to see if anyone noticed and reached into her shoulder bag for a throwaway cell phone, a phone she wasn't supposed to have. When hired, Charles Claussen made it clear there would be no unapproved communication devices, for her, or anyone else working for him.

It was written into her employment contract, allowing the company to tap any personal communication devices, her personal cell and land-line. Claussen, founder of Enseûrtech, built the network of communications personally. His communication channels were the only ones used, even the special channels used by his security staff.

He had a burning need to know everything that happened anywhere within his company's operations.

It was Angela's job to enforce the rules of no unapproved com devices. She was about to break that rule.

Claussen had a monitor to listen in to all wireless transmissions and read any text messages. His staff were used to the soft click to indicate Claussen was listening to their phone call.

"I have this one with me twenty-four hours a day," he'd once told her, producing a small handheld receiver. "I listen to conversations at ran-dom—or target a particular employee, if necessary," he'd said with a smile that bordered on a smirk. "I developed a software program to alert me to keywords. I scan 24/7, on the alert for attempts at using code or making any attempts at deception or betrayal." He continued. "I keep track of small details. Believe me, I have an uncanny way of knowing when to listen in on someone."

Angela Vaughn knew he browsed through e-mails. He would send a blistering message to a department supervisor, and the person named on his email usually disappeared from the Enseûrtech payroll.

Knowing Claussen monitored two-way radio traffic, she used a series of clicks to signal her field teams. He would certainly be listening tonight, eager for news about the TV reporter, her cameraman, and especially any sighting of Matt Tremain.

Screw him, she thought. She never said that aloud.

Angela had ways of communicating off-line with trusted security connections, without his knowing...she hoped.

The barely perceptible double-click on her two-way radio was a signal to her—one her boss would hear as random noise. She felt her heart do a double-beat copy of the sound as she acknowledged it with quick double-clicks, turning the squelch knob to create static, followed by a single click.

Angela looked at the time.

She palmed a small phone she took out of a desk drawer. Angela slid it into a pocket, glancing at strategically placed surveillance cameras in her work area. She knew where they were. She'd personally supervised every installation. Other cameras swept each corner of the building: offices, hallways, and stairwells.

Angela tried to ignore the cameras, making extra effort to appear to casual. She tapped a command on her keyboard, ordering the video surveillance system to place seven cameras into loop mode. They would constantly display empty offices, except one pre-taped video showing her at her desk, hard at work. She'd been careful tonight to wear the same clothes as the video.

Tanner Woodson, the young computer systems engineer, taught her the secret to programming the cameras just before his 'unfortunate' accident.

Why did he give all our secrets away to that blogger, Matt Tremain? She wondered. *Why did Tanner show me how to get around camera sur-*

veillance? Why did he trust me with and know I would use the deception? And why did I keep it from Claussen? I he ever finds out, I'm a dead woman.

Angela's guilt about Tanner's accident wouldn't go away. What she did to Tanner went against everything—all the pride at police academy graduation, that pledge to protect and serve. She tried to push the guilt away, but it remained, like a pesky, buzzing fly.

The shame, Tanner Woodson's accident, she thought, knowing full well it hadn't really been an accident.

She'd orchestrated Tanner's accident. Angela wanted to believe she didn't have a choice. She'd made her choice, the devil's handshake with Charles Claussen. Angela knew she'd never feel right about it. She hadn't attempted to warn him. Worse, it never crossed her mind to warn him. Disobeying orders wasn't in her DNA—until now. Angela realized when she'd issued the kill order, it marked her fall from the ethical cliff. She was coming to terms with how far she'd had fallen since her days as a cop.

Angela Vaughn was thinking about breaking her oath of loyalty to Claussen.

• • •

Angela had to trust the security camera showed her at her desk. She stepped into the hallway, walking rapidly to the stairwell to the roof. She looked at the cameras overhead, her fingers crossed the cameras were spoofed. Racing up the stairs, she stepped onto the roof. The view, though usually breathtaking, didn't interest her tonight. She tried to rub tension from her forehead, her hand shaking. Angela knew the rooftop was the one place in the building Claussen failed to install cameras. Taking no chance, she hid in the shadows next to the massive ventilation-fan housing. Angela turned on her clandestine phone.

I must control this and take charge. If I can bring in Matt Tremain, I can redeem myself, she thought.

"Talk to me," she whispered. "What do you mean, they aren't there? Did your men—" She stared at the phone in disbelief and held it to her ear again. "Don't ever interrupt me again! How many people do you have watching the motel?" She listened, her face a study in concentration. "I want all the details."

After hanging up, she called back. "Click code when you find him."

Ten minutes later, back at her desk, she pushed the Enter key, and all cameras returned to live feeds. Drops of moisture had formed under her arms, steeling her nerves as cameras were back on.

Angry at the call she just had, she tried to hide her emotions.

• • •

Sam was her best agent. Angela knew it must have been important enough to warrant sending her a double-click warning. They both knew Claussen was glued to his monitor. As it turned out, this report would enrage him, making their jobs even tougher.

If we still have jobs, he thought.

"It's my fault, boss," Sam said. "I should have anticipated what happened. That cameraman is no fool, and the reporter, Payne, didn't get where she is on looks. I clearly underestimated them. I thought we used enough shock and awe in the garage to keep them in place. We had the front. No one expected that back door. It looked like it hadn't been used in years, crusted with a layer of rust. When we checked, it was too late," he said.

She heard him pause, waiting for reassurance all would be forgiven. When he didn't get it, he continued. "I've personally taken care of our two agents who were supposed to be watching them. We call them Frick and Frack, not our A-team. I should've known. I have teams at their apartments, in case they return. *If* they return." Sam knew he was responsible for entrusting the charges to the two men who had let the duo slip out of their grasp.

"On a positive note, they can't get far walking," he said. "I have cars scouring a ten-block area. Our phone tech picked up a wireless call. The cameraman and Tremain talked about meeting the same place they met before." Sam explained, hoping he was back in her graces. "I remember Tremain met the videographer at a grubby motel on Lakeshore. I've sent my best," he said, trying to make the situation sound better than it really was. "One is already a room next to the one they used before. We have the parking lot covered. One agent has replaced the desk clerk. Can you think of anything else?"

She couldn't.

Angela sat at her desk, regretting her fast-food dinner mapping a journey through her intestines. *There're too many places for the targets to hide. I'm afraid of what Claussen will do when he hears I don't have a clue. How do I tell him we can only wait for them to come out into the open?* she thought.

They're together right now, the three of them. This isn't going to end well; Claussen's going to eat me alive.

CHAPTER 12

READY TO RECORD

"**D**amn, *now* the camcorder runs out of juice," Remy said as he tossed the camera back into his bag.

Room 231 at the Europa Motel was quiet. Quiet, that is, if you ignored distorted, tinny music coming from the bedside radio, water in the tap constantly running full on, and the relentless *drip, drip* of the leaky shower head.

Remy adjusted the radio tuning, making a racket. They all tried to ignore it, but it grated on their nerves.

Remy picked up his smartphone.

"Our instructor once said a good videographer makes do with whatever's at hand," he said, aiming the device. "This makes a decent video while the camera recharges."

Susan stretched back, trying not to think about stains on the bedspread, its collection of DNA samples.

"Ready to record," Remy said. "The phone is fully charged."

Susan sat up again. "What happened to Tanner is terrible. Matt, I know you two grew close. Hearing his death was no accident must have come as a shock," Susan said, reading paper copies of the reports. "Why do you think Tanner finally came forward with the story—why he chose you to tell it?"

Matt rubbed the stubble on his chin, as if considering where to start. "One night, we started sharing personal stuff, nothing directly related to Claussen or CleanSweep. Tanner took up the challenge to force my kitchen window open; the smell of smoke in the air was fading. I remember it was a bird of some kind chirping away. I don't know anything about birds. Tanner said it was a catbird. Man, the silly shit you remember…"

Remy held the smartphone camera steady, waiting for Matt to start.

"Tanner asked about my family, how I started blogging," Matt said. "My life until CleanSweep had been pretty boring. A kid like me, raised by both parents in a stable relationship, living in the Chicago suburbs? No pain or suffering enough to write tragic poetry. What experience did I have to tackle a break-out novel? I didn't even have a reason why I moved to Toronto. I expected it to be different living in Toronto. It was different, but a lot of the same. Toronto goes from polite to road rage as quickly as any American city."

Matt paused, thinking.

"You need angst—to suffer—to sing the blues. What did I ever do that was dangerous or sad, let alone tragic?" Matt shrugged. "The closest I'd come to writing about anything worth mentioning was blogging about CleanSweep. Look where that got me.

"Tanner had the creds. He came from hardier stock, a family tree tracing to the Netherlands. He had generations of family lore, the way it was in days past. Hell, I hardly knew my grandparents before they died. We were well into the single malt that night." Matt explained, smiling at the special memory.

"Tanner not only had root; he inherited courage. His family's blood coursed through his veins. His grandfather told him stories about Holland during the German occupation. His grandfather was in his early teens, forced to work for the Germans, making uniforms. He helped the underground, not directly at first, using his youth and delivering messages on his bicycle.

"Tanner heard stories about horrible things his grandfather witnessed, the sight of men in leather coats who stood, supervising soldiers dragging people from their homes, pulling them screaming into the streets."

Matt stood, pacing the room, as Remy kept him framed in the shot.

"Tanner never told me directly," Matt said. "I asked him, did he really do as he claimed, infiltrating Ensûrtech from the start? In any event, he paid for it with his life, producing these documents."

They sat quietly, thinking about what Matt said.

Matt paced some more, revealing his anxiety. "Why did he pick me? It could've been pure chance, surfing the web, happening across my blog posts, that story striking the right note. Maybe he chose me because he knew I would believe. I'd written that I eat and breathe conspiracy theories. Did he think I'd comprehend the massive scale of evil? I'll never know the real reason...."

Remy turned off the camera and stood. He walked to the drapes, pulling one side back with his finger enough to peek into the parking lot.

"Nothing," he reported. "I guess I'm feeling jumpy for no reason."

"It's after midnight," Susan said, sounding surprised. "Could anyone else use a coffee?" Her question went unanswered; they had more than coffee on their minds.

"Did you bring the flash drive from before?" Matt asked Remy.

"I copied it," Remy said. He pulled the media cards from his pocket. "The interviews between you and Susan are on two, the contents from your flash drives on this last one."

"I brought a media player," Matt said, Matt reached into the satchel he'd brought. He handed it to Remy. "Will the card work on this? It's another video of me talking with Tanner."

"No problem," Remy said.

In the video, Tanner appeared holding a copy of an e-mail, displaying a PDF attachment to the email. "This is where Claussen talked about PRO-FUNC, a 1950s government plan to watch, arrest, and detain Communists and other sympathizers thought to be subversive. There were a surprising number of high-profile national leaders on the list. The name at the top was Tommy Douglas, leader of the first Socialist government elected in Canada," Tanner explained. "I've always thought it ironic that many years later Douglas, considered the father of healthcare, would have a CBC poll declare him 'the Greatest Canadian.'"

"It gave Claussen the idea for CleanSweep?" Matt asked.

"You can see he used some of its details. His versions proposed secret detachments of private security forces sweeping across the country after it was successfully demonstrated in Toronto."

"The plan was to be implemented on M-Day, Mobilization Day. People arrested would be placed in temporary staging facilities. Once processed, they would be transferred to permanent internment camps, called reeducation centers," Matt said. "Claussen planned on using empty buildings in run-down urban neighborhoods as temporary holding facilities, walling them off like the Warsaw Ghetto. Sites would be segregated by gender," Matt said, reading from the PDF. "One coed camp used for propaganda purposes, ensuring, in Claussen's words, the scum not be allowed to procreate."

Remy and Susan tried to absorb the implications of what they were seeing.

"He was salivating when he read the PROFUNC camp rules," Tanner said. "An eleven-page document from PROFUNC outlined harsh rules for the camps. People were held indefinitely. If they tried to escape, they would be shot. Claussen added a margin note on that."

Matt paused the video. "There's more," he said as he handed over copies of the PROFUNC plan, along with an outline of CleanSweep.

After giving them a chance to look at the plans, Matt broke the silence. "Look at this newspaper account he cites."

Susan and Remy read a story about the 2010 rioting in Toronto during the G8 summit.

Matt read it aloud. "'Sources report hundreds of citizens detained and documented by police during the 2010 summit. During a three-day period, people were stopped without cause, questioned, and documented. Police in key patrol areas downtown collected names, ages, names of associates, and places of birth. Police also took notes on skin color: white, black, brown, or other (specify).'"

"*This* is where he got the idea?" Susan asked it as a question, knowing the answer.

"Read this next part." Remy said. "'Arranging for the government to host a similar event, he would bring in a militia of trained agitators to stir up hatred. There would be widespread destruction to sow panic in the general population. People would demand protection. The government would pass emergency legislation giving CleanSweep the contract, granting police powers like the Wartime Measures Act.' Guess who got the contract to implement CleanSweep? Good-bye, habeas corpus," Remy muttered.

"I still can't believe it," Susan whispered. "Tanner said it wasn't about the money. Imagine the power Claussen could exercise."

"Look at this, too," Matt said, pointing. "Claussen's advising the government committee to nationalize four zones in the city. One would include the city center between Bloor Street to the north, Front Street to the south, Bathurst to the west, and Parliament Street to the east."

"Here's an e-mail," Susan said. "Claussen's proposal, bankrolling demonstrations, riots, and hooliganism to stir the public. He said they'd infiltrate crowds in Nathan Phillips Square. Claussen's goons would work their evil. When the police moved, it would be easy to herd crowds into a marshaling area, a fenced-in area bordering a streetcar line. Another nationalized zone would lie farther to the west, another to the east."

"Streetcars could be designed as prisoner transports," Remy said. "Detainees could be quickly processed and transported to holding facilities—three warehouses in the western zone."

"As evil as it is, it's brilliant," Matt said. "Claussen committed his entire fortune to secretly buying properties and constructing facilities to support CleanSweep. It would look like ordinary construction taking place. Anyone curious might even see it as a good sign—the economy finally on the way to full recovery."

"I saw a warehouse like that, and that's exactly what I thought," Susan said.

"Claussen is a poster boy for evil," Matt said. "The worst thing, he looks and acts normal. Every news story about him sings high praise. Who would suspect anything like this coming from Charles Claussen? Sure, his extreme-right leanings are well known, but that by itself doesn't make someone evil. It's the...." Matt paused, searching for the right words. "It's taking the final step to remove elements of society he doesn't like, to this." He pointed at the screen. "He's planning their eradication. Claussen views the unworthy as no more than cockroaches. He sees himself as the exterminator called in to fumigate society."

Matt wasn't given to talking much, but talking about Claussen's evil genius brought out his emotions. He rubbed his temples, scowling.

"This is like fitting together pieces of a jigsaw puzzle," Remy said. "I need to charge the phone again." Once plugged in, he nodded.

"Do you know who else is supporting him, giving him money?" Susan asked. "Who are the other backers?"

"I don't know," Matt admitted. "Even Tanner didn't know. Claussen's obsession for secrecy took over. He used private communications channels, not through Enseûrtech. Tanner might have monitored. Richard Waverly was on my list of suspects. He's the only one in the government with enough clout. But I'm not sure; it's a guess."

Susan gasped at Waverly's name. "He's slime. We tried doing background on him. There are questionable things in his past, but the trail disappeared down a rabbit hole. He pulls a lot of political strings. I was told to back off. I heard from colleagues at other stations, even regional and national networks. They were told the same. Stay away from anything to do with Waverly, Claussen, or CleanSweep."

"I can't get anyone to listen to me, either," Matt said. "There's a massive news blanket over this. I tried contacting news bloggers and CNN and got stonewalled. The guy at Fox News laughed and hung up on me."

The three sat quietly. The soundtrack was the tinny AM radio music, competing with the running toilet. An unpleasant mixture of smells filled the room; tension sweat, fear, disinfectant, and the cigarette smoke embedded in the furniture and drapes.

The beam of a car's headlights filled the room. Dimness returned when the headlights were turned off a moment later. The car stopped directly outside the room. They waited for the sound of multiple car doors opening and closing—a signal of impending arrest.

CHAPTER 13

CLOSE CALL

Two men sat in the car, gazing at nothing in particular. Both had an end-of-shift bleary stare. The sharp pings from the cooling engine were the only sounds, until the man in the passenger seat took a loud slurp from his takeout coffee cup.

"I gotta piss!" The driver grunted, releasing his seat belt. "Be right back. You OK with that, boss?"

"A man's gotta do what a man's gotta do. Take your time, Jimbo. The Westside guys are having all the fun anyway while we cruise around doing next to nothing." He winced as the door slammed shut.

Jerk. Why does he insist on calling me boss?

His phone vibrated.

What'd Sam's call it? C-phone? He never came right out and said it, but we all got the idea. The C doesn't mean cell. They're phones Mr. Big can't listen in on.

A phone without bells or whistles—a basic voice, text, and photo phone.

And we're not supposed to have the not-so-smart phones, Brian thought, squinting at the small screen.

He pressed with his thumb and read the text just as Jimbo returned, slamming the door again.

"Zup with that, boss?" He asked, nodding at the phone.

"Why do you always have to slam the door? We got an alert. This is a picture of the two we're supposed to be on the lookout for. Look. It's

Susan Payne and Carl Remington. She's the one on TV, *Action 21 News*. The guy is her cameraman."

"She's the one I go to for the news," Jimbo said. "I wonder what she's done wrong."

The two men squinted; the dim dome light didn't help much.

"Them's the two that Sammy let get away?" Jimbo asked.

"I'm sure of it. Sammy was sure they headed west. Our guys staked out a motel on Lakeshore, but so far, no show. Wait." He held his hand up. "There's more." He read while Jimbo tried to look over.

"What's it say?" Jimbo asked.

"We're supposed to be on lookout. This is miles from that parking deck. What're we supposed to find here? There's nobody around this time of the night. The streets are deserted. What if they're hiding out in this motel? Yeah...right." He started laughing.

"There's nothing going on in this dump," Jimbo said, wiping his hands on the tail of his shirt. "There wasn't anybody in the office. It was locked tight. I had to piss on the side of that wall," he said, pointing out his make-do urinal. "At least I found a corner with a shadow. Hey, boss, wouldn't it be something if they *were* in this shithole? You think they might be here? They could be in that room right in front of us."

"Get serious," the boss said. "This coffee tastes like crap." He rolled down the window and turned the cup on end, letting the dregs spatter on the asphalt. He carefully placed the empty cup into a recycling bag he kept next to the seat.

The phone vibrated again.

"Now they say that Matt Tremain is on the move," Brian said. "Damn, I sure wish we were the ones catching him, eh?"

"Do they have any idea where he might be, boss?"

"If they do," Brian snorted, "they're not keeping us in the loop. Can you believe it? The TV lady got away like that. They had Tremain's building cased but nobody bothered to look for a back door. That would have been the *first* thing I looked for if it was up to me. Sometimes I think we work with amateurs."

He gave little thought to being in the same amateur category, sitting in a car with someone named Jimbo, assigned to the far edge of the story and not on Angela Vaughn's A-list.

"The two of us driving around like this," Jimbo said. "We're useless as teats on a boar hog." The chill night air began seeping in. Jimbo started the car, turning on the heater. "Screw green and saving the planet." He laughed, letting the car idle until the vents spewed warm air.

At the end of a ten-hour shift, they were bored. It'd been a dreary ten hours. When boredom creeps in, monotony leads to a lack of focus. The two men sat in the car, their minds wandering to thoughts of their day off tomorrow.

"Remember that couple we saw back there?" Brian broke the silence. "It was an hour or so ago. Did you see how they ducked into that doorway damn fast? I don't think it was these two in the picture, but maybe we should cruise back to that place we saw them. It ain't far from here."

"Why not?" Jimbo turned on the headlights, flicking on the high beams. "I love shining high beams into a motel room like this," he said, backing out of the parking spot. "You never know whose fun you're spoiling."

Neither of them noticed the slight movement of the drapes directly in front of their car.

CHAPTER 14

DETECTIVE CARLING

He wasn't happy. He wasn't one bit happy. Wallace Carling couldn't remember what it was like not being a cop. Some of his colleagues didn't like being called *cops*, preferring to be called *policeman* or *policewoman*, *police officer*, or *detective*—always insisting on getting the rank just so. Not Carling. He was a cop first. Everything else came next.

Rank and respect didn't matter; He was all about catching the bad guys, but not tonight.

Tonight, he sat in a seedy bar, nursing a whiskey. He knew this place from his days walking a beat as a rookie. It had gone through many owners, but it didn't change. It was seedy back then, and it was the same now.

Carling wasn't drunk, but he was slipping to the edge of sobriety.

"Too many cops today are a bunch of dickheads," he slightly slurred to his new best friend, an anonymous drinking buddy, an old man sitting on the next stool, sporting a week's growth of graying beard.

"They strut around, pumping one another up with self-importance, claiming they are protecting the peace and keeping everyone safe," Carling said. "Protect and serve, my ass." The old pensioner didn't look up from his drink, pretending to listen to what Carling was saying. After all, Carling was buying the drinks.

"Another for my buddy here, one more for me," he waved two fingers to the barkeep, patting the old man on the shoulder. The old man tried fixating on his free drinks. He never quite managed to focus his attention on Carling's story.

"The justice system is a revolving door, a joke," Carling said. "We push our way through the door, and the bad guys push their way back out. We go around...and around...and around." Carling caught himself from falling from the chair.

The old pensioner sat next to him and stared ahead, trying to nod when he thought it was needed.

• • •

Leaving the bar, Carling walked back to headquarters, leaving his car keys with the bartender. Three in the morning, while sitting at his desk, he was sorry he still felt sober. He reached into his pocket for some heavy-duty headache pills.

It was dark. The quiet was interrupted by phones ringing before going to voicemail. His workstation was situated among a cluster of writing desks. He liked being alone. He often did his best thinking at this hour. Stale coffee was always available in the squad room, but he reached into his desk's bottom-right drawer instead. He stared at a whiskey flask and closed the drawer without picking it up.

He was trying to figure out how he got in the middle of this story.

Carling, a veteran cop, rose from his uniform days to become a detective in SIS, Special Investigative Services. His personal history was littered with debris of four failed marriages. It all came down to this: a desk at three in the morning, trying to ignore whiskey calling and trying not to think about ex-wives. First was Angela. Second Brittany. Charlene was the one he still missed. She'd remarried and moved to the coast. His biggest blunder was marrying Tiffany. That marriage lasted three weeks. He'd realized it was a mistake while saying, "I do."

"Rule number one," he told a friend. "Always be sober at the altar."

Carling liked to pretend his current state of celibacy was by choice, but hard drinking combined with a lack of personal grooming didn't make him a babe magnet.

He was one helluva cop, he thought. What set him apart from other detectives was subtle, but significant: *patience*. He coupled that trait with the tenacity of a snarling pit bull.

Carling remained at crime scenes long after other officers, detectives, and forensic specialists were gone. He'd sit in the middle of a crime scene for hours, saying nothing and appearing to look at nothing in particular. If anyone intruded, he'd turn with an angry scowl, telling them to buzz off. *Buzz* wasn't the precise word; meddlers left with their ears burning.

He would be the first to admit he didn't know how he solved crimes. He approached them as crossword puzzles, extended periods of silence leading him to an important clue, a trail leading to closing a case.

"What is it, Carling? A Zen thing?" someone asked.

Carling never bothered answering questions like that.

The taste of cheap whiskey, memories of ex-wives, and current events all converged that morning. Rage built like steam in an overheating boiler, the meter registering dangerously high readings. His blood pressure kept pace. He put his hand on his chest, feeling his heart throbbing. He wanted to blame it on caffeine, but he knew better. He wondered if there was a safety valve for rage.

"Fuck it."

He pulled out the flask and took a long sip, swishing the whiskey like mouthwash. Liquid heat scraped his throat, distracting him from his anger. He swallowed and recapped the flask. The whiskey didn't quell his anxiety, however, nor his false sense of sobriety.

It would be dawn soon. Daytime would bring other stories.

Splashing water on his face, he changed into clean clothes kept in a locker, putting on his professional face. He never anyone see last night's version of Detective Wallace Carling.

He knew why he was angry. Most of all, he knew the target of his anger. He looked at the first page in a file folder. A photograph was stapled to the upper-left-hand corner. Everyone told him it was all about computers these days, but Carling preferred the feel of paper in a file.

"It makes a case more real to me," he'd told a rookie detective. "I like to hold something tangible."

"He's a dinosaur," someone said behind his back once.

I very well may be, he thought, looking at the neatly printed case number on top this new file. Using a marker, Carling wrote Matthew Tremain's name on the bottom of the photo.

Why are we investigating this guy? What has he done, really? So, some guy claims to be a blogger. What law's he broken?

He printed out Google searches on Matthew Tremain and scanned his Facebook and Twitter accounts. Carling pretended to be old school, but he was savvy when it came to computers, smartphones, and social networking.

He reread an e-mail from Angela Vaughn, director of security for Enseûrtech Corporation.

"With regard your investigation of Matthew Tremain, be advised that Operation CleanSweep has first standing in this matter. Attached is Article 7 of the new National Security Act. In broad strokes, further police investigation will cease. Forward all records to the address below, including personal notes.

"Failure to comply is not an option."

Carling squeezed the e-mail copy into a ball, trying to smooth out the wrinkles.

This guy hasn't broken any law, but now I'm to send all my case material to this new...whatever. He read the last sentence again. *Failure to comply is not an option. This bitch is more officious than most cops.*

Holding the crinkled e-mail, he walked to a window, looking at dawn competing with city lights.

"What have you done, Matthew Tremain?" Carling said aloud.

He went back to his desk, looking page by page one more time. A thought was creeping into his awareness in silence and stealth—like a cat lowering its belly to slink upon an unsuspecting bird.

It came to him. *This guy has something on CleanSweep, and they don't like it one little bit.*

He stood and began pacing. The flask in the drawer would wait until this mystery was solved. Once Carling sank his teeth into a case, he put all thoughts of drinking aside.

I might change my mind about Matthew Tremain, Carling thought. *The little shit's like I was back in the sixties. All he needs is my old tie-dye shirt, an Afro, and his fingers in a peace sign.* Carling smiled as he paged through the file, although he knew the situation wasn't one bit funny. *Tremain knows something. I can't blame him for not trusting anyone.*

Carling had sent Matt an email with some questions. Matt answered back. "CleanSweep isn't clean, but it is sure sweeping."

Carling was beginning to agree. Carling was old school and proud of it. He'd wanted to be like that cop in the Norman Rockwell painting. *The Runaway* depicted a friendly police officer and young boy sitting at a soda fountain together. He laughed, knowing how corny that sounded. Still, that's the way his inner compass pointed.

Carling realized if he started to like Matt, it could make things complicated. He even entertained the idea of he and Matt becoming friends. The absence of meaningful relationships in his life played into such thinking. Carling didn't have any real friends except for Scotty. He would take a bullet for Scotty. He knew better than try to analyze the sudden feeling about Matt. In truth, he didn't try to at all.

He trusted his instincts. Matt wasn't one of the bad guys, and Carling was satisfied with that conclusion. Returning to his desk, he opened his laptop. He started to type an e-mail to Matt. Carling stopped four words in. It was addressed to wordster@verite.com. He quickly deleted the address and closed his computer.

It hit him like a shock wave. "They're monitoring everything I do."

Instead, he composed a handwritten note in neat, deliberate printing. When he finished, he put it in a small envelope, sealing it.

"Matt," it read, "We need to talk. Watch your back." He finished the note and signed it "KBO, Carling."

He picked up his battered fedora to leave.

Screw Angela Vaughn, he thought, making copies of all his field notes and official records. Wondering if there were surveillance cameras watching, he put them in a large folder and grabbed his hat and envelope with the note to Matt. He hid the folder under the spare and drove to The Beaches, parking near Matt's building. He looked around for any sign of a tail. Satisfied there was none, he walked into the building's lobby. He used a master key to open a mailbox door, sliding the envelope into Matt's mailbox.

He decided he wouldn't mention where Matt lived to the high-and-mighty Angela Vaughn. *Let her people find him.* He walked back to his car laughing. *It took everything I could think of to find where he lives,* he thought with a grin. *They don't know the city like I do.*

Matt made it back to his apartment without being arrested. Cyberia messaged his apartment was safe, but he took precautions. He picked groceries at random, filling three bags to make it look like he returned from shopping. Carrying the bags, he backed through the door. "Thanks," he said to the woman holding the door for him. He watched her walk out and was starting for the stairway when he decided to check his mailbox. Placing the groceries on the floor, he searched his pocket for the key.

Matt's mail was usually stacks of advertisements. He didn't check it on a regular basis. He was about to throw it all in the communal trash bin when he noticed a small envelope.

"That's odd."

He threw the ads away, opened the envelope, and read Carling's note.

"What dirty laundry have you turned over? How did this CleanSweep business start? I think you know. They don't know where you live, yet. Watch your back.

"KBO, Carling.

Carling? That's the detective that sent me the email.

CHAPTER 15

LION'S HEAD

The breathtaking escarpment forming the distinctive Lion's Head loomed over the shoulder of the solitary angler. He sat in his boat, a beer in one hand, a fishing rod in the other. The man wasn't given to introspection, but thought about how he'd ended up in this place anway.

Getting out of Detroit wasn't an option. That decision was made when a friend whispered, "Big Julie's looking for you. Word is, you owe over forty large."

Big Julie—Leg Breaker Julie—worked for a notorious loan shark. He got his nickname persuading people to repay their loans. Big Julie was a man to be feared.

Putting distance between himself and Big Julie, the fisherman drove until he reached the small village of Lion's Head on the Bruce Peninsula in Canada's Ontario Province. It only took a tad under six hours, but it was like being separated by an ocean. At least that's what he hoped.

Hitting his mother up for travel money and Big Julie hot on his trail, he took what he hoped was an ingenious route. There are five ways to get from Lower Michigan to Ontario: two bridges, a tunnel, and two ferries. Guessing Big Julie would have eyes on the bridges and tunnel, the angler chose the Bluewater Ferry.

"Fishing trip," he fibbed to the Customs and Immigration officer on the Canadian side.

That was a little over two years ago, but thinking about Big Julie still gave him the shivers.

The locals didn't ask many questions. His talent as a carpenter and willingness to help others soon made his reputation. Living on a cash-only footing kept curious immigration questions diverted.

Today, he was anchored in the shade of the escarpment, under the outline with the shape of a lion's head. Amazed at his luck, he admired a string of fish. The day seemed nearly perfect. The boat rocked gently as he placed the stringer back over the gunwale, then twisted the cap off a bottle of Cracked Canoe beer. He was about to take a swallow when a helicopter rounded the face of the escarpment. Sounding like a she-devil as it passed low overhead, the angler almost pissed himself.

The sight and sound caused him to do something unimaginable. He dropped his beer, the bottle clanking on the aluminum hull, spinning, and vomiting froth. The helicopter passed overhead so low, downdraft from the chopper's rotor rocked the boat. Scotty put his hands over his ears, ducking in reflex.

With a mixture of fear and awe, he saw the sky beast rise abruptly, turn north as if rotating on a pin, and pass over the government dock.

"What the—"

• • •

Charles Claussen looked at his map. A straight line marked the flight path from Toronto to Lion's Head. Claussen traveled 133 miles in slightly less than forty minutes. He was at the controls of the fastest helicopter money could buy. It'd been custom built, based on the Sikorsky X2, powered with an ultra-light helicopter turbine engine. The craft utilized advanced blade technology to both dampen noise and maximize speed.

He'd asked for the best, and the designer adapted an antitorque system instead of a conventional tail rotor. That made it one of the quietest and fastest helicopters on the market.

Earlier, his corporate jet landed at Billy Bishop Airport. Clearing customs, he gave his pilot instructions. "I'll return day after tomorrow," he said. Claussen walked through the flight center to file a flight plan detailing a route taking him past Owen Sound, toward Tobermory—the tip of the Bruce Peninsula—where Georgian Bay emptied into Lake Huron. He added his intention to stop on private property near Tobermory.

Flight plan filed, he walked to a waiting helicopter.

"I'm looking forward to some diving and hiking," he said. He started the engine, waiting for the turbine to begin its low whine. He knew the mechanic was an avid diver who often explored the shipwrecks that made Tobermory a location well-liked for diving.

"I envy you, man!" the mechanic shouted above the engine noise.

Claussen had other plans for the trip, however—nothing to do with diving. He made sure his attaché case and overnight bag were secure. With full power, he adjusted the controls, the craft lifting gracefully from the tarmac. He turned the helicopter in a 360-degree sweep of the area, checking for other air traffic. Satisfied it was clear, he pulled back on the controls.

Gaining altitude, he dipped the nose and pointed northwest. He wasn't interested in the city passing below, soon replaced by farmland. He cross-checked his progress with GPS, marking the chart as he passed Orangeville. Everything was going as planned.

Finally, over the crystal-clear blue waters of Georgian Bay, his solitude was only interrupted as traffic controllers acknowledged his path.

He needed all his concentration. Showtime started when he landed.

In the distance, he saw an outline on the horizon, rising until he made out the scarp forming the striking rock formation shaped like the head of a lion. The Niagara Escarpment seemed to rise majestically from the waters of Georgian Bay. From his angle, it looked like a stately lion.

He knew other locations in the world had their own Lion's Head, but the splendor of limestone jutting from the lake, formed spectacular cliffs and caves. He believed *this* lion's head was unique.

He nudged the nose of the helicopter toward the formation of the cliff.

Not given to sport, Claussen allowed a moment of amusement and excitement. He'd staked everything on Operation CleanSweep. He'd committed his all, and the idea of his dreams coming true was intoxicating. He was meeting the people who would hand over the keys to the power to complete his vision.

Overtaken by a feeling of exhilaration, he gave in to impulse; he pushed the stick forward, nosing the helicopter into a steep descent.

He experienced the thrill of high-speed flight at wave top as he banked around the face of the lion. Rounding the turn, he saw a man in a skiff passing underneath. Claussen laughed at the man's obvious alarm, pulling back on the controls. *Too fast and dangerously low,* he thought, glancing at the altimeter. He'd passed over the boat at seventy-five feet, realizing he'd given the man quite a fright.

Amusement over, he gained altitude, glancing at the large power yacht docked at the government wharf.

Ah, Spencer is here, he thought, smiling.

Claussen passed Dyer's Bay on his left, making a sharp turn to skirt the escarpment, hugging the pebble beach until he reached Cabot Head lighthouse and his destination a few miles to the north and west.

He turned inland until spotting a small lake. The privately-owned lake was surrounded by hectares of wilderness, accessible by a single paved road. On final approach, he waved to men guarding the entrance. Nobody ever made it uninvited.

The house wasn't a cabin in the woods. It was a majestic lodge on the edge of the lake. Jutting from stony outcroppings, it was a masterful combination of granite and wood, blending seamlessly with the rustic surroundings.

The heliport was situated behind the carriage house, exquisite landscaping shielding it from view at ground level. Landing, he listened to the turbine engine pinging to rest.

Claussen raised the Plexiglas door, picked up his attaché case, and stepped out. He raised his arm, waving and smiling. His host stood watching from a large deck extending from the lodge. Claussen was pleased to see two other men standing there as well.

"It's time—and I'm ready."

CHAPTER 16

MEN OF MYSTERY

Claussen unfolded his dinner napkin, glancing around the table, feeling smug.

I could buy and sell them all—well, maybe not Winston, he thought. His lips curled into a small smile.

He speared a piece of stewed elk. Chewing slowly, he savored the flavor, infused with a juniper-and-cranberry reduction. He reached for his glass of wine. Claussen loved to display his knowledge of wine. "Hmm," he said. "I taste red cherries and oak, with a hint of olives and smoke. Wonderfully complex, I'd say."

Holding his bottle of Chateau Petrus Pomerol, he examined the label. *Only Winston would have the rare 1961 vintage in his cellar—at a price tag of $4,000 a bottle.*

The host, Winston Overstreet sat one leg casually crossed over the other. His chair was turned so he could glance over the lake as they talked. He held his wineglass in a lackadaisical manner that fooled nobody at the table. Nothing was ever nonchalant with Overstreet.

Spencer Abbot sat to Winston's left, looking uncomfortable in outdoor recreational clothing, likely purchased in a hurried trip to an outfitting store. Claussen sneered. Spencer was at home in yachting whites and a captain's hat. *That man never touched any controls on his yacht,* Claussen guessed. "I have people to do that," was Spencer Abbot's default saying.

Abbot tossed nautical terms around. "The twin engines give her twenty-three knots cruising speed, fast enough for waterskiing." He snorted wine, wiping his face. "They said I only needed a crew of three. They forgot about the chef," he said, patting his ample stomach.

The fourth man said little. He kept himself behind a scrim of silence. Like the audience watching a play, the curtain hid the levers, pulleys, and costume changes going on backstage.

Richard Waverly was fourth-generation politician. Often referred to as "über-conservative," he delighted in the label. He quietly used his family fortune to back his right-wing views. He confided to Claussen he'd studied the great tyrants and dictators of history. "We need to learn from their mistakes, where they went wrong, how to avoid the same mistakes when our time comes."

A veteran politician, Waverly knew what it was like to both win and lose elections. He liked winning better. In fact, he'd only lost one election. The experience taught him that lots of money—and a lack of ethics—were surefire ways of staying in office.

He was called "Sir Waverly" derisively behind his back; his own staff detested him almost as much as his opponents did.

Richard Waverly's value was belonging to an elite inner circle at the epicenter of power. Claussen knew while party leaders and power brokers considered themselves in charge when it came to the nation's coffers, when Waverly pointed, money would move wherever the man indicated.

• • •

Claussen considered his dinner companions. He respected Winston, a man he thought of as his equal.

Spencer possessed substantial financial assets, making him easy to tolerate. He also shared Claussen's political leaning.

Claussen thought Richard Waverly fit the definition of a sleazy politician, someone who enjoyed spending taxpayer's money. Waverly made Claussen pucker as if he'd taken a bite of a lemon. *There's something about him*, Claussen thought. *Power and money slip through the man's fingers like sand, his promises as hard to hold onto as quicksilver. What choice do I have, though? Waverly's crucial to making CleanSweep a reality.*

"Ulrich," Overstreet said, turning to the server. "We're finished. Put the other wine and glasses by the fireplace. We'll need this table cleared for later."

"Certainly, sir. As you wish." Ulrich said, bowing slightly. He ordered the table staff to the kitchen. "Mr. Overstreet and his guests are not to be disturbed." As if choreographed, they turned and left the room.

Ulrich returned, carrying a silver tray, four bottles, and glasses expertly balanced. With an exaggerated bow, he returned to the kitchen, leaving the four in front of a fire blazing in the granite fireplace. The silence was broken by the occasional hiss and spit as burning logs settled in the grate.

"Can he be trusted?" Claussen asked. "Your man, Ulrich?"

"My majordomo's been with me for thirty-seven years now. I have absolute confidence in his discretion. He'll see to our privacy."

Charles Claussen wasn't convinced, but said nothing.

Overstreet prodded the dwindling fire, stimulating more flame. He peered at the flames, as if trying to recall something. Finally, he placed the poker in the stand and turned.

The other three watched him pour wine, swirl it in the glass, and breathe its aroma.

"Gentlemen." He raised his glass.

The other three got to their feet like marionettes whose strings had been pulled. They raised their glasses.

"Like the vintner of this fine wine, we've toiled in our vineyards, waiting for a vintage crop. It's time," he said. "Our project isn't merely good wine, but *outstanding* wine. And Charles here," he said, placing his hand on Claussen's shoulder, "is our master vintner."

Charles Claussen basked in the praise.

They engaged in small talk but were all eager to hear what Claussen had to say about the project.

"Why don't we take our wine and glasses," Winston said. "Ulrich is finished cleaning. Let's adjourn to the dining table and hear what our friend has prepared. You haven't let that shoulder bag out of your sight, Charles."

I've waited years for this moment. Oh yes. I do have something prepared, he thought.

The other three tried to outdo one another appearing nonchalant. In truth, they were like children in a candy store. Charles could hardly contain his excitement. Tension and anticipation filled the room as he put his case on the table.

Ulrich waited nearby.

"I'll use the radio if we need anything," Winston Overstreet said. Before sitting, he ensured the door was locked. "We won't be disturbed."

• • •

Ulrich stood outside the room, his hand resting on the butt of his Israeli Jericho 941 semiautomatic pistol, a .357 Magnum special. The kitchen staff were gone, driven away in a minibus. The security team radioed the compound was in lockdown and secure. Ulrich left nothing to chance.

• • •

Overstreet put his elbows on the table, leaning to watch his protégé remove four tablets.

"Operation CleanSweep in high definition," Claussen said. Murmurs of astonishment greeted the screen image, a bold logo, artfully designed to appear benevolent, *CleanSweep*, embedded in the border.

He handed each man a wireless headset. "I personally fabricated these to a specially calibrated, fixed frequency. I've tested each one, making sure they're secure from eavesdropping," he said. "If you step away from the table, you'll lose the audio."

Spencer stepped back to test it and nodded. "Nothing but static at this distance."

Ready, Claussen pushed play, the four tablets displaying a synchronized video.

The logo faded away, and the soundtrack began. Claussen personally selected Henryk Gorecki's Symphony No. 3, known as the *Symphony of Sorrowful Songs*. He relished the subtle irony, the composer inspired by the words a prisoner scratched on the wall of a Gestapo prison cell during World War II.

Troubling images filled the screen. The first, a man in the terminal stage of AIDS, taken just before his death. The three men flinched, Spencer turning away from the screen.

"Watch carefully, my friends," Claussen insisted. "This is what we fight to excise, like the social cancer it is."

The next image was two men embracing, quickly changing to two women kissing.

"Disgusting," Waverly muttered. "We need a strong law defining marriage as a pact between man and woman...as God intended."

Following images showed gangs of young men of color. Another, an elderly Asian woman struggling to carry a string shopping bag. A toothless man wrapped in a blanket sat on a park bench, holding a coffee can in outstretched hands, begging for money.

"This man's so lazy he can't even get up to beg," said the voice-over, dripping sarcasm. More examples followed, each photo chosen to depict people considered detritus—social misfits. The images were carefully chosen to evoke loathing.

The last image showed two men walking away, the camera smoothly zooming in on yarmulkes as the video faded to a pastoral setting, flowers and bright sunlight.

"Wouldn't we all be better off without such people?" the voice-over said.

Gorecki's haunting melody segued into an edgy beat, a musical statement: something new, something to pay attention to.

The screens were filled with graphic videos, scenes of rioting and destruction so familiar now. The first were scenes from newscasts during the Toronto economic conference in 2010, followed by video from political riots and sporting events.

Images blended long shots and close-ups, frame after frame capturing people wearing balaclavas and other disguises to avoid identification. A soundtrack of sirens and police whistles played scenes of windows smashed, stores looted, and cars overturned. The final riot scene was a long camera pan of hoodlums setting a police cruiser on fire.

Waverly sneered, watching police officers form a phalanx, moving in and swinging batons. Sounds of clubs hitting flesh could be clearly heard over the shouting and sirens.

"See that?" Waverly stood and pointed to an officer delivering a brutal blow with his baton. "That thug's getting what he deserves."

The other three nodded in agreement and made no comment as the camera zoomed in to show police officers using black tape to cover their badge numbers.

The sound effects on the video faded, and a voice-over condemned the protesters as gangsters, Communists, agitators, thugs, mercenaries, and criminals. There was no reference to the thousands of peaceful demonstrators: mothers, fathers, children, aunts, and uncles. Ordinary people wanting to address grievences wanted to vent displeasure, believing the ruling class was ruining the economy and their way of life.

Claussen made sure any such views were edited from this presentation. He paused the video, knowing the men at the table needed no further convincing.

"Someone has to stand up to hoodlums," Winston said smoothly, and the others harrumphed agreement. "Decades of permissive parenting led us to this point. It's time to remind spoiled-rotten youth their party is over."

"Hear, hear," Spencer said with a self-important sputter.

"That was the background. Watch this next part," Claussen said, resuming the video.

How Great Thou Art, playing in the background, was his choice as the uplifting soundtrack needed. Claussen's plan—CleanSweep—would rescue society from itself.

They won't get the joke, he thought, *the similarities of that music to the Horst Wessel Lied, the infamous Nazi rallying song. A careful listener might recognize the parallels between the two melodies.* Claussen thought it the perfect touch—his evil plan camouflaged by a great religious hymn.

Music rose in volume as architectural renderings appeared. The voice-over described modification of existing buildings, scenes bathed in a warm glow. People could be seen strolling along beautiful walkways meandering through landscaped atria.

"The centerpiece of CleanSweep," the voice-over stated. "This is headquarters for our new national security service." An image of a multi-story, glass and chrome building filled the screen.

The scene shifted to renderings of other structures. "This is what the intake centers will be like," the voice-over said, adding an excited tone. Background music played the soothing, repetitive melody of a Philip Glass composition.

"The centers will have the highest security safeguards without sacrificing detainee comfort. Inmates can expect clean accommodations," the voice-over explained as a picture of dormitory rooms appeared on the screen. "Each person is entitled to a healthy meal and orderly accommodations. No smoking or drugs will be allowed. Each detainee will be thoroughly searched at entry, and subject to random searches during their stay.

"You will, however, note the absence of luxury items. For example," the voice went on, "strategically placed TV screens will broadcast educational messages and important announcements. Sorry, detainees," the voice added in the manner of a sports commentator giving a play-by-play, "you won't be watching any games or movies on *these* televisions."

The video continued. "Buses will be wrapped with CleanSweep logo and graphics, windows tinted to thwart anyone looking inside. We don't need good citizens to be bothered with the sight of undesirables." A streetcar image filled the screen. "Specially designed trolleys will be wrapped with graphics. Buses and trolleys will have controlled entrances and exits to prevent escape."

A passenger train appeared without the familiar VIA Rail logo. Darkened windows screened passengers from curious onlookers. The voice-over described the scene. "It will depart from a dedicated railroad terminal. It will travel non-stop until reaching a top-secret location. A reeducation camp," the voice-over intoned. "This is designed for reforming misbehavior, eventually returning them to society as contributing members."

The men watched their tablets, a flyover of a large facility under construction. "This is a state-of-the-art design, where internees can develop healthy bodies and minds, free from influences of human parasites breeding in today's urban milieu."

The four men watched the final segue, and the capitol appeared. An army officer in dress uniform stood with jutting chin, his hands behind his back at parade rest. As the camera panned to a waving flag, a rousing rendition of the national anthem played while credits scrolled on the screen.

Claussen turned the player off, watching each man sitting in quiet contemplation. He saw it on their faces. They'd been given a glimpse of the future—and were delighted.

"Impressive," Winston said, breaking the silence. "What about the details, Charles? That place where the devil hides?"

"Where *is* that camp?" Waverly interrupted, insistent. "I've never heard of anything like that."

"The details are on these flash drives, gentlemen," Claussen said. "I assure you the plans have been thoroughly vetted. I've gone over them personally, the details polished until the last *i* was dotted and the final *t* was crossed."

Claussen picked up his glass, taking a satisfied drink before continuing. "The camp, my dear Waverly, was built with my own money. My construction team will keep the secret. It was constructed in a place where formalities like building permits don't exist. Let me put it this way: the construction workers had to travel far to the south to warm up after they were finished."

That brought out a hearty laugh.

"You really expect to rehabilitate those people?" Spencer Abbot wanted to know.

"Impossible," Waverly insisted.

"Gentlemen." Claussen held up his hand and smirked. "I left out one or two small details. The site was designed with...." He paused for the right words. "How can I put this? I have planned certain, ah, disposal facilities. We all know many of these people are beyond redemption."

"Let's take a break and adjourn to the fire," Winston said. "Some more wine, eh?"

Claussen realized it was like fishing. He'd cast the line, and they'd swallowed the bait. His challenge now was to carefully reel them in, keeping them on the hook until they were safely in his net.

• • •

It was late when they returned to the table, but they were eager for another session before the evening ended.

"Terrific! Absolutely brilliant." Spencer said, his words slurred. "That's an outstanding video. My board of directors would love to hire your video team. It'd like to make Spencer Enterprises look that good." He made it sound like the joke it wasn't.

Waverly offered a different critique, waving his wine glass with an arrogant gesture. It was a practiced motion, used to impress his political devotees—as well as rivals. It had no effect on the other three men in the room, but they tolerated Waverly's mannerisms. They needed Waverly's political connections—especially his access to the treasury.

Claussen recalled a conversation with Winston Overstreet when they planned this meeting. "Sir Richard always looks like he has a broomstick jammed up his backside," Winston confided. "Still, we need him."

"He sold his soul to get elected and reelected. His deal with the devil will fund our project now," Claussen said. "You, Spencer, and I, know what it is to earn money. When we spend, it's gone. We must go back to work if we want more. But Waverly lines his pockets with taxpayer money. For him, taxpayers are a gift that keeps on giving."

Unlike Spencer, Waverly seemed unaffected by wine, his glass nearly full, Claussen noted.

"Your media people might rival Hollywood, Claussen, but a video is nothing more than a fantasy. I need details if I am going to recommend funding, Waverly said."

You're salivating, you pompous ass, Claussen thought. *You'll be the easiest fish of all to reel in.*

Claussen turned to the host. "Waverly wants details. Let's get some much-needed sleep. Wait until tomorrow. You'll need your wits about you, Waverly," he said, his tone close to a sneer. "You'll get all the details you need—then some."

CHAPTER 17
BREAKFAST WITH FRIENDS

Sunlight filtered through glass panes, tinted to mute the light. Ulrich served breakfast with consummate skill; coffee refills and additional portions were placed without the guests being aware of his presence. Plush carpeting softened his footsteps. With a nod from Winston, the majordomo quietly removed plates and flatware.

Ulrich returned from the kitchen with a carafe of coffee. Winston insisted on a robust blend, shipped in weekly from Columbia. The plantation manager personally attended to roasting and shipping. The reason he was so attentive: Winston Overstreet made sure he always had the very best coffee and bought the company.

Claussen peered over the rim of his cup. The coffee lived up to Winston's description, but Claussen savored the moment. Today was the day he would reveal final details of Project CleanSweep. If the day went as planned, he would begin implementation within weeks, if not days.

Highly caffeinated coffee combined with nervous tension raised his heart rate perceptibly; he felt his entire body pulsing.

I'm ready, he thought.

"Gentlemen," Claussen said, placing his cup down. "I promised details. Before we begin, however...."

He set the leather attaché case onto the table, the case never out of his sight. Two fasteners opened with a click, and he raised the lid. He removed an electronic device the size of a compact digital camera. He extended an antenna and turned on the apparatus.

"I've been thinking about your radio, Winston, the one used to communicate with the kitchen," Claussen said. "I must guarantee complete privacy. You're about to hear critical, sensitive details. My research team was compartmentalized, each working on components of the plan. Nobody but me had the *entire* picture. By the time we break for lunch, the future will be in our grasp." He paused for effect, looking at each in turn.

Winston sat back, trying to look nonchalant. Spencer gave his impression of casualcy, but his eyes gave him away—the intense look of a predator. Bleary-eyed from the night before, he looked keen to hear.

Charles looked across the table at Waverly, a man willing to do anything to stay in office. Claussen wanted access to Waverly's political empire, the one hiding in the shadows. Waverly was power incarnate—a private network free from public scrutiny and the wearisome media. The sneer from last night was replaced by squint, a palpable desire to increase power and curiosity on how he could bend CleanSweep to fit his purposes.

Judging the moment, Charles Claussen handed a folder to each man. The cover displayed the same logo that opened last night's video presentation.

"Before I begin," Claussen said, "I would like to make a personal observation. You're about to hear details of a far-reaching plan that'll shape our world for the better. It is not without some risk, however. Previous attempts at social engineering on this scale have each contained a fatal flaw—or two."

The other three men waited, willing to let Claussen set the pace.

"Take Joseph Stalin and Adolf Hitler, the Big Two. They let personal rivalry become a vendetta. They were both blindsided by greed. They worshiped at the altar of expansion. They each believed achieving global supremacy was their destiny, obsessed with ideology. It didn't help that they were megalomaniacs with oversized egos. Their issues were distractions, taking attention from an essential internal goal. They should have focused on eliminating the undesirable elements eating away at their countries from the inside, like cancer." He paused, searching for the right words.

"To be frank, they didn't *invent* ethnic cleansing. Stalin swung a blunt hammer, getting rid of enemies, real and imagined. He had little, if any, regard for what he considered the disagreeable detritus of the Soviet

Union. He became obsessed with his *imaginary* enemies, eliminating his best military thinkers just before he needed them the most.

"Hitler was a visionary. He told everyone what he intended to do and did it. He insisted on systematic processes. First, his police infiltrated groups, gathering intelligence and identifying negative elements in their midst, both political and social. They arrested criminals and dissidents, sending them to camps. Their organized network of work camps was brilliant. He was well on target to rid Germany of Communists, Jews, Gypsies, and the mentally retarded.

"Imagine what he could have accomplished without the unnecessary wars for *Lebensraum*, the German word translated as 'living room.' He should have finished the internal cleansing, before expanding Germany's borders.

"My grandfather was an engineer, committed to Hitler's values, proud to be instrumental designing many of the camps. He supervised construction of walled ghettos in Poland. He created spaces that funneled people into a single location, making it easier to transport them to so-called labor camps."

Claussen's eyes filled with tears, an unexpected display of emotion. "He's the inspiration for CleanSweep. He offered advice, how to avoid the pitfalls, the mistakes both Hitler and Stalin made."

Waverly started to say something, but Claussen held up his hand.

"Let me finish, please. Germans are skilled craftsmen by nature, but they misused their tools. People in camps were valuable resources, like tools. With a minimum of food and minimal health care, they would be productive workers. My grandfather even devised a formula. He calculated the number of daily calories needed to keep people strong enough to work."

"Camps in Germany were turned into killing machines," Winston said.

"That was their mistake," Claussen said. "They worked able-bodied internees to death, convinced they could be replaced by the next trainload of workers. That was inefficient—something any engineer could tell them. As camps became overcrowded, they needed to eliminate non-productive workers. The extermination techniques they used, while necessary, were ghastly." He pointed to the folder. "Our procedures have been designed to ensure necessary 'eliminations' are compassionate."

He looked at each of them, judging their reactions.

"CleanSweep isn't about world domination," Claussen said. "I will, however, serve as a template. Once the potential for social engineering is effective... Well..." He stopped. "Open your folder and take out the map."

He waited while the others unfolded a full-color map.

"You'll note the thick red line. That marks the border of the area initially covered by CleanSweep." Charles sniggered. "Compare yours to *this* map," he said, displaying a map of the entire country. "Our region," he began, "will provide a sufficient statistical sample, enough to prove viability. If we make CleanSweep work here, it can be transplanted to any city. More than eighty-five percent of the nation's crime and social evils occur in urban areas. The figures you see listed, outline the problems.

"Start with immigration," Claussen continued. "This metropolitan area leads the nation's largest increase of immigrants. How many are illegal?"

Sir Waverly nodded eagerly as Claussen continued.

"Immigrants arrive thinking the country owes them something. Remember when we once screened applications, making sure they fit in? Immigrants used to embrace true conservative values, believe in hard-working families, and Christian faith.

"Today we're worse than our good American neighbors to the south. So-called refugees crawl through our porous borders like cockroaches. Liberals in charge even pay airfare for terrorists disguised as refugees!"

Spencer and Waverly both harrumphed in stereophonic unison.

My amen corner, Claussen thought.

"In addition to immigrants, we've seen the surge in gang-related crime. We have homosexuals, mentally ill, homeless, and other blood-suckers, all feeding at the trough of welfare programs. Claiming to be victims of an uncaring government and society, they protest, waving signs and demanding their so-called entitlements."

Claussen refilled his coffee cup, watching steam curling up like smoke signals. *Time for details*, Claussen thought.

"That's part of the background," he said. I will tell you more after a break, when the idea for CleanSweep originated."

* * *

"It was the summer of our discontent," Claussen said when they reconvened. "My apology to Shakespeare and Steinbeck." He paused. "Turn to page three. We were proud to sponsor the 2010 international financial conference. It would spotlight the country and city on the international stage."

The others nodded in understanding.

"Instead, the liberal media had a field day. Scenes of rioting showed photographs and videos of burning cars, broken windows, and crowds on the rampage. Those scenes can still be seen on liberal news shows, YouTube, Facebook, and the like. We'll never know the extent on private instant messaging and texting."

Claussen consulted some notes. "Our fine police did their best. The local force was bolstered by hundreds of officers from across the country. The integrated security force was *still* outmaneuvered. Turn to page eleven and the map." He waited. "Patrol areas were established with the aim of documenting people, finding out who the troublemakers were. Anyone not passing the checkpoints were subject to questioning."

"There were plenty of those," Waverly sniffed. "Agitators slipped past roadblocks. They were looking for ways to make us look bad."

"Our police officers were busy," Claussen went on. "They used a manual carding system to interview thousands before the conference. Of course, civil libertarians whined and complained, as expected."

"Don't they always?" Spencer asked.

"Documenting citizens in noncriminal interactions has always been a valuable tool. The police can sift through data, weeding out criminals." Claussen smiled. "All they did was record names, ages, names of associates, religion, and skin color. There was nothing sinister. They coded by categories: routine investigation, keep under observation, or suspicious activity. It's a practice used by police all over the world—and has been for decades. We weren't surprised at the predictable knee-jerk reaction from liberals." Claussen's voice dripped with venom.

"They want police to look like the bad guys," Waverly added.

Claussen glared at the interruption. "My security team gained access to the police records preceding that 2010 summit. It's a treasure trove; those so-called interactions with the public yielded thousands of pocket-size cards called field information reports."

"If someone isn't doing anything wrong, they shouldn't object," Spencer Abbot said.

Claussen was annoyed at this second interruption, but kept his bristling hidden. "In 2010, temporary jail locations were set to handle the sudden surge of arrests if there was rioting. There were over eleven hundred it turned out, the largest mass arrest in the city's history. What I'm about to tell you is t known only to a handful of my most trusted aides...." Claussen paused.

The others leaned forward, eager to hear this part. Claussen talked in a low, dramatic voice. The others would need to concentrate, giving him full attention.

"My head of security, Angela Vaughn, uncovered a report, detailing security planning, in place for two years leading up to this international summit. Armed with that, she used a contact in a nearby city.

"She reported there was a man we might use, Gustav Brunner, really Ralph Patterson. He didn't think his real name sounded Germanic, thus Brunner. He led a close-knit group of goose-stepping, heil saluting skinheads. Hanging swastika flags from their apartment balcony railing was too much.

"The authorities moved quickly, ordering them to be removed. Officials claimed the flags were symbols of hatred, another example of misguided thinking, banning the right to free expression. Do-gooder activists made it impossible for Brunner and his group.

"When Brunner tried to organize rallies and marches, their Antifa enemies made sure they didn't get the attention they craved." Claussen paused, saying, "You take excellent care of your plants." He pointed to Winston's greenhouse, visible near the garage. "You cultivate, prune, and fertilize your plant life. That's what I did with Brunner. I made him an offer he couldn't refuse," Claussen said, laughing at the movie reference. "We trained the man in the art of recruiting. We sent experts to show him how to indoctrinate his recruits. We funded him with assets and money beyond his wildest dreams. He became my Judas goat.

"He moved west, to a province with fertile soil for recruiting. The political climate and soil proved perfect for him. Citizens tilted to the right," Claussen added, "pollinated by talk shows fanning our beliefs. It wasn't long before Brunner has a small-but-growing group.

"Brunner organized rallies, using his gift of oration, seducing new recruits to join the movement. To put a fine point to it, I provided all the financing. I ordered Brunner to train teams in preparation for this next summit. Most destruction during the earlier summit was instigated by a small group—and look at the public outrage *that* caused.

"We learned from that summit's experience. This upcoming global conference will play into my—I'm sorry, *our*—hands. Brunner's hooligans, his Free Eagle Militia, will create conditions so frightening, everyone, even the sniveling liberals, will beg for enhanced security. CleanSweep will answer their pleas, public disturbance will be put down, and order will be restored. Citizens will thank us.

"I've visited Brunner's camp, observing the training of his private army. I can testify they are some frightening men and women. They're the dangerous-looking sorts we cross the street to avoid.

"What happens after our planned rioting? Let me show you about the planned infrastructure, in detail. I've developed a plan to facilitate CleanSweep's swift implementation. I've already funded the operation with my own resources—along with some help from Winston, here."

Winston stood. "Well done, my friend. I am sure I speak for the others when I say I am impressed. Perhaps we need a lunch break."

Claussen would have preferred to get to the next part, the heart of the proposal. He couldn't risk alienating his host, however.

"Of course. Please hand back your folders, gentlemen."

"You're a stickler for security," Waverly replied, handing his copy to Claussen. "I like that."

Copies of the proposal safely locked, Claussen saw Winston take a small radio from his pocket, whispering. "Bring in our lunch now, Ulrich," he said, releasing the transmit key.

Claussen looked at the small radio with alarm. "May I see that, please?" He turned it over, looking carefully at the transmit key. He tried to hide a frown. Finally, he asked politely if he could remove the battery cover.

"Of course you may. What's the worry? Is there a problem?" Winston said. He respected Claussen's fixation with security. "I only use it to call Ulrich."

Claussen scrutinized the radio, trying to do mental reverse-engineering.

This is a nightmare, he thought. *The fool has an outdated radio so old its transmissions aren't safeguarded by the security protocol built into my signal-jamming program. Still,* he thought...*what harm can it really cause? It can't have much range.* He put the radio back together and handed it back to Winston.

"I wish you'd told me you were using that, Winston." Claussen was careful to keep anxiety out of his voice.

"Is it a serious problem?" Winston asked. "It only reaches Ulrich, and I trust him without reservation.

"Problem? Probably not," Claussen said—but he wasn't sure.

● ● ●

Hearing what Winston said, Ulrich smirked. He placed a second radio into a locked drawer. It was like the one the boss used to call him. Safely locked in the drawer, the twin had an aditional feature. Tuned to the same frequency, it recorded conversations in the next room. State-of-the-art miniscule receptors were located throughout the lodge, transmitting every word.

The majordomo walked into the dining room with a tray. He'd placed food on the table and reached into his pocket to set the harmless radio on the table while he returned to the kitchen for wine. He knew Claussen would examine it. Once Claussen did, Ulrich thought it would placate any concerns Claussen might have. It worked.

Ulrich thought about the recorder in the drawer, humming softly as he carried the empty tray back to the kitchen. Someone with sensitive hearing would have detected—in spite of the off-key version—what he was humming: *The Internationale.*

CHAPTER 18

HIDDEN IN THE DETAILS

"**I**'m stuffed—and tired," Spencer grumbled as Ulrich cleared the lunch table. "I need time with my personal trainer after one of your meals, Winston."

Claussen knew Spencer's idea of exercise was moving his chair closer to the table, and his personal trainer was a chef, equally rotund.

Claussen was still annoyed his presentation had been interrupted as he'd been getting to the best part. "Spencer, it's clear you've missed most appointments with your trainer," he said, intending it to be lighthearted, but he was immediately sorry—Spencer frowned.

"Will that be all, gentlemen?" Ulrich asked.

"Bring coffee in a carafe. We need the afternoon to be interruption-free," Winston said.

Ulrich returned, and when everything was to his satisfaction, he left the room.

All attention returned to Claussen. He wasted no time outlining details of CleanSweep. "Teams will patrol streets, as well as patrol the back roads on the outskirts. We've first called the teams auditors. They *will* be performing a special kind of audit, after all. Angela Vaughn came up with calling them Sweepers, after CleanSweep."

Claussen paused, sipping coffee. "CleanSweep sweeper teams are comprised of driver, computer analyst, and two officers—Cleaners—for arrest and detention.

"I specified customized Sprinter vans on Mercedes-Benz frames. The driver and computer specialist, in front, the specialist with immediate access to arrest and detention warrants. The two 'cleaners' sit immediately behind, separated from the back by a wire mesh screen. The van is designed to accommodate eight detainees, four seats on each side, U-bolts welded to the frame. Cleaners make sure any high-risk prisoners are handcuffed, unable to escape.

"To keep them from looking like Black Marias, the vans are painted white with no identifying logos or signage."

Claussen explained how the sweeper teams were trained, handing his friends a tablet and starting another video.

"Watch this demonstration. We set up a trial operation using actual subjects," he said, the camera aimed over the driver's shoulder. As the van braked, two cleaners jumped out, apprehending a homeless man. He was handcuffed and placed into one of the van's holding seats before surprise registered on the man's face.

"Excellent. Exactly as planned," an excited Claussen said over the video's commentary.

When the van was at capacity, the detainees were driven to a neighborhood holding facility nearby. "We've set up small holding units throughout the greater metropolitan area," Claussen boasted.

"Were those people actors?" Waverly wanted to know.

"No. I said earlier they were actual subjects, eight insects no longer befouling our city," Claussen said.

Turning back to the video, they watched the sweeper van unload passengers.

"It looks like an ambulance pulling into any hospital emergency room." Spencer Abbot sounded impressed.

They saw a pointed difference inside, however. The detainees were directed to various lanes. Each lane was designated for certain categories; homeless in one lane, mentally ill in another, other handicapped prisoners in another.

Claussen explained. "Criminals were divided into subcategories, depending on the type of crime committed."

The camera zoomed in to follow a prisoner directed into a dormitory-type room.

"He's waiting there to be interviewed one-on-one," Claussen explained.

The video showed detainees boarding a bus. They listened to the voice-over. "Detainees are taken to the central intake facility where they await final assessment. Once final determination is complete, each person will have an electronic chip implanted, subcutaneously above the right elbow. Every person detained will be monitored with a mouse click.

"Bluetooth technology feeds vital signs to the nearest cellular tower: pulse, blood pressure, and anxiety measurements. That data is relayed to our central computer," the narrator said.

"Give me a report on detainee 12-4577," a voice commanded.

The screen filled while a disembodied voice said, "Detainee 12-4577 is currently residing at the Spadina Avenue intake facility. She's designated potentially homeless, no known family of record. The detainee is scheduled for transfer to the Lakeside facility in seventeen days." More examples followed, and the men around the table seemed very pleased indeed.

"That's how it will work, once in place," Claussen said. "What you saw in the video is a pilot project set up to demonstrate CleanSweep. When CleanSweep is fully operational, a network of busses and streetcars will transport detainees to the transit center. It can accommodate the larger numbers we expect. Trains will be used to transfer the to the purification camp—I mean, facility."

Claussen was spitting out a fine spray as he talked. "With this online, expect immediate, visible results. When the template is adopted, imagine fathers taking wives, children, even mothers-in-law out for a stroll. No worries about gangs, panhandlers, or all the ugliness civil libertarians and liberal advocates have forced on us.

"With this operation, we've become advocates supporting real families, those willing to contribute to our world. Good riddance of bloodsuckers who leech away precious resources."

"Excellent," Waverly said.

"You're right, Waverly. It will be excellent when we finally interrupt the generational cycle of welfare dependence. We'll simply stop them from breeding."

When he finished, he looked around the room. There was no reaction. For a moment Claussen feared the worst—until Spencer leaped to his feet.

"That's brilliant, Charles. More than that, it's brilliant beyond my wildest expectations. My checkbook is open. I'm giving you a blank check."

"You have actually put your plan into practice—beta tested it?" Waverly tried not to show he was impressed.

"We've run beta tests, getting it right," Claussen said. He couldn't suppress his glee.

Waverly wiped a tear away. "I've dreamed about this for years. We finally get rid of scum sucking taxpayers dry. You'll have my full backing. I'm talking billions I can divert from secret accounts."

Winston Overstreet sat back, quiet, letting his broad smile spoke for him. He nodded to his protégé. Finally, he lifted his hand for silence. "This marks a solemn occasion, gentlemen. This country's been on a slippery slope since the Great Depression tilted our great country to the extreme left. What our great friend Charles Claussen's done..." Winston said, patting Claussen on the shoulder, "is give this great nation the backbone needed to set things *right* again, no pun intended!" He laughed heartily. "I'm proud to call him my friend, and we can do it. Let's give this scheme our full support."

"Like I said, done!" shouted Spencer.

"You can count on me," Waverly added.

"I propose," Winston said, "since you're all leaving early tomorrow, we should get some rest. Early to bed, as the saying goes..." He turned to Charles. "Do we have the okay to take the proposal to our rooms? We can digest it in private and make final recommendations over breakfast?"

Charles Claussen already knew they supported him. He was only too happy to let them take the proposals if it would help them feel like part of a team.

Spencer and Waverly headed along the hallways toward their respective suites.

Winston stopped Claussen. "Now with Spencer and Waverly gone, we have some time alone. I've ordered coffee and digestive biscuits to accompany a fine cognac. Please, join me in front of the fire. 'The time has come,' the Walrus said, 'to talk of many things: of shoes—and ships—and sealing wax—of cabbages—and kings—'"

• • •

Ulrich watched the two men in wingback chairs in front of the blazing fire. Backing out of the room, he closed the door with the consummate quiet expected of a majordomo. He was, after all, a highly trained professional.

He unlocked the drawer containing the secret recorder. He tested the recording, listening for a few minutes. Satisfied every word could be heard clearly, he put the recorder back into the drawer. When he reached his rooms, he opened a suitcase and took out a shipping envelope. He placed a label on a FedCo Courier envelope. When the conference was over, he'd seal the recorder and enjoy a leisurely bicycle ride into Lion's Head.

Always cautious, Ulrich would create a copy on his computer, in case.

He hummed his off-key version of *The Internationale* as he undressed for bed.

• • •

Two friends sat in the dim light, the room's quiet occasionally shattered by a strong, sputtering *hiss-sss-sss*. It sounded like a coiled snake preparing to strike. Charles and Winston watched a log roll over in the fireplace, and a burst of flame momentarily chased shadows of the room. With a whimper, the flame dwindled, silence returning.

Longtime comrades, they were comfortable with lengthy periods of silence. Each held his snifter in the practiced, casual manner that men of privilege seem to adopt so well. From time to time, one of them would raise his glass to take a sip, mostly in silence, with the occasional sigh of satisfaction.

"L'Essence de Courvoisier cognac," Winston said when Claussen asked. "I was staying with a friend in Zurich. You know him—Wilhelm."

Charles nodded.

"I was surprised at the superior taste." He held the bottle for inspection. "Wilhelm said its teardrop decanter and finely crafted crystal stopper were inspired by signet rings Napoleon Bonaparte gave his commanders in recognition of noble acts."

The two sat back in silence, enjoying the flavor. Winston looked over at Claussen as if judging whether the moment was right to ask a question. "I've been curious about something. Perhaps it's impolite, but—"

"I would never think you impolite." Charles held up his hand to reassure him.

"It's your family's background," Winston finally said. "There's always been an aura of mystery, parts of the story hidden from view."

"My family history is a carefully guarded secret," Claussen said.

"Excuse my asking," Winston said. "Please, forgive my inquisitive nature."

The silence resumed between the two men, broken only by the occasional sizzle from a burning ember.

"There is a reason for my self-imposed secrecy," Claussen said, finally breaking the stillness. "My grandfather's name was Otto Klausmann before records were altered. He subtracted a letter and changed the *K* to a *C*. Otto made his Nazi records disappear as the war ended." Claussen sipped his cognac, considering what to tell his friend. "He was a high-ranking member of the National Socialist Party. The old man still has his membership card. He even received a medal from Der Führer in person. He's quite proud of his work, designing work camps and ghettos."

"It's all misconstrued today, twisted to make it sound worse than it was," Winston said. "Was he ever under suspicion, you know, with immigration?"

"A warrant was issued for Otto Klausmann as you can imagine, branding him a war criminal," Charles said. "Fortunately, Otto Claussman, spelled with a *C* and one *N*, was good enough."

Winston nodded.

Claussen continued. "People have been brainwashed to think Nazis invented the idea of racial purity. My grandfather said there was nothing inherently wrong with certain forms of ethnic cleansing—population relocation for example. Workers with special skills could be assigned jobs accordingly. Those with general skills could be assigned menial labor, and the rest..." Claussen let the words trail off.

"Killing for its own sake was a mistake. Certain races can be used for labor and other services. He'd calculated minimal caloric intakes keeping people at healthy work capacity. If he'd had his way, wasteful killings wouldn't have occurred. It was a distraction. He knew it wouldn't be tolerated by the outside world.

"Eradicating,' he told me, should be targeted," Claussen said, "applied to those who would never be contribute to society. I promised him we won't make that mistake with CleanSweep. Eliminations will be humane and discreet. We aren't monsters, after all. Charles smiled. "Did you know the history of ethnic cleansing goes back to the early Crusades?"

"That far? Winston said.

"Turkey, Russia, Germany, Bosnia are late to the game. Even the Americans had a go at it. Read about the Trail of Tears, the Seminoles, and life on the reservations. Mexicans were seen as roadblocks to American westward expansion. Perhaps that explains the continuing backlash against Spanish speaking immigrants."

Winston nodded and sipped cognac, listening intently.

"The United States slipped over the line with a bit of genocide—if stories from the early American involvement in the Philippines are accurate. Not to mention Wounded Knee."

"And slavery?" Winston said.

"Its own category," Charles admitted with a wave of his hand. He did something highly uncharacteristic next. He loosened his tie and removed his loafers, using toe-to-heel to ease them off. He frowned, annoyed by a small hole in the toe of his left sock.

"I've never seen you so relaxed," Winston said.

"Thanks to you," Charles said, holding his glass in a faux salute. "Thanks to you, my dear friend, this weekend went exactly as we'd hoped. Maybe even better."

"Waverly simply had to go through the motions," Winston said. "He never makes a move without knowing he has a strong tailwind at his backs."

"He's behind CleanSweep completely, though, yes?" Claussen asked.

"From the beginning, Charles. He only needed you to flesh out the details, so he could spin the facts. He's possibly the most powerful man in government. Rarely in the public eye, he knew if he controlled money, it would yield the ultimate influence in power."

"He turned down all the offers of a cabinet appointment, didn't he?" Claussen said.

"And he knew exactly what he was doing," Winston replied, nodding.

"And you're sure he's on board with CleanSweep?"

"Let me show you something." Winston walked to a small table, taking a small key from his pocket, and unlocked its single drawer. He pulled out an envelope, a notarized seal straddling the flap. "Take a look at this," he said. "Here's an opener."

Charles sliced open the envelope, pulling out a single sheet of paper. His eyes widened, and a broad smile graced his face.

"Read it aloud, Charles," Winston said.

● ● ●

LION'S HEAD ACCORD

Whereas the Government recognizes the threat to national security, this accord serves to define the formal agreement between the federal government and CleanSweep Enterprises, Ltd., and contracts with Clean-Sweep, Ltd. to implement and manage a pilot project ensuring the security of citizens living in the area designated as the Greater Toronto Area (GTA).

By special order of the government, this confidential decree grants agents of CleanSweep emergency powers to conduct inquiries, make arrests, interrogate detainees, and keep in confinement persons found to be a danger to the public order.

Agents of CleanSweep shall be armed and carry warrant cards that establish their powers of arrest and detention. Persons detained by such officers will not be entitled to appeal. The right to habeas corpus is hereby suspended for individuals identified by CleanSweep as enemies of good order.

Agents of CleanSweep are authorized to operate proprietary surveillance systems, with the authority to analyze all information acquired thereby, as needed to meet the terms of this accord.

Further, agents of CleanSweep will have access to the databases and surveillance records compiled by any local, regional, and federal police agencies.

The agents are granted instant subpoena power to obtain any private surveillance records of commercial establishments, banks, ATMs, traffic cameras, and any other recording equipment used within the GTA.

This order is granted by emergency legislation, enacted in secret session, for the well-being of the people.

Signed and dated,

Richard Waverly,
Special Government Counsel

• • •

"You've had this all along, damn you!" Claussen said. His smile contradicted his attempt to sound annoyed.

Winston knew his protégé was ecstatic. "That's my copy," he said. "Waverly and I prepared them for this meeting. The decree is ready for quick implementation. Let him have his moment tomorrow when he officially hands you your personal copy. Can you act surprised?"

"What? Surprised at what? I have no idea what you're talking about." He grinned as he handed the paper back to Winston.

• • •

Ulrich's radio recorded the two men laughing, and the sound of paper scraping as the accord went back into the envelope.

"I need my sleep," Winston said.

The hole in his sock no longer bothered Charles. He savored the last of the Courvoisier. "This is the best night of my life, Winston. The best night of my life."

CHAPTER 19

ONCE IN MOTION

Winston Overstreet, hands clasped tightly behind his back, watched his last guest leave—Charles Claussen. Winston listened to the helicopter's engine whine, the rotors turning slowly as it gradually picked up speed.

Claussen sat, his hand on the controls. He knew the windshield's reflection concealed his face, keeping his grin from showing.

His corporate jet sat ready to go as Claussen set the computer for a course to Billy Bishop Airport in Toronto. *Toronto's the perfect choice for a trial run. The city had no idea what lays in store*, he thought.

Once airborne, he pressed the microphone key. Flight-plan formalities complete, he changed to another frequency.

"It's a go. I want the compliance team assembled in the conference room," he said, looking at the clock, "in two hours and thirty-six minutes. I expect all implementation details. Make it happen."

He didn't wait for an answer.

Annoyed didn't begin to describe his reaction when traffic control gave instructions delaying his arrival by seventeen minutes. He was furious, learning the reason. It was due to the huge annual gay pride parade—airspace needed for television helicopters in the air.

Altering course out over Lake Ontario, a view of Niagara Falls over his shoulder, he turned back for an approach to the airport. He forced himself to remain seated until rotating blades came to a stop.

He unfastened his shoulder harness, picked up his leather case, and stepped onto the tarmac. He leaned forward, head down, racing sideways until he reached the jet. The door scissor-folded into the fuselage as he fastened his seatbelt. When they reached altitude, he undid the strap and walked forward, tapping the pilot on the shoulder.

"That damn parade had to be today, didn't it? Can we make up the time?"

"Easily," said the pilot as he contacted international air traffic control.

• • •

Once landed, the pilot taxied at the maximum allowed speed, arriving at the corporate hangar, a limousine waiting. Claussen didn't bother acknowledging the slight bow of the driver holding the door.

Two men squeezed into side jump seats, muscled arms straining their suit fabric. Claussen joined Angela Vaughn, waiting in the rear seat.

"Tell me," he said, waiting for someone to start.

His chief of operations, started first. "We're on target. Training is complete. Squad leaders are pouring over every detail, making sure their teams are prepared to hit the ground running."

"Are the facilities operational?" Charles snapped.

"The signs are going up," the second man said. "Substations are ready. The Spadina detention center is already open for business, and business is booming." He waited for a laugh. Nobody did. "Headquarters on Broad Street is drawing lots looky-loos," he added. "They're in for a big surprise."

"What about transportation?" Charles said.

"Everything's been tested, retested, and tested again. Sweeper vans have been inspected. Buses and streetcars are ready," said his chief of operations.

"What about our...northern facilities?"

"The Moon Lake facility's fully operational. All personnel, from manager to cook's helper, have been trained—"

"Security?" Claussen broke in.

"Tight," the second man said, sounding offended. "The Moon Lake perimeter is secure. Surveillance countermeasures are in place. With the government using your program, satellites are tricked into seeing images of pine forest, as it looked before construction."

Angela Vaughn nodded. "Everything is in place," she said.

"No planning is ever perfect. There's always a small detail or two overlooked. What about the northern contractors?" Claussen continued, firing questions in a machine-gun staccato. "Will they keep it secret?"

"They have all been relocated," the chief of operations said. Nobody needed to ask for a definition of *relocated*.

Charles hid his excitement behind his harsh questioning. Finally, he relaxed, turning to Angela Vaughn. "What about our distraction?"

"The e-mail from Waverly's staffer came in." She held up her tablet. "The global economic conference is in full swing, conference headquarters at the Royal York, overflow resources and rooms at your friend's hotel, Trump Tower. Most people attending will like the old-school feel of the historic Royal York, while some prefer the gold-plated feel at the Trump Hotel. They've arranged an outdoor ceremony in Nathan Phillips Square in front of City Hall. That'll funnel thousands of people into a contained area. It'll be perfect."

"It *has* to be," Charles almost spat as he spoke.

"I've sent the order. Brunner and his hoodlums are ready to go," Vaughn said. "Some'll fly in. Others by train or bus. The rest will arrive in cars or vans."

Vaughn showed Claussen her tablet. "Say the word. At my command, they'll start creating chaos. The police think they're ready." Vaughn sneered. "What they don't know, Brunner and the nine thousand militia coming were trained to create maximum violence."

Nobody spoke, watching Charles Claussen digesting the information. "What about secondary targets?"

"We're ready, sir," the second man said. "The Distillery District is a primary target. We'll take out two key subway stations," he said, working hard to avoid looking smug. "Explosives are set to bring down the overhead expressway west of the Spadina ramp." He smiled. "That'll mess things up for a long time."

"Waverly has committed," Claussen said. "When we demonstrate the police have been totally overwhelmed, the federal government will implement a new Emergency Powers Act. The entire metro area—and beyond—under national control, CleanSweep will come to life at last."

Claussen looked at the caller ID on his personal phone. He squeezed the phone, his face turning white. The others, fearing the worst, waited.

Finally, he spoke. *"Mein Grossvater ist tot!"*

Claussen stared at the phone, as if waiting for another call telling him it was a mistake. He looked up. "I'm dedicating CleanSweep to *SS-Gruppenführer,* Otto Klausmann." He choked back emotion.

The only sound was the hum of tires.

CHAPTER 20

CAMP FREE EAGLE

"I don't trust the reports."

The following morning, Angela Vaughn stood motionless, watching her boss pacing from one side of his office to the other. He stopped to stare out the window. Eventually, he wheeled around. "I want to see the training camp for myself. Make it happen!"

Should I offer condolences? She thought. *He's not showing any signs of grief. I know he controls his emotions like that—*

"Yes, sir." Vaughn nodded. The meeting clearly over, she turned to the door. She started a mental to-do list for the trip to Brunner's camp. Her boss wanted to see Camp Free Eagle. She grimaced. *How did Brunner ever come up with that name?*

Angela was uncomfortable around Brunner. He always insisted she call him "Gustav," trying to be ingratiating. *His real name's Ralph*, she thought, laughing inwardly. *He wants a Germanic-sounding name.* She'd purposely annoy him, calling him Gus, watching him blush in anger.

Angela Vaughn didn't want to acknowledge her discomfort with Brunner was based on a gnawing sense of guilt. Graduating from police academy was profound; she and the other new officers shouted, tossing their caps in the air. She was never prouder. She'd taken an oath to protect and serve and thought her conviction was unshakable.

Now she was serving to protect Charles Claussen and his Operation CleanSweep. The man calling himself Gustav Brunner was the poster boy for the evil of Claussen's ideas.

I've mortgaged my soul, accepting Claussen's job offer as head of security operations, she thought. *I'm on a slippery ethical slope, with Camp Free Eagle and Operation CleanSweep waiting for me at the bottom.*

• • •

At her desk, she knew she couldn't delay the unavoidable. She reached for the phone, calling the pilot. When she had flight details arranged, she placed another call.

"Vaughn here." She didn't wait for a reply. "Put me through to Brunner." Her gruff words should have been enough for immediate action on the other end. She squeezed the phone. She wrinkled her nose as if a foul odor were invading her office.

"I don't give a rat's—" She didn't finish; the receiver on the other end hit the desk, and a young man shouted for Major Brunner.

"*Major Brunner?*" She laughed at his self-appointed rank.

When Major Brunner answered, she didn't offer explanations. "The General of the Army will be landing"—glancing at a clock—"In three hours, sixteen minutes. Have a car ready at the airport."

Not waiting for a response, Vaughn disconnected the call without ceremony. She smiled. The general far outranked Major Brunner, likely in a state of high froth.

• • •

Claussen was quiet on the ride to the airport. Vaughn assumed he was thinking about his late grandfather and didn't intrude on his grief.

If we're on time, it'll be wheels down in three hours and sixteen minutes, she thought. *Overnight at Brunner's camp, back to civilization tomorrow morning.*

Aboard the jet, Vaughn waved away the copilot's offer of coffee. Claussen didn't speak. Grunting, he gestured to be left alone. The copilot returned to the cockpit. Soon, the jet was airborne, Claussen silent as

Vaughn settled back, caressed by expensive leather. She drifted into an uncomfortable sleep.

Her eyes opened as the plane shuddered, the pilot banking on approach to the small airport. Angela saw spiked peaks of a snow-capped mountain range, a dramatic sight she usually enjoyed. Today, her mind was on more important matters.

"Will he be there to meet us?" Claussen said. He looked at her, but she couldn't read his face.

"I told him to make sure he is. He's calling himself *Major* Brunner these days," she said. "I promoted you to General of the Army to outrank him."

She saw a hint of a smirk. They both tightened their seatbelts as the plane lurched through.

"Sorry, boss," the pilot said on the intercom. "I have to counteract thermals rising between those mountains." The plane shuddered again as they descended.

"Wheels down shortly," the copilot said, sounding calm over the speaker.

The wheels screeched in protest, the jet bouncing, then bouncing again, finally gripping the tarmac. Reverse thrusters and brakes brought the jet to a stop at the end of the runway. The pilot taxied to one of the hangars, a ramshackle structure attached to the side serving as a terminal.

Angela was glad to see Brunner standing there, next to a Hummer.

The fool even has small flags fastened to the front fenders, she observed.

He was standing next to a woman. Stiffly at attention, both tried to look "military" in camouflage uniforms.

"He's a jerk, but he's *my* jerk," Claussen said, not bothering to hide his sarcasm.

"Please wait until the ramp is completely down, sir," the pilot said. He stood in the cockpit doorway. "We'll be ready at 0800 tomorrow morning." The pilot tucked his hat under his left arm.

The exit door opened, the hydraulic steps unfolded, and Angela led the way. At the bottom of the steps, she looked at Brunner, half expecting him to salute. Instead, he ordered his assistant to carry luggage and bowed as he opened a rear door for Claussen. He gave Angela Vaughn a look that implied she could open her own door.

Vaughn and Claussen shared eye rolls, listening to Brunner's nonstop monologue. It was obvious the Major was nervous, hoping a running commentary on the history of the valley would cover that up.

Blond hair pulled back in a severe ponytail, his assistant sat at attention. She didn't speak, but now and again looked at Brunner with obvious reverence.

Brunner was an expert driver—Vaughn conceded him that—easily managing the Hummer as the road grew more demanding. At an unmarked side road, he turned left. This road leading to the foothills wasn't paved. They reached a steep incline, rising steadily until the road reached a dense stand of pines. Exiting the woodland, the road curved and twisted until bright yellow flowers reflected sunlight.

The road leveled as they drove through a meadow. Ahead, Vaughn saw a checkpoint, a small kiosk to the side. There were no signs warning curious drivers to turn back. There was no barrier to stop curious drivers. As they approached, two men stepped out from the guardhouse. They were armed and looked as if they took their jobs seriously; she guessed their automatic weapons would have discouraged any unauthorized person from driving past.

The guards, recognizing Brunner, snapped to attention, saluting as the Hummer sped past. *That looked well-rehearsed,* Angela Vaughn thought. At the edge of a small depression, Brunner turned sharply to take a road along its rim. Brunner slowed as they reached a dense grove of trees, spanning the road like a canopy, tress outlining the view of the camp gate like a picture frame.

Angela saw a high, electrified fence. The gate remained closed as Brunner braked to a stop. Two guards came out of a kiosk; one walked to the driver's side, the other to the passenger's side. They didn't open the remote-controlled gate until all IDs were confirmed.

"I would have their heads if they weren't thorough," Brunner said over his shoulder.

The camp was comprised of five buildings. "That's headquarters," Brunner said, pointing to one. "That larger one doubles as mess hall and lecture room." He pointed to one farther away. "That houses operations and facilities. We have the capacity to go for a week without power with that bad-boy generator. The other two buildings are barracks."

They came to an open area occupied by men and women wearing camouflage uniforms, grouped in various stages of training. One squad ran in a crouch, shooting at cut-out targets. Faux storefronts depicted an urban street scene.

"That's some good shooting," Angela Vaughn commented.

Another group on the right was engaged in a form of martial arts training. Vaughn saw one man standing to the side, clutching his arm in pain.

Brunner braked. An unsmiling woman appeared in front of the Hummer, waving a red flag to stop them. Brunner directed Claussen to look to the left.

They watched a man running past an open doorway, pausing to throw an object through the door. As the man tumbled for cover, a strong blast shattered the silence. Flames and smoke spiraled above.

"Good job..." Brunner grumbled.

"How many people do you have in training?" Claussen asked, even though he knew.

"Sergeant?" Brunner said, snapping his finger.

"Sir. Two thousand and forty-eight, sir!" the assistant said. "Sir. The others are in transit as ordered, sir! Four thousand two hundred are fully trained are heading east, or already waiting on the outskirts of Toronto."

Brunner stopped the Hummer and looked back at Claussen.

"How many are trained to do *that*, the maneuver with a grenade? That's what I was asking."

"They all are," Brunner said, smirking at the young sergeant sitting next to him.

Claussen smiled for the first time. Angela saw his broad, beaming smirk and relaxed.

Once settled in guest quarters, they walked with Brunner to head-quarters. The sergeant walked at Brunner's side. *Like a dog at heel*, Angela Vaughn thought. When they entered the building, seventy-five personnel jumped to their feet, standing in rigid poses.

"At ease," Brunner said. There was the sound of sliding chairs as the men and woman sat. Brunner led his guests to another room—a conference room. Five men and two women stood at attention, waiting for Claussen to take a seat at the head of the table.

"Sir," Brunner looked at Claussen. "I have asked these team leaders to brief you."

By the time the meeting finished, Angela heard them each tell Claussen what their teams were ready to do. Over nine thousand men and women were preparing an attack on the city of Toronto, timed at the start of the global summit.

Brunner and each team leader outlined their task. "Team Spearhead will start with a bang." Brunner laughed. Angela didn't think it was funny. She knew Team Spearhead was to set off the first bomb in the Distillery District, as the summit was getting underway. The plan was to create enough destruction to draw the police and security forces away from surveilling the crowds assembled to watch the dignitaries arrive.

"Collateral damage is unavoidable," Brunner said. The tone of his words, however, implied he didn't care who got hurt. "The bombings will be the signal. Operation Short Fuse will be in high gear. Five key areas are pinpointed as specific targets for violence and destruction. The Free Eagle operatives will cause as much confusion and destruction as possible. We're more than ready." Brunner assured his guests that the army of hired thugs looked forward to smashing skulls and teeth. He grinned.

Angela didn't sleep well that night. This was her city being discussed as if it was the object of an exercise. Her feeling as a former police officer bubbled under the surface of her awareness. She was grateful her boss was not in a talkative mood as they were driven back to the airport. She did note, however, he smiled a lot on the flight back.

• • •

Three days after that visit to Camp Free Eagle, the media reported that tens of thousands were expected to gather as the summit opened. Drawn to the spectacle and ceremony, spectators would crowd into the city center, hoping to get a view of the dignitaries as they arrived. TV cameras prepared to focus on signs, some protesting politics of certain delegates, some to cheer their favorite celebrity. The crowd seemed to be in a festive mood, but police security forces were on high alert. Undercover agents melted into the crowd, ready to sound the alarm if someone looked threatening. Despite all the preparation, nobody was prepared for what happened.

Several Free Eagle agents began pushing and shoving. Their job was to stir up resentment, careful to avoid violence...until the signal was given.

The crowd surged to the front of the plaza as the first celebrity limousines arrived. Television cameras, reporters with microphones, and bloggers using smartphones to record the event formed phalanxes, swarming around each dignitary. Alarm, fear, and terror came uninvited murder and mayhem was unleashed on the unsuspecting city.

"What are those guys doing?" a curious subway passenger asked, turning to a stranger. They stared at some men who were stripping away their outer layers of clothing, revealing military-style uniforms featuring Free Eagle Militia insignia.

At Saint Patrick station, men jumped up, drawing an assortment of weapons from their belts: police batons, lead pipes, and a formidable array of knives. One reached into his pocket for a set of brass knuckles, glaring at other passengers.

Shrieking brakes blended with screams. Rough-looking men left unarmed passengers bleeding and clutching at broken bones. They laughed at an old woman, whimpering in fear.

Other cars spewed out thugs. A woman in uniform smirked as she clasped a bloodstained baton. Holding up their hands in self-styled salutes, they assembled at street level, surging toward Nathan Phillips square. Uniformed hooligans speared into the crowd, raising their arms and smashing weapons on unsuspecting heads. Bone-crushing sounds combined with screams. People turned away from the limos, hearing the commotion behind them.

"Let's bash some heads in," a thug said. Looking at his watch, he gave a signal. "Now!"

His command was timed to the first explosion. The crowd panicked, trying to scatter, trampling those underfoot.

A small child with pleading eyes stretched her arms for help only to be kicked aside. When the crowd dispersed, she was lying still on the concrete—blank eyes that would never see a future.

The first blast came from a high-explosive bomb strategically placed in the Distillery District, its position calculated to generate maximum damage as well as spread panic and confusion.

The walls of the historic brick building—a former factory—seemed to belch outward as shock waves heaved away from the point of detonation. Walls collapsed inward as the trailing vacuum sucked them back in, overpressure creating an earsplitting sonic boom.

Heat from the explosion released a thermal wave, as newly exposed, combustible material incinerated in microseconds. Fragments of bricks, plumbing pipes, window frames, and furniture vomited small shards expelled at supersonic speed.

For those closest to the blast, death came mercifully fast, internal organs ravaged, shrapnel from debris shredding body tissue, the fireball immolating whatever remained.

Over the next seven minutes, five other regions in greater Toronto were targeted with similar results. Blast waves could be heard and felt over the entire metropolitan area. Entire blocks were leveled and left in flames. Transportation was disrupted. Three freeway bridges were destroyed.

Psychological shock waves, however, had yet to begin to spread.

• • •

A coded terrorism alert signal from police headquarters placed the city's nine regional offices on a war-measures footing. All uniformed officers—on duty and off—received a text message, ordering them to report to emergency stations immediately. Uniformed officers, detectives, command officers, and support personnel were mobilized for the duration, each with a preassigned task.

Over seven thousand men and women were activated. Rumors were rampant; few bothered to hide their apprehension.

The first clash between police and Free Eagle Militia ended with injuries on both sides.

A police commander screamed, "They're storming a hospital." He ordered officers onto buses.

Radio traffic depicted confrontations with rioters. Medical clinics were raided, with patients and staff beaten. Firefighters watched helplessly as buildings burned and collapsed. Many were seen kneeling, heads in hands, weeping at the destruction.

Emergency medical technicians rushed ambulances through thick smoke, dodging debris. They could be heard on radio yelling, "I can't hear you. Say again?" Radio communications faded out and in.

• • •

"Implement exit strategy" was the Free Eagle Militia's final broadcast.

With that, militia men and women began withdrawal. Like ghosts fading into shadows, they disappeared, leaving a stunned populace, the sounds of hissing embers, sighing buildings on their way to collapse, and the haunting sound of screams—human screams that no longer seemed human.

• • •

By day's end, fire and explosives destroyed the trendy Distillery District, the Kensington Market area, the Spadina corridor, the near-west factory region, and the area surrounding Allan Gardens—one of the oldest parks in Toronto.

Statistics were appalling, 337 deaths and over seven hundred people seriously injured. Overburdened authorities were unable to tabulate the number of missing.

Television reports included interviews with witnesses.

"This is the terrorism violence we've long feared. Attacks were well coordinated, and particular groups were targeted," noted an anonymous government source. "Hospitals and clinics were stormed."

"I saw a homeless woman beaten and dragged into a van," an eyewitness said, describing armed men and women in camouflage-style uniforms.

"I saw their uniform patches, clear as anything," a man told reporters. "Free Eagle Militia. I've never heard of such a thing."

Another eyewitness said, "I watched them torch a Jewish church—what do you call it? A synagogue. It was like something out of an old newsreel."

The television announcer continued. "The clash between police and uniformed mobs lasted over seventy-four hours. Order was restored when special agents from a new program called Operation CleanSweep took control of security. Free Eagle Militia began to withdraw, leaving behind a city of dazed citizens, shrouded in smoke. Curiously, not one militia member was ever arrested."

• • •

After the first blast, panic erupted in Nathan Phillips Square and the city center. Police security forces spread out, attempting to protect dignitaries. They opened passageways through crowds, waving frantically, often giving contradictory orders. The convoys of bullet-proof limousines began speeding away, smoked-glass windows rolling up for protection. Dignitaries caught flat-footed between their cars and the hotel were rushed back to limousines, bodyguards forcing them inside with rough shoves. TV cameras and smartphone videos captured the commotion.

Someone in the crowd cried out as Free Eagle agents took their cue from the initial blast, jostling people, using batons and sticks to bash heads. Soon, people were screaming. The crowd began stampeding. They trampled falling bodies, unmindful of who was hurt—their only thought: safety.

Blood pools accompanied sounds of bones breaking and horrible screams of pain and terror. The second blast sounded to the east, quickly followed by a black cloud of smoke.

Police radios crackled with tension; instructions issued in voices close to panic.

"Units one and three, stay where you are."

"Proceed to the Distillery District."

"Captain, have your men cover the medical clinics."

That was only the beginning. Rioting, vandalism, beatings, and even worse extended over the next two days.

• • •

"This is Leonard Paulsen reporting for Action 21 News. I apologize for the poor quality of the video. We are operating from our temporary studio using portable generators."

Leonard Paulsen looked stunned.

"The city's been the scene of unprecedented rioting over the past ninety-six hours. We don't have a latest count. Known dead are in the hundreds. Over twenty-five hundred serious injuries reported. There is no way to estimate the damage in dollar terms, but the destruction of property has been enormous.

"Metropolitan Police Services Chief Claude Randall is urging calm, asking all residents to remain in their homes unless needed on urgent business or assigned to critical services."

The background showed scenes of destruction, one building still blazing, smoke belching from windows, firefighters helpless.

"We're also required to announce formation of a new security organization," the newscaster said, looking down at his notes. "When the all-clear is sounded, each citizen is to report to your neighborhood Clean-Sweep office to be documented and issued with a new photo ID. There are no exceptions to this order. You're ordered to comply with three days."

A map of The Greater Toronto Area appeared as background, showing the locations of CleanSweep stations. "The map is also streaming online."

"Reports from the field indicate the city is returning to normal. Four areas of the city received significant damage, with the Distillery District the hardest hit. All hospital and emergency rooms are operational except Central Hospital; its patients transferred to other facilities. The hospital is badly damaged and not expected to reopen soon.

"This story just in," the newsreader said next. "Police have tentatively identified the person who apparently jumped to his death from the City View condominium building last night. According to a detective on the scene, it was Matthew Tremain, a well-liked investigative blogger. No further information is available, but a source reports Tremain was undergoing treatment for depression.

"In addition to Tremain, the total suicide count is now fifteen, according to reports. Since the rioting began, it's been difficult to access official records. Stringent privacy protocols established by CleanSweep make access to information unattainable.

"In other news, there's still no word on the disappearance of Action 21's own reporter Susan Payne, along with her cameraman. Payne was working on an investigation about the new organization, Operation Clean-Sweep."

After a moment, the screen went dark.

CHAPTER 21

AFTER THE RIOTS

The Ten-Eight was a saloon, never pretending style or class. Most would call it a dive, a dump, a place decent people should avoid. "Keep walking," mothers would say, passing by, noses turned up in disgust as they held children's hands tightly.

The Ten-Eight was a place deliberately uninviting. Smoked-glass windows discouraged examination, a solitary digital sign winking its indifferent invitation to anyone happening by. The door was hard to open, perhaps intended to discourage all but the most tenacious visitors.

The flashing sign displayed 10-8, the saloon's call sign.

10-8 was unofficial police headquarters, a place for a select group of off-duty police officers and detectives, rank left at the front door. 10-8 in cop code meant "officer on duty," adding more than a touch of irony—that only patrons of this cop bar appreciated.

Tonight, the 10-8 was deserted except the barkeep and two men sitting at the counter.

"The worst seventy-two hours of my life," Carling grumbled. "The city's ruined. I don't know if it will ever recover. Look around—there's nobody here."

"Where were you when the balloon went up?" his companion said.

Carling turned and stared. "What the fuck are you talking about? What balloon?"

Detective Sergeant Wallace Carling was nursing a beer, sitting next to Scotty, his closest friend.

"I heard it in a movie," Scott said. "You know, when a battle was starting, they would say the balloon was going up—something big was about to happen. So, where were you?" he asked, gesturing with an upward spiral. "You know, when this balloon went up?"

Carling thought considered the question. "Alone, at my desk," he finally said. "It was quiet. The other guys were either off duty or out in the field when all hell broke loose. Phones started ringing on everybody's desk at the same time. There was no one except me to answer them. Shortly after the phones rang, the emergency Klaxon sounded. That made an awful racket...a horrible sound."

Carling raised his glass for a drink.

"With all the freakin' paranoia about terrorism, we've expected a disturbance like this, even trained for it. The assholes organizing the international conference should have known better—that something like this would happen. The summit is an open invitation to hooligans. What were they thinking?"

It wasn't a question.

"There was bound to be a repeat of the 2010 riots. But this was far more serious than we ever imagined." He took a slow sip of beer, wiping foam from his lips as he looked in the mirror behind the bar.

Do I really look that tired? he thought.

"Some wiseass planner had the bright idea any detectives not working undercover should have uniforms nearby, ready to suit up it there was trouble. They were prepping us for a riot. Hell, it wasn't a riot, it was *riots*—plural. Someone at the top of our food chain thinks the mere presence of uniforms provides a feeling of security. So when the alarm sounded, I hurried to my locker and put on my uniform."

Carling took a long drink and grunted. "I haven't worn mine in years, and it was too tight for comfort. I saw my reflection." He grimaced at the thought. "Yeah, my uniform was way too tight. Where the fuck did all those rioters come from anyway?" Carling said, asking an unanswerable question. "They were prepared, I tell you—organized."

Scotty just nodded.

"I needed this break. We all did," Carling said. "This is the first breather I've had since the riots started."

"Same for me," Scotty mumbled. "All I've had time for is a quick bite and smoke breaks." Scotty rubbed his glass on his forehead to cool it. "Damn, it's hot for this time of the year. I'm beat."

"How could this have happened? We heard rumors. There was intelligence pointing to a riot or disorder, but this went so far beyond that!" Carling was almost shouting. "The other riot back in 2010 was a child's game next to this. This was prearranged, I tell you." He banged his empty mug down on the counter.

For the usually taciturn Carling, this amounted to a soapbox speech.

"I haven't had much sleep in the past seventy-two hours, and I know it's the same for you," Scotty said. He signaled Randy, the bartender, for another round. "I'm surprised you're still open," Scotty said as the aproned man placed two beers on the counter.

"I'm totally out of draught beer," Randy, the bartender barked grunted. "I'm down to a few cases of bottled beer, mostly the crap nobody will buy—except in an emergency. When my inventory's gone, it'll be last call, lights out. I'll call it quits. Hell, I've sent my people home. What's the use even locking the door? The city's gone to crap now. What's left of it? I just don't care anymore." He hid tears behind indignant words.

Randy walked away, picked up a cloth, and started polishing empty glasses while muttering obscenities. Watching the pointless cleaning, Carling knew people often filled a vacuum with ritual, especially when they were at a complete loss.

"How much sleep have any of us had?" Carling said to Scotty. "I fell asleep at my desk a couple of hours ago, right in the middle of filling out a form. I snapped awake to someone coughing, deciding it was time to head here."

Scott nodded. "I know what you mean," he said. "I was almost asleep behind the wheel, waiting to get waved through a snarled intersection. I looked up at a uniform rapping his nightstick on the window. He started to yell at me, so I held up my cap and badge. He walked away, mumbling about how wrinkled and crappy I looked in my out-of-date uniform."

"There's something strange about this riot," Carling said, strident. "It's like the UK riots, where people used instant messages, cell phones, and the like—you know, to orchestrate stuff. This time, it was clear from the get-go that someone was directing things, calling the shots." He stared at the beer glass in front of him. He hadn't taken a drink from his new pour yet. "This was well organized, I tell you."

"I sensed that, too," Scott agreed.

"We know the usual student troublemakers from intelligence reports," Carling said. "They have a certain look about them. It wasn't them, not this time. These new guys didn't fit a terrorism profile. A lot of them looked like bikers in camouflage. I saw more than one prison tat, for sure—"

Carling was about to add something more when the door burst open. Two men were framed by the doorway, the bright sunlight silhouetting them from behind.

"We thought we would find you two here," one said.

"It's about time we got a break," the other one added as they walked in. "Ain't this a freakin' awful mess?"

"Jimmy. Brian. It's a relief to see you're OK. You'd better hurry and order before Randy runs out of beer," Scotty said. "On me."

Carling turned to his friend. *I can't remember the last time the notoriously thrifty Scot picked up a tab.*

After ordering, the foursome moved to a booth. Nobody spoke at first; they sat, drinking, four veteran cops with a total of eighty-seven service years between them. All wore the same shocked expressions, with pale and drawn faces.

"Before you guys got here, Carling and I were talking about where we were when this all began," Scotty said.

"I was in the middle of the sweetest dream, you know, getting laid," Jimmy said. "At least I think it was a dream, because I was alone in bed. My cell rang with the alarm. It always means trouble that time of the night. My feet hit the floor. Chasing sleep away, trying to remember where my uniform was."

"I thought we'd be assigned together," Carling said. "But with all hell breaking loose, I ended up with a bunch of rookies. We were on a bus heading to the north end. The smoke was so thick in some places the driver had to slow to a crawl."

"They handed out riot gear when I got to my assigned post," Jimmy said. "It was downtown. I didn't see anyone I knew. We could hear gunfire—a lot of gunfire. There were a lot of worried looks exchanged."

Scotty jumped in. "I was watching TV, nothing special, surfing for something to watch, when my phone started to vibrate. I didn't want to wake Karen."

They all knew Karen was a nurse at General, and rumors it was one of two hospitals mobbed, ER patients beaten, some killed. At least that was the buzz.

"Karen's phone rang soon after mine," Scotty went on. "We both rushed to get ready. At least she knew where her uniform was." It wasn't meant to be humorous, and no one took it that way.

"I think we're facing an organized attack," Carling said. "This was orchestrated. Mark my words. We're going to be told this was the work of terrorists. Watch the government lay down the law—hard."

Randy, the bartender, yelled, "Hey, guys!" He held up his hand and removed his earbuds. "They're announcing something on the radio. It sounds something like, I don't know, they mentioned a War Measures Act—at least I think that's what they said." They all waited as he held an earpiece in place. "All civil liberties are suspended," the bartender said. "Now they're saying something about CleanSweep. Do any of you guys know about some program like that?"

Carling's head snapped up, suddenly on full alert. "That blogger warned me about that! He tried to tell me CleanSweep was something to worry about. I didn't take him seriously at first..."

Is Charles Claussen behind this somehow—CleanSweep? Carling considered that thought. Something tugged at the edge of his memory. He reached for his cell phone holster.

"I have an old message stored." He tugged the phone out and saw it was working. "Hey, phones are back up."

Everyone was frantic, each scrolling through messages in a frenzy.

"Karen's safe!" Scott said, starting to cry. Nobody thought any less of him for it.

At the same time, the television screen flickered on. "Action 21 News," an announcer said.

Before the loss of power went off, the volume was turned up to be audible in the always-crowded bar. Now it came back on so loudly, the four yelled at Randy to turn it down.

"We're broadcasting from a mobile trailer," the announcer said. "Television and radio studios have been destroyed. We're hoping for a report from Susan Payne on scene at Nathan Phillips Square. So far there's been no contact."

The screen filled with riveting and heartbreaking aerial views, parts of Toronto in ruins, smoke still curling from buildings, scenes reminiscent of bombed-out cities during World War Two. The worst was destruction around the center of the Distillery District. That popular restaurant and entertainment area was reduced to scorched buildings with most of their windows broken out.

"Look at Allan Gardens," Carling said. Video showed the botanical conservatory and gardens. "Look what they've done to that beautiful old structure—it's in ruins."

"Karen and I were married there," Scotty said. "Now...it's gone."

They watched the newscaster pause as he was handed a note. "There's still no word from Susan Payne, not since the police raid on our studio earlier."

"That wasn't a police raid," Carling corrected.

The four turned back to the television. Behind the anchor, the screen projected background videos showing protesters gathering in Nathan Phillips Square. The backdrop changed to B-roll footage, hundreds of people parading back and forth on the sidewalk in front of the Royal York Hotel, carrying signs protesting every conceivable cause.

"Thugs and hooligans appeared without warning," the announcer said. "It was like a flash mob. But this militia had more than protest in mind."

The screen behind the announcer showed another view of the carnage. Hundreds of fear-provoking men and women wearing militia-type uniforms could be seen smashing windows, overturning cars, and firing weapons into the air. Suddenly, the screen went dark.

"That was the last footage we received before our station and studio came under attack. We now know that at least five major sections of the city have been targeted. The destruction was significant—" His voice broke, no longer dispassionate. "The latest numbers now available, over four hundred and seventy-five people have been killed—no accurate count of injured. Emergency rooms and all medical clinics have been overwhelmed. They appear to be the intended targets of attacks as well.

"There are confirmed reports of people awaiting treatment pulled from their chairs and attacked, many beaten severely. One clinic that received particularly vicious assaults was Lifeline Clinic, popular with street people and the homeless. Another clinic that was attacked offered abortion services."

The announcer stopped reading and looked up at the camera, the skin on his face stretched tight in a grimace. "This just in," he said, looking at another sheet of paper handed to him from off camera. "The federal government has now enacted emergency legislation. All citizens are to report to one of the following sites to be documented and receive individual identification cards."

The screen behind him flashed the CleanSweep logo and changed to a map showing the location of the CleanSweep district administrative offices. "This station will keep you informed when we have more information about the locations of sites that will be issuing ID cards. Mark Spears, reporting." He kept staring at the camera until the cutaway.

As the newscast faded to black, the first real CleanSweep operation got underway.

Near the intersection of Danforth Avenue and Dewhurst Boulevard, on the eastern edge of the Valley neighborhood, a two-story, red-brick building displayed bright-red doors that glistened in the sunlight. Neighbors had been pleased to learn someone purchased the abandoned fire station, delighted at the care taken to restore it to like-new condition.

"The landscaping and renovations make it look like it used to years ago," a longtime neighborhood resident said. "I used to go there as a kid and ask the firemen if I could slide down the pole. But budget cuts..."

Others nodded, accepting his venerable word on the matter. The mortar joints of the bricks had been renewed, carefully tuck-pointed, the window and door frames freshly painted. Flowers graced large planters along the front wall.

Passersby were often treated to the clanging of the alarm bell behind closed doors. The chiming had a comforting aspect to it—it signaled help would soon be on the way. With the overhead door open, they might have seen young men and women in khaki uniforms sliding down the pole. But this was no game.

When the station alarm rang on the first day of Operation Clean-Sweep, as it would become known, Sweeper Team Alpha scrambled to duty. The captain jumped from his chair, sending dishes and cutlery sliding.

"This is it, for real!" the station captain shouted. He checked a form on his clipboard and watched the driver, computer analyst, and two sweepers slide down the pole one after the other, just as they had rehearsed.

The main garage door opened, and a Sprinter van emerged. The driver turned the vehicle north first, then east. They were making history with orders to proceed to an address flashing on the computer screen, sending the van's GPS coordinates, detailing the distance and directions in a robotic voice. "Three minutes to destination...two minutes to destination...one minute to destination."

Doug, the team's computer analyst, was hunched over a keyboard. His job was to provide the two sweepers with intelligence information, keeping them constantly updated.

"We're after two men," he said. "They live on the second floor. It's a walk-up. Apartment two hundred and two, first door on the right at the top of the stairs. They're in the apartment now. I have confirmation."

"What's the charge?" one of the sweepers asked.

Doug wasn't supposed to reveal any charges, but let the information slip in his enthusiasm. "They're two lead organizers of the gay pride parade, charged with contributing to moral decay. As if *we* need a reason. We're going after several more after these two," he said, looking at the monitor.

The van glided to a stop in front of a small three-story apartment building. The sweepers picked up the equipment needed for an arrest and ran for the door.

CHAPTER 22
VÉRITÉ

Matt sat at his computer. He'd never experienced this feeling of being utterly cut off from friends he could trust. He wished he was back at Le Rôti Français, standing in line, the barista ready to hand him his order. That seemed ages ago now.

Did Cyberia's warning come soon enough?

He'd asked himself that question so many times in the past few hours. He'd made it through the destruction to the safety of this basement room serving as computer central. So far, no knocking—no agents with hand-cuffs.

The brief communication with his cyber team hadn't helped, the admonitions of their final words a warning—both explicit and implicit. Matt was cut off from help, and he knew it. He knew he was in danger, targeted because he'd investigated CleanSweep, trying to expose the ugliness. His investigation cut too close to the bone, as some might say. Now the fury generated by his probing meant the considerable resources of Enseûrtech and CleanSweep were pointing at him like an arrow aimed at a bullseye.

I have to think of a way to get in touch with Carl and Susan, he thought.

He wrinkled his nose, annoyed at the lingering stench of smoke and decay leftover from the riots. The odor permeated everything, even seeping through the cracks in the building's foundation and finding a way into his basement hidey-hole. He knew he wouldn't be safe for long. His narrow escape from the subway was only the beginning. Someone was sure to spot him soon. At that point? Game over.

He needed to keep his mind occupied so he could think clearly. For something to do, he turned on one of his computers, the one with his blog files. With a mouse click, his computer screen filled with the opening page of his very first blog. Matt read the words, feeling melancholy and chagrin.

Was I that naive? My city was still intact. How did we let this business with CleanSweep go so far?

Reading that first blog was like returning to an innocence that likely never existed. *Who wrote that you can never go home again? Well, the genie's out of the bottle now,* he thought as he began to read.

● ● ●

April 28. VÉRITÉ, a blog by Matt Tremain

Let me tell you about my adopted city, the place I call home. I've walked its streets and lanes, leaving few, if any, neighborhoods unexplored.

By far, my favorite activity is riding the streetcar. I love riding the 501 streetcars between Long Branch loop and corresponding turnaround loop on the east end. I sometimes ride that trolly back and forth, hours at a time. It's an opportunity to breathe in the rich diversity of the city.

That ride captures our diversity.

Colorful silk wraps reveal cultural roots of women wearing them. Men wearing stiff-necked suits sit next to students wearing predistressed designer jeans—blending together as the car glides east, turning around to head back west, only to turn around and head east. The streetcar does that day after day. I'm reassured by the constancy.

Looking out the window, I'm always curious about a man. Most days I regularly see him, waving his arms as if trying to gather crowds to follow him. Is he guiding them away from a danger only he knows about? If so, I've never seen anybody follow him. You may have noticed him if you ride the 501. Next time, look for him, standing at the corner of Berkeley and Queen.

My favorite character, however, is a woman I call the Dancing Lady. I don't know if she's dancing, but I imagine her attempting a plié, perhaps a demi plié, or maybe a not-so-grand jeté. I admit to a limited acquaintance with ballet terminology. I silently pray her dancing gives her pleasure. Somehow, I doubt it. Look for her if you ride the 501. She can be seen dancing in her private dance studio, mown grass at the edge of Moss Park.

If you live in any large city, you know what I mean by a rich tapestry of colors, styles, and circumstances. If you don't live in a large city, I hope reading this blog will provide context for my stories.

Born and raised in Chicago, this Midwesterner hand-picked Toronto as home. In many ways, it's different from my home town, but in some ways, the same. My roots were planted elsewhere, but I love my Toronto.

Lately, though, something doesn't feel right. I realized arm-waving man was no longer at his corner, urging us to follow him. Most bothersome to me, Dancing Lady's no longer there either. What's become of them?

There's a new CRO thing. If you haven't heard, we're all supposed to comply with the CRO, the Citizen's Registration Order. All newspapers, radio and television stations, transit advertising, and billboards say everyone living in the Greater Toronto Area must pre-register with a new program called "CleanSweep."

Yours in truth,
Matthew Tremain

Matt put the computer to sleep and walked up to his apartment to make some coffee. A feeling of dread followed him up the stairs.

• • •

Matt wasn't the only one experiencing near-panic. Susan and Remy were trying to avoid detection, carefully keeping away from main streets and surveillance cameras. Stopping, Carl tested the door of a parked vehi-cle. It was unlocked.

"Where did you learn that?" Susan asked, watching Remy pull a panel away from the dashboard of a Nissan Versa.

"Who leaves a car parked on the street anymore—since the riots? One reason, is what I'm doing now: hot-wire the car to borrow it," Remy said. "Maybe there's a lot about me you don't know," he snapped. "Sorry—nerves. I'm almost done. Keep a lookout."

Nothing happened as he touched two wires together. "These cars are too sophisticated any more. Closing the door, he saw something metal poking out under the floor mat. Laughing, he saw it wat the key fob. The car started, and they both swiveled their heads to see if anyone noticed.

"If we make it out of the city, I know a hide-out: my uncle's farm. He called two days ago. He was packing and heading to Florida to get away from the rioting, even though the farm's hours away from all this."

Three hours later, Carl turned off the paved road, following a dirt road down a slope, over a homemade bridge, and finally up a steep hill. He stopped in front of a barn that hadn't been painted in years.

"Uncle Frank hasn't mowed lately," Carl said, pointing to the weeds. "Uncle Frank's always been meticulous the lawn. He wasn't going to waste money on paint, though. Those boards would soak up paint like a sponge."

The gray barn siding was silent testimony to years of bad weather; several boards warped enough to allow wind and light to pass through with ease.

"Open the door." The curtness of his order reflected the tension they were both feeling.

Susan didn't retort, doing as instructed. The barn door resisted at first. She tugged until it finally gave in. She pushed the door to the side, and Carl drove the car in. They embraced, the only sound from pigeons, cooing as if to applaud.

Finally, Remy stepped back, pulling his Blackberry from his pocket.

"Hardly any signal. I wonder what Matt's doing?"

CHAPTER 23

TAKE ME OUT TO THE BALL GAME

Matt was rereading that first blog post when his backup phone started to vibrate, skittering across the surface of the desk. He picked it up, answering before the ringtone chirped.

"'Sup?" he said, still focused on reading that first blog.

He heard silence, looking to see if there was a connection. He was on good terms with crank calls—a reality for provocative bloggers. Only three people had this phone number: Cyberia, Carl, and Susan.

He started to close the phone when he heard a man's voice.

"Matt? Is this Matt Tremain? I have something...I need to tell you. We have to talk," a man said. Something, the tone of the voice, the hesitation, brought memories of Tanner flooding back. It was the pause and guarded phrasing. Matt sensed the man on the other end, searching for the exact words needed.

"Who is this?" But he knew the caller wouldn't tell him. Not yet.

"You're investigating Claussen...CleanSweep?"

Matt didn't say anything. *Who is this?* he wondered, on guard. Some people used silence to gather thoughts and words together, suspecting that was the case with this caller.

"The man, Claussen," the caller continued, "and his ideas—they scare me. What happened to your friend Tanner was not an *accident*. The accelerator had been tampered with."

Mentioning Tanner had Matt's full attention. The cryptic reference to Tanner's accident was tantalizing. Matt couldn't resist. Matt knew he had to hear more. He had to know. "You asked me a question, if I'm investigating Claussen and CleanSweep. It only sounds like a question. You already know the answer. You hint about Tanner, that what happened to him wasn't an accident." Matt gripped the phone. "I'm being hunted, and it scares the hell out of me. I need to know who you are before this conversation goes further." Matt said it with as much bravado as he could muster. "If you don't—"

The caller cut Matt off from finishing.

"I won't give my name over the phone. Open the website for Metro Police Services; tell me when you're on the home page."

Matt followed the instructions, squeezing the phone between his left shoulder and chin while he typed. "I'm there."

"Click on the heading for departments. Use the dropdown box and click Investigative Services."

"Done," Matt said.

"There's a heading for staff. That takes you to divisional command site. You'll need a username and password," the mystery caller said.

Matt landed on a page devoted to detectives in the major cases squad, he saw a log-in box in the upper right corner.

"Use the name of the man you interviewed as the sign-in name."

Matt typed *Tanner*.

"Do you remember the address of the garage where you first met Tanner?"

"Yes," Matt said.

"Use the address number for the password."

How had someone found out these details? This guy's either para-noid or careful—or both.

Matt entered the number. He was at a page and profile of Detective Wallace Carling.

Matt was unprepared—it was like being sucker-punched.

This guy is a freakin' cop, he thought. "I'm on the page," he finally said.

"Now you know who I am. I need time to change the access code back."

The screen refreshed, and Matt was redirected to some new generic page encouraging citizens to report any suspicious activity in their neighborhood.

"I know who you are, Tremain, and now you know who I am. Will you agree to meet now?"

"You're better at this sort of thing than I am." Matt knew that sounded lame. "How can we with everyone walking around with my photograph—"

"Assume they're monitoring your calls. It wasn't hard for me to track down the number of this phone you thought was private. They use a program to go through phone calls, instant messages, and e-mail messages, sorting by keywords. Take one of your streetcar rides."

It was hard to keep grasping the phone; Matt's palms were sweaty. "Won't someone recognize me?"

"Somebody jammed all the electronic signals for you. Your photo was up for an instant. *Poof,* it vanished. Besides, you don't have much time—or choice. When you leave your building, walk east to the nearest corner. Board the eastbound streetcar. Ride until it loops back to the stop by your apartment building. You might want to do that right now. It's an excellent afternoon for a streetcar ride. Isn't riding streetcars something you write about in your blogs?"

The line went silent, and Matt looked down at the phone's screen. The call had been disconnected. He tried to think. *The caller's a cop, a detective named Carling, and he knows something about Tanner's death. He knows about Claussen,* Matt thought. Words flashed in front of his eyes, like mental three-by-five cards.

I'll meet with the detective. I must. But how?

• • •

Matt didn't need a jacket, but for some reason, he grabbed one as he left. In the lobby, he paused at the door. This meant taking an even larger risk than meeting Tanner.

Stepping outside, he looked up at a perfect-weather sky; there wasn't a cloud to be seen. With his jacket over his shoulder, he pushed thoughts of Tanner to the side, walking to the corner as directed. Soon, a trolley arrived, the front door opening like an accordion. Hardly anybody rode east this time of day. Matt scanned his monthly pass, almost making it to a seat before the car lurched ahead, the driver indifferent.

He looked around. *Will I see the detective?* None of the passengers matched the photograph of Detective Carling, the one on his web page. A sour-looking young woman sat close to the driver, chewing gum at a ferocious rate.

Two young boys sat across from her, talking, grasping their backpacks as if daring anyone to take them. They gave Matt a suspicious look when they saw him staring. He turned away, embarrassed they might think he was a pervert.

Matt tried to lower the window for ventilation without success. He folded his jacket across his lap.

Looking to the back, he saw a skinny guy with long hair, nodding to a rhythmic beat only he could hear. That was it—no other passengers.

The transit system's not taking in much revenue on this trip.

Matt saw a heavyset man waiting at the next stop.

That's not Carling.

As the streetcar approached the stop, someone pulled the cord, a signal to get off. Matt turned again and saw the scrawny man standing. The man reached overhead to a strap, balancing as the car slowed. Instead of exiting through the rear door as expected, Matt watched him lurch toward the front of the car.

When the car stopped, the fat man boarded and fast-walked toward the back. Fat and skinny passed each other next to Matt. They collided, putting their hands up as if launching into a boxing match. It was almost laughable, seeing them clutch at each other. One fell to the side. Matt was glad it was the scrawny one who almost fell into his lap.

"Get off my car if you're going to fight!" the driver stood and yelled, hands on hips, glaring.

The fat man mumbled an apology to Matt, walking to a seat at the rear. Skinny did his best to swagger his way to the front door and step off.

After that bit of drama, the ride to the east end was uneventful. The car circled the eastern loop and headed back west. The trolley made several stops, passengers getting off or on. Matt didn't see anything unusual, wondering why Carling told him to take this ride.

Matt looked down at the jacket folded in his lap. He spotted something white—a paper wedged in the folds. It was the corner of an envelope. Reckoning it would be unwise to read it on the streetcar, he refolded the jacket to hide it. As directed, he signaled a stop.

Was it from the fat man? The skinny one? Were they both in on it?

Before exiting, he resisted the urge to look where the fat man must be sitting. He'd no doubt now the two hadn't bumped into each other by accident. It was well choreographed, one of them slipping him the envelope. *It doesn't matter which one it was*, he thought.

Matt stepped off and crossed the street to board a streetcar heading back toward his apartment. Matt was walking toward his building when he spotted the surveillance team. It wasn't his imagination. He lived in a close-knit neighborhood, and the two men stood out. No one wore suits in this neighborhood—an area that was more suited to jeans and flip-flops—never dressed like the pair standing by their car. One wore a gray suit, too heavy for the season. The other had on a hideous-looking sports coat that would have been out of place in *any* season or location. They each held a photograph, looking at Matt's apartment building. Intent, they didn't notice Matt walking toward them on the other side of the street.

Matt swiveled, turning his back to them. He walked away, hunching over to disguise his height. He felt his pulse racing. When he reached the corner, he decided. He saw the sign ahead. It was Java Jivery, a neighborhood favorite, and Matt's go to place for good coffee. The only other customers were a couple looking as if they qualified for celebrating a golden wedding anniversary.

"Hello, Matt. Hey, I saw a photograph on TV and thought it looked just like you," the barista said.

"That's a funny coincidence," Matt said, mumbling.

He carried his cup to an overstuffed chair in a corner. He turned the chair to observe the door, alert to strangers walking past the street-side window. His hand started to shake, coffee spilling over. He placed the cup on a side table and tried to steady his shaking.

Looking around to make sure no one was paying attention, Matt retrieved the envelope. He turned it over, front and back. There were two initials printed on the front: MT. Nothing more. It was sealed, but opened easily as Matt slid a finger under the edge of the flap. He pulled out the enclosed note. The handwriting was neatly printed.

• • •

Dear Mr. Tremain,

Claussen loves his high-tech toys. I've been giving this some thought. If we want to avoid detection, we need to go low-tech and stay off his radar. He's quite unhappy with your snooping. I don't have to tell you that. He wants to make it dangerous for you. I'm sure we both know what happened to Tanner, even if I can't prove it.

There will be a letter in your mailbox. It contains some basic codes we can use when we are writing each other. I will also include keywords we can use on the phone. If one of us doesn't hear the keywords, there's an impostor on the other end. It's old school, I know. But people today only think about the latest technology. They're expecting us to use new school, hi-tech communications. We need to avoid that whenever we can.

I wasn't a fan of your blog at first. I realized we share a passion for truth. I also believe in justice. There's something terrifying about Claussen. I'm frightened, ever since I learned what CleanSweep was up to.

I'll send directions, setting up a meeting place and time. I'll be there, regardless of whether you show up or not. It's up to you, my blogging friend.

Signed, KBO, Carling

• • •

Matt refolded the note, putting it back into the envelope, and tucked it into the back pocket of his jeans. He used a napkin to soak up the spilled coffee and sipped on more coffee. He thought about the note as he kept watch for any out-of-place activity on the street. Seeing nothing out of the ordinary, he walked to the door to look around. There was no sign of the two strangers he'd spotted earlier, and he returned to his chair.

Java Jivery coffee usually agreed with him, but today he grimaced as he sipped. It left a bitter aftertaste. When he finished his coffee, he read Carling's note one more time. "Look in your mailbox tomorrow. I'm sending instructions for our first face-to-face."

Matt wondered if all police had access to mailbox passkeys, but didn't question Carling's directions. Walking back to his building, he thought about Tanner and fought back an urge to cry.

What the hell does KBO stand for? Matt wondered why the detective signed off with those initials.

When he got back to his building, he reassured himself the watchers were gone. Matt knew there would be others.

• • •

He couldn't stay in the basement forever, so he risked going up to his apartment. He was tired and needed sleep. After a restless night, Matt walked down to check his mailbox.

Toast and cold cereal had been all he could tolerate, his stomach meter registering sour. He pushed the breakfast bowl to the side and thought again about the strange phone call from Detective Carling, followed by his note.

He looked at his phone, checking the weather report. A cold front was expected, along with falling temperatures. He grabbed his jacket and headed for the elevator. He changed his mind. The elevator was antique. The residents—including Matt—were apprehensive about its strange noises, fits and starts, and the way it often stopped with an unsettling shudder. His apartment was on the third floor, and he viewed the walk up and down as good exercise.

They met on the second-floor landing, and he tried to think of something witty but could only manage "Hey." It wasn't at all witty; he always felt inadequate around her.

"Hey," she replied, her response's tone hovering halfway between sarcastic and mocking.

Matt walked on, muttering under his breath, wondering when he was ever going to get up the nerve to tell her he found her attractive—and then to ask her out. *Probably never,* he admitted to himself.

The growing sense of uneasiness about yesterday's note from Carling took all his attention.

Cyberia said the CleanSweep agents still didn't know where he lived, but they were getting close. "You need to be careful, always," Cyberia said.

When he got to the lobby, he looked at the bank of mailboxes. Many of the doors were bent from tenants forcing them open when they didn't have a key. In today's online environment, few worried about getting critical mail via the post office anymore. Management wasn't about to spend money to repair them anyway. Matt's box didn't even have a nameplate anymore, a victim of someone's warped amusement. He'd scrawled the number of his apartment with a marker on masking tape, mostly to help the letter carrier.

Though expecting to find it, Matt was still surprised to see a corner of white poking from the side of his mailbox door. It was early for mail delivery, and Matt rarely had any snail mail other than junk advertisements. He opened the mailbox, seeing the envelope with Carling's now-familiar handwriting on the front.

At the door, Matt looked up and down the street, but didn't see anything suspicious. Electing to be careful, Matt didn't leave by the front door. He walked toward the rear entrance. Before he got to the rear exit, he stopped on instinct. He unlocked the door to the basement. Down the steep stairs and past the large furnace, he used another key, unlocking the door to his hidey-hole. He stepped back to check the stairs. Nobody was following. He stepped into the room, locking the door behind him.

Computers and electronics hummed a catlike purr in the climate-controlled environment. Turning on the desk light, he opened Carling's envelope and began reading.

Carling's instructions included code words and ways of communicating. A ticket was inside the folded page—a ticket for today's baseball game at the enclosed domed stadium, now called Toronto Sports Complex. The Toronto Screech Owls were playing an afternoon game. Matt checked the seating chart on his smartphone app. *The cheap seats,* he thought, *Section 510, the uppermost lever.* They were in the next-to-last row. *Big spender.*

Matt wasn't a sport fan. Baseball was like watching paint dry—except watching paint dry was more fun. He didn't have a choice. Matt knew he must go. This note was also signed "KBO, Carling." Matt made a mental note to ask Carling what *KBO* stood for.

Carling sure as hell didn't need to add that postscript about being careful to avoid being seen.

To appear that he was working—certainly not at a baseball game—Matt made changes to the computer settings. It would look like blogs were posted at random times while he was away. It would be a diversion—or it wouldn't. He shrugged, locking the doors as he left.

He saw a baseball cap someone left on a shelf by the back door. He picked it up and walked out the door.

He hoped the cap might provide concealment, but wasn't naive. He knew CCTV cameras fed facial images back to a central computer. Clean-Sweep technicians continuously matched faces with images in a massive database.

The hat was probably ineffective, but it was all he could think of. Approaching the stadium, he laughed. Gathering fans wore similar hats. *Maybe I will blend in*, he thought, hearing crowd sounds.

"Hey, man—ya want a hot dog?"

"Yeah, grab one for me. Meet me at the beer booth."

A small-but-festive pregame crowd congregated at the entrance. "This sure beats a day at the office," he overheard a man say.

"A lot of sick calls this afternoon—the 'Screech Owl Eagle flu' is contagious."

Matt remembered reading about the former team, the Blue Jays, in the World Series a few years ago. Over fifty thousand fans lined up to see, standing room only. This team, the Screech Owls, would be lucky to draw five thousand. There was no gridlock at the entrance and no lines at concession stands. Even a free ticket giveaway had done little to boost the numbers.

Matt handed his ticket to a young woman. She barely glanced at it as she scanned it, returning it with a tired look.

She needs a mouthful of chewing gum to complete the picture, he thought. *At least she didn't pay any attention to me.*

He followed signage arrows. One sign indicated the escalator was out of order. It was a long climb to Section 510. Stopping at a concession stand, he ordered a beer, believing sports fans consumed copious amounts of beer during games. He didn't want to stand out.

By the time he reached the top level, he was wheezing. *Crap*, he thought, looking up at steps to his seat.

Matt counted ten, a noisy group of avid fans sat at the railing in the front row.

One was squinting at the field far below. "Shoulda brought binos, man," the man said.

"Who's up for a beer run?" another yelled.

Matt looked up. The seats were empty, other than the men at the railing. Matt saw a man sitting alone at the top. *It must be Carling*, Matt thought, taking a deep breath as he started the final climb.

Carling was aware of Matt's approach, but he didn't look up, stand, or offer to shake hands. He kept his attention action on the field far below.

The detective seems intent on ignoring me, his invited guest.

Carling didn't look particularly tall. *He's better dressed than I expected*, Matt thought. Carling had on expensive-looking slacks and a stylish sports coat. Matt assumed Carling would have a rumpled wardrobe like cops on television shows. Carling sported a fedora, sloped in a casual manner. Matt wasn't sure, but Carling looked in shape and guessed the detective watched his diet.

Matt jumped at the sound of a loud crack, bat meeting ball, hearing oohs as the batter hit a practice pitch into the upper deck.

"If he could do that during a game, we wouldn't be in last place," Carling said, not looking up. "The only time to watch this team is during warm-up."

His face was unreadable when Carling looked up. Matt didn't sense hostility. Neither did he feel anything approaching warmth. He couldn't turn his eyes away from this man, feeling a sudden urge to confess something. *He must be excellent at detecting and interrogation*, Matt thought.

"Detective Carling?" Matt suddenly felt foolish, a cup of beer in his left hand, holding out his right to shake hands.

"Detective Sergeant Carling." The reply carried a hint of droll humor. "Are you going to stand for the whole game?" Carling said, still no effort to shake Matt's hand.

Not having a quick retort, Matt sat down, sipping beer as they watched the team warming up. Matt didn't know one team from the other.

What was it someone told me about the color of the uniforms? Matt wondered. He asked the detective sergeant.

Carling didn't reply; he kept muttering something about poor hitting stats. "Bunch of overpaid deadbeats," he added.

Matt looked up at the dome roof, gaping half open, a light rain adding to the dismal atmosphere.

Carling saw him looking up. "That damn roof hasn't worked for over three years now. They don't make that public. It's like a lot of other infrastructure, things that aren't in working order these days. They still seem to find money for surveillance and detention facilities. See that?" Carling pointed at the roof. "It sits there like an oversize case of lockjaw. You can bet it'll be raining hard when the game is over."

The announcer's voice echoed in the stadium, urging everyone to stand, remove their hats, and join in singing the national anthem. Carling removed his fedora, holding it to the side. It was hard to tell from where they were sitting, but a few voices were attempting to sing along to the recorded version. When the music faded, some fans gave a desultory cheer, sat down, and waited for the first pitch. Matt wondered if they'd cheered the end of the anthem or the beginning of the game.

"You like baseball?" Carling asked.

"Not really, but who passes up a free ticket," Matt said, unable to resist his turn at sarcasm.

"I used to love the game," Carling said." Now it's just a bunch of whiners waiting for their next contract negotiation. Still, there's something about the sport..." He let the words trail off.

The two men watched the game in a silence more comfortable than either expected. The home team finally took to the field at the bottom of the first inning, chasing a three-run lead.

"If you think our pitching stinks, wait until you see how awful our hitting is," Carling grunted.

Matt didn't say anything. He knew they weren't at the game to talk about baseball.

"Don't make it obvious, but look around. You'll see surveillance cameras everywhere. CleanSweep's obsessed with them." After a pause, Carling saw Matt starting to turn despite the warning. "Don't look for them, dammit. When we talk, lean forward and look down at your feet. Few people watch the game, anyway."

"Surely they can't—"

"Lean forward and look down, dammit."

"Sorry," Matt mumbled. He obeyed. It felt awkward. "They can't watch our lips moving, can they?"

"Probably not, but why take the chance?" Carling held his program up to shield his face while he talked.

The second half of the first inning didn't take long. The Screech Owls went three up and three out. A collective moan went up from the crowd.

"What can you tell me about CleanSweep? What have you learned?" Carling finally got to the point.

Matt thought about his answer. *Should I trust this guy?* He made his choice. "I know Charles Claussen's the driving force behind it. Street people are disappearing, and nobody seems to know why. Something feels wrong, sinister in fact." It felt good saying it out loud.

"If we only knew the half of it." Carling snorted. "Do you trust anybody?"

That was a question Matt needed to answer with care. Two other people knew what he knew—Susan and Remy. They'd vowed to trust no one. *Now I'm sitting next to a cop, asking me to talk about them,* he thought.

"Why should I trust you? Why all the secrecy? You make this sound like we're in the middle of a freakin' spy novel. Besides, you're a cop," Matt said, stating the obvious.

"I know it calls for a leap of faith. It's hard to trust me. That's logical." Carling kept the program in front of his face while talking. "I didn't expect to like or trust you either, based on your blog. But here we are. We need to step over the line that divides us."

Matt thought that was a remarkable thing to hear.

"When I started to dig into your background and read between the lines of your writing, I saw common ground," the detective said. "Clean-

Sweep is a game changer, new and dangerous. Sure, some cops support that kind of radical, hardline thinking. Most of us don't. There's inherent danger in CleanSweep. That's what my instinct is telling me. My instincts are rarely wrong. We're giving away far too much power at the expense of our...liberty—"

"Two people from Action 21 News. Susan Payne and her cameraman, Carl Remington," Matt said, interrupting. "You asked me if I had help."

Matt decided to trust the man he sat next to.

"I hope the three of you have been very careful."

"I thought we were. But now you've scaring the hell out of me," Matt said. He paused. "I hope we've been. I hope so."

"What're you going to tell them about me?" Carling seemed to be thinking. "Do you trust them? How can you be sure?"

Matt leaned forward, looking down at his shoes. He stepped on popcorn and peanut shells, brushing remnants away with his foot. He told Carling how he'd met them. "I didn't believe or trust them. Not at first," Matt said. He stopped whispering as a female security guard walked up the steps toward them. She stopped halfway up.

Apparently, she didn't see any threat from two fans alone at the top of the third level in a mostly empty stadium.

Matt continued after she started back down the stairs. He held his program up to shield his face, mimicking the detective.

"Watching Susan Payne on the news, I figured she was just another empty talking head," Matt said. I didn't think she did anything more than reading a script. I was wrong. She's smart with steely resolve. Her cameraman's a straight shooter." Matt wondered how he came up with a cliché like that, something from an old Western movie.

"Check me out," Carling said. "Ask around. When you're convinced we're all on the same side of this story, tell them about me. But I don't think it's wise for the four of us to meet. Payne's interviewed me in the past. She seems OK, as far as I can tell."

"Why would a cop help me? Why would *you*?" Matt asked.

"I took an oath to uphold the law—to protect and serve. I took that oath very seriously. I still do. CleanSweep's doing an end run around due process, and it stinks."

Matt looked over. He saw something on Carling's face. *Fear, sadness,* and *disillusionment* were three words that came to mind.

"In your blogs, you mentioned people disappearing. Do you have any idea what has happened to them?" When Matt shook his head, Carling went on. "It's far worse than you think. I'm outta here. Before we make contact again, tell Susan Payne you met with me. Convince her we need to work together."

Matt was shaken by the anxious tone in the man's voice. The detective coughed a fake cough, dropping something by Matt's left foot.

Carling stood, squeezed past Matt, and started down the steps. Matt expected him to turn around and wave. Instead, Carling paused by the ramp wall, taking a flask from his jacket pocket. He took a long swallow, recapped the flask, put on his fedora, and disappeared.

What spooked him? Matt wondered.

Before he got up, he looked down at another white envelope. Matt waited three painful innings before reaching to pick it up. The Screech Owls were trailing by fourteen runs. Matt had watched enough paint dry. He stood and walked to the exit with the envelope folded and secure in his pocket.

Oh hell, I forgot to ask what KBO means, he thought. *I really do need to Google it.*

CHAPTER 24

DO YOU TRUST HIM?

"What're you thinking—talking to a cop? I don't care if I *have* interviewed him, or if he said we've met before," Hurricane Susan exploded, living up to her name. She was livid, furious with Matt. "What made you think you could trust him?"

"I didn't at first—"

Susan cut him off with a withering look.

"Let him talk," Remy said, but his words had little impact on her anger.

"We're sticking our necks out," she told Remy. She turned to Matt. "What were you *thinking*?"

"If you take a breath, I'll tell you!"

They sat in a luxury suite of rooms at Loon Lake Resort. They chose this location because it was unlike the seedy motels they'd used before. Seventy miles north, Matt was glad to be out of Toronto for a while, far enough there was no lingering smell of smoke.

Matt scanned the golf course. Despite rain, a foursome was getting ready to tee off. When he saw a vivid flash of lightning, Matt questioned the collective wisdom of the group. He closed the curtain. Susan's angry words still echoed. When she stopped venting, he told them about Carling's phone call, the streetcar adventure, and first note. Matt decided to tell them about meeting Carling at the baseball game.

"He's apprehensive...no frightened. Just like us. He didn't come right out and say it at first. Why'd he lay out ways to avoid surveillance? He wants me to tell you guys he's on our side."

"I remember him now," Susan said, her tone calmer. "He's the one who wears that fedora. I asked him about it once."

"What choice do we have now, anyway?" Remy asked. "If he knows about us, he could've turned us in already." He stood, pacing. "But he hasn't...yet. Why don't we have some coffee before it gets cold?" He got up and went to a nearby serving table. Picking up the carafe, Remy filled the cups, mist rising like smoke.

Sipping, they each sat quietly with their own thoughts.

I enjoy good coffee, but this stuff tastes bitter. It's crap, Matt thought. He kept quiet, not wanting to offend Remy, who seemed to think it was gourmet quality.

"I was following a lead," Susan said.

"*We* were following a lead," Carl snapped.

Matt noticed a difference, the two swapping gibes like a married couple.

Susan ignored Remy. "Looking at my notes about people vanishing, I began to see a pattern. It was the *kind* of people disappearing. Isn't it curious?" She ran her fingers through her hair. "There's an old bag lady I passed on the way to the newsroom. You know who I mean, Remy— near our studio's entrance. Maybe she's not that old, but looked it. I tried speaking to her, but she kept talking to some invisible friends."

Susan wrinkled her nose and continued, "She smelled as bad as she looked. People avoided her, pretending she wasn't there. She sat close to one of those subway ventilator grates, emitting warm air. One day, she wasn't there. Just like that." Susan snapped her fingers for emphasis.

"Her name's Ellie—or was," Remy said. "She's harmless. In fact, she has an interesting backstory."

Susan cut him off. "Have you seen her lately, this Ellie person? No, you haven't."

"I've noticed stuff like that, too," Matt said. He told them about the ballet lady and the gesturing man, there one day, gone the next. "What's going on?" He showed them the envelope Carling had dropped at the stadium. "He made sure I got this before he left the game."

He held up two pages, summarizing the contents for Remy and Susan. "This," he said, waving a page, "is copy of an order to police services. They're to turn over all notes and files they have. They have a list of specific names they're to hand over to CleanSweep agents. The order lists names by category: homeless, persons with known mental illnesses, petty criminals. It doesn't stop there. CleanSweep is also interested in individuals. They're also keen to know about felons and serious criminals, especially those with gang affiliations."

"Distinct skin tones, accents, cultural characteristics other than white European," Susan said.

"Get this," Matt continued, reading. "CleanSweep agents have extraordinary powers to arrest and detain *without a warrant.*"

"Damn, this scares me. It's worse than I thought," Susan said.

"Amen to that," Remy added.

"There's more," Matt said. "Police are ordered not to interfere with CleanSweep agents transporting detainees."

"That's why Carling's so afraid of us," Susan said. "If word gets out... By the time activists realized what was happening, it was too late. Demonstrations were stopped with emergency court orders. If you're reading that right, the special policing powers given to CleanSweep agents are like provisions in the War Measures Act, that holdover from 1914, the beginning of the First World War."

Matt looked up from a page he was reading and nodded. "Apparently it's now OK to suspend habeas corpus and other legal protections. They've done it in the name of making us feel safe. I don't feel very safe right now. Do you?"

The three sat in uneasy silence, their despair aggravated by the growing darkness. Remy turned on a lamp. It did little to cheer the room.

"I have a question," Remy said. "What do we know about the building renovations along Spadina Avenue? What are they for? I'm talking about the ones being renovated over the past couple of years. Usually there's a sign, something coming soon. Not these. It looks like they're a secret."

"You're right," Matt said. "There's something queer about the one just north of Sullivan Street. Why would a new streetcar track spur lead to an overhead door at the front that building?"

"I saw that but didn't pay any attention," Susan said.

"There's a logo on the cornerstone of the building," Remy said. "I was on a southbound streetcar one morning when we had to stop for an approaching tram turning into the building. The trolley was painted dark gray, the windows screened to keep who or what concealed. I watched the door, like an oversize garage door, go up. After the trolley entered, that door came down—fast. I tried to get a glimpse inside the building. No luck. Most unusual, wouldn't you say?"

Susan nodded. "Did you get footage?"

Remy gave her a look. "Of course," he said, showing his smartphone. "No video at first, but just photos showing the rear of the trolley entering the building. I finally got a video of the door being lowered.

"I didn't know what to think at the time, but now..." Susan stared at one of the photos. "There's something about that streetcar..." she said. Her finger traced a line on the screen. "I saw one like it last Wednesday, the windows shielded so you couldn't see in. It's the kind of tinting on car windows when the driver wants to stay hidden. I wondered what it was, possibly a test car, or maybe a training car. I made a note to check with my contact at transit and forgot." She took a notebook out of her purse.

She fanned pages until she found what she was looking for. "Here it is," she said, holding it up for them to see. "Last Wednesday. Here's my note to call Sal Petrecelli. He's my contact at transit headquarters— remember him, Carl?"

"There's more," Matt said. "I got an e-mail from an anonymous source. I almost put it in the file I reserve for crackpots. The source claimed vans were driving around at night. Whoever wrote the email claims to have seen at least two people handcuffed and taken away." Matt shook his head. "I found it hard to believe. Why would anyone be taken away like that? It sounded over the top. I guess I don't *want* to believe it."

"Things are starting to add up," Susan said. "I don't feel comfortable with what I'm thinking now."

"I don't know about you two," Remy said, "but I think it might be a good idea to have Detective Carling on our side."

Susan and Matt nodded agreement.

"We need to be extra careful from here on out," Carl said.

"Tell me something I don't know," Matt snapped. He leaned back in a chair, fingers laced behind his head. "We need to put our notes together now. There's never been a better time for teamwork," he said. He picked up his note, turning to a blank page, his pen poised.

"What do we really know so far?" Susan asked.

"The Screech Owls apparently are an awful team," Matt said. His attempt at lightening their burden didn't work. Susan and Remy stared, at a loss for words.

• • •

The three worked through the night. When they finished, papers were spread on the bed, on chairs, and on tables. To someone walking in, it might seem as if documents were scattered at random. The collaborators knew the papers tracked a pattern back to the beginning. Matt had certain facts previously unknown to Susan and Remy. They, in turn, had bits and pieces Matt was unaware of. They found similarities uncovered—overlapping events painting an ugly picture of Charles Claussen and Operation CleanSweep.

Matt spoke first. "Claussen is the key. He used his money and connections within the government. What else explains the order, the police and government so readily giving CleanSweep such sweeping—pun intended—power to arrest and detain?"

"Agreed," Susan said. "What we don't have is a look inside his organization. The information Tanner gave you is important, but not proof of a conspiracy. I hate to use the cliché, but we don't have the smoking gun—yet. The lid's been sealed tight since the rioting began."

"Who will believe us with this?" Matt said, sweeping his arm around the room. "Claussen's reputation is rock solid. Who believes Matt Tremain except for some loyal blog readers? We need more, and it's out there."

Susan Payne closed her eyes to think. "I tried to pitch an investigation, using studio and network resources. I was called into the boardroom, and a team of lawyers told me to drop the inquiries. If not, my job was on the line, despite my ratings."

"The union sent me an email with the same warning," Remy said. "We're on our own.

• • •

Susan's phone started ringing, a ringtone set loud enough to be heard over background noise. In the quiet of the room, however, it howled like a blaring fire truck siren.

She looked at the phone number displayed. "It's not a number I recognize," she said, holding it up for Remy.

"I don't recognize it. What about you, Matt?"

"Nope. Not a clue."

Susan let the call go to voicemail, and the three went back to work, reexamining everything, finally creating a master list.

"Let's have our next meeting at the farmhouse," Remy said. "If anyone's following us, we'll know. He gave Matt directions.

As Susan put her phone away, they all agreed it'd been a night of hard work.

Matt's phone suddenly chirped. He looked at a text. "I'm heading back to the city. Carling's set up another meeting."

They picked up documents, notes, and photographs, preserving their order. Finally, there was nothing to say or do. Matt watched Susan place her hands on her hips, leaning back to stretch tired muscles. He saw tension leave her face when Carl rested his hand on her shoulder.

"By the way," Matt asked as they were all leaving, "do either one of you know what *KBO* means?" His question was met with blank stares and shrugs. "No idea," they said at the same time.

They walked to their car, laughing to relieve the tension.

CHAPTER 25

TWO NAMES

Matt's felt like he was rounding a dangerous corner, meeting Carling near the foot of the arches at Nathan Phillips Square. "Make sure you're on the east side of the square," Carling had insisted.

The detective's red-faced, foul mood was visible. Holding his fedora in his right hand, Carling used his sleeve to wipe sweat from his brow.

Despite the heat, Matt wore a hoodie to keep his head covered to avoid detection.

"Not having a good day?" Matt asked.

"How about bad day, dreadful week, and awful month?" Carling snarled.

"CleanSweep?"

"What else?"

Carling pointed to an empty bench. There wasn't any shade, and the temperature was nudging toward the eighty-degree mark, hot for that time of the year. "Take that hoodie off," he said, raising his voice. "In this heat, you stand out like polar bear in the Sahara."

The seasoned detective knew something about tailing suspects. Now he wondered who tailed him. He remained standing, casually sweeping his gaze to see if he could spot surveillance.

When they were seated, he said, "I've no idea if anyone's following us or not. I'm good, but these guys are well trained. I'm not sure I'd spot them."

Matt told him about Remy and Susan's response when they heard about Matt and Carling meeting. "We need to work together."

"More than you know, Matt. I tried to kick CleanSweep up the command structure. There's some serious cover up. All the way to the government. I was told, in no uncertain terms, to lay off anything to do with investigating the operations. I'm guessing they now have me under surveillance."

He leaned over slightly. "It's an odd word, Matt. Did you know *surveillance* wasn't even a word until Edgar Allan Poe invented it?" Carling sounded unsettled. "I don't have much time, and I have no idea why I just said that about Poe. It's nerves. I should know better; acting nervous often gives my suspects away. See that takeout container?"

It was sitting on a railing as if abandoned. It made Matt realize how litter-free the city was now. *Why haven't I noticed that before, the absence of litter?* he thought. *That's new.*

"You'll find a bagel and a diet cola in that container," Carling whispered before he stood abruptly and starting walking Queen street. He looked back, giving Matt a brief nod before boarding a streetcar. His poignant look spoke more loudly than words. *He's carrying a heavy burden,* Matt thought. *Aren't we all.*

Matt turned back in time to see a young woman in a uniform striding toward the take-out container. It was clearly her duty to make sure no trash was left behind by some rude person. Matt hurried; he needed to get to the container first. He stepped to the railing, picking up the container before she could get to it.

He gave a how-could-anyone-leave-this-here look. She smiled, waving her approval of his good citizenship. She did an about-turn, directing her inspection to another part of the square.

Matt settled his breathing, hoping nobody noticed his odd behavior. He walked to the nearest trash container. Picking out the bagel first, he inspected it, saw nothing unusual, and dropped it into the bin. Next, he looked at the takeout cup. It felt light; in fact, it was empty. He removed the lid and peered into the container. Matt was about to drop the cup and lid into the trash receptacle when he looked closer at the lid in his right hand. A note was taped to its underside.

So that's where he put it, Matt thought. He gave his best acting performance, a man casual looking around. He slipped the lid into his pocket and tossed the cup away, along with the notorious hoodie.

He took a meandering walk before catching a streetcar heading east. *Anyone following me will think I'm out and about for an afternoon stroll, a flâneur.*

Yeah. Fat chance.

An hour later, he sat in his favored overstuffed chair at Java Jivery. He needed a caffeine fix. He watched Connie behind the counter, getting ready for the late-afternoon customers. Making sandwiches, her back to Matt, he listened to her humming as she worked. Her arms and shoulders moved in a steady cadence: bread, meat, lettuce, mayo, bread, meat, lettuce, mayo, bread, meat, lettuce, mayo.

● ● ●

Unfolding Carling's note, Matt began reading.

Here're two names that should help your investigation. I met Mattie Reynolds when I was a beat cop. She must be in her late sixties now. She might not seem the sharpest knife in the drawer. Don't let that fool you. She's a survivor, wise to the street.

Clifford Horne is a guy I met during a homicide investigation. He turned out to be a good witness. He's a stand-up guy and tough as nails, but you'd never guess by looking at him.

Both have gone to ground. If they agree to meet you and tell you their stories, it'll go a long way toward explaining why they're in hiding. They have both escaped the clutches of CleanSweep.

To talk to them, you'll have to go through their network of gatekeepers. They'll vet you and let you pass—or they won't. It's up to them. They won't trust you. Hell, they don't trust me all that much. But these are people I've helped in the past.

We shouldn't be treating marginalized people as criminals. Criminal is a word reserved for the bad guys. People like Mattie and Clifford aren't bad, just overwhelmed. Criminal is a word we should reserve for someone like Claussen.

I've passed along word you're a stand-up guy, on the right side of the story. Like I said though, whatever they decide is up to them.

You'll be met in one of the coffee chains with the distinctive red-and-white logo. They have a store at the corner on Sherbourne Street, south of Bloor. Be there at nine tonight. I know it sounds stupid, but it's their rule. Order a blueberry fritter. Order an extra-large, double-double coffee. The person meeting you doesn't know what you look like, but when he hears you order, he'll know it's as a signal from me. That's as much as I can do. I vouched for you.

If they decide you're good to go, a man called Stinky will sit down at your table. You won't have to wonder how he got that name. If you pass their test, he'll be your conductor. If not, enjoy your fritter and coffee and go home.

KBO, Carling

• • •

There it is again, Matt thought. *What the hell does KBO mean?*

Matt tore the note to pieces and hoped Connie wouldn't look up from making sandwiches, seeing distributing random pieces of it in several wastebaskets.

"Bye, Connie!" Matt shouted as he walked to the door.

"See ya, Matt," Connie said over her shoulder. "When's this smoke going to clear?"

Matt used his tablet to contacted Cyberia. "Your apartment is still safe," Cyberia responded by text.

• • •

Matt sat in darkness, time seeming to pass in slow motion. He stared at the clock. The digital readout flashed 7:17 PM. Only three minutes had passed since he'd last checked. He'd figured out when he needed to leave to get to the coffee shop by 9 PM. He visualized his route to pass the time.

What am I setting myself up for? he wondered. *Trust's a rare commodity these days.*

Matt wanted to soothe his nerves. He poured a glass of single malt, neat. The whiskey left a warm trail as he swallowed. His eyes moistened, remembering the drink he'd shared with Tanner. The whiskey did little to calm him; nothing would, he realized. He took his drink back to the living room and picked up the TV remote. He didn't turn it on, though. He just stared at the blank screen, wondering if he'd nerve enough to keep going on.

A noisy crash-bang shattered the silence. He almost dropped the glass, liquid splashing over its rim. Matt heard shouting and tiptoed to the window. A car had smashed against a parking meter. It was a minor car accident, but he couldn't steady his hand enough to finish the drink.

He looked at the clock again. *It still isn't time.* He began to pace—*thirty more minutes.*

A phone rang in the next apartment. A door opened and closed in another. They were typical apartment-living sounds, but they added to his panic. He walked into the bathroom to splash water on his face. It didn't help.

He was watching numbers on the clock change when he heard a siren. It almost tipped his emotional scale into the red. CleanSweep vehicles used a distinctive European-type siren that growled from high pitched to low. He realized it wasn't getting closer, but it made him tremble. The siren faded, and silence returned until it was finally time to go—afraid or not.

Standing at the trolley stop, he heard the familiar clanging bell signaling the next streetcar. In the dusk, street lighting was under attack, storm clouds forming to the west. A strong gust of wind whipped his shirt collar as Matt boarded. The operator glanced at Matt's monthly pass, nodding to the rear.

As the trolley approached Sherbourne Street, the first hint of rain came in fits and starts. Matt felt that electric sensation in advance of an approaching storm.

At least I won't have to pass through the destruction zone, Matt thought.

With the first powerful burst of wind, rain lashed against the window. Fierce lightning made the streets look like a scene from an old black and white movie. The lightning conjured images of a scrum of old-time news photographers using flashbulbs, each flash glaring reflections on the pavement ahead. Sparks from the trolley pole connected to overhead wires completed the film noire look. *All I need is seeing Orson Wells appear,* Matt thought.

He hurried to transfer to the Number 75 bus, heading north on Sherbourne.

Matt stepped off at the designated corner. The sign of the coffee chain looked like a lighthouse directing ships to safe harbor. He shivered as he ran, sheeting rain quickly soaking him. Inside, conditioned air made his shivering worse. He didn't see anyone in the coffee shop looking like a Stinky. Matt's nose was on high alert for any noxious smell.

An old man sat in one corner, staring at his cup. *A lonely pensioner thinking about someone from his past,* Matt wondered. A young couple sat at a window table. *The boy looks tentative,* Matt thought. *He's getting ready to propose something—either marriage—or maybe just a night together.*

Glancing at the girl, Matt decided her answer would be no to either one. Trying to stem his shivering, Matt stepped into the line of customers waiting to place orders.

What am I was supposed to order again? he asked himself.

When it was his turn, he muttered, "I'll have a fritter." He rushed to add, "Blueberry. A blueberry fritter, please." The young man behind the counter looked at him blankly, and Matt realized he was whispering through chattering teeth.

"I'll have a blueberry fritter and a large double-double coffee—with double cream and double sugar. A double-double," he said, almost shouting. He looked around to see if anyone was paying attention to his cue.

He carried his order to an empty table next to the door. Matt looked at the coffee and was revolted. He drank coffee black, and the thought of cream, let alone sugar, was...well, appalling.

He wasn't sure what a fritter was, but his fingers felt sticky after he picked it up for a taste. *Damn, it's pretty good,* he thought. He was too nervous to eat more than a taste, determined to never order a double-double coffee again. He sat, shivering, thinking this'd been a big waste of time.

He flinched at movement to his right. A man appeared like an apparition. Matt didn't have to ask. Stench from the man sitting down rated somewhere between septic tank and compost heap.

What was that punch line from a George Carlin routine? Matt thought. *Something about odor strong enough to knock a buzzard off a shit wagon?*

That applied to the man called Stinky.

CHAPTER 26

VOICE MAIL

Another abandoned farm? How does Remy come up with places like this? Susan thought, pulling a blanket up to offset the morning chill. A slate-colored sky did little to brighten the room. Embers from the fireplace hissed and popped, a dying fire barely giving off heat. She felt Remy stirring next to her and smiled. Welcoming the memory of making love for the first time, her night-to-morning transition was truly magical.

Remy turned out to be a sensitive lover. A strong sensation flooded over her as she remembered a blazing fire and her surprise at romantic music on Remy's playlist. They'd been giddy, tossing clothes with abandon.

Remy turned as she draped her arm over his bare shoulder, revealing a broad smile.

"We've changed hiding places so many times, I'm losing track of them all," Susan said. "I wake up with no idea where I am."

"You're next to me...now."

"Does this place have any food?" she asked, standing. The blanket fell away. Susan blushed when she saw Carl grinning, fingers locked behind his head.

Rewrapping the blanket tight around her, she walked to the kitchen. Rummaging through cupboards and drawers, she said, "There has to be food somewhere." She opened the last cupboard.

"Some dry cereal. It's always the last place you look, eh?" The shelves were empty, except the top one. "Look. Our absentee host liked coffee."

Susan found a well-worn, old coffeepot. She turned it around. "Where's the power cord?" She opened the lid, peering inside. "Nothing but a metal basket on top of a metal rod."

"City girl!" Remy said. "That's used over an outdoor fire; you can see from the stains. I use one like that for camping." He took it from her. "Someday, there won't be anyone who knows how to make coffee this way. I've got a friend who bought a car recently, insisting on an adapter to plug in his gourmet electric coffee maker. I don't usually wish ill, but I imagine him waking up to a drained car battery. I can even picture his petulance, a car that won't start, and no coffee." Remy laughed at the thought. "In case you haven't noticed, there's no electricity, Susan."

Standing at the sink, Remy worked the arm of the pump until a stream of water came out. He filled the pot. "I think that's about enough," he said. Remy poured coffee into the basket. "I'm guessing, but that should be enough," he said. He positioned the basket on the metal rod and closed the lid. "Fire might be a problem." He opened a storage door. Inside was a box of firewood. "This wood's cut especially for use in that cookstove."

Carrying an armful of kindling, he opened the door to the old-fashioned cookstove. Finding matches, he soon had a fire going. Holding his hand over the stove, he judged it hot enough and placed the coffeepot on top.

"I love places like this," he said, holding his hands over the range to warm them. "They don't need electricity or city water service. This is back to the basics. I love it."

"You love it here, don't you?" Susan asked.

"Well, I've never made a fire naked before." Remy laughed. "Yes, I love it away from the city."

"I guess we should get dressed," Susan said, grinning.

Minutes later, Remy estimated how long the coffee percolated. He lifted the coffee pot, a towel around the handle for protection. "This sucker gets hot." He filled two cups Susan found in a lower cupboard.

"This is great coffee!" Susan said, sounding surprised. They munched handfuls of dried cereal, using the open door to the cookstove as a fireplace. "And you do make excellent fires...naked."

She leaned against Remy, his arm around her shoulder. They'd reached this high level of comfort without effort. Susan almost forgot why they were here—the danger prowling outside. It came back to her in a blinding flash.

"I wonder if we can get a signal here…" Susan said. "Grab my handbag for me." She pointed. "It's in the other room."

"A *please* would be nice." Remy smiled as he said it.

"Two bars," she shouted. I didn't expect *any* signal here. It's not that rustic after all. I haven't had my phone on since we were back at the resort." She looked at the screen. "Whew, the battery's still good… But damn…over twenty-five voice mail messages." Susan looked through the list. "I don't need to listen to any of them."

Susan had her finger on the master delete icon when something stopped her. She saw the time-stamp, the call that'd come in while they were working with Matt at the Loon Lake Lodge.

"I got a call from this number two days ago and didn't answer. There's no caller ID number." She held it out. "Do you recognize it?"

"It's not one I've ever seen."

"I'm going to delete it," she said. But she couldn't. Her finger just wouldn't click the icon.

Curiosity is a potent drug.

She deleted the rest until one remained, the one tugging at her inquisitive nature. Finally, she clicked on the message, listening to the voicemail.

"That was interesting. In fact, *most* interesting. Have you ever heard of a man named Roger Ulrich? Here—you listen," she said. She played the message again, turning on the phone's speaker.

Remy stood next to her, listening.

"My name is Ulrich—Roger Ulrich. You don't know me, but please don't hang up. I can't keep silent anymore. The riots were even worse than I thought they'd be." The line went silent, and Susan and Remy wondered if the message was over. Ulrich continued. "I overheard it all. I was in the next room, when they planned and decided. I know how Charles Claussen engineered CleanSweep. I have it all recorded. I'll call you back in two days. If you answer, I'll know you're interested. If not," Ulrich left the statement unfinished. I won't leave another message." The line went dead.

Remy looked at Susan. "What do you think about that?"

"I have to follow-up," she said.

"That was two days ago."

"I *just* did the same math," she said.

"If he meant what he said, he'll call today."

"That's exactly what I was thinking," Susan said, staring at the phone. "I'm willing it to ring."

"In movies," Remy said, "the phone always rings on cue."

When nothing happened, they decided to clean up the kitchen and packed their belongings. Remy stepped outside.

"The storm's over. We need to get on the road. Uncle Bruce left an old pick up in a shed. There's not much gas, but enough to start. I was looking around while you were brushing your teeth."

They loaded their belongings into the pickup truck, their car hidden in the same shed.

"A better-than-even trade, I would say. This truck's so old it was easy to hot-wire," Remy said. "I think there's just enough fuel to get us to the city."

Even though they were hoping for a call, they both flinched when the ringtone blared.

Susan was holding the phone to her ear when a wheel hit a rut. "Dammit, Carl. Be careful."

"What?" No, I wasn't talking to you. I'm sorry," she said. "We just hit a bump. This is Susan Payne." She recognized the voice from the message, the man calling himself Roger Ulrich. "Who are you?" she asked.

"You know who this is. Why act coy?"

"Any person can leave a message like that and claim a fake name," she said. "If you know who *I* am, you know I'm a serious reporter. I verify sources."

"I have something for your story, facts you can verify. You won't be sorry."

"How do I know I can trust you?"

"You will, or you won't. I'll give you instructions for a meeting. I won't stay on this phone much longer. CleanSweep programs are scanning calls like this. We have precious little time establishing bona fides. Decide, Ms. Payne. I'll be there. If you don't show, I will be gone like a wisp of smoke."

Susan told Remy about the despair in the man's voice. She gave him the man's directions. "I know where it is. We may blend in. Our stalkers won't be looking for a battered, old truck. We have two hours; it's going to be close."

Remy drove carefully to avoid attention. They passed several patrol cars, Remy's hands white from gripping the steering wheel.

At the meeting place, they saw a man standing ramrod straight. "It must be him," Susan said, whispering for some reason. Roger Ulrich stood next to a gazebo in a small neighborhood park—exactly where he'd told Susan he'd be.

"Look at him," Susan whispered. "People walk around with a depressed, unkempt look since the riots. It's incredible to see a man dressed like this." Ulrich wore an elegant suit, and sunlight flashed briefly from perfectly shined shoes.

"I have to ask," she said as she approached him. "Why are your shoes so highly polished?"

"What can I say?" he said with an indifferent shrug. "If you must, I'm a manservant, schooled in the old ways. It was my father's profession, and his father did before him. None of that matters now.

"What you need to know is who my employer is, or I should say, *was*. I served Winston Overstreet for over thirty-seven years. Four years ago, things began changing. I skimmed some envelopes one day, correspondence left unattended. I was arranging them in the order he preferred, when I noticed an envelope on top. I did something I'd never done before. Reading other's correspondence is—how should I say it—indecorous. What made me break the professional valet's code? Call it accidental curiosity, if you have to put a label to it."

Roger Ulrich was well spoken, but Susan detected an intriguing accent between the words.

Ulrich continued, "I read that letter. Charles Claussen sent it by courier. Everything I admired about Winston Overstreet turned on a dime. I'll make this quick. I contacted trusted comrades, telling them what I'd read." Ulrich had a wistful look as he continued. "My life changed direction. Given instructions, I stayed in Overstreet's service, never letting on what I knew. I made plans—plans to expose him for the snake he is."

Ulrich looked composed, but nervous glances from side to side gave him away.

"When I learned he was inviting a group of coconspirators to his remote lodge near Lion's Head, I realized I was in position to get more details about the plan. I was shown how to secretly record them—something I'd never dreamed I would do...until now.

"I saw and heard how sinister Operation CleanSweep really is. You'll want to know who else was in attendance that weekend. Charles Claussen was there, of course. The whole evil plan was his idea. The meeting included Spencer Abbot. We can only imagine how much money *he* has. He wastes more money than most millionaires make.

"The shocker was Richard Waverly. Did you know he calls himself *Sir Richard Waverly*? Can you believe that? They met for two days. Claussen laid out his entire CleanSweep scheme. They're a bunch of raving fascists. They're fanatics—and I have proof. Somebody must go public. Do you have the guts?"

"I hope so," Susan said.

"I hoped for a stronger affirmation," Ulrich said. "I tried to get it to that blogger Tremain. I know, however, he's in imminent danger as we speak. I couldn't risk contacting him."

"We're working with him," Remy said. Both Susan and Ulrich were surprised by Remy's words. "You asked if we have the guts," Remy went on. "Afraid? Yes. Do we have the guts? Yes. Do any of us have a choice? I don't think so. No!"

Hearing that, Ulrich reached into a coat pocket and took out a recorder. "It's what young people call 'old-school'—a cassette tape." Ulrich almost smiled as he said that. Remy assured him he could play it. Ulrich handed over the tape with a formality that matched his attire.

Susan watched tears forming in Ulrich's eyes. The manservant, former majordomo to Winston Overstreet, turned away. He walked to a waiting van with a military bearing. They saw Ulrich motion to the driver and passenger in the front. The side door slid closed, and the truck sped away.

Susan broke the silence. "I don't see actual smoke coming from that tape you're holding, but I think it's the fucking smoking gun we've been looking for."

Hurricane Sue, Force Five, when she uses that word, Remy thought, looking around to gauge danger.

CHAPTER 27

WHERE ARE WE GOING, STINKY?

"Ya got's ta follow me...stay close," Stinky whispered. Matt was convinced staying close to that man wasn't something people did willingly. Matt held his breath, but it didn't help. A synapse transmitted warning messages from Matt's survival center—telling him to turn around, go home, drink a lot of single-malt scotch, and get much-needed sleep.

He thought about Tanner, Susan, Remy—and Carling. Despite his urge to run, Matt couldn't let them down. The memory of Tanner's sacrifice gave him resolve.

"When I give orders, follow them. When I tell you what to do—do it—no questions. Got it?"

"Understood." Matt added a nod for emphasis.

"The rain's nearly over," Stinky said, peering through the window.

Matt considered finishing the fritter but gave up, licking frosting from his fingers. *That tasted pretty good after all,* he thought again.

He got up when Stinky walked toward a trash receptacle. Before he knew it, Stinky was out the door, Matt racing to catch up. They walked south, Matt shuddering at sirens in the distance.

"I told ya to stay close," Stinky said. He sounded annoyed. Walking fast, almost running, he abruptly turned into a side street. Matt stayed within hearing distance. Ever since the riots, street lighting was spotty; many of the city's streets were dark by this time of night.

With the storm as a backdrop, it looks evil, like a film noir scene by Orson Welles, Matt thought. *Didn't I feel like that earlier?*

Bright street lighting was just a memory in this part of Toronto. Streetlights worked on the main streets, but most side streets were still shrouded in smoky darkness. Matt thought the one they were on now was a nightscape of shadows and discomfiting noises. The storm, almost cleared, generated occasional bursts of lightning, creating an eerie scene. Matt shoved fear to the side and hurried to keep pace with his tour guide.

Stinky stopped unexpectedly and held up his hand. In the gloom, Matt saw a look on his guide's face—Stinky was alerted to something.

"Quick, behind that dumpster!" Stinky said, pointing.

"What?"

"Shut up, dammit. What did I tell you? No questions, man. Just do what I say."

As he ducked down, Matt saw a CleanSweep van speeding past the intersection they'd just crossed. The van's roof lights flashed red and blue colors, piercing the shadows.

"They ain't using a siren. That's too freakin' close," Stinky said as he unclipped an antique pager attached to his belt.

"Does that still work? I haven't seen one of those in—" Matt said.

"Old-school trumps high tech when it comes to avoiding Clean-Sweep. That's the law according to Stinky. These days, low-tech is best. CleanSweep's so fixated on the latest and greatest gadgets and anything high-tech, we learned how to slip under their radar by using one of these things."

Matt heard an almost-laugh.

"Who even remembers old pagers from years back? Hell, they still work. When someone sends a signal, it vibrates a warning that a Clean-Sweep team's close. We have spotters all over town. We use numeric codes."

"What's your real name?" It was the investigative blogger asking.

"If you needed to know, I woulda told you."

"Does it bother you, you know, to be called Stinky?"

"How close do you think people want to get to me? It even keeps CleanSweep agents away." He snorted. "It's my secret weapon, like wearing garlic to ward off vampires. I've been stopped twice, but they just back off. It won't last, though. I know they'll get me sooner or later."

"How do you know Carling, the detective?" Matt asked.

"That cop sees right through me. It's spooky, like he can tell what I'm going to say before I say it. Carling ignores my stink." After turning his head to listen for danger, he continued. "We can go on now, but get your hurry on; they're really on the prowl tonight. Probably looking for *you*."

He started laughing at Matt's discomfort.

Matt knew only too well Stinky was right.

"Pay close attention. I'm taking you into the worst riot zone. It's dangerous, and not from CleanSweep. Ain't gonna make any promises how far we get."

All of Matt's instincts screamed, "Turn back; it's not too late." He was on a mission, a pilgrimage to the heart of the truth.

Matt followed Stinky through darkened streets, so many turns Matt lost count. As well as he knew Toronto, destruction and darkness made the path baffling; he'd only a guess where they were. When they crossed a main street, Stinky stopped and peered both ways. He yelled, "Run!" They sprinted across, slowing to walking pace down another lightless side street.

Matt was out of breath, wondering how Stinky ran with apparent ease.

I thought I knew the city, Matt thought, *but I've never tried navigating in complete darkness like this.*

Turning a corner, Matt recognized where he was. *It looks so different since the riots,* Matt thought. *This used to be a lively entertainment area. Now look at the buildings. They're missing window glass, freshly nailed plywood boarding over the doorways.* He thought the building fronts looked like they were standing sentinel, guarding skeletal insides, with still-glowing piles burping smoke.

Stopping in front of a building with walls still intact, Stinky pulled aside plywood sheeting nailed over a doorway, motioning Matt inside. Matt hesitated. He could only imagine who or what was waiting for him inside.

Stinky walked ahead, waving at Matt to follow. He led down a hallway, showing Matt where to step over debris.

Stinky stopped, listening. "This is it," he said.

It was dark, an inky nothingness inside the yawning door.

"Move it, asshole," Stinky said, shoving Matt through the doorway.

Inside, Matt felt a hand on his shoulder, stopping him. His knees felt weak, fearing a knife or maybe a lead pipe to the head. Instead, a man whispered, "Wait for your eyes to adjust." *It's not Stinky. Who?* Matt's eyes slowly adjusted to the low light. He looked at this new tour guide.

Matt and Stinky helped replace the large sheet of plywood covering the entrance. Matt was almost blinded when the man turned on a small flashlight; the glow seemed as bright as sunlight in the inky darkness.

On the left, he heard Stinky whisper. "My name's Earl." He added nothing more.

The new conductor stopped at a door. He paused and knocked—three quick raps.

"Come," a voice of authority said from behind the door.

Inside, two men stood waiting, on the alert. Both held police truncheons, and Matt felt his heart pumping. A small propane lamp on a nearby table hissed like a cobra.

The man on the right was huge. Matt guessed well over six-foot-eight. A black T-shirt strained to cover muscular, thick arms and shoulders a professional football lineman would envy. It wasn't his size that unsettled Matt. The man wore a certain expression—the look of a feral beast prepared to attack.

The shorter man held a truncheon in his right hand, tapping a rhythmic beat on the palm of his left hand. He used the baton, pointing at the giant. "He'll take over now. He won't say much, but if he does—"

"I know, ask no questions—just do as I'm told," Matt said. He saw a hint of a smile when he said that.

"He's your conductor to the next station," the man went back to tap-tapping the truncheon.

I've passed their test, Matt thought.

He turned to say good-bye to Stinky, but the man was nowhere to be seen. "How did he manage to leave without making a sound?" Matt asked. "Thanks...Earl."

"Now," the large man said. He started toward the door, moving with surprising grace.

"What's your name?" Matt stammered as he raced to keep up. "Does everybody have to go so fast?" All Matt heard in response was a grunt. "Got it—no name," he said to the man's back.

Matt decided to give the giant a name anyway. *Gigantis, from the Gigantes tribe in Greek mythology.* Matt followed the man whose shoulders were so wide he had to turn sideways to get through a doorway.

Matt faced a labyrinth of dark streets, no lighted intersections here. When Gigantis stopped, Matt stopped. When Gigantis moved, Matt kept pace. He was soon huffing, out of breath. Gigantis took long, loping strides with the ease of someone out for a casual stroll in the park.

"Wait here!"

Matt was stunned to hear his guide speak and hadn't expected a voice that sounded...normal.

"Somebody will meet you here; be on the lookout for a motor scooter. The driver won't stop for long. Be ready. If you hesitate, they'll drive on without you. In the meantime, stay in the shadows and don't move around."

With a catlike move, Gigantis faded into the mist, swallowed by darkness.

· · ·

This's someone's idea of a snipe hunt, a trick to lure me into Clean-Sweep's trap. It was a chilling thought to a man standing alone in the dark.

Noticing a glow of city lights in the distant sky, he reminded himself large parts of Toronto were intact. Listening closely, he heard faint sounds of traffic, occasionally pierced by the *whoop-whoop-whoop* of a distinctive CleanSweep siren.

Was that gunfire? He chose to chalk that sound up to his imagination, now running in overdrive.

The rain had stopped. Matt tugged his jacket tight to fend off the chill of his rain-dampened clothes. He paced back and forth to warm up, taking care to stay close to his assigned spot. After a few minutes, he had to pee. That caused him to laugh out loud.

"Who's going to see me pissing, anyway?"

After relieving himself, he tried to think, his mind jumping from panic to dread and back. Matt imagined the worst when he heard something, and recognized the sound—the distinctive *putt-putt-putt* of the vintage Vespa scooter his friend Bryan used to own.

Growing in intensity, the sound soon echoed from the walls of nearby abandoned structures. A headlight flickered as the scooter careened around a corner. Dark shadows flashed on the sides of buildings, and once again, Matt felt as if he were in the middle of a film noir scene, the one from *The Third Man*, Orson Welles' character, running through the streets of postwar Vienna, evil personified.

The scooter skidded to a stop.

"Hurry, get on." It was a woman's voice. "Get on or walk," she said.

Matt ran from his hiding place and jumped on. *She can't be much more than seventeen or eighteen,* he thought. Reaching around her for support as the scooter accelerated, he felt his ears burning red as he blushed. He didn't know where to place his hands, self-conscious of where he grabbed her to avoid falling back. With no time for apologies, he held tight as she sped. He went from embarrassed to terrified as she raced along at a breakneck pace, hurtling through narrow, litter-strewn streets.

He flinched when she turned to warn him. "We're almost there," she yelled.

Watch the road! Matt screamed on the inside.

"Up ahead," she said, "I'll turn left on Gerrard. When I slow, jump off and run across the street to what's left of the Allan Gardens Conservatory. It'll be light soon; you won't have much time."

They raced through deserted streets until they approached a street Matt recognized. *I know where I am,* Matt thought. *For the first time since the coffee shop meeting with Stinky.*

"Gerrard!" she yelled, the scooter skidding, crablike, to a stop. Matt jumped off and started to say good-bye. He heard the scooter's engine growl. By the time he looked up, she was turning into another dim side street, the scooter's sound quickly receding.

Matt looked across the street, the now-abandoned horticultural conservatory bringing tears to his eyes.

Now well-schooled in looking both ways, he raced across a street, into the softer light of the park. At the main entrance to the conservatory, he paused. He pushed through the east door, stepping over shards of glass and rotting vegetation. It needed full concentration.

What in the hell am I doing here?

He didn't have time to answer. He was startled by a woman stepping out of a side room. *She looks familiar*, Matt thought.

She looked at him with a piercing stare. The woman wore a long dress that Matt thought of as quaint. Despite the temperature, she wore several cardigans over her dress, one layered over another. On her feet, mid-calf high woolen socks and hiking boots. Her long, gray hair was tied back in a ponytail, errant strands poking out like antennas.

Where've I seen her before? Matt wondered.

She moved her head with a slight tic; it jerked to her left every few seconds. Matt wondered if she was directing him somewhere using head gestures, but he soon realized it was a permanent affliction.

"You Matt? Carling say you be an OK guy—"

Matt absorbed her peculiar speech pattern when a sound interrupted, a shrill CleanSweep siren in the distance. A cloud of fear scudded across her eyes. "I's been there," she nodded toward the sound. "I's rode in one of their trucks. I knowed what they was wantin' to do with me."

This had to be the one Carling sent me to meet. When she didn't say anything more, Matt asked the question. "Are you Mattie Reynolds?"

"Mattie, yes, yes, yes, Mattie," she said, her head moving from side to side with each *yes*. "They saids I was ta meetcha."

"Matt, Mattie—our names are almost the same," he said.

He knew why this woman looked familiar. The knowledge hit him with a sledgehammer wallop. Standing in front of him, was the Dancing Lady, the ballet dancer he watched from the streetcar.

Now she had a name—Mattie Reynolds—and Matt wanted to hear her story.

CHAPTER 28

THE DANCING LADY

Matt couldn't believe he was looking at the same dancing lady, the one from his streetcar rides, but her words jarred him back to reality.

"We need to get to the backa this place," she said.

He reached up to touch her arm, and she drew back as if his hand were electrified. "Nooooo," she hissed. "I don't like nobody I don't know touching me."

He dropped his arm and held up his hands to show respect. He followed her further into the conservatory. The floor was littered with wreckage. They stepped over rotting palm fronds and other vegetation. Matt looked around at the once-magnificent, stately building. It now smelled like it was bathed in a musky, unpleasant perfume.

The storm clearing, Matt made out the symmetrical system of steel supports, framing, and trusses overhead. Some of the frames held intact panes of glass, while others, admitting defeat, simply let their sheets of glass fall to the floor below. Walkways were decorated with slivers of broken glass, fragments large and small. Shards crunched underfoot. Matt felt as if he were trampling on history. Sunlight used to stream through those panes, he recalled, giving the conservatory plants and musty smells of soil a special charm.

Now it's reduced to this.

Mattie stopped abruptly, drawing Matt out of his thoughts. He listened to her unique manner of speaking. Her lack of syntax and odd words, jarring at first, still told a story. As much as he thought about correcting her speech, he knew it would be the wrong thing to do. He listened to her.

"This conservatory was builded in 1879. They had to do it again after a fire—1902, I think." Matt couldn't miss the melancholy in her voice. "I wonder if it ever be rebuilded after this..."

He'd nothing to add, so he nodded and listened.

"Important peoples talked here. They say Oscar Wilde did once." Matt was surprised at the reference. "Maybe he was looking for new words growing here, or finding commas hiding among the tropicals."

Matt thought he was beyond surprise, but those literary observations flummoxed him. Detective Carling warned him not to judge her by appearance or to assume ignorance. "If you do, you'll fail to hear her story," Carling had said. "People tend to do that when they see a homeless person—you know, misjudge them."

He thought about that, looking at Mattie Reynolds. "Where did you learn stuff like that?" he asked.

"Homeless peoples spends a lot of time at the library. We used to, anyways."

He was still trying to put her in context when he looked around.

"Where are we now, Mattie?" They were passing an entrance that Matt guessed was on the north side and came to a door.

"Used to be the cactus room," Mattie said. "It was my favorite. I liked the prickles." She looked around. "It's getting lighter; we need to hide." She opened a door that revealed letters on a dangling sign that spelled out "Cactus House" and under that, "Cacti and Succulents."

They walked into the room, past ruined displays, now reduced to remains of potting soil, broken pots, and boards torn from the shelving. Mattie was in a hurry and led the way directly to another door. It squealed in protest as she pulled it open.

"We're safe in here. Nobody comes into the ruins this far, usually. Except for the teams on foot, those vans just spend their time driving around the streets looking for people like me."

"And me," a man's voice boomed from the shadows.

"Damn, I almost pissed myself," Matt said. "How about some warning? I'm sure my heart skipped a beat—or three."

"Clifford," a wiry man said as he stepped out of the shadows. "If you need to write it in one of your notebooks, I'm Clifford Horne, with an *e*." He looked at Matt with a steady gaze as he walked over, draping a protective arm around Mattie's shoulders.

She didn't pull back and shout at him like she did when I reached out. He felt irrationally annoyed, thinking that.

"You two know each other?" Matt asked. *This nightmare would've made Alice Kingsleigh feel at home with the Mad Hatter.*

"We didn't. Not until this business with CleanSweep brought us together." Clifford said, brushing glass from the top of a box. Satisfied, he looked like he was going to sit.

"We friends now." Mattie looked at Clifford; her voice had a softness that surprised Matt.

Instead of sitting, Clifford motioned them to a far corner. The threesome squatted, leaning back against the walls. It was the first time in hours Matt relaxed, but he felt cramping in his right leg. An involuntary pang shot a bolt of pain through the muscles in his leg, and he yelped, jumping up to shake out the cramp. When the pain eased, he sat down again.

Nobody talked, but it was a comfortable silence. Matt prepared his emotional strength for what was ahead.

Mattie and Clifford seemed to be hyperalert to sounds. She swiveled her head from side to side, reminding Matt of a radar dish on the mast of a ship, spinning around and scanning as if peering into the distance for hazards.

"We listen for those van sirens," Mattie said. "We listen for car doors slamming. But we don't really worry until we hears footsteps." She didn't finish—and didn't need to.

"We hide in different hiding places every night," Clifford added. "So far, we've stayed safe." His voice lacked conviction about the "safe" part.

"May I call you Cliff?" Matt wanted to know.

"Clifford will be just fine, thank you."

Matt looked at the two of them. He realized he'd no idea what time it was; the ambient light was coming from the unspoiled part of the city.

Their collective gloomy moods suddenly filled the Cactus House room.

"What can you tell me?" Matt finally asked. "Carling—Detective Carling—said you two *escaped* from CleanSweep. How's that possible?"

Neither answered immediately, and Matt started to worry this was all going to be zilch, a waste of time, an excursion through hell for nothing.

"We each done it different," Mattie said finally. "You know, escaped. It was different for each of us."

"Like she said, we each escaped their clutches in different ways," Clifford added.

Matt, getting used to Mattie's speech pattern, waved off Clifford's need to explain. She had an odd way of speaking, but her meaning was quite clear.

"What happened to you? How did you get out, Mattie?" Matt asked.

She grimaced and sniffed as if detecting a foul odor. "I was sleeping in a doorway near my regular corner, cold, needed more blankets. I heard the tires screech. Their van stopped, and three mens jumped out." She paused, wrapping her arms around herself. "I grabbed onta my bag and held it tight. I knowed they wasn't up to no good. One of the mens grabbed me by my arms, one held my feet together. They throwed me into the van like a sack of potatoes. One of them threw 'way my bag." The sadness of its loss was etched on her face.

She was quiet for a long time then, and Matt wondered if she was going to continue. Pain was fixed on her face. He knew enough to wait.

"They had another man already in there. He was tied to the wall with bracelets."

"Handcuffs," Clifford said, "locked to U-bolts welded onto the wall."

Matt gave him a withering look for the needless explanation, but Mattie kept talking.

"This guy and me was locked in the back of the van together. He kept yelling as we slid around corners, but I kept quiet. Then they locked in another man and drove us around some more. We ended up at some building. I couldn't see much, but I think we were still on the east side."

Matt was scribbling in his notebook as fast as he could write, using his own cryptic version of shorthand.

"They dragged us out of the van, and then we was all inside a building, in a big room. The lights hurted my eyes. They marched us in a line."

Her pain at telling this was evident.

"You know how it was, don't you, Clifford?" she asked.

"Yep, they took me to the same building. I wasn't sure where it was, but I guessed we were east of Parliament Street. I will never forget the smell. You know how it is when people are nervous. They have a nervous smell. Some of the people reeked because they hadn't bathed in days. Add an overlay of an aroma called 'eau de cleaning solvent.' Phew. And the stink from all the smoke in the air..."

Mattie picked up her story again. "There musta been ten or more of us in a line. As we got to a counter, they had us take all our clothes off. It was embarrassing—mens and womens all naked like that together. It wasn't sexy or anything like that, just embarrassing.

"They took everything I had in my pockets and throwed it in a bin. I never saw any of it again. I lost the only picture I ever had of my two kids." She started a low, mournful keening at the memory. She wrapped her arms around herself again and began to rock forward and back.

"You have children?" Matt asked with his pen poised.

"They live with their father, back east. Last time I seen them, they was with their nana. Nobody wanted me to see them."

Matt was intrigued by this new glimpse of Mattie's life, but he knew he had to stay focused on CleanSweep. Her full background story would have to wait for another time.

He noticed her wardrobe was unique, but she kept things clean. He wanted to ask her about her ballet, the dancing he used to see from the streetcar, but he didn't want to distract her. *It's a question for another time*, he thought again.

Mattie was in constant motion as she talked, her head jerking to one side and back to the front, like she was turning to listen to something neither Clifford nor Matt could hear. She kept biting her fingernails. Matt looked carefully at her hands; her nails were bleeding and raw. He knew it was painful for her, like her life.

Clifford, sitting at her side, placed a comforting hand on her shoulder.

"How did you escape? What happened?" Matt prodded again.

"They put us in those orange suits. You remember, Cliff?"

Clifford nodded.

I must remember to call him Clifford, Matt thought, letting his annoyance drift away like a balloon. *I was just trying to be friendly.*

She went on. "When they moved us to the other place, there were four of us womens chained together in a van when we started out. They told us we were going to the Spadina place. They didn't use no bracelets, though—just locked us inside. One woman was crying, and another told her to shut up. One pounded on the door, but it didn't do any good. I learned a long time ago that quiet was best. I kept my mouth shut."

She screwed up her face in thought. "Partway there, we gots hit from the side. The dumb driver wasn't looking, and a streetcar hit us. We were throwed all over. The van was pushed almost a block, and we ended up on the side. The back door flew open. I took one look at the driver and guard and knowed they was both hurt bad. I crawled to an alley. It was dark there, and I curled up like I was a baby. I just laid down real still and acted dead."

"Go ahead, Mattie," Clifford said. "Tell him the rest."

"The other women tried to run, but a patrol van was following us and saw the accident and stopped. Men jumped out of the van and started shooting. They killed them other womens. I saw it. One man talked on his radio, and soon another truck pulled up. The bodies were tossed in the back of that truck, and they all left. Nobody saw me in the dark. Wouldn't youd'a figured they kept some kind of count?

"After a long time in the dark, I heard voices. I heard three other different men's voices and knowed they was talking about me. I squeezed my eyes tight. Someone picked me up, and I musta passed out. Next thing, I was in a garage, behind a burned-out house. The one that picked me up was a giant, but he was so gentle. Then I passed out again. I'd been blessed. When I woke up, a skinny guy was sitting next to me. Lord, how that guy stunk."

Matt knew she described Gigantis and Stinky perfectly.

CHAPTER 29

CLIFFORD AND MATTIE

Mattie stopped talking and leaned back against the wall. Matt watched her draw her knees up to her chest, her eyes staring over his shoulder at some secret place only she knew about. He rested his notebook on the ground, placing his pen on it.

He wondered, *Is it sadness I see? No, far more than sadness. I see melancholy so deep it can't be measured. Is she thinking about seeing the women murdered, shot down trying to escape? Perhaps she's thinking about her children, long ago lost to her? Possibly she's thinking about dancing her ballet at the park.*

Clifford patted her arm. It was a simple gesture, but it seemed to carry a lot of significance. Mattie closed her eyes, absorbing Clifford's contact.

Distant traffic sounds and other city noises pierced the stillness. Off and on, Matt heard distinctive sirens rising and falling, singing a frightful musical scale.

"That's an ambulance," Clifford said, describing one siren wail. "We've learned to recognize different sirens." His voice seemed louder than necessary in the quiet darkness. "The police use a warbling siren. It makes a noise like they're always in a hurry.

"CleanSweep vans are the ones to fear. They use a siren sounding like the honking of a giant goose. At least that's what it sounds like to me." Clifford shivered and crossed his arms to grasp his own shoulders. "It will be full light soon. What do you think, Mattie? Is it time to hunker down?"

She nodded agreement but didn't say anything. Matt saw her stand and pick up the belongings she carried in a tattered pillowcase. She reached inside and pulled out a plastic food container. In the growing light, Matt could see an assortment of carrots and other vegetables. She turned without speaking and left the room. She'd pulled back a sheet of plywood serving as a door.

"I need to get you settled," Clifford said. He saw Matt's questioning look. "It's not good to be out and about during the day. We'll hide here, in the conservatory. We've used it before. It's as safe a place as anywhere."

Matt didn't feel reassured. "I didn't realize—"

Clifford stopped him by gesturing to follow. Matt gathered up his notebook, hurrying to put it in his backpack.

"It took you too much time to get here. That's not good. We'll hide today. You can finish your interview tonight, unless…"

He didn't finish as he led Matt past the detritus of plants. Most were dead or dying, but some were trying to recover. Matt was surprised they could thrive without a gardener's touch.

They turned right, left, and left again, until Matt lost count. They came to a hallway. Clifford pushed on a metal door. They both winced at the scraping noise. Looking around, Clifford appeared satisfied.

"Crawl under that table," he said, pointing. "Stay quiet, and do your best to remain still. If CleanSweep auditors come nosing around, they'll use heat and motion detectors."

"Auditors?"

Clifford laughed. "Isn't that someone's idea of a cosmic joke? They're called auditors, but they're just teams of CleanSweep agents, scouring the city for people like Mattie and me—anyone considered redundant."

Redundant? Matt never thought about that word applying to people.

"How's that for a word describing people like Mattie—people like me? They look for people disturbing Claussen's ideal of perfection, then remove us from sight. Claussen and men like him," Clifford spat the words, "hide evil behind innocent-sounding terms like that. If you ever feared an audit by the tax man, that's nothing compared to a CleanSweep audit."

Clifford Matt a brown paper bag. "Here's some food. It's not much, but it will have to do. If you have a need to pee or anything, well, just be quiet about it." He pointed to a corner. "That's your fancy pissoir," he said with a laugh then turned serious again. "Don't answer to anyone. Make sure it's me or Mattie—no one else."

Matt got down on his knees and crawled under the table. He clutched the brown bag, suddenly famished. Adjusting his position, he looked back to say something, but Clifford was gone. *It's going to be a long wait*, Matt thought. *I hope I don't want to be audited.*

A siren pierced the quiet, and Matt was racked with fear, trying to remember what Clifford said about the differing sirens.

It was uncomfortable on a dank concrete floor. His hips and elbows soon became pressure points. *Flesh and concrete don't make good partners*, he decided. Slowly drifting toward sleep, his thoughts were like a recording, playing an endless loop. *Where am I? What am I doing here?*

"Whaaat?" Matt almost shouted, waking to the sound of breaking glass. Muffled voices and the sound of wrenching metal caused him to sit up quickly, hitting his head on the underside of the table.

"Damn, that hurts," he said aloud, then realized where he was.

Matt's waking-up fog passed quickly. *Is it night or day now? Did I sleep the day away?* He wondered.

It was dark, his every nerve ending on high alert. He braced himself— *but for what?* He remembered where he was. Matt heard noises, but the voices and the sound of twisting metal receded. Silence returned, distant city sounds and birds chirping the only sounds he heard. He peered through an opening in the roof and judged the time.

A sharp hunger pang reminded him of the brown paper bag. *What's on the menu?* he wondered. Expecting something inedible between slices of moldy bread, he unwrapped a pastrami sandwich, a small package of chips, and a requisite dill pickle in its own plastic pouch. Matt looked at the wrapping. It was from a deli Matt knew and liked. *How did Clifford arrange this?* he thought, beyond surprise.

When it happened, it came uninvited. Matt started to cry.

It wasn't a faint, sobbing cry. This came from deep inside. *I'm in so deep over my head.*

Matt tensed at a new sound: a rattle of scraping footsteps. He counted the steps. One, two, three...stop. One, two, three...stop. His stomach contracted at the sound of wood paneling ripped away. He heard excited talking but couldn't make out words. He was relieved when Mattie and

Clifford appeared. His feeling of relief vaporized when he heard fear in their voices—exposed, naked fear.

"Hurry—this way—follow us!" The urgency of Clifford's command was all Matt needed.

"Them's be CleanSweep sirens!" Mattie yelled as a siren grew in intensity. "We heard them earlier, auditors, walking all around here," she said, waving her arms. Matt saw her face drawn tight and pale. Her eyes flitted around. She hopped from one foot to the other as if she had to pee.

"We don't have time," Clifford said. "They're close. Damn, I don't know why I went to sleep. Still, no time to think about that now. Keep up with us," Clifford said to Matt, breathing hard. "Run. It's getting dark, but not dark enough yet. Damn."

They raced through the conservatory until Clifford stopped at the south entrance. Matt looked over his shoulder. Bright beams of powerful flashlights swept away dark at the far end of the building, swinging up, down, right and left.

"Don't let them get you in the light!" Clifford called out. Matt didn't need the warning.

Clifford held up his hand as they paused. They were at the south entrance, looking at the grass between the conservatory and Gerrard Street.

"They not on this side of the building yet!" Mattie yelled. "Hurry! Run!" She didn't wait for a response. Moving with surprising speed, she ran toward the intersection with George street. Matt shouted encouragement. If she made it to the shadows on the other side of the street, she'd find cover and safety.

"This way!" Clifford shouted. He pointed Pembroke Street. He was breathing hard. "She knows we had to split up. Better chance that way."

It was getting hard to suck in oxygen as Matt urged his out-of-shape body to run. They crossed Gerrard Street, almost to the shadows of Pembroke Street when Matt heard the first shots fired.

Matt felt a sudden warmth as his bladder let go. He knew they had to keep running, but he was afraid for Mattie. Shouting for Clifford to stop, he turned in her direction—wishing he hadn't.

Gunshots pierced the dark—evil streams of tracers, flaming threads. Like bumblebees, the lights stretched out deadly stingers, reaching out.

When the fiery malignancy caught up with Mattie, she stumbled. Matt desperately hoped she'd only tripped. But he knew better.

Worse than anything he'd ever imagined, Matt watched the fusillade of bullets, appalling shots turning her body over...and over. An arm separated from her body, blood showering the air like a garden sprinkler.

"No time to stop and stare." Clifford grabbed Matt's arm, yanking him into the shadows. "Your tears won't help her. But now you see the evil for what it is."

Matt bid a silent good-bye to Dancing Lady and her grotesque ballet finale.

CHAPTER 30

DARK ALLEYS

Clifford pulled Matt back into the shadows, turned him around, and pushed him into a hard run. Matt wanted to erase the image of bullets hammering Mattie's body, her obscene ballet. His crying blinded him as he started to run, rushing without regard, holding his hands out in front. It didn't help. He collided with a dumpster, his head slamming against the hard steel. It hurt like hell, blood pooling on his chin.

"That's just a scratch—no time to stop!" a hard-breathing Clifford yelled. "Keep moving. Damn it, pay attention. They're close. They know we came down this street. We need deep cover. They'll be coming at us, hard!"

Matt held a sleeve against his chin to stanch the blood. Now, with wide-open eyes, he chased after Clifford. He was moving fast, and Matt raced to catch up. Terror, Matt discovered, provided a newfound ability to run...without limping.

Clifford's prediction was right. Bullets ricocheted from brickwork, Matt seeing a flash when a slug scraped and caromed off the side of a building. He thought of Mattie as sparks tracing a lethal path. Matt heard rapid-fire shots.

"Those are guns set on automatic," Clifford said. He'd stopped, and Matt almost ran into him.

Clifford headed into a side alley, running until they came to a narrow lane. It wasn't much more than a gap between two buildings. Matt guessed it wasn't any more than two feet wide. A piece of sheet metal served as a flap concealing access, making it unnoticeable from the alley, especially in the dark. Clifford seemed familiar with it; he reached out and pulled the sheet metal back. The shrieking sound of the twisting metal was masked by gunfire.

"This way—hurry!"

They had to turn sideways, Clifford, pushing Matt ahead, closed the flap behind them. They sidled, crablike, the laneway too narrow. They came to an alcove, a space wide enough for both of them.

"This was designed as an access for utilities," Clifford said, breathing hard. Matt thought he detected distress in Clifford's words. "I was a building inspector—"

He stopped talking as he heard footsteps beyond the sheet metal at the opening. The steps faded. They heard running again, then stopping. Someone shouted in a command voice.

"I know they came down this alley. You men, check the far end. The rest of you, start look for any place they might be hiding. Break down any door or window they could use. Get on the radio. We need searchlights set up here. It's black as ink, and these flashlights are doing sweet fanny all."

Clifford urged Matt to keep moving. They came to a door on their right.

"Damn, it won't open," Clifford whispered, looking for something. "I need a pry bar."

"Can I help?" Matt said.

They put their shoulders to the door, trying to push it open. It inched open slightly. They stepped back and lunged in unison. It finally gave way.

It looked pitch black inside. On faith, Matt followed Clifford. Stepping through, he barely saw Clifford's hand motioning the way.

"Careful," Clifford warned over his shoulder. "Two steps down, and we'll be on a platform. These buildings have been death traps since the riots. Hell, they weren't much better before. This isn't the fancy Distillery District, after all."

Matt followed, easing himself down the steps until standing chest-to-chest with Clifford on the platform, smelling their combined fear, a rancid perfume of terror. To his surprise, Clifford embraced Matt as if to reassure him.

"We *have* to make it," he whispered. "You have to tell Mattie's story."

Matt felt tears on his cheeks—Clifford's.

If Clifford's intent was to calm Matt, it worked.

"Maybe we gained some time," Clifford said. "Do you have your phone?"

"We can't risk a call. They must be monitoring signals."

"You people, with your technology, never seem to have common sense," he said. "Just give me the damn phone."

Clifford turned it on, using the light it emitted to see in the gloom.

"Why don't you use the flashlight app?" Matt said.

"That's what I meant, lacking common sense," Clifford said. "The flashlight's too bright. We only need enough light to see our way."

Two sets of stairs led from the platform: one to the right and another straight ahead. He pointed to the one on the right, which led down.

"There," Clifford said, using the phone to light the way. "This building was slated to be rehabbed, deserted since the economy tanked...now the riots. Look for rotting flooring."

They tiptoed through the basement. Clifford led the way up another set of stairs to the ground floor. He paused at the top of the steps, listening to make sure CleanSweep agents weren't waiting for them. He waved Matt to follow, holding a finger to his lips as they crept along the main-floor hallway.

Matt whispered, "We sound like a herd of elephants."

"Especially if you keep yakking," Clifford retorted.

Near the front of the building, they heard loud shouts and the urgent voices from CleanSweep agents on the street.

Someone yelled in his command voice again, "Report, dammit. Where are they?"

Another voice relayed commands, directing the agents in their search.

Clifford turned the phone off and whispered. "I'm sure they can't see us, but I'm not taking any chances. There's enough light now." He held his hand to cover his mouth, the way people do when they whisper. "We're going up. They probably can't hear us with all the noise they're making, but be careful. Watch your step; like I said, the flooring can't be trusted."

Probably? Matt thought.

The building had three floors. Clifford seemed to know exactly where he was going. He needed the phone as a light again once they reached the top level. "Let's go to the back, overlooking the ally," Clifford directed.

Glass panes were broken away, a few pieces hanging tenaciously to the frames. Clifford turned the phone off and signaled. They stepped to a window, the two men carefully peering down.

"Look at that," Clifford whispered. "There're more than a dozen agents."

They ducked back as a beam of light swept past the window.

"This's no time for foolish," Clifford said with a chuckle. Matt heard a different tone now. Not as fearful, Clifford took charge. "We'll use that door?" Clifford walked over and pulled it open. A skywalk led over the alley to another building. "We might make noise, but we have to chance it. Be careful and walk softly."

Taking off their shoes, they walked across in stocking feet. On the other side, they put their shoes on again, both grunting as they tied laces.

"Follow me. It's getting light here. It'll be daylight soon," Clifford said.

When they got to the top floor, they opened a fire door.

"Three steps, and we're on the roof."

Clifford opened the door and peered out, satisfied it was safe. "C'mon," he said in a low voice. The roofing gravel crunched underfoot. "That can't be helped. We need to hurry."

Matt scurried behind Clifford until they came to the edge of the roof and a low wall. The rooftop to the adjacent building was divided from theirs by a two-foot-high brick wall. They stepped over it and continued running. They jumped over several more divider walls, reaching the roof ten buildings away from where they'd started. Clifford stopped suddenly, looking up.

"What's wrong?" Matt asked, his fear returning.

"Helicopter. We have to get off the roof." A searchlight began shining a bright beam, sweeping across rooftops and streets below.

Matt was gripped by fear again. "How did you know?"

"I don't know. I just sensed it somehow. They use sound-suppressing helicopters. You don't hear those devils until they're right overhead."

The two ran across the last roof, reaching the access to the floor below. They made it just in time. Clifford closed the door as the searchlight swept over the roof behind them.

"They didn't see us, but they'll be searching every building, calling in reinforcements as soon as it's light. We need to be long gone by then."

"How did you know your way around like this?"

"I told you, I used to be a building inspector," Clifford said. "I know these buildings like the back of my hand, better than the architects who drew the plans back in the last nineteenth century. This building's basement has a passageway under the street."

Matt must have looked doubtful.

"Don't worry," Clifford laughed. "We're far enough now. Once we're in the next building, we walk out and board the Dundas streetcar—just two guys looking for work."

Matt's shirt was clammy under his jacket. He smelled the stench from pissing himself. Still carrying his backpack, he dropped it to the ground when they stopped. He took out his notebook.

"I wanted to check and make sure I still had this."

The first morning light began slinking past the slats of the boarded-up window beside them.

The distorted image of Dancing Lady's dance of death came uninvited. "I have to write a note while the memory's still fresh, something to honor her.

"Hold it." Clifford held up his hand as Matt finished writing. "I think we can go now. The light makes it easier to see," he said, peering through window slats. "We have to stay on our toes. You reek, by the way," Clifford said, holding his nose.

Matt was too nervous to be embarrassed and remembered Stinky. *Was it only a few hours ago, or a few days?*

"What's your size? Let's see what we can find for you." Clifford nodded in the direction of a door and waved for Matt to follow.

"I'm well past being surprised at anything anymore," Matt said, looking around a room. He saw shelves holding parcels wrapped in brown butcher's paper and tied with cording. He watched Clifford sort through parcels, looking at labels until he found one, tossing it to Matt. "Here," he said, handing over a small pocketknife.

"What is this place?" Matt asked.

"A warehouse for some nonprofit organization. They distributed clothing to homeless shelters or anyone needing clothing. Mattie got her dress..." After he'd composed himself, Clifford went on. "Funding ran out. The government said churches and charities would take up the slack helping the needy. Like that happened, eh?"

Matt nodded understanding.

"The foundation couldn't pay the rent," Clifford said. "They walked away from all this. That was over two years ago. They're out of business, bankrupt. There're hundreds of similar stories. Stuff abandoned. People are afraid to come here, even looters—except for them," he said, referring to a rat that scurried past them, running from one hiding place to another.

"What about churches and charities?" Matt asked. "Surely they can use this."

"Churches are still building grand sanctuaries. Charities are paying comfy salaries. People in need are screwed. Always have been. Always will be."

Matt believed Clifford was mostly right.

"Now with the riots—" Clifford stopped. "This may be your size," he said.

Matt sliced through the string. Inside, he found underwear, jeans, and a shirt. He checked the size and shrugged. "Close enough," he said, stripping. *At least my new underwear's dry*, he thought. The jeans were too big around the waist, the legs dragging on the floor.

"This might help." Clifford picked up the cord used to wrap the parcel, handing it to Matt. "Double up, pull tight, and tie it off. Back in the day that was called a hobo's belt."

It held the pants up, the leg bottoms rolled up to avoid tripping. The shirt was a size too large; the shirt tail concealed the rope belt at least. Matt pulled on his socks and tied his shoes, turning to model his new wardrobe.

"You don't stink quite as much," Clifford said, having a good laugh at Matt's expense. "Look like someone going to work. Between the economy and the riots, there are lots of people dressed like us."

Clifford walked over to the corner. "You might want to use this, too," he said and picked up a black workman's cap. "It has the right look, and it might help to conceal your face a little."

There was an opening where the flooring had rotted away. Clifford pulled the boards apart just enough to throw in the old clothes, watching them tumble toward the basement. "A lot of people aren't bathing and don't smell too good these days. It won't be noticeable until we get to the undamaged sections. It's time to go. Just do what I do." He seemed to consider something. "What choice do you have?"

Exactly, Matt thought.

Matt intended to do whatever Clifford did, to follow every move as if joined at the hip.

Last night's rain was a faint memory.

Or was it two nights ago? Matt tried to think back. The cold front departed without notice—now history. Stepping onto the sidewalk, the brilliant morning sky was Hollywood perfect, a breathtaking cerulean, cloudless blue.

"Walk. Never hurry," Clifford said. "They're looking for hurry. Odd thing—they don't have checkpoints, stopping people for identification. I heard they trust facial recognition technology now."

People who live in a city with streetcars know their unique sound, a reverberating metal-on-metal cadence, a sound Matt associated with a children's book, a long-age gift from his nana. He'd grown up reading and rereading his cherished book, *Barbapapa*. It was a story chock-full of characters capable of shape-shifting, accompanied by chanting. *"Clickety-click—barba-trick...clickety-click—barba-trick...clickety-click—barba-trick."* Matt wished the chant would work for him.

● ● ●

Brought back to the present, Matt saw the streetcar approach from the east, a clanging bell to warn jaywalkers. The car rumbled to the stop where Clifford and Matt stood waiting, the door *whooshing* open. An old woman glared as she stepped down, shouldering between the two of them in their haste to board. The streetcar was near-full. Matt followed

Clifford as they edged back, grabbing for a handhold as the car lurched forward.

Five stops later, the trolley passed through an opening in a newly erected fence, leaving the burned-out district behind. The transformation was magical. This part of the city was still in pristine condition. People walked the streets as if the destructive riots had never taken place.

The streetcar gradually emptied. When there was a vacancy, Clifford joined Matt taking a seat.

Clifford leaned and whispered. "Don't hold your face up and stare. You don't want to let those cameras get a view of your face." He looked out the window, observing an office building they passed. "We should be safe on this part, but past Spadina, we'll be back in the western riot area. Agents will be riding, looking for anyone standing out. That'll be us."

They rode in silence. Most of the riders got off at the City Center. Matt counted seven other passengers.

"You can call me Cliff."

Matt reddened, feeling as if he'd passed a school exam. To deflect his embarrassment, he changed topics. "If you squint, it all looks normal," Matt said.

"Just wait," Cliff said. Each stop was the same—until they reached Spadina Avenue.

They approached another fence, this one separating the city core from the riot's destructive path through the west end. The streetcar rattled through the gateway.

"It's just like the east end," Matt said, "in some ways even worse." In contrast to the undamaged midtown, they entered the west end. Unlike the trendy Distillery District, this was a street lined with modest store-fronts: their own stark reminders of the destruction caused by the riots.

"Here, fire caused most of the damage. Look at that building," Clifford pointed. "That looks like arson to me. A fire of that intensity...the building's skeleton frames stripped bare of their facades..." Cliff kept look-ing. "I used to inspect these buildings when I first started."

Twenty minutes later, the car passed another threshold and fence. "Look," Matt said. "This far west, it's still undamaged, except for that sooty film on storefronts."

"That's from heavy smoke," Cliff said.

A camera mounted over the driver started blinking red.

"Get off. I don't like that light blinking," he said, a panicky edge in his voice.

"I'm right behind you," Matt said in a muffled voice.

They disembarked, trying not to hurry, and walked to a side street.

Rounding the corner, they saw an alcove at the back door of a café. A man wearing a stained apron walked out, tossed garbage in a large dumpster, and went back in without looking at them. They stood by the trash container, ignoring the stench from the garbage.

"Who knows?" Cliff said when Matt asked if it was safe there.

"Do you have any idea where I can get a burner phone?" Matt said.

"That's hard," Cliff said. "They're outlawed now. We were all supposed to turn in all phones, remember? CleanSweep's database had a list of everyone's phone when they banned all future sales." He thought for a moment. "There's always someone willing to take a chance for the right money. For some, it's always about money. I know a place we might try. It's a long walk—even longer using side streets."

"How're you fixed for money?" Cliff asked.

Matt dug into his backpack, pulling out a roll of bills. "I need to contact Susan and Cyberia."

Cliff looked at Matt. If he was curious about names he didn't recognize, he didn't show it. "I'm glad to hear that sound in your voice," he said. "You don't seem so damn scared now."

"I'm scared as hell. Like you said earlier, we don't have a choice, do we?"

"No," Cliff said, "we don't."

"I need a couple of phones. Then get back to my apartment?"

"Where do you live?" Cliff asked.

"The Beaches," Matt said.

"That's back the way we came, then some. I don't think we can... Wait." Matt watched Cliff as he thought. "We're on the opposite side of town, and the streetcar is out—with that red light we saw blinking. Let me think."

Arriving at a swirling sign advertising Chuck's Barber Shop, Matt tried to remember when he'd last seen a barber pole. As they walked in, a bell on the door jangled, Matt remembering a similar bell at the Europa Motel. They waited until the single customer paid and left.

"What'll you have, gents?" The barber blew clippings from a comb and wiped it on his apron.

Cliff walked over, talking in a voice so low Matt couldn't hear, but knew it was some sort of negotiation. Finally, the barber nodded and walked toward a door in the back of the store. He returned and handed a box to Cliff. When they walked out, Matt had the two phones.

Cliff borrowed one to make a call. When he finished, he said, "It shouldn't take long, fifteen minutes, tops. We're going back to that dumpster. That barber will sell us out if the price is right."

A truck pulled up at the dumpster, parking in shadows. It was a truck for delivering bottled water—a precious commodity in high demand since the riots. The driver nodded to Cliff. The driver got out, showing them where to duck under the bed of the truck. "Pull on that handle," the man said to Cliff. There was a compartment. "It's not visible from the top," the driver said. "Besides, they don't stop the water trucks; they just wave us through. Hunker down, best you can."

The driver made so many stops Matt lost count. Finally, the driver shouted, "We're here!" He crawled under the truck and opened the compartment to help them down. Cliff and Matt crawled out, stretching away cramps from riding in that small compartment.

"I owe you," Cliff said as he embraced the driver.

"Is he worth it?" the driver asked, nodding at Matt.

"More than you will ever know. I know the risk you took getting us here." Cliff paused. "This's Tremain, Matt Tremain. Is he worth it?"

The driver looked at Matt, his chin thrust up. "Money's no good with me," he said, waving away Cliff's offer to pay. "Take care of this guy, Cliff."

Matt was amazed. They stood in a familiar alley, a block from his building.

He took the lead, showing Cliff the way. They hurried to the apartment building, hugging the shadows of storefronts.

A woman in a doorway next door took a phone out of her bag and began making a call.

CHAPTER 31

A NAGGING THOUGHT

Leaving Cliff in the apartment, Matt walked to the basement—to his safe room.

Matt sat at his computer, waiting for Cyberia to respond. He remembered an earlier conversation; something Cyberia said nagged at him.

"I don't know how close they are to finding your location," the Russian had warned. "I think they're very close."

How much time do I have, Matt wondered.

The screen flickered a messaging from his friend.

"I was in line, waiting for coffee, when I first got your warning," Matt typed, the memory of reading that SOS warning text was still fresh in his mind. He'd managed to avoid detection—so far. He lost track of everything that followed that warning: the riots, Stinky, Mattie, Cliff. It was all a blur.

Now, back in the security of his safe room, he started to feel safe once more. *Or do I?* he thought. Matt remembered an earlier chat with Cyberia.

"Is our connection secure?" Matt typed.

Matt knew his online Russian friend—screen name Cyberia—lived somewhere in the greater Moscow area. Cyberia was moderator of Matt's close-knit group of six electronic friends.

Matt once asked Cyberia how secure their chatroom was. "We can never be sure," Cyberia typed his unnerving response. "The best we can do is keep communication under six minutes, in case."

• • •

"How did you find out they were after me?" Matt typed.

"Thank Tanner. The password I needed was in that file he gave you." Matt watched the words scrolling on the monitor. "Tanner created a back door to the CleanSweep master computer system. I use it to monitor their communication traffic. Using Matt Tremain blogger as keywords, I know when your name's mentioned. When the alarm went off, I read the order for your arrest. It came directly from Vaughn, Claussen's head of security. The good news? Claussen wants you alive."

"When I saw my photograph flashing on the subway," Matt typed, "I was sure it was over. Then the screens went all wonky—nothing but snow."

"I cut the connections just in time. I deleted the feed," Cyberia typed and then stopped, the screen patiently waiting for Matt to type to respond.

Matt typed quickly. "I made it back to my building and didn't know what to do next. I can't begin to tell you what I've been through, and I still don't know what to do. I can't tell you how important—"

"What about the reporter?" Cyberia cut in. "What do you know about her, what she knows?"

"I used to think she just chased the latest headline. Now I know she's serious. Her cameraman, Remy, is stand up. The detective came out of the blue," Matt typed. "It's weird, but the cop is on to something. He gave me names of two people to interview. I met them and..." Matt couldn't tell anyone about Mattie, not yet.

"Be careful about police," Cyberia typed. "An inherent distrust of the authorities is hardwired in our Russian DNA. How do you think we survived the czars—and what's come after? I'll see if I can get into the police computers and check him out for you."

"I don't know what I would do without you, Cyberia. Thanks, but I trust him. It's a gut feeling." Matt looked at the screen after he finished typing. He didn't trust anyone the way he did Cyberia, however.

A new message box popped up. It was from Ubari, another member of Matt's Internet circle. Ubari could be male, female, young, or old—he'd no idea. Ubari's electronic trail led to a public computer in the lobby of a hospital in Central Africa.

"I've been monitoring the time. You need to finish soon," Ubari's message flashed and disappeared.

Matt typed as fast as he could. "If I can't get CleanSweep exposed, their success will serve as a template for others to adopt the CleanSweep concept. They'll export it to other urban areas. Soon others will think they can do the same. Claussen's behind the riot, but we need proof."

"Be careful. Don't get burned by the sun," Cyberia answered, then the screen went blank.

Matt turned the computer off. *What did Cyberia mean, burned by the sun?* Matt wondered.

• • •

Charles Claussen was trying to forget an angry episode with his son at breakfast. As he stepped off the elevator, he saw a young woman waving a paper, blocking his path. She told him about the alarm.

Claussen bellowed, "I want the bastard in handcuffs before my coffee gets cold!" He stomped into his office.

Vaughn heard yelling and ran to his office, knowing she needed to tell her boss they were close, but lacked details about his precise location. Claussen would be furious—or worse—with another dead-end.

Standing in front of his desk, she tried to think of something to reassure her boss. She knew it was better to tell this man bad news straight, with no chaser. It would be a mistake to misinform him, to wrap bad news in a fib. She thought about what she needed to say. The report from the field confirmed her worst fears. Her agents still had no idea where Matt Tremain was. They didn't know where he lived—they were going on sketchy reports.

Angela Vaughn never put full trust in technology or electronic surveillance. Her experience as a police officer taught her the value of boots on the ground. She looked across the desk at the man supposed to be a master of electronic data gathering. She didn't know how to voice her suspicion Matthew Tremain was getting help in avoiding his sophisticated methods, staying off the electronic grid.

"We still don't know where he lives."

Claussen's look was cold enough to make her wish she had a sweater.

"I'll be in the field. I'm taking charge, personally."

• • •

The call came in while she was driving. It was from John Bristol, her best agent. He oversaw the teams looking for Tremain.

"He's nobody's fool, boss. He's changed his location and hidden his identity; he dropped out of sight. Our computer records are being altered by someone and we have no idea how *that's* happening. We're at a dead end. Whoever the hacker is...is damn good. We can't seem to get a handle on him."

Angela Vaughn stopped herself from reprimanding him. She knew he was good at his job. This wasn't the time to undermine his momentum. She listened.

"We may have finally caught a break, though," Bristol went on. "One of my...our...spotters claims to have seen him this morning. She made sure she wasn't seen and called it in. If it's him, Tremain's being careful; she didn't think he noticed her."

"Why didn't we catch him at the coffee shop?" Angela Vaughn demanded.

"Two businessmen walked past him and started talking to someone, blocking the way on the sidewalk. We managed to get down to the subway platform as the train pulled out. They saw him plain as day. I know what you're going to ask," Bristol said. "Our cameras were starting to come back online, and before they went down again, we think we got a shot of him getting off at the next stop.

"A camera shows him walking past two police officers. They saw him and didn't take any action. I tell you, the cops aren't helping like they're supposed to. Anyway, another camera got a glimpse of him waiting for a bus. We've no idea whether he went north or south from there."

Bristol was the only one on a first-name basis. He continued, "Angela, we had two agents near that subway stop. They interviewed those two cops. They two of them shrugged and said they hadn't seen a thing. I'm getting tired of the police not cooperating with us."

"What about his latest sighting?" she asked.

"Queen Street, the Beaches," Bristol said.

"Leave the police to me," Angela said as she hung up.

We have you this time, Matthew Tremain, she thought. *Yes, this is a real lead. We might have him.*

• • •

Matt, not knowing how secure his basement safe-house was, assumed it wasn't safe. He'd been painstaking in designing safeguards for his hidey-hole. No one could connect his name to the apartment lease. He'd spent his own money designing the safe room in the basement of the building, but he knew it was worth it.

The apartment manager's name tag said Ronny. It could have said Greedy. He took Matt's money under the table. He told Matt he was reluctant to go down to the basement anyway. "Spiders and all kinds of creepy shit down there," he'd told Matt.

Matt thought about the warning from Cyberia. It gave him some comfort to know Cyberia might be able to warn him in time to escape. That didn't seem like enough now. It was time to say good-bye to his safe room. He'd published his blogs from here, using electronic skips bouncing through offshore locations. All the data he needed was stored in a darknet cloud account Cyberia established.

He'd given this next step a lot of consideration, planning his escape. Shuddering, *Time to pull the plug,* he thought.

When finished, all the equipment was destroyed.

First, he used a huge magnet to obliterate all traces of data. He pulled wiring from the wall, severing all electrical contact with the outside.

Then, he poured industrial-strength acid over his collection of electronics, modems, hard drives, peripherals, everything electronic.

Matt was careful, following warnings on the bottle, wearing a breathing apparatus while he worked.

Before leaving, he checked the coal room hidden behind wall paneling. *Ready, if needed,* he thought. He kicked at the paneling with his right foot, causing it to open slightly. Thanks to a set of building blueprints left on a shelf in the basement, he knew the former coal room had a sloping chute once used for delivering coal for the furnace. Long abandoned, Matt suspected it would provide a possible escape route.

Acrid fumes filled the room, his eyes watering as he walked out, locking the door behind him. It felt he'd destroyed a part of himself, his own history.

CHAPTER 32

IS THIS LINE SECURE?

Matt climbed the stairs to his apartment lobby. He looked right and left with a renewed sense of dread. *It's as if someone's watching,* he thought, *waiting around the next corner with handcuffs. Is it always going to be like this now?*

He ran steps two at a time, gasping for breath when he reached his floor. He listened for anything out of the ordinary. Satisfied, he unlocked the door to his apartment. Cliff hadn't returned with food yet.

He was filling a glass with water when his phone rang. He looked at the number and relaxed.

"Talk to me. We have to make it fast," Matt said.

"Remy and I are fine, thank you," Susan said, pushing her sarcasm to the side. "Do you remember that call I got at the resort—you know—Loon Lodge? I let it go to voice mail. Surely you remember it ringing."

Matt tried to think. "I've had so much going on. Wait—I remember now. What about it?" Matt heard Remy in the background. "What's he saying?" Matt asked.

"Remy says we need to change phones. I think he's right. Do you have our other number, the next one?"

"Yeah, I'll call you back—and I *am* glad to know you two are OK."

Matt went into the bedroom, retrieving the burner phones from the barber shop. He set one to the side and packed the other in a shoulder bag. His hands were shaking, his palms slippery. He dialed.

"I hope this is secure," Matt said.

"We've been careful. I spend as much time looking in the rearview mirror as I do the road ahead now." She sucked in a breath. "I have it, Matt," she said, and he heard exhilaration in her voice. "That voice message I almost ignored back at the lodge was from a man with inside knowledge. We have the smoking gun, and no wisecracks about the cliché." She told him about almost deleting the voice mail. "It was instructions for meeting this guy, Ulrich."

"Who's Ulrich?"

"What do they call it? A manservant or bodyguard—something like that," she said. A muffled voice could be heard in the background. "Remy said Ulrich's a majordomo. Wait. Make that former. He'd been with Winston Overstreet for years. Overstreet's a major part of the funding behind CleanSweep; Claussen had quite a gang of backers."

The excitement in Susan's voice was palpable. "This guy, Ulrich, had it all. Recorded. Can you believe it—the man recorded everything? All the sordid details of how they planned CleanSweep. Claussen can be heard talking about funding a secret militia. That's why the riots were so bad— he wanted our city destroyed so he'd be given the green light to provide Toronto with CleanSweep's protection."

"Freakin' unreal!" Matt said. "That explains what I found out—"

"I'm sorry to cut you off, Matt, but this means we have proof. I know it's a cliché, but like I said, we have the smoking gun. We can go public. The world has to listen to us now. The authorities and media can't turn a blind eye now."

"I have two personal stories—firsthand accounts—a man and a woman who were arrested and put into the CleanSweep system. They managed to escape. I've had a harrowing couple of days myself," Matt said.

"That's terrific, a firsthand account to go with the recording from Ulrich. Are you safe? I've been worried for us all," Susan said. "What did you find out?"

Matt told her about Stinky and his tour through the ruins of the Distillery District. He told her about Clifford and Mattie, choking back sobs describing her death. He told her about his own narrow escape.

There was a soft knocking on the door then, a code agreed to earlier.

"Cliff's back with food. We're starving."

"Be safe, Matt. We need each other more than ever now."

Safety was at the top of Matt's worry list as he unlocked the door.

"Hurry," he said, pulling Cliff into the room. Matt leaned out, looking both directions before relocking.

Washing down sandwiches with tap water, Matt turned to Cliff. "This feels more and more like the plot of a bad spy movie. I'll grab some things. Let's out of here."

"We don't have any time to waste," Cliff said. "I'm getting a bad feeling."

Matt told him about his conversation with Susan. "We have it, Cliff. We have the proof we need—and it's all on record."

"You don't need me, then?" Cliff asked. "Was Mattie worth it? We gave up our safe places to meet with you." There was a bitter tone to his words.

"Yes, it was worth it. I hate what happened, but with your stories and now the recording, we can move forward. I'm a truth-seeker, a blogger. But you and Mattie gave me your personal back-up." Matt paced as he talked. The passion in his voice was unmistakable. "For all we know, Claussen has a team of experts on his payroll who will prove the recording Ulrich made is a fake."

"Who's Ulrich?"

"He's the guy who made the recording. If his audio is discredited, people can just say we were acting out of spite—a vendetta. After all, who would doubt the word of a genius like Charles Claussen? But with you and Mattie to corroborate..."

Trying to sound reassuring, Matt continued, "For any hope of bringing CleanSweep down, we'll need as many layers of truth as possible. Each level of truth is a layer over the main story, like frosting on a cake. The recording Ulrich made, along with Tanner's background material, serve as the ingredients for the cake. You and Mattie made the icing."

"I hope so." Cliff's voice lacked conviction.

"All of this isn't worth *anything* without the icing," Matt said. "Claussen will do everything in his power to get to us. Tanner's death is proof enough of that. Susan and I may know how to dig for a story, but we're all out of our depth now. We've stayed ahead of them by luck and instinct."

"Don't I know that!" Cliff said. "We were only seconds away from meeting the same fate Mattie did."

"Somehow it doesn't feel comforting to think it's mere luck, does it?"

Clifford started to laugh when Matt said that, an undertone of hysteria. Cliff laughed until he began to cough, but the coughing soon turned to a mournful crying, painful to Matt's ears.

When Cliff finished venting his anxiety and fear, Matt had a question for him.

"How did *you* escape? You never told me."

"I wish I could say it was a brave act on my part. I was never in the danger Mattie was..."

Matt waited.

"It wasn't dramatic," Cliff said. "When I was locked up—*arrested* is too nice a word—I was taken to a holding station to await transfer. The only explanation given was that my name was on a list. Mattie talked about the vans with the hard seats and handcuff restraints. The van I rode in was filled with men, the smell of our sweat overpowering. It had to be because of our anxiety.

"At a larger intake facility, we were separated and lined up in some predetermined order. I was interviewed alone in a sort of interrogation room. The man interrogating me looked at some papers, saying he didn't know why I'd been detained. The other one, a woman, said she'd double-check the details. It was apparent they didn't know what to do with me. She left, the other interrogator following, leaving me with my thoughts. Finally, the man came back and handed me a form and instructions to go to another room." Cliff started to laugh. This time a derisive laugh.

"You'd think they'd had things all figured out," Cliff said. "Looking back, I think a lot was put together in haste. You've heard about the devil hiding in the details? They're enamored with all kinds of high-tech gadgets, but they let me walk down a hall, alone, with a yellow slip of paper in my hand.

"While I was walking, I saw an alcove on my right, leading to a door. I was curious, no one was around, so why not, right? I looked both ways, making sure I wasn't seen, and I checked. It was *unlocked.* Can you believe that? The door wasn't locked; I just walked out. It was as simple as that.

That's why I know they're vulnerable. I still have it." Cliff reached into his back pocket and pulled out a sheet of carefully folded yellow paper.

Matt unfolded it. The information on it wasn't critical, but the very existence of such evidence was.

They were sitting in silence when Matt's phone chimed. He looked down at the screen.

"It's Cyberia."

"Cyberia?" Cliff's eyebrows rose.

"I'll tell you about him when I'm finished." Without a QWERTY keyboard, sending a message was a lesson in patience. Matt cringed at his typos, but turned off his internal editor, typing fast, to keep the contact brief. After he was finished, Matt closed the phone and turned back to Cliff.

"I've never told anyone about Cyberia. He's part of a special group that trusts one another. Each one of us recognizes the danger around us."

"How did you meet?"

"It was gradual, Cliff. I joined a forum, an online group. It was a hangout for bloggers like me, calling ourselves journalists. I soon learned to recognize the ones who really were."

Matt started pacing. "I was drawn to the screen name *Cyberia*, spelled like a combination of "cyber" and Siberia. A unique name, wouldn't you agree? One day he suggested a private chat. We've shared some personal stuff, but not much, for safety. He's still an enigma." Matt chuckled.

"What was it Winston Churchill said about Russia?" Cliff said. "'Russia's a riddle, wrapped in a mystery, inside an enigma."

"That's Cyberia," Matt said. "What I do know, he's saved my life—and yours." Matt hesitated before continuing, "Our group's learned Claussen has plans beyond our borders. He wants to spread his gospel of evil. People in other countries recognize the strategic value of a concept like CleanSweep."

Matt paused. "One goal of anarchy is disrupting social or political order. If you create enough chaos and aren't concerned about collateral damage or human casualties, you can bring down governments quickly. In the chaos, the cries begin. People want a leader to make our country great again. They're drawn to someone with a plan to create order from chaos, regardless the cost."

"History's littered with stories like that," Cliff said with a shrug.

"This time, Claussen and funders think they have the key to making it work. Cyberia knows about a CleanSweep replica being started in another capital."

"I had no idea," Cliff said.

"Hell, none of us did. We all assumed it was local."

"Have they had riots in the other place? Has it happened anywhere else?"

"We don't think it's gone that far. Cyberia thinks those people are waiting to see how it works here."

"It must be hard, communicating like that," Cliff said, pointing to the phone.

"What choice do we have? We've always kept the time we spent chatting online to an agreed-upon limit."

"What do we do now?" Cliff asked.

"Not much, I suppose," Matt said. "I think of this all like a jigsaw puzzle—no piece of the puzzle is unimportant."

Sitting back, Matt laced his hands behind his head. "It's been a long day. With some luck, I may be able to find something to drink."

"What's next?" asked Cliff, something they were both wondering.

"I know it isn't safe to stay here," Matt said. "I've kept this place a secret, but is it still? It's safer than the streets, anyway."

"Claussen's turning over every rock, looking for you," Cliff said. "I know what that's like. One of their recognition cameras is bound to pick us up once they're running again. That's why I was so worried about that blinking red light on the streetcar camera. You said Cyberia wouldn't be able to turn them off again, once they were back in operation..." Cliff said.

Matt stared out the window, his thinking hidden from Cliff. He closed his eyes finally, pinching the skin on his forehead.

"A damn headache," he said. "I agree it'll be dangerous on the streets. I don't think it's safe at all."

"What if they find out where you live and come knocking? What then?"

Matt was almost tempted to tell him about the safe room, the destruction he'd wreaked on his computers, and the escape hatch.

One of the phones on the side table started ringing.

CHAPTER 33

ANOTHER CLOSE CALL

"Who's that?" Clifford wanted to know, sounding apprehensive.

"It's Carling!" Matt held the phone to his ear and listened.

"No hello or how are you?'"

Matt motioned to Cliff it was safe.

"Your name;s lighting up radio traffic and streaming to all police computers," Carling said. "They've issued a direct electronic order to locate one Matt Tremain. Police are ordered to pool resources with CleanSweep agents, no exceptions. You, my friend, have made it to the top of the list. How's that for a laugh? I think I'm probably committing treason talking to you now. Ask me if I care."

"Am I safe here?"

"Who knows?" Carling said. "Maybe, for the moment. That's the best I can say."

"Those names you gave me at the baseball game," Matt said. "One was Mattie's. Did you hear what happened to her?"

When Carling replied in the negative, Matt told him about meeting Stinky. "He led me to the conservatory." Taking a deep breath, Matt described Dancing Lady's final moments.

"Fuck. I was afraid of something like that. What about Cliff?"

"He's here, with me."

"If I found out where you live, CleanSweep agents will too. They're following the same paper trail I did. You guys are in danger—"

Matt jerked around at the sound of his front door closing. Clifford was gone. An empty beer bottle sat on the coffee table, where he'd been sitting.

"Hold on," Matt said. He ran to the door. Cliff was nowhere to be seen. He closed the door, turned, and saw a note sitting next to the bottle.

"Shit," Matt said. "Cliff's just taken off. He left a note, saying he's gone to ground. He knows a place they'll never find him. Damn. I'm short on friends—and I couldn't even say thanks or good-bye."

"He's good, but if he gets caught, he knows he'll lead them back to you. There's no time for sentiment now."

"I don't have much time, do I?"

"Sit tight," Carling said. "I'm in my car. Look out your side window." Matt did as he was told.

"See the sign for the bakery in the next block? I'm parked in the alley behind. There's a garage with a door open. I'm backing the car in now. I'll be at your place in a couple of minutes. Keep watching for anything out of the ordinary. I'll case the area to see if anyone is keeping watch on your building. Got it? Is there somewhere you can go now if you have to make a run for it?"

Matt started to tell him about the basement but didn't get past the first word before being cut off.

"Not now!" Carling yelled. "Not over the phone. Do you have an escape route?"

"Yes," Matt said, then described it using the code words Carling wrote in that note. *How long ago was that?* Matt wondered.

It was enough to let Carling know he'd be waiting in the basement.

"Get the hell out of the apartment, right away," said Carling. "If they come at you from the front, how will you get out? You can't. You told me nobody uses the back stairs. Take that way down and wait there. If you hear steps, it will either be CleanSweep agents—or me." He gave a short laugh. "You can only hope it's me."

"What if they're first, before you get here?"

"Kiss your ass good-bye. They want you alive for a reason, and I don't think it's a good reason."

Matt stared at the phone, Carling disconnecting suddenly. Knowing it was the detective's style, Matt didn't take it personally.

He grabbed his shoulder bag and a carry-all. Looking around, he realized it was the last time he'd see where he and Tanner had shared drinks. It seemed like ages ago.

He didn't bother locking the door as he dashed to the rear stairwell. Matt didn't hesitate or look around to see if anybody was there.

He almost stumbled in his hurry to get to the basement. *This is no time to fall down the stairs.*

He was about to open the door to the basement when the front lobby door thumped open. Matt froze, his hand on the doorknob.

"I'm sorry," a girl said. "I didn't mean to bang the door like that."

"Give me some of those bags," her male companion said, looking at Matt.

"Sorry, dude. Too many groceries," he said. They disappeared up the front stairs.

Matt ran to the front and looked out. He didn't see anything and returned to the door to the basement stairs.

What's taking Carling so long?

Matt unlocked the basement door. Downstairs, the door to the safe room was hanging on one hinge. He was surprised at the extent of the damage caused by the acid he'd used earlier.

Carborane superacid mixed with a dash of triflic acid, he remembered the recipe. A chemist he knew promised it was a million times stronger than sulfuric acid. Matt saw what that really meant. It'd even dissolved glass and metal. Luckily, he'd worn his protective face mask and jumpsuit.

He jumped at the sound of heavy footsteps overhead. The door to the basement opened and slammed shut. Matt let out a long breath when he saw Carling hunched forward, racing down the stairs.

"I don't think anyone saw me," Carling said. "I came in the back door. It took time to check the car for a GPS tracker. The department tracks all police vehicles, but I'm driving a car that hasn't been used in ages. I couldn't detect one. Who knows?"

"It's good to see you, too," Matt said, not bothering to hide his sarcasm. He knew it was only Carling being Carling.

"Look, skip the tender feelings. There are very few people you can count on right now, and you're damn lucky I'm one of them. I won't waste words, especially not on a civilian. Don't get your knickers in a knot."

"I'm not ungrateful," Matt said. "I'm so scared I almost pissed myself when I heard your footsteps."

"We both need to ease off," the detective said. "I'm sorry. Let's start over. How the fuck are you?" Carling said, smirking.

Matt's shoulders sagged as the tension released. "Do you have any plan at all?"

"I was hoping you did," said Carling. He stopped. "I'm sorry, I was just jamming your gears." He looked around. "What a fucking mess. To answer your question, yes, I have a plan, but we need a way to get out of here. I bet they're getting ready to hit the building now, heading to your apartment."

"It's all gone." Matt swept his arm in a circle. "Everything I used to publish my blog and writing. It's all there in a gooey pile."

"And the smell!" Carling sniffed. "Whew."

"How much time do you think we have?"

"We'll know when we hear them. And we're trapped in a basement with no way out."

They heard the first CleanSweep siren approaching.

"We're screwed. Unless..." Carling paused. "If you know a way out, now's a good time to let me in on it."

They heard more sirens, a chorus of howling, all stopping in front of Matt's building. Muffled voices and shouted commands were followed by the sound of agents gathering.

Matt's phones rang. Matt listened as Carling watched.

"Cyberia couldn't get the warning to us in time," Matt said. "He says they've dispatched a command bus and vans carrying agents. We're about to be totally surrounded."

Carling didn't bother asking who Cyberia was or why he even knew such things. He pulled his jacket open, reaching behind his back for his service weapon. "I don't think this'll do any good," he said. He shrugged and put it back.

"We have one chance," Matt said, "I have a way out—maybe. If they haven't thought to check the opening to the coal chute, we may have a chance. It's been boarded up for years."

"Let's go for it. No choice," Carling shouted.

With that, Matt kicked at the wood panel covering the escape door. The panel fell to the side, and Matt nodded to Carling, leading the way. Spiders had taken possession of the space. Matt forced aside his fear of creepy-crawly things, brushing cobwebs aside. Carling was close behind.

"Pull that panel shut behind us," Matt ordered. "If it works as a cover, it may give us more time. Pull that rope," he said, and pointed. "The wood panel should fall back in place and hide the door—I hope."

After Carling did as told, it was almost completely dark in the tunnel. "Don't turn on your phone," Matt whispered. "See glimmer of light?" he said. "That's our way out."

Matt crawled up the sloping wood ramp, turning to help Carling.

He remembered as a boy, trying to climb a slide in the park and kept slipping back down. The former coal chute provided the same challenge. Unused for decades, the chute was covered with coal-dust residue. The two men looked like minstrels in blackface by the time they scrambled into the attached shed. They did their best to brush the dust off without success. The shed was in a narrow alley at street level. Matt hoped his camouflage made the shed appear it was permanently boarded up.

They heard voices nearby. "There's nothing back here, boss."

"Or here," said another voice, from a different direction—the back of the building.

"Post someone at the back. The rest, follow me."

"I just heard on the radio," someone said. "There's nobody in the apartment. Now they're searching the building floor by floor," one of the agents said.

"Some old lady shit herself when we busted into her place," a voice on the radio said. It sounded as if he thought it was funny.

Matt and Carling held their breath as silence returned. They heard activity in the front and back of the building, but no sounds in the side lane.

"I only tested this once," Matt admitted. He pulled a board away and motioned to Carling for help. They peered out.

"I don't see any...no...nobody here," Carling whispered.

"Back here either." Matt said. He pulled at an old door. "Fingers crossed we're alone."

It opened without effort.

Carling made the decision. "What do we have to lose? I really hope you have something more in mind. Otherwise, your escape plan really sucks."

"I do have something. I've planned this. Follow me." Matt felt a rush at being in charge. He knew exactly where to go.

In a few quick strides, they crossed to the shadows on the other side of the narrow lane. They stood by a side door to the next building. Matt had covered that door's lock striker with duct tape, so it wouldn't lock. He pulled the door open. They were both holding their breath, feeling vulnerable. Matt tore the tape away and pushed the door closed. They heard a satisfying *clunk* as it locked.

"If they try the door, they'll find it locked. I'm hoping they won't bother to check further."

"What's this place?"

"My friendly neighborhood dry cleaner," Matt said. As their vision adjusted to the low light, he said, "Follow me."

They dodged plastic-covered bundles of clothes hanging from overhanging rails. "The owner divided the space and subleases that part to a nail salon," Matt said, pointing with his chin. "It's been painted over. There's a door between the stores. It's here." It took both kicking and lunging to break through, but soon they were standing in the back of the nail salon.

"Stand back," Carling said. He edged his way to the front window. "I see them," he snorted. "There must be twenty or more standing around."

"The command bus will be here soon," he said, urging Matt to hurry. We need to get from here to that garage behind the bakery."

"There's another door leading to the side street," Matt said. "I hope they don't have it covered yet. Maybe they're all concentrating on my building." Matt turned the handle and they stepped out. "Nobody," Matt speaking softly.

"No time to waste," Carling whispered. It was dark, large trees covering the street like an umbrella. "I don't see anyone," he said, leaning close, "so far..."

He didn't finish.

"It'll be dicey getting across," Matt said. "Queen Street's well lit." They inched their way to the corner. To Matt, their footsteps sounded like a drum banging. Carling reclaimed the lead and peered around the corner, judging the moment.

"When I give the signal, we just run, got it? As fast as you can. Ready? *Now!*"

They sprinted two doors to the left, staying in the shadows. Matt was already panting as they zigzagged right, crossing the street between parked cars. "They're all looking at your building," Carling said as they ran, turning right into a dark side street.

It wasn't far to an alley, where a quick turn had them safe from discovery. No longer worried about being as quiet, they ran down the alley, stopping at a garage ahead, on the left.

Matt's eyes adjusted to the dark. He saw the grille, recognizing the unmarked car Carling drove.

"I parked here before coming to the apartment," Carling said. They stepped toward the garage door and looked in, exhaling a loud breath, in stereo, when they didn't see anyone waiting to arrest them.

"Throw your stuff in the backseat and buckle up," Carling said. "The door won't close completely. I'll shut it best I can. We aren't going anywhere yet. But be ready. If we must try and outrun them, you will be glad you're wearing that," Carling said, tugging at Matt's seat belt.

Matt felt his leg starting to spasm. He leaned his head back, closed his eyes, and urged himself to be calm.

"So far, so good," Carling said.

CHAPTER 34

WE HAVE HIM...WE HAVE HIM NOT

Angela was on the carpet—make that the hot seat. Called to Claussen's office, she was desperate for good news to pass along. When her phone rang, she listened intently; a smile curled her lips as she did.

"We've got him. We know where he is, boss. We have his building surrounded. He can't get out." Bristol couldn't keep the excitement from his voice.

"Where—?" she started, but he cut her off.

"The Beaches, some crap building that hasn't been upgraded in years. One of our spotters saw him and called it in. One of our facial-recognition cameras matched him. The camera spotted shows him going in the front door. I sent agent Reznat to check it out. She showed his photo to a couple walking up to the building, carrying groceries. They said he lives in Apartment 304. We've been chasing a ghost, but now we have him, boss. Reznat said she hasn't seen anyone except an unknown male leave since she's been there, and he was way too old to be Tremain."

Angela Vaughn didn't realize she'd been holding her breath. She exhaled. "Are you sure he's still there?"

"He hasn't left the building, and I see a light from one of his apartment windows."

"We take him alive. No rough stuff. You have a green light. Let me know when you have him in custody."

"The watcher said there's a man with him. We have nothing on him."

"Do you know who?" Angela was curious.

"No idea, boss. Reznat used her phone to send us his photograph, and the techs are starting to match it with our database now. What about him? What do you want us to do with him if we catch him?"

"He's expendable," Angela Vaughn said.

• • •

"Now!" Bristol said after calling Angela Vaughn. He turned to his second in command. "The boss says it's a go. He's in there," he said, pointing. "Apartment 304."

He stood back and watched men running to the front door of the building, yanking it open. Men and women wearing protective vests stormed the lobby, guns drawn. "You two, front stairs! And I want four more right behind. When you get to the third floor, call me on the C frequency. You two, take the back stairs and make sure nobody comes down!"

Bristol stepped into the lobby and looked at his number two, holding a radio to his ear. "Roger that," his assistant said, looking at Bristol. "We're ready to go in."

Bristol gave a nod, and his assistant clicked the radio, shouting, "Go, go, go!"

It was an agonizing wait for Bristol.

"Fuck." It was Adams, his second in command. "He's not in his apartment, sir. Teams have searched all four floors. Matt Tremain's nowhere to be seen."

"Where is he?" Bristol shouted. "The basement. Have you checked the basement?"

Agents ran to the back of the hallway and began prying the locked basement door open. Bristol stood at the top as they crowded down the steps. He saw them stop, then he ran down to see.

"It's a total mess down here, boss. No sign of Tremain."

Bristol ran down, looking around at the destruction.

"It's impossible," Adams said. "He has to—"

"You have to see this, boss," an agent yelled.

The agent stood by a strip of wood paneling. He pulled it back from the wall, exposing a door. Kicking the door open, the two officers darted inside the coal chute, shining their flashlights on the ramp. They could clearly see the trail, two sets of footprints Matt and Carling had left behind.

"Who the hell is with him now?" someone asked.

"This isn't going to end well for us," Bristol said. "Vaughn is going to have us for breakfast, lunch, *and* dinner."

"And dessert." Adams groaned as he watched Bristol dial her number.

● ● ●

Angela looked at the mirror, admiring her broad smile, when the phone rang again. *That means they have Tremain at last. I can look forward to my meeting with Claussen,* she thought. *This must be Bristol with the details.* She watched her reflection change, her smile fading, color draining from her face.

"How—*how*? You said you had him!"

She listened for a moment and clicked the phone off without a word. She pressed a number on speed dial. It was the number for Amber, her part-time lover and the only person she could confide in.

"It's over, Amber, when I tell Claussen we let Tremain get away. Again." She listened, the commiseration not helping. "My team tracked him to an apartment building. The building was covered front and back. They found an escape route through the basement."

She didn't recognize the woman in the mirror.

"It's no use," Angela said. "It's far too late for excuses. When the dry cleaners next door opened for business, they heard a commotion. It was apparent Tremain escaped through there, broke into a shop next to it, and poof. Gone, like a puff of smoke. We've no idea where he went from there."

She contemplated the woman in the mirror, not believing it was her own image staring back.

"Bristol mentioned something else, Amber. Bristol said there're *two* people. We know that there was a man with Tremain earlier. But we looked at the surveillance tapes. That man left before we moved in. That man got on a streetcar, and nobody thought to follow him. We have evidence of someone else is with him. Who in the hell is he collaborating with now?" It was a question she knew Amber couldn't answer.

"Thanks, Amber, but I have to get it over with. I have to give Claussen his bad news, gone worse," Vaughn said.

She disconnected the call and took one last look at the face in the mirror. Her eyes were swollen and red, frizzy curls hanging over her right eye. It looked nothing like the consummate professional she was.

Another woman walked into the room and looked startled when Angela muttered, "I might as well tell him and get it over with."

Dead man walking, she thought, slinking down the hallway to Claussen's office. *Dead* woman *walking, is more like it*. She walked slowly. When she arrived at the door, she paused, then knocked softly.

"Come."

Claussen looked up and started to smile—until, that is, he noticed her appearance. Her red eyes were a clear warning sign. His smile changed to a grimace. He stood, leaning forward with his hands on his desk. He'd guessed what she was about to tell him, and he knew it wasn't what he wanted to hear.

Angela saw his jaw tighten and a flush of crimson climb his face like mercury in a thermometer.

"I depended on you." His voice was cold.

She knew it was useless to offer excuses. Her options expired with this last missed chance. She didn't bother to straighten her hair or fix her appearance. She stretched back her shoulders, standing at attention, like she was standing before a firing squad. *I'll face my demise with dignity*.

"I depended on you," Claussen repeated. This time, his frozen tone thawed. Not exactly warm, but not as cold, either. "If Tremain links up with that damn news reporter..."

Angela was still holding her shoulders back at strict attention. *Wait...I'm still alive,* she thought. With neither one speaking, silence fueled her unease. *This's worse than being yelled at. When's he going to explode?*

"It's imperative. We must find him and stop him. Find Susan Payne as well," Claussen said, breaking the quiet. "Whatever it takes. Alive is no longer an option. You must stop them. Do you have what it takes, or—?"

Angela realized she'd been given one last chance. "I'm taking direct charge, sir. This is too important to handle from my office."

Claussen looked at her for a long time. It was a gaze, just short of a stare. Angela couldn't see behind the expression. Finally, she nodded and attempted to execute a precise military about-face. It would have been perfect, except her heels didn't click together as intended. She tilted to one side with an awkward motion.

What the hell am I trying to do? she thought. She turned and walked out the door, letting it close behind her. *Just when I thought he was going to explode at me, he didn't. Why?*

She pulled her phone from her pocket. "I want a car, now!"

CHAPTER 35

NEVER TRUST A DRUNK

"**D**ispatch, three-one-two-five is ten-fifteen this location. I need a supervisor ten-twelve, make it forthwith." The radio went quiet. Sitting in the undercover police car, Matt and Carling listened to the radio call.

Matt turned to Carling with a questioning look.

They were sitting, a police services handheld radio resting on the dashboard. The detective reached into his coat pocket and pulled out another radio, smaller and sleeker, placing it alongside. He explained.

"'Ten-fifteen's code for prisoner in custody. But there must be witnesses observing the arrest, taking videos on their smartphones, no doubt. They're warning their supervisor to use utmost discretion when he gets there," Carling explained. He chuckled. "That's what ten-twelve meant."

"How do you make sense of all the calls? It's a jumble of noise to me."

"Anyone working radios develops the knack," Carling said. "Your mind learns to ignore all the chatter, the useless noise, until you hear your call sign. That call you just heard was from a car in the thirty-one division. That was my first post as a rookie. That's why I heard. I still pay attention to their calls."

Matt tried to ignore the radio traffic noises, to concentrate on why they were sitting in the garage.

"I could use a drink," Carling said.

Matt didn't bother responding. They'd been in the car for over forty-five minutes, listening to the sounds of search parties getting closer.

Twice, cars drove slowly down the alley, shining flashlights between buildings and into open garages. Carling managed to get their garage's door most of the way down. So far, they'd gone undetected.

They were both startled by a voice blasting from one of the handheld radios on the dashboard. "We have him. We know where he is now, boss. We're going in now."

Matt looked over, his eyebrows arching in surprise.

"That's the CleanSweep radio and frequency," Carling said.

The two men listened to Bristol reporting to Angela Vaughn. Moments later, they heard him calling back to report the unsuccessful search of Matt's apartment and building. They heard the undertone in Angela Vaughn's voice when she heard that last piece of information.

"They're going to find our way escape, our way out," Matt said. They listened to the description of the basement and his former safe room.

"But that's all they'll know," Carling said. "They don't know where we went after that nail salon. We must stay put. The worst thing we can do is run. That's how suckers always get caught."

"I'm scared."

"We both are," Carling said. "We'd be fools not to be."

The CleanSweep radio blared again. Carling lowered the volume. He looked suddenly worried.

"I'm on my way." It was Angela Vaughn's voice. "I'm taking charge. I want every building and alley in a ten-square-block area of that apartment surrounded and searched. Tremain couldn't have gotten far. I want *every* nook and cranny, *every* dark corner, *every* shadow searched. Don't leave anything to chance. We're getting this guy, or else. Claussen's issued the order. Tremain's now a Code Blue target."

That made Carling sit as if jolted with an electrical shock. "That's an order to kill on sight."

"There's somebody with him," John Bristol said.

"Do you have any idea who?" Vaughn demanded.

"Damn if I know, boss. What about him? Is he a Code Blue target, too?"

"Disposable," came the one-word response from the boss.

The radio hissed, and Carling adjusted the squelch knob until the white noise stopped. "Hmm, they don't have an ID on me yet, but they've raised the stakes. We're both code blue targets."

"I never thought you looked like a cop," Matt said. "I just realized, you're not wearing your trademark fedora.

"And that may work for us...with luck. You can hear it in Vaughn's words. She's running scared."

"And we aren't?"

"Like I said, we'd be fools *not* to be scared. But we have the advantage."

"Oh really? Do tell. I would *love* to know what advantage we have."

"We know where they are," Carling said, laughing. "They don't know where we are."

"Some plan. Some advantage."

"It's better than no plan, wouldn't you say? KBO," Carling hissed.

Minutes passed listening to radio reports from search parties. It turned ominous. "Check all the alleys," Vaughn said. "Any open door you see."

"It's only be a matter of time until someone opens the door to this garage," Carling said. "They'll find their targets sitting here. I need to get something out of the trunk, Matt. Get out, and join me at the back of the car."

They heard voices and footsteps approaching, so they closed the car doors as quietly as possible. Carling opened the trunk and pointed to a satchel. He reached in and pulled out a bottle of whiskey. He tipped the bottle over his head, letting it wash down over his hair and shirt. Then he took a large swallow, gasping as the heat of the liquor caused him to sputter.

"Damn," he muttered, "what a waste of good whiskey."

A surprised Matt watched as Carling deliberately began pissing his pants, the spreading, wet splotch visible in the dim light. Finished, Carling grabbed dirt from a discarded flower pot and rubbed it all over his face. His coal-stained clothes reeked with urine. He was transformed into a disheveled, smelly man, looking very homeless indeed.

"Now," he said, pointing. "Jump on the trunk and haul your sorry ass up there."

Matt looked up at the rafters overhead. Scraps of wood, old doors and windows, and other debris piled on top of them. Matt got on the trunk, then the top of the car, finally hoisting himself up. He curled behind a plywood slab, as invisible as he could be.

"Stay quiet," Carling shushed.

Matt didn't need the reminder. He watched Carling walk to the front of the garage and slide down the wall until he was slumped on the ground. It was an award-winning imitation of a drunk.

The agents conducting the search made no attempt to be quiet. They reminded Matt of scenes from jungle films and safaris, with beaters thrashing the bush in front of the hunters, hoping to scare up the game.

"Has anyone looked in here?" someone said.

Suddenly, the door was yanked open. A flashlight beam shone on the dirty car and swept around the garage until it landed on Carling, looking like a drunk, leaning there against the wall.

"What the fuck?" Carling demanded, but it sound more like "Wha' de fuuuk?" He shielded his eyes from a flashlight. "Turn off those fuckin' lights—"

"What are you doing in here, old man?" a man yelled.

Another agent came in, dragging Carling up to a standing position. Carling staggered and weaved to the side. As Matt looked down through the debris, he witnessed a remarkable display of near-projectile vomiting. Carling puked down the shirt and pants of one of the searchers, looking puzzled by how that'd happened.

"Damn! Fuck! Damn!" the agent yelled. "Some dirtbag just puked all over me!" he yelled, his hand on the radio switch.

The agents with him started laughing. "You got it good, Billy—and they heard it all back at the bus."

"Too bad we have to find Tremain. I'd love sending this guy to a detention center," Billy said. Then, he punched Carling in the gut, pushing the detective onto the ground. He pulled his leg back, ready to kick the drunk, when he stopped himself. "Screw it. Let's get out of here. I need to clean up. You guys finish the alley."

Footsteps, banging doors, and other noises associated with a search receded. The alley returned to quiet. Carling motioned to Matt to climb down. At the open door, Carling looked both directions and then nodded. He walked back and reached into the trunk. He picked up a towel and wiped his hands and face. He stripped off his shirt and replaced it with a clean one from the duffel bag in the trunk.

"How did you—"

"Not another word." Carling's voice was cold, a matching look on his face. "We need to warn Payne and Remy."

CHAPTER 36

PLAN C

Matt and Carling waited until the dawn made a slow transition into daytime. Streaks of sunlight became visible through a dusty garage window.

"How much longer do we wait?" Matt asked.

"There's nothing more on the radio," Carling said, placing the hand-held police set on the seat. "Same for the police calls. Let's wait a bit longer."

"Someone's sure to spot us. What are we going to do when they come back this way? Won't somebody recognize this car—and you?" Matt tried to keep fear out of his voice.

"Listen up," Carling said. "I spent time undercover, learning tricks of changing my appearance. There's only a handful of cops who'd recognize me looking like this, and those are the guys I trust."

They were startled by a radio blast. It was the police band, a routine traffic call.

"Like I thought," Carling went on, "I'd counted on looking dirty—and the smell added a nice perfume, eh? They won't invite anyone like that close."

"You smell as bad as Stinky," Matt said. He wondered where that man was this morning. "What about the car?"

"I figured if I was breaking rules, it might as well be something big." Carling smiled. "I waited in the station garage for shift change. I picked out this old car because I'd used it for undercover surveillance. This piece of crap hasn't been out of the garage in years. It was sitting in the back, covered with enough grime to give it character—wouldn't you agree?"

Matt nodded.

"I've had my eye on this car since hearing about CleanSweep. I carried a can of gas in one day, making sure it was topped up with fuel. Luckily the battery was charged. I had a dupe—you know, a duplicate key made. The old-timer on security never noticed a thing when I drove it out last night.

Carling grimaced. "We have to do something about your look first."

By the time Carling opened the garage door, Matt was covered in grime, a good match to the detective's appearance. The ten-year-old car was rusting in several spots, a long, angry crease marked the hood, and the windshield was cracked. Despite its looks, the motor purred with a quiet fury. Matt guessed undercover cops using vehicles like this depended on perfect running order.

"Get out and look down the alley. Tell me what you see."

"Right," Matt said. He tiptoed to the doorway as if expecting agents to be waiting. "Nothing but normal-looking traffic at the end of the alley," he said in a loud whisper. He gave a thumbs-up sign and walked back to the car. He was careful to shut the door with care, just in case.

Carling eased the car partway out. Matt watched him decide to turn to the right.

"Guess we have to find out sooner or later." He didn't sound encouraging.

It another of those days of perfect weather—for anyone liking a cloudless blue sky, temperature at 16 Celsius. They reached the end of the alley. Carling paused, his foot on the brake. Glancing in both directions, he turned away from the traffic on Queen Street, rush hour complicated by the CleanSweep and police presence.

"I saw a car at the corner. I'm sure it's a stakeout car. I saw the front. It's where I would be if it was me doing the looking. I'm not taking any chances." Carling drove through narrow residential streets, dodging parked cars and waste bins. Matt tried convincing himself they just might make it—get away.

"Where are we going?" Matt finally asked.

"I have a place in mind, but I'm not taking a direct route."

The smallest handheld radio crackled, and Carling adjusted the squelch filter.

"Status report." Angela Vaughn's voice broke through the noise.

"There's nothing on Tremain. Nada. It's like the guy's a ghost."

"What area have you covered?"

"I had over a hundred agents on the ground. We covered it all. They didn't find anything except for an old drunk sleeping in a garage. He puked all over Crandall's shirt."

"Did they bring the drunk in on spec? Did anyone question him? We know Tremain was *with someone*?"

Carling and Matt heard a whimper in the reply. Bishop was a man without a job.

"Williams, are you listening?"

"Yes, boss," replied a new voice.

"You're in charge now. Take over from Bishop. I want as much of the area covered again. I want people out of their cars, off their lazy butts, and walking the neighborhood. How could—?" There was no need for her to finish. "And have somebody bring in that drunk."

"Copy that, boss."

"We're shifting the focus to Payne and Remington. They're going to meet up with Tremain. I'm sure of it. I'm putting out an all-points bulletin over a 100-kilometer radius."

The police radio traffic came alive. Everyone on patrol was ordered to action. "We are sending photographs. They're high-priority targets."

"But one's a cop," someone said, "it's says so on the printout."

"Code blue, both targets," Angela Vaughn said.

Matt and Carling looked at each other. Carling pulled to a stop. "We're still on a side street. Before we get into traffic, I need to think."

"What do you have in mind, Detective?" Matt waited for an answer, but Carling just stared out through the windshield. Matt was hoping a plan was forming behind that stare. "My name's Wallace."

Matt knew the relationship changed. He'd just been given permission to cross a line, a courtesy Carling granted few civilians.

"My friends call me Brick, but my first name's Wallace. Don't ever put that in one of your damn blogs."

"Brick?"

Carling held up his hand. "I hated being called 'Wallace.' That changed to Brick Wall, and then just Wall. My friend, Scotty, said bad guys were up against a brick wall when they met me."

Both radios erupted with traffic, broadcasting orders for a widening search, adding Susan and Carl to the list.

"I don't think they know about me," Carling said. "It's apparent they haven't pieced together my role. That's our edge. Try reaching Susan and Remy?"

Matt reached to get his backpack. "I almost forgot this. I don't know what made me remember it, with all that was happening." He pulled out two phones and looked at them. "I'm going to try this one." He started to punch in numbers.

"Wait," Carling said.

Matt had been just about to press the Enter key.

Carling carried his cell phone in a holster. He used it to place a call.

"Scotty. You know who this is." Carling listened. "Do you still have that friend working at the morgue?" He said, "I'll call you back. I need your help. Thanks, Scotty. You too, more than you know."

He turned to Matt. "OK, call your friends. Tell them, 66 Tilson Avenue, the sooner the better. Tell them to be careful. Hell, don't bother. They already know that. Tell them to park behind the building. The back door is locked, but there's a spare key taped inside the electrical panel to the right of the door. It's an abandoned day-care center. The owners lost everything in the riots. It's called Tiny Tots, or something like that. Remy and Susan can't miss it."

Matt started to dial again when Carling muttered. "I may have a plan that might give us some breathing room." Matt waited, but Carling didn't offer any further information. Matt finally dialed the number and pressed Enter.

"Remy?" Matt whispered. "It's Matt here. How are you guys holding up?"

He signed "OK" to Carling as he listened.

"It's the same here," Matt said, telling Remy about their close call escape. He gave directions to the day-care center.

"Carl's north of the city," Matt said, turning to Carling.

"Brick says come down Leslie and turn at Eglinton." He started to laugh. "Oh yeah, Brick's Carling's nickname. That's another story. See you guys there. Wait—"

He looked at Carling, who signaled him not to hang up yet.

"Tell them to wait until it gets dark," Carling said. "Make sure they know about the APB out on them."

Matt relayed the message and turned off the cell. "I know these things have GPS built into them. Can the SIM card really be traced?" Carling nodded. Matt took out the SIM card and tossed it out the open window.

Carling's made another call. "Scotty, Brick again. How about the back row of the theater? Right, that's it. I'm going to ask a huge favor. See you then. Oh, Scotty, I'm with someone, and we haven't eaten since yesterday. One more thing," he said, looking at Matt. "He's five-nine or five-ten, medium build. I'd guess large for shirt size. We both need some clothes. You know my size. Thanks, Scotty. You da bomb, my man." He ended the call.

He turned to Matt, explained. "We're meeting him this afternoon. Now we need to take our phones apart. Take the battery and SIM card out like you did on that other phone. We'll toss them as we drive."

Matt did, except for one. "I'll keep this one. It's analog, so old it doesn't use a SIM card, so it should be safe to use." He put it into his pocket. "Do you trust him, this Scotty?"

"With my life—and yours."

Carling took his phone apart as he was driving. A dump truck was coming in the other lane. As they passed, Carling made a perfect three-point toss, his phone heading to the landfill.

• • •

Carling drove up a steep access road. Matt recognized the location, the Nordheimer Ravine. The two men spent the rest of the day at Sir Winston Churchill Park well back from St. Clair.

"Hardly anyone ever comes here this time of the morning, except the dog walkers. And, there's a washroom facility. We need rest," Carling said. He parked by the steps leading down to the ravine. "One sleeps, the other stays awake. I'm not sure what good that'll do. At least we'll see them coming. You sleep first."

"Why this place?" Matt asked. "I heard you tell Scotty something about a theater."

"It's our cop thing. Scotty and I have our inside jokes. If we use the word *theater* on radio, it means this park. All cops have secret hideaways."

Matt smiled. "A doctor told me about a code used when he was an intern. A page for Dr. Better meant a poker game was on."

He tried easing the tension, but it didn't help much. He tilted the seat back and closed his eyes. The next thing he knew, Carling was punching him in the arm.

"It's my turn, Blogster."

Matt stood watch while Carling stretched and walked to the toilet. When he came back, Carling laid down on the backseat. Matt sat behind the steering wheel, trying to turn on the radio for some music. "It hasn't worked for years," Carling said. In an instant, Matt heard a jet airliner trying to take off. It was his friend's snoring.

He attempted to ignore it, but gave up. Sitting on the hood, Matt turned his face to the morning sun, the CN Tower rising over the tree line. Matt savored the warmth. Any doubts about staying awake on guard duty were dispelled by snoring from the back seat.

Nervous energy combined with all he'd been through was catching up with Matt. His legs cramping, he had to stand and walk. He circled the car but didn't venture far. He looked up at the St. Clair bridge overhead. Even the traffic noise couldn't cover up the snoring.

Instantly alert, Matt heard a car approaching well before he saw it. Like gasping for breath, it sounded like the car wasn't up to its task.

"It's his personal car, a Fifty-six Peugeot." Carling's voice caused Matt to whirl around. "It makes an awful racket, but Scotty loves that car. Fortunately, it runs better than it sounds or looks. He knew better than using a cop car, if that's what you're wondering."

The car crunched over the gravel. Scotty braked and opened the door. He was wiry, stepping out like a man ready for a fight, strutting to where Matt and Carling waited. The two detectives embraced.

"Thanks, Scotty."

Scotty looked at Matt. "You're the guy we've all been on the look-out for, eh? Public Enemy Number One—through Ten—and all at once!"

Matt felt uncomfortable until Scotty laughed and draped his hand around Carling's shoulder.

"If this man says you're OK, you're OK."

The three men walked over to a picnic table. The wood was warped and weathered. Matt looked at the variety of names and comments carved onto its surface.

"You two smell like chimpanzee shit," Scotty said.

"You should've smelled him *before* he washed," Matt said.

"Tell me about it," Scotty said. "I spent too many times undercover with him, Matt. He likes to get into character. I didn't forget what you asked for, Brick." He walked back to the Peugeot, reached into the back-seat, and retrieved four large takeout bags, carrying them back to the table.

"Here's food," he said, pulling Styrofoam containers from one of the bags. From another, he removed cups. "Coffee, hot and black." Matt watched steam curling from the lids. "I wasn't sure, so I brought this as well," Scotty said, setting two metal cans on the table. Carling and Matt both put their coffee down and lunged for the beer.

"I brought clothes you asked for. I suppose a shower is out of the question, but you both could use one," Scotty said.

When Matt and Carling finished eating, Carling motioned Scotty to sit next to Matt. Matt watched Brick flip the plastic lid from his coffee, take a sip, and bigan to outline his plan.

"Who's your contact at the morgue?" he asked Scotty.

"Marsha Liner. You remember her? The one with the big tits—"

"Yeah," Carling cut him off. "Can she keep her mouth shut? Will she do what you ask without going weird on us?"

"It always helps to have a trump card," Scotty said. "It must've been about four years ago. I was working vice when an informer gave me a tip on what a woman at the morgue was doing with corpses. I have a video and selfies she doesn't want to see posted on YouTube. She'll keep her mouth shut. What are you thinking? You always have some devious scheme when I see that look."

Matt's was curious, but waited for the two friends to spell out the plan.

Carling pulled a face. "We need a body—a dead body. What better place to find one than the morgue? Give her a call on your backup phone."

"What do you want?" Scotty said.

"The first question. Does she have a male on ice, roughly the size of our friend, Matt?"

"I'm beginning to see where this's going." Scotty gave a broad grin. "I love it. We're gonna make Matt dead, right?"

"In a unique way," Carling said. "I'm thinking a jumper—a suicide. After all, Matt Tremain's been under investigation, and according to the story circulated, friends have noticed how depressed he is." He turned to examine Matt. "We need to ask Marsha to check her inventory. Here's the skinny," Carling said, laying out the plan in more detail. "If Marsha has a candidate, we'll take Matt's clothes and dress the cadaver."

Matt shuddered at the thought of dressing a cadaver.

"The key will be how to move it without being noticed." Carling said.

"I can borrow a van," Scott replied. "I know the owner of a carpet-cleaning company. We can use his truck—no questions asked."

"Yeah, let's make it work," Carling said. "Do you have one of those master entry cards we use to get into condominium buildings?"

"Never leave home without it." Scotty patted his pocket.

"We need your help, Matt. Are you game?"

"It all depends..." Matt said. A touch of concern in his voice caused both detectives to stare. "But I don't have a choice."

"I thought of a place that'll be perfect," Carling said. "It's one of the new ones." He turned to Scotty. "What do you think about using City View Condominiums?"

"The one on the Esplanade, right?" Scotty nodded. "One of those tiny places could pay for three or four regular homes." The tone in his voice implied a distaste for the snobby occupants.

"We'll use it then," Carling said. "There's a steep driveway leading down to the service entrance. We wait until just before dark. The sun will set a little after seven thirty tonight. There won't be much traffic, and it's a dead-end street anyway."

Matt started to ask a question, but Carling stopped him.

"Let me finish. Then you can ask questions. We'll dress John Doe at the morgue and carry him in a body bag. This building has a large service elevator at the back. You don't have to worry about any residents getting on. They're all so damn uppity, they probably don't even know such a thing exists. Chances are you two can make it in and out without notice. There's a keypad you can use to disable the computer. The owners installed a video cam. You can reach it with a spray can."

"What are we going to do?" Matt finally exploded.

"This may offend your delicate sensibilities about the truth, but we need to convince everyone you're dead," Carling snapped. "We're arranging that unless you want CleanSweep to make it real for you. This isn't a plan for the long run. It'll only be a distraction to buy us some time."

Matt leaned back, holding his hands in surrender.

"Scotty, you and Matt carry the package to the roof. Our police-issue entry cards will get you through the roof access door. Take the soon-to-be-dead Matt Tremain out of the bag. When you hear three clicks on the handheld radio, toss the body over the edge. Make sure it comes down at the front of the building—the Esplanade side."

"OK," Scotty said. He looked at Matt for confirmation.

Matt, realizing what he was about to do, felt numb. "Go on...let's get it over with."

"I'll wait at in the next block," Carling explained. "When the call comes from dispatch, I'll be first one on scene. I'll make a quick ruling that it's an obvious suicide—a jumper. What else could it be? I'll call Marsha and have the body transported to the morgue—ironic as that sounds. I'll file a report that it looks like Matt Tremain, but make a note we have to wait for final confirmation. Wait. Why didn't I think of it?" Carling thought for a moment. "Matt, give me your wallet. It'll give me your identification when I check the body."

Matt was beyond arguing. He handed it over. "Just my license and a couple of bucks," he said. "What the hell...here."

Scotty checked his watch. "We have a couple of hours. Matt, come with me. We can walk from here." He threw the keys to Carling. "Still remember how to drive a stick?" Carling then turned to Matt. "Call Susan and Carl. Tell them not to believe everything they hear on the news." He started to laugh.

● ● ●

"Ted Johnson, Action 21 News, reporting. A young man, estimated to be in his early thirties, fell to his death tonight. Police have not confirmed identity, but it's rumored to be Matthew Tremain, a popular investigative journalist. It appears he jumped to his death from the roof of a condominium. Sources tell us Mr. Tremain has been undergoing treatment for depression.

"There's been considerable damage to the body. We're told it will take fingerprints and DNA to confirm identity. Investigators at the scene recovered a wallet. An anonymous police insider said they're officially treating this as a John Doe case, the investigation ongoing. But our source confirmed Matt Tremain's name and photo on the ID."

● ● ●

Matt tried calling Susan several times without success. *I hope I can explain before they hear it on the news,* he thought.

CHAPTER 37

DAY CARE

Remy shook his head, trying to focus on the road. "Hand me something to wipe the windshield with." He rubbed condensation forming on the glass, dropped the tissue, and began rubbing his forehead. "I need sleep."

Susan started to say something when her phone rang. She listened. "We've been lucky so far," she said. "We're scared. I'm putting you on speaker."

"CleanSweep issued an all-points. We're in deep." Matt's voice came through clearly. "We have to assume they're capable of listening in now. Carling said they monitor everyone's movements using SIM cards, even when we're not talking."

"It doesn't matter. Tell them we don't have a choice," Carling's voice boomed in the background. "Give them the address again, and be quick about it. We're running out of chances."

"66 Tilson Avenue," Matt said. "Park in the alley behind." The phone went quiet after Matt told them the name of the day care center and location of the key. Susan sat staring at her phone, looking like she was praying.

● ● ●

Two men monitoring communications traffic at CleanSweep headquarters were at the end of their double shift, and caffeine wasn't helping them stay alert.

"Did you catch that?"

"All I could make out was 66 Till-something. Do you think we should tell Vaughn? It sounded like that TV lady talking. Fuck me sideways, we didn't have the recorder on."

"I'm not trying to explain that to anyone."

The two sat at a monitoring console. One had his headphones off and was staring at a screen. He pointed.

"The call to them originated downtown, near Casa Loma." He tapped the mouse, and another screen came up. "Payne and the camera guy are well north of the city. I saw their signal moving while they talked. Crap, they must have taken the card out."

"There's an all-points out on them. We *have* to let Vaughn know."

They played a round of rock-paper-scissors, and the loser started to dial.

"We're in trouble; you should have been paying attention," the winner said, pushing the blame away.

• • •

"What's our plan?" Susan sounded tired.

Remy pulled to the side of the road and looked at her. *I've never seen her look so disheveled*, he thought. He reached over to touch her cheek. "Hand me the map."

There was enough light to make out details. He traced a road with his finger, shaking his head no. He followed another. "I don't see any way to avoid detection."

"What're we going to do?"

Remy sat, drumming his fingers on the wheel.

"You always come through in a tight spot," Susan said.

"We need another ride. We've had this car too long already. I saw an old pickup parked at a feed store we passed. As soon as it gets dark..." He looked at the map again. "I know what Carling warned, but it may work. If we take this road, it'll be rough, but I don't see any other way. Look," he said, sharing the map. "We can get into the city on this utility access road. The last time I went hunting, I walked that fire-lane corridor running under high-tension wires.

"There's no telling how well maintained it is. If we follow it here, we come out by the river. The utility road goes under the freeway. If the truck's up to it, and that's a big *if*, we face a pretty steep climb. The good news is, if we make it, we'll end up within half a mile of the address Matt gave us. Let's hope that old truck is up to it, and enough fuel would help."

Susan started to cry, softly at first, but then broke into sobs. She waved her hand, motioning help away. "I'm sorry…"

"I hope there's enough gas in that truck. It wasn't covered in dust, so someone must have used it lately. We're both beat, and I need to rest. Can you stay awake?"

"There's no way I can sleep. I'm more wired than tired."

"Wake me when it's dark." Remy leaned back and was asleep in seconds.

Two hours later, Susan pushed his arm. "Now?" she asked. "It's getting darker.

Remy rubbed sleep away and sat up. "Has anyone driven past? I was hoping this road wasn't used much."

"A couple of cars heading that way." She pointed behind. "They didn't slow down or notice us."

Remy started the car and made a U-turn. Five minutes later, he coasted to a stop. "There it is, and there's nobody around." He parked to the far side of the deserted parking lot. "Grab your stuff and stand by the truck. We need to make this fast."

Susan stood to the side while he tested the door.

"It's unlocked at least," he said. "I hate to do this to someone, but we need—"

He was looking under the driver's seat, but stopped when he heard a dog barking in the distance. When it was quiet again, Remy looked in all the usual hiding places. "No key. I'll have to hot-wire it. It should be easy with an old crate like this."

He crouched under the dash panel and pulled a harness of wires down. He told Susan to reach in his left pocket and hand him his knife. He stripped two wires, touched them together, and the truck sputtered, then started. He quickly twisted the wires together and motioned Susan into the passenger seat.

"There's enough gas. Now all we must do is not get caught. This damn pickup needs a tune-up. I lose respect for people who don't take better care of their trucks." He drove past the place they'd rested earlier. "It shouldn't be much farther," Remy said. "See those power lines? That's where the road is."

The utility road ran off to the right, toward the city. Remy steered the truck into the ditch and up the far side. They came to a fence blocking their way. He didn't pause; he accelerated and smashed through the barrier. The left headlight got twisted in the crash and now dangled, pointing down and to the left, but one light was enough.

The truck bounced over potholes and ruts, its springs moaning in protest. Susan held on with both hands without complaining.

The light from the city skyline was chasing darkness away. Remy turned the headlights off.

"No need to have that broken light drawing attention. I can make out enough to see the road." He slowed until his vision adjusted to the light, then accelerated again. "That's the freeway up there," he said.

They followed the utility road and high-tension wires, parallel with the river. They passed under the freeway overhead.

"I don't think anyone can see us. Why would they have anyone posted on that bridge as look-out? I can't imagine why they would, but..."

The bridge was behind them. The river curved to the west, the utility road and high-tension lines curving with it. "That red-brick building ahead is a power substation. As I recall, there's an access road that veers to the right. The address Matt gave us shouldn't be far—if we make it up the hill."

"What if a cop sees the damage—the broken headlight—and stops us?"

"What option do we have?"

When they came to the substation, the main string of high-tension lines continued, but other lines branched to the right. Remy stopped the truck and got out. After looking around, he got back in and put the truck in gear. The access road wasn't as steep as remembered, and the old truck made it to the top with only a whimper.

Remy paused before entering the road. "There's more traffic than I expected. If I can turn left, there's another road off to the right we can take—not far. It's back streets from there."

He turned on the lights and drove, Susan holding on. Remy turned corners faster than she thought was safe. "I'm lost," she said.

"Almost there."

Remy's forehead was creased in concentration. He made a turn to the left, spotting the sign for Tilson Avenue.

"There it is!" Susan yelled. "We made it."

Carl slowed the truck and coasted past the storefront for Tiny Tots Day Care Center.

"That's so sad," Susan said. "The windows are all covered with newspapers."

Remy didn't say anything. He'd spotted a lane ahead, between two buildings. "I think that leads to the alley in back. I'd just as soon get off the street anyway."

He drove back between a hardware store and a convenience store, both closed. Reaching the lane, he turned right, driving a short distance. "I can park in that alcove behind the day care center, just wide enough. I can't believe it! I think we've made it," he said, his shoulders sagging.

They got out of the truck and stretched. It was dusk, but there was just enough ambient light to illuminate the electrical panel. Remy pulled open the rusty panel door. It sounded like a scream as it opened. He reached in for the key.

"That could really use some spray lubricant."

Remy unlocked the door and they stepped through, pulling it closed behind. Lighting from the street pierced the newsprint-lined front windows, casting the interior in a ghostly light. They stepped over randomly strewn toys, walking between an assortment of tables and overturned chairs. "You can tell they left in a hurry," Remy said.

A front window was cracked, gusting wind trying to find a way into the room. One of the newspaper corners flapped in protest.

Susan was tough, but she appreciated it when Remy pulled her close, drawing her to his shoulder, stroking her hair.

"Whatever happens, I love you with all my heart," he whispered.

CHAPTER 38

BREAKING NEWS

"How long do we wait?"

Remy walked back from the bathroom when Susan asked. He looked at his watch.

"It hasn't even been two hours." Remy helped Susan up from the floor. "I wonder how long it'll take them to get here. If they get here," he added.

"I've had softer beds," she said and grimaced. Rubbing her left arm, she leaned to stretch her back. "Thanks for letting me sleep. What time is it?"

"Almost half past three," Carl said. "There hasn't been any traffic on Tilson. Maybe a car or two and a delivery truck. None stopped, though. I don't—"

The quiet was shattered by the back door opening, slamming against the wall. Matt stepped out of the shadows and looked around, adjusting to the light. Holding his phone, he waved them over.

"You have to hear this," he said, putting it on speaker.

"520AM All News Radio. This just in. Police have *not* confirmed the identity, but Matthew Tremain, a popular investigative journalist, apparently jumped to his death from a condominium rooftop earlier this evening. Detective Wallace Carling is quoted as saying he thinks it was a suicide, but he won't issue a formal statement until later. A witness described a body damaged beyond recognition. Our reporter saw the detective removing a wallet from the jumper. Tremain has not posted on his blog lately, and there have been rumors he's suffering from severe depression."

"Freaking unbelievable," Matt sputtered. "You guys will *never* believe what I just had to do." He turned the radio off and started to cry—a muffled sobbing. "It was awful, let me tell you."

Matt began to shake and turned away, walking to the front of the room and back, pacing and crying.

Remy and Susan shrugged, trying to make sense of what they were hearing. Susan started to say something, but Remy motioned her to hold her questions. They waited for Matt to wind down. Finally, he turned to them.

"Carling had this crazy-ass plan. Then he called a friend of his, Scotty. It turns out Scotty has a contact at the morgue. They have these thick plastic bags to carry corpses. Look at these clothes I'm wearing. They're not *my* clothes, not even close. I think they belonged to a dead guy I helped carry—"

"PTSD," Remy said. "Post traumatic—"

"I know what PTSD is," Susan barked.

Matt walked to the front window, pulling back a corner of a newspaper taped there. He peered out and finally turned around.

"It's beyond crazy." His voice was now under control.

"Who's Scotty again?" Susan asked.

Matt filled them in about the close call at his apartment building. He told them about Clifford leaving, then hiding in the basement until Carling arrived. He told them how they escaped through an abandoned coal chute and hid in the garage. Matt managed a half-laugh as he described Carling's projectile vomiting.

"It *was* an outstanding display," he said.

He told them about reservoir park and meeting Scotty.

"He's another cop. A guy Carling trusts," Matt added. "You won't believe the plan Carling came up with."

Susan didn't remind him he was repeating himself; they just waited.

"We went to the morgue. Some crazy woman who apparently takes selfies while she does indecent things with corpses...anyway...she let us in and showed us which drawer to open. When we slid a tray out, a naked guy was lying there. It was just like they show it on TV or in a movie. I stripped and was embarrassed to be standing there in front of the morgue woman, but apparently, I wasn't dead enough to interest her that way...

"Where was I? His clothes. The dead guy's clothes were on a shelf. The woman, Marsha..." Matt took a deep breath. "She handed me these clothes. It's an unnerving feeling wearing them," he said, pulling at a pant leg. "Just knowing they came from a dead guy. Anyway, Scotty gave her some money, and we dressed the dead man in *my* clothes. Then we put him into a body bag and zipped shut.

"Carling said he had to go and disappeared like a cat. That left Scotty and me to carry the body bag to a van. Then it got *really* weird. We drove to this condominium, and Scotty used his key card to get us in. All cops seem to have masters.

"We took a service elevator to the roof and unzipped the bag. I held the body by the feet, and Scotty held it under the shoulders. Scotty waited until his radio chirped, a preordained signal, and we crab-walked to the edge of the roof and just threw the body over the side. Then he drove me here, and he took off. I don't—"

Matt told the story at a machine gun pace. It fell quiet when he stopped. Nobody spoke.

Finally, Susan chimed in. "That's the suicide they're reporting on the news?" she said. "That's absolutely diabolical. It's brilliant. You're now officially dead," she said, looking at Matt.

"I could use a little help here!" Carling was outside the back door of the day care, kicking it to get their attention. "A little help here!" he yelled again.

Remy rushed to the door. The detective stood with a large brown bag in one hand and a tray of coffee cups balanced in the other. "I figured you guys could use some nourishment."

"Oh...my... god," Susan said. She stepped forward and took the tray of cups. "You're a lifesaver."

Carling reached into a pocket and handed over creamers and sugar packets. Susan took one, and Remy noticed her hand shaking as she tore a corner from the sugar package, dumping the sweetener into her cup.

While they were drinking, Carling walked over to a small table and began laying out breakfast sandwiches and donuts. The scene was surreal: Carl, Susan, and Matt sat on child-size chairs, munching breakfast in an abandoned day-care center, the morning light a gauzy-beige tint filtered through the newsprint taped to the storefront windows.

Yes, Matt thought. *Alice Kingsleigh and her Wonderland friends would be right at home here.*

Carling perched on a desk and lit a cigarette, waving the smoke away from his face as he inhaled. "My first smoke in seven years," he said, ignoring Susan's scowl.

"Did you hear the news report?" he finally asked.

They nodded.

"I made sure I was first responder on scene. It wasn't a problem. Great job with the body, by the way," he said, looking at Matt. "I know it wasn't easy for you. Something like that isn't easy for anyone. The 35-story fall made quite a mess of the John Doe. His face was smashed up pretty bad, but that was the plan, eh?"

He took a long draw on his smoke and exhaled slowly, puffing rings into the air. "I felt sorry for the woman who saw the body hitting the ground. She was shaken. I made sure everyone saw me remove your wallet from the body," Carling said.

Carling went on. "I called Marsha. She was already driving the van from the medical examiner's office, parking a few blocks away. She arrived in a rush. I think she wanted to get the body back to the drawer as soon as possible, before the morning shift discovered the gap in their inventory. I heard a few sharp-elbow comments from the brass about the speed of my investigation, but everyone seemed pleased to be rid of Matt Tremain." He smiled at Matt's discomfort.

"What's next?" Carl asked.

Susan stood up so fast, her coffee cup turned on edge; the remaining liquid drained off the table and spilled into a rapidly widening puddle on the floor. "I've had enough of this crap."

The three men looked at her.

"We have evidence now." She looked to her left. "Remy has our investigations recorded on media cards. Matt, you have your latest stuff. Then, the final nail in CleanSweep's coffin when we met Ulrich. It all adds up. It's time to go public. I dated a guy once—you might say we were more than good friends. He's a major talent at World News Network now.

Oh, don't give me that look, Remy," she said with a laugh. "WNN will make sure this goes viral. We need a way to get this to him somehow."

• • •

Carling extended his police-issue radio to a sputtering fluorescent light fixture and clicked the Transmit button.

"I just saw the TV reporter and...her camera guy..." He kept the radio near the light. "They're driving...a red Camry, heading west...on Lakeshore." There was more static as he clicked the transmit button. "I can't keep...up with the car. They're west of the city...heading toward the old refinery at..."

He started a chuckle that turned into a belly laugh when he heard another, similar, report a minute later. "That's Scotty. He's also claiming he saw people that looked like you two." He pointed to Susan and Remy. "We just sent them all chasing shadows. A clever diversion, wouldn't you say? Now we'll find out how much time we just bought."

He described the fluorescent-bulb prank. "That's an old trick. When I saw the tube flickering, I knew it would cause static, make it seem like my radio message was breaking up."

They listened to the escalating radio traffic. "All units respond, per CleanSweep orders. Be advised. All cars. This is a red alert. Use open frequency in plain language." The radio was alive with calls and clicks.

When they realized what Carling had just done, the other three breathed a collective sigh of relief.

"Absolutely fucking brilliant," Susan said.

Carl looked at her from the side. In all the time he'd worked with her, he'd never heard her use the *f*-word.

CHAPTER 39

CLAUSSEN, WE HAVE A PROBLEM

Charles Claussen built his financial empire by imposing strict self-control, demanding the same from people he hired. He couldn't think of many mistakes choosing management personnel. If he discovered a mistake, it meant someone's immediate dismissal. He considered himself a master at reading potential hires.

He realized he'd made two wrong hires: Tanner Woodson and Angela Vaughn. He never regretted the order to arrange Tanner's death. Angela Vaughn, however, presented a dilemma for him. He placed the blame on all that was going wrong on her shoulders. What he couldn't do was come to term with his feelings for her. The one fantasy he allowed himself to have? When CleanSweep proved itself, he would leave his wife. He envisioned a tropical island estate, Angela lounging by his side as they sipped fruity drinks.

Claussen turned his chair toward the window and stared south. Inky, angry clouds gathered over Lake Ontario, waves rearing back as if recoiling from the wind. It hinted at the whirlwind blowing toward him, a low-pressure system, sucking the life from Operation CleanSweep. A view that usually gave him pleasure, he couldn't see past the turmoil—what he dreaded most: failure.

Angela Vaughn had let me down, he thought. He learned someone was infiltrating CleanSweep's communications and security.

Who's the hacker helping Matt Tremain evade capture?

Claussen didn't know, but he acknowledged the skill and genius it took to penetrate a system he'd personally designed and implemented. He'd created a masterful surveillance system relying on state-of-the-art computer technology. Despite that, someone slipped in the backdoor. All he knew was a location of the hacker, Eastern Europe.

He'd no way of locating him. Claussen created an impregnable electronic wall, but it was a wall with a secret door. Tanner had a key to that door, the key allowing the hacker access. Claussen knew Tanner was a traitor, slow to recognize that fact. He was now beginning to fully realize how complete the damage was.

It felt easier to blame Angela Vaughn, the woman he loved.

Looking out the window, he felt overwhelmed, reluctant to accept what needed to be done. He must pick up the phone and call his co-conspirators. *I'd promised them the future, and they put their collective finances and personal reputations on the line,* he thought. Today, the memory of his glowing media presentation at Winston's lodge near Lion's Head haunted him.

How quickly the CleanSweep plan is unraveling!

Something else worried him even more. He'd never told the others about his second mortgage on CleanSweep—another secret group of backers. Informing them was far more daunting, admitting their investment was at risk. *They're people who have special ways of recovering their losses,* he thought. He knew the rumors of what they'd done to anyone who crossed them.

When additional funding was needed, Claussen made discreet inquiries using the dark net. It'd led him to a secret world and a small group of four, each with more money than Charles, his coconspirators, and the government's contribution combined.

He remembered the icy smiles as they readily loaned him the money. They'd demanded collateral. The loan was secured by everything Claussen owned—and his life. It was a contract Faust could identify with—a contract signed in blood, a soul for collateral.

After the launch, the rioting had gone as planned, he thought. *Soon CleanSweep was cleansing the city of undesirables, as planned. It had been going so...*

His thoughts trailed off. *My beloved plan's going off the rails.*

He swiveled and looked at three photographs on a nearby bookshelf. He frowned at his wife's photo. *How did she let herself get so fat?* He considered the second photo, the faces of his two children. *Look at those Teutonic features; the eldest would have been a poster boy for Hitler's Germany.*

The last photograph showed his grandfather's stern look.

It was all for you, he thought, his eyes blurring. *Especially for you, Mein Grossvater.*

Claussen held a mahogany box on his lap. Its brass plate was engraved with double eights. The numbers were chosen to honor his hero. The eighth letter of the alphabet representing Herr Hitler.

Claussen placed the box on his desktop. He opened the case, looking at the weapon resting on felt lining. It was a gift from his grandfather, reportedly by the famous gun maker Georg Luger himself. His grandfather presented it to Claussen on his sixteenth birthday. It was a .9mm pistol Claussen cleaned at the end of each day before returning it to its mahogany case.

The pistol exerted a mystical power over Claussen.

"Angela Vaughn," he hissed, saying the name out loud. "This is *entirely* your fault. If only you..."

He quickly closed the lid and picked up the telephone. Claussen arranged a conference call and waited for Waverly, Spencer, and his best friend, Winston, to join.

"Charles?" It was Winston who spoke first. The steely, questioning tone unmistakable.

"Spencer here. What's up? Why the call? You said we shouldn't talk like this."

"Waverly's in some committee meeting. I ordered him called out; he should be with us shortly." Claussen tried keeping his voice modulated, sounding a calm he didn't feel.

"Is something wrong?" As Claussen suspected, Winston was the one to guess there was a problem.

"Let's want to until we're all—"

"What's so important?" Waverly's voice broke in, sounding breathless. "You had me called out of a critical meeting."

Claussen hesitated, unsure of how to begin. He decided the best way was direct. "There's no way to sugarcoat this," he started. "We have a problem—"

"What do you mean by *we*?" It was Winston who interrupted, and Claussen didn't like the chill in his voice.

"That blogger got wind of what we were planning with CleanSweep. I thought we had him neutralized, but he connected with that TV reporter, Susan Payne. They started digging around, and..."

The line was silent except for a slight electronic hum. Claussen could hear them breathing.

"I ordered my security team to confiscate any incriminating evidence, verification, or proof that Tremain and Payne may have uncovered. We never had a clue how slippery they would prove to be. We got close, but..." Claussen took a deep breath before continuing. "All that doesn't matter now. They know what we planned, how we planned it, and they have our names. We are in deep. At first, my team was ordered just to retrieve their evidence, but they've gone to ground. If the reports of Tremain's suicide are true, I've ordered the others eliminated: Payne, Remington, and especially Carling. He's a traitor."

● ● ●

The men on the conference call didn't hear a click, or electronic noise, to hint someone was listening in. There was none. Cyberia made sure his eavesdropping was seamless. At his desk in Moscow, staring at the monitor, he recorded the conversation in high-definition audio. It was a documented admission of guilt, CleanSweep agents tasked with assassinations.

Cyberia was crying, mourning the suicide of his friend, unaware of the ruse the detective and Matt created. All Cyberia heard was the news account of Matt's apparent suicide.

He clicked the mouse on his texting program and started the message for the remaining three friends of Matt.

SNAFU! You're a target now. Orders to kill. Claussen behind it, and sent the message flying, hoping it would reach them in time. He smirked at SNAFU, the expression American soldiers invented during World War Two. It meant "situation normal all fucked up." It seemed appropriate.

• • •

"What evidence do they have?" Winston demanded.

"Tremain was initially contacted by a young man I'd trusted to manage my computer systems. His name *was* Tanner Woodson," Claussen said, stressing the past tense. "He turned out to be a whistleblower, giving information to intrigue Tremain. Then, Tremain started to dig for more. Apparently, Payne was sniffing around as well and started her own independent investigation. My communications team overheard Payne and Tremain talking. Now, I know the knife-in-the-back came from Ulrich."

He heard a gasp when he said that. "What're you saying?" Winston shouted. "What did my man Ulrich have to do with any of this?"

"He's a bloody traitor, you fool. His family roots go back to Russia. He's a dyed-in-the-wool Socialist. That's the man you trusted. I *told* you I was worried about the radios the two of you used at our meeting at your lodge. Now you know why I was suspicious. He somehow recorded everything—every damn word. Now Payne has all the proof they need to bring us down."

"I have connections," Winston whispered. They all heard the evil in his words. "Ulrich is a dead man. Nobody fucks with me."

"It's too late, my friend. Ulrich is a ghost. All traces of him gone. Someone vaguely resembling him was thought to be on a flight to Copenhagen, but that's the only hint we have of his whereabouts. From there—nothing. Gone, like smoke. Your trusted majordomo was the worm in the apple."

"That's preposterous!" Waverly sputtered. "I'm contacting my source in the government. We will track them all down. I knew we should never have relied on a private—"

"Shut up. You're nothing but a gasconading booby." Spencer said. He'd been silent until that point. "We all knew what we were getting into. Fortunes are made to be lost. What we must do now is save ourselves from the fallout. We need a PR plan."

Claussen started to laugh, but it wasn't a pleasant laugh.

"We are so far beyond putting a positive spin on this, it's pathetic to even consider that's an option." Claussen's CleanSweep radio started to blink. "Hold on, I may have a report. I told Vaughn not to contact me unless she had good news."

Finally, he came back on the line. "That was Vaughn. We may have caught a break. After a wild-goose chase involving a suspicious car, we've zeroed in, surrounding a storefront on the east side. They're apparently hiding in an abandoned day-care center. A neighbor was putting out the trash and saw a man going in the back door with a tray of coffee and take-out food. She was suspicious; the center had been closed since the riots. Vaughn issued a silent alarm. Agents should be there now. The witness is waiting for them at the nearest intersection."

"Why didn't you keep us up-to-date with these problems before?"

"I make no apology, Winston. You didn't presume to micromanage me, and you can't start now. It was your man who tipped the scales, after all." Claussen realized he was trying to shift the blame. "I'll call you back as soon as I have news. I want to concentrate on overseeing my team in the field."

• • •

Claussen didn't listen to his field radio, however. He lifted the lid on the mahogany case again. He removed the gun, feeling the cold metal. He looked at it for a long time. Holding it in his right hand, he reached with his left to pull the slide back, cocking the Luger. He placed it carefully on the desktop and swiveled to look out over the lake again.

"Angela Vaughn." He kept repeating her name.

• • •

From 4,647 miles to the east, an eight-hour time difference, Cyberia sent another warning to Matt.

CHAPTER 40

SKIN OF THE TEETH

"They have us!" the panic in Matt's voice was palpable. "Cyberia says they are closing in! About to surround the building now!"

Carling ran to the front window, peeling back a corner of the newspaper. "I don't see any activity. What exactly did Cyberia say?"

"Someone saw you come in, describing a man carrying food trays. It was reported as suspicious, and now agents are on the way."

Carling looked out again. "The only thing I see is a car parked across the street, but it was there when I came in."

Carl and Susan stood together, holding hands, their faces taut.

"We have to do something," Carling said. "Let me think." He began outlining a plan. "It's simple, but simple may be best." They gathered their belongings. Carling opened the rear door and leaned out. He didn't see any activity. He yelled. "Hurry! Now!"

They heard sirens, faint, but getting louder. Carling barked orders. "Payne, down on the backseat! Now!" He ran over to a dumpster and carried back an assortment of cardboard. He covered her, then opened the trunk. He motioned Remy and Matt to get in. "It's time for you two to become very close friends." He closed the trunk after they curled up together inside. "No funny stuff, you two," Carling laughed, as he banged his hand on the trunk lid.

Carling started the engine, and, looking over his shoulder, reversed at a high rate of speed, tires smoking. At the far end of the alley, he kept it in reverse, backing into a side street, street lighting filtering through leaves.

Deciding, he drove forward, south on Bayshore, then left.

When Carling saw a CleanSweep car at the next corner, he turned the emergency lights on and activated the *whoop-whoop* of his siren. He braked as if he just arrived on scene. He got out of the car, holding his badge, and waved at the two agents.

"Hey guys, that way." He pointed behind him. "They're running, three of them. I couldn't get turned around in time. They were on a side street—Belcourt, I think."

"Jimbo!" one of the agents yelled. "Get back to the car. Call it in. Let everyone know they're on foot, heading toward Manor Road. Tell them a cop's seen them running. They can't be far." He turned to Carling for confirmation.

"Just seconds ago," Carling said, nodding his head. "Quick. I saw them, and they looked dog tired." Carling smiled when the two agents jumped in their CleanSweep cruiser and drove off, tires screeching.

"I hear sirens, squealing brakes, and excited voices," Carling leaned in to tell the other three. "The entire posse's shifted direction." The two agents didn't seem to notice the undercover car hadn't joined in the chase. "Those two aren't the sharpest knives in the drawer," he said, laughing.

Carling jumped into the car and drove off in the opposite direction, and down another side street. After several turns, he began whistling softly and kept a slow pace until they were many blocks away. He rolled the window down, listening to the sirens in the distance, and grinned.

"I wonder what they will find where they get there."

He turned his head and told Susan to stay put. "I hope carbon monoxide isn't seeping into the trunk," he added, joking.

He heard her gasp. "I never even thought about—"

Carling assured her the two men were OK. He watched the city skyline receding in the rearview mirror. In the city, the bad guys knew undercover cars when they saw them. Carling hoped their country cousins weren't as perceptive.

• • •

Two hours later, he spotted a roadside park and pulled over. He was glad to see a portable toilet near the parking area. The pressure on his bladder was beyond uncomfortable.

After he had pissed, he helped Susan from the car and grinned, watching her race to the toilet. He opened the trunk to help Matt and Remy out. Remy got out first, then turned to give a hand to Matt, who was rubbing a cramp in his leg.

"I heard what you said to those agents," Remy said to Carling. "You think pretty damn fast for an old guy." He smiled, and that took the edge off the barb.

Carling ignored him. "We should all feel grateful to have made it this far—another close call behind us. You're right, I may be getting too old for this. I disabled the GPS, but who knows? The agents will give a description. By now, they'll know it was me. We have to make our move—and fast."

"Do you have a map? We had one in the truck, but it's still parked behind the day-care center," Susan said.

"Check the glove box. I don't know if there's anything other than a map of the city."

Susan pulled everything out. "This is disgusting." She sorted through candy wrappers, donut crumbs, and police forms. Finally, she pulled two maps out. "We're in luck. This's a city map," she said, tossing it aside. "This, however, is the map we need."

Matt jumped up and started waving his arm in a windmill. "It's Cyberia!"

They all turned to see him grinning.

"You won't believe this, but I sent a text to let him know we're safe—for now. But this is the cool part. It turns out Ulrich's related to Cyberia! Go figure. How freaking mind-boggling—all the spiderweb connections."

"Using the phone was really stupid," Carling said. "CleanSweep will be onto us."

"That makes it more imperative to get moving," Susan said. "Let's look at a map. How much fuel do you have, Carling?"

He walked to the car and turned the key on. "It depends on whether you're an optimist or a pessimist. The needle is between half empty and half full," he shouted back as he returned to the table.

"Here," Susan said, pointing to a place on the map. "It's not too far. There used to be a TV station there—I was the weather girl when I first started. It used to be a network affiliate. Now it's a studio for the local cable company. Their equipment may be well past the sell-by date. But that shouldn't be a problem—isn't that correct, Remy? All we need is a place to link-up to national."

Remy agreed.

"What's that station manager's name? Let me think." Susan's face was a study in concentration.

Remy was surprised. Susan had absolute recall when it came to names.

"Jensen, that's it," she said. "I wonder if he's still there. He always acted like one of those gruff newspaper editors—always yelling at his minions—but Jensen's a softy, a marshmallow at heart. How long will it take us?"

They all looked at the map. Carling and Matt suggested one route, but Remy said they were both wrong and pointed out a shortcut.

"See that?" he said, his finger tracing a dotted line. "That's a gravel road. It curves a lot, but it will shave almost an hour."

They all looked at Carling. It was his car after all—actually, the city's car—but he was driving. That meant he made the final choice.

"What the hell?" he said. "They likely have the main roads covered anyway."

• • •

Back roads from Toronto to Kitchener can be puzzling drivers not used to the area. Following old cow paths and wagon trails, they often headed in unexpected directions. Carling kept a tight grip on the wheel, and his three passengers held their breath, careening around curves. They sped past fences, enclosing pastures. Cows gazed at them with looks that could have been curiosity.

The road ran past rushing streams, through a small valley, over the Grand River, and finally up a slight rise on the other side. When they crested a tall hill, they saw city lights in the distance.

"That's it!" Susan exclaimed, excitement rising in her voice. "Once past Waterloo, the studio is on the boundary with Kitchener."

Remy looked at his watch. "This time of the day is perfect. Morning news is going off-air about now. My guess is they'll go into reruns to shave production costs. That means the newsroom will be quiet. What do you think, Susan?"

"I don't know, Remy. It's only used for local news. But you should be able to upload stuff while I'm on the phone. You two," she said, turning to Carling and Matt. "Stay out of our way." She didn't try to hide her smile. Hurricane Sue was back in business.

It's game on, she thought. She leaned forward to make the car go faster.

Carling followed Susan's directions, parking behind a small building with cedar-shake siding. It was shaded by two large elm trees.

"The last time I was here, they didn't have a receptionist," Susan said. "They keep the door locked. Wait here." She walked up to the door and pressed her forehead against the glass, peering in. She tried knocking. "There's no intercom," she yelled back.

She looked at the keypad at the side of the door. She hesitated, then pushed some keys.

"Remy," she shouted back, holding the door open. "Hurry—my old code still works!"

Carling and Matt weren't going to wait in the car, however. They raced to the door, following Susan through a warren of cubicles. "These were all used by the news team, crowded and busy 24/7," she said. As they rounded the last partition, they came upon four men and a woman. They looked up, clearly frightened to see strangers.

Carling had seen equally frightened looks on the faces of crime victims. Holding up his police badge, he said, "Don't be alarmed. This is police business." He tried to strike a balance between authority and reassurance. This was so far out of his jurisdiction that it should have been obvious to them he was a fake—but it worked.

"Well, shut the front door," a man shouted. "Susan, is that really you?"

She turned. "Mr. Jensen. You're still here."

Jensen had a beard that Hemingway would've envied, except for pairing it with a shaggy head of white hair, for a Hemingway-meet-Einstein look. It wasn't a good mix.

"Susan Payne, I'll be damned. Who are those guys with you? I recognize Remington."

"Carling's a detective from Toronto," she said pointing. "This's Matt Tremain—"

"That Matt Tremain," the woman standing next to the station manager shrieked. "This guy was—is—famous. Hey, aren't you supposed to be *dead*?"

"Don't believe everything you hear on the news," Susan said.

Jensen suddenly fixed her with a hard stare. "We've heard the police scanners. Lady and gentlemen, we're looking at Public Enemies One, Two, Three, and Four—all wrapped in one burrito."

"We can explain," Susan said. "Hear us out."

Susan hurried through the details, Matt adding details. The looks of the audience change from skepticism, to curiosity, to anger. Jensen and the others crowded around to hear.

"There's a problem," Jensen said.

Susan and Matt started to ask what.

"CleanSweep! There's a total clamp down," Jensen said. "All news about CleanSweep is spiked. The feds have issued a blackout order. We can't touch it. We'll have regional, provincial police, and the horsemen here as soon as we try to go on air."

"That can't be," Susan protested. "I'm making a call."

The only sound was someone's radio playing country music while Susan went to the side to call.

"It's worse than I thought," she said, after disconnecting the calls. "My contact at CBC won't touch the story. I tried Syd at CNN. He said it's the same. Syd told me they're hunkered down at CNN, waiting for police raids."

"CleanSweep's the first step in a coup," Carling said. "No wonder we've had so much trouble getting anyone to believe us."

"I have an idea," Susan said. She started to scroll through her phone contacts. They watched as she placed a call.

"Marius? It's Susan Payne. Awful, thanks. I have to skip the niceties, sorry." She explained the story, making notes while she talked. When she finished, she closed the phone and told the others.

"That was Marius Walderhaug. He's station manager of TV 2 in Bergen, Norway. I was there when they launched in 1992. They're a full active member of the European Broadcasting Union." She looked at her notes. "If we can upload from here, they will air it."

Jensen barked out orders. "They have full use of our facilities. We may be taking a risk, but when this story hits the air, everyone will know about us. If anybody wants out, leave now." Nobody left.

"Hurry, Richard. Show Remy to whatever he needs."

"Remy," Susan interrupted. "Marius gave me this: 16:9 (720p, HDTV) (576i, SDTV). The upload code is 7222/5020."

"Got it," Remy said. OK, Richard, let's move it."

"Linda, help Susan with the phone—you'll see a pro in action. If I'm judging this correctly, she'll also need makeup, if you know where it is."

If Linda was insulted, she ignored it. "I can't believe it, Susan Payne."

Susan's reporter shoes were back on the ground. She was in her element.

Jensen turned to Matt and Carling and pointed to the coffee bar. "It's fresh. I made it myself just before you got here. We may be a small-market station, but we have a great coffee supplier. They import the beans, and..."

Carling and Matt let him ramble on about the coffee. They suspected this was the brass ring for him—a last chance at fame. They sipped coffee, watching the action of people heading in different directions. It looked like chaos, but they both knew they were witnessing a magnificent ballet.

That thought reminded Matt of the Dancing Lady. He fought back tears. When he regained composure, he turned to Carling.

"Brick, we might make it after all."

CHAPTER 41

SUSAN PAYNE REPORTING

Financial cutbacks had stripped the station of equipment and personnel. Jensen told them he knew he was captain of a sinking ship. "But if this gets out, I will end my career at peace with the decision. This's the biggest story this old studio in the twin cities will ever be a part of, and we all know it."

The newsroom was crowded. Field reporters rushed back when they got word. Everyone kept a respectful distance, watching Remy work his magic on a video console behind soundproofing glass. It was obvious he was a master of his craft, his fingers moving expertly over the keyboard and switches. He transferred details from the media cards and uploaded them to the station computers at TV 2 in Bergen, Norway.

Susan walked on set, wearing fresh makeup—reading the cut sheet, her lips silently mouthing the words of her report. She showed no signs of the past seventy-two hours. She held sheets of notes with a steady hand and paced back and forth; the floor director pulled back to give her room. Sometimes, she folded the corner of a page and wrote a correction. They watched her lips as she spoke her lines in silence, her forehead wrinkled in concentration.

If anyone was curious about Carling, they didn't show it, except with a furtive glance in his direction every now and then.

"Time!" someone shouted. The room was instantly quiet, and all eyes turned to the clock, the second hand sweeping to the top. "We're going live in five, four, three, two, and...*now!*"

The central monitor had been displaying bars and tones, changed to show a man's face in high definition—a man with a serious look. It changed to a split-screen with two announcers.

"From TV 2 in Bergen, Norway, this is Marius Walderhaug," the man on the left said.

"From headquarters of the European Broadcasting Union in Geneva, Switzerland, this is Jean-Paul Calvert."

A third image appeared.

"Reporting live from Channel Five in the Waterloo region, this is Susan Payne."

Remy hoisted a camera on his shoulder. They agreed earlier a shoulder cam would lend authenticity. It was something they'd done together for years now, each knowing what to expect from the other.

He signaled Susan, and Matt saw the broad grin on the cameraman's face. All eyes turned toward the monitor.

"Thank you, Marius and Jean-Paul. This is Susan Payne, reporting from the twin cities in Ontario, Canada," she said, pausing to brush a wisp of hair back. It was unneeded. Remy knew it was her signature on-air move. "Everyone here in the studio knows the risk. Two great North American countries have tried to stop us, to ban this report. Thanks to our European colleagues, here's the story.

"Today, you're going to hear about the *real* story behind something called Operation CleanSweep…" She paused for dramatic effect before continuing. "Designed to undermine everything free men and women everywhere value—peace, security and the rule of law—CleanSweep almost succeeded. This is a story of how it almost brought a great city to its knees."

By the time she finished her report, the world was aware of the deception and the roles of Charles Claussen, Waverly, Overstreet, and Spencer. The conspiracy was laid bare, naked, exposed.

"It's a public-private conspiracy at its very worst. From now on, dictionaries will have a picture of CleanSweep next to the definition of conspiracy." She paused for dramatic effect, turning to camera one, the floor camera.

"Will they claim it was a simple case of the government misjudging the damage to the very core of our civil liberties? I tell you, a secret inner circle judged it quite accurately. With help from people like Charles Claussen and his cronies, and Waverly greasing the wheels of a rogue government cabal, it almost worked. While Toronto was the intended target *this* time, the conspirators hoped this become a template to be used worldwide."

Turning back to Remy's camera, using poise and her evenly modulated voice, she laid out the facts for viewers like a verbal buffet. She started with Tanner's death, pointing out that it wasn't an accident as had been reported earlier. She honored his bravery, explaining his role as the first one to bring the evil of CleanSweep to light. She described Matt's investigations into CleanSweep and his story about Mattie, the Dancing Lady.

"Key to this story is a fellow journalist I'm proud to call my friend and fellow journalist, Matthew Tremain." Pausing for emphasis, she continued, "Matt Tremain brought this to the attention of our government and was rebuffed. They claimed the story was preposterous. However, our parallel efforts uncovered the facts, and now show it was indeed, not only preposterous, but it was pure evil."

Matt lowered his head as he listened, tears streaming on his cheeks. It wasn't from hearing his name or Susan's praise. It was the memory of Tanner, pain rising to the surface. *I hope this brings some comfort to Tanner's wife and serve as a legacy his children can be proud of.* Carling put a hand on his arm, an offering of both comfort and congratulations.

Susan reported on her role in the investigations, then surprised Remy. "It was a team effort. The viewers never see the man behind the camera now: Carl Remington." Carl's red face failed to hide his embarrassment when she explained his role.

Viewers may have noticed a slight shudder as Carl's rock-steady camerawork developed a short-lived, but quite uncharacteristic wobble.

Carling's head snapped up when he heard about his role. He was sheepish, his face turning crimson.

"Now, listen to portions of a recording made by four conspirators at a weekend retreat. The voices of Charles Claussen, Winston Overstreet, Richard Waverly, and Donald Spencer can be heard distinctly, as they plan a diabolical conspiracy."

A hastily prepared graphic filled the screen behind her.

Susan looked to the side and down. Remy captured the perfect image of her striking a thoughtful pose while the recordings played. She turned back to the camera when the audio finished. She remained quiet for four seconds, an eternity during electronic news. Finally, "Back to you, Marius and Jean-Paul."

Her image on the monitor faded.

• • •

Landline phones started ringing. Smartphone ringtones started a chorus of sounds. Susan shouted for silence. "Quick, the monitors. The world-famous logo faded to show a familiar face, bold graphics forming a backdrop. "This is Roger Follet reporting from WNN." He looked down at the script on his news desk. "The prime minister of Canada and president of the United States have released a joint statement denying any knowledge of this plot.

"An emergency combined task force of special agents from the Royal Canadian Mounted Police and the Federal Bureau of Investigation have begun making arrests over the past half-hour."

Roger Follet turned toward a side camera, maintaining his signature solemn gaze, and concluded his story. "We'll be back after a word from our sponsors."

The newsroom at channel 5 was silent, hushed-church quiet. Someone applauded. It began as a slow clap, others joining in, until everyone was on their feet and shouting. They realized they'd just played a part in history.

"Bravo!" someone yelled.

The station cameramen rushed up to Remy to shake hands and acknowledge his professionalism. Aware of their roles, news persons then turned to Matt and Carling. Soon, the blogger and detective were mobbed with backslaps and shouts of "Well done!"

Susan stood alone in front of the bank of monitors. It'd provided the perfect backdrop for her report. Now, people honored her privacy with a reverence for a person of high office, someone you didn't approach unless invited.

She started trembling, the script in her hand shaking, then dropping from her hand. Remy set his camera down, rushing to her side. There was a hush as they embraced, clinging to each other as he caressed the back of her head. Susan sobbed her relief.

"It's done, Susan," he said. "You did it—*we* did it."

Then he led her through the crowd until they reached Matt and Carling. The four joined in a circle. They could have been bowing their heads in prayer or huddling like a football team. It could have been either of those, but none of them ever revealed what they said to each other in that moment.

The newsroom exploded again with the sound of ringing telephones. As they were answered, people started to shout.

"Susan, it's for you on lines one and two and four."

"Matt, can you take line three?"

"Remy, it's the WNN on line five."

"Detective Carling, it's your chief wants you to call, soonest."

Carling didn't look happy, hearing that.

CHAPTER 42

ARRESTING DEVELOPMENTS

Friday morning rush hour was usually a crunch of traffic clogging freeways and major roads leading into the heart of Toronto. This day, however, it was an eerie quiet gripping the city, the roads empty except for emergency vehicles. Social media, television, radio, newspaper, and mass internet mailings advised people to stay home. Cars equipped with loudspeakers roamed the streets with a single message: "Stay home unless it's an emergency."

Remy squinted at the sunlight as they drove from the west. "Damn few pedestrians," he said. "It's downright spooky. If it weren't for the military or police, there wouldn't be any vehicles on the road at all."

They all wondered what to expect as they arrived at the first checkpoint.

"It's them," a woman shouted. "I heard they were coming this way."

She wore a camouflage uniform and waved over a squad of soldiers. They started cheering, while other soldiers tried to maintain a stoical pose, clutching weapons at the ready. Any civilians out and about were treated to the sight of a massive military and police presence. Military scout cars, usually only seen in television in war footage, lined curbs. Troops were stationed at intersections and other strategic points.

A man in a police uniform ran to the car and peered in. "That's Carling!" he said as he reached through the open window to slap the detective on the shoulder. "We've got your six," the officer said. "You're one of us."

Their surprise was complete. An officer signaled, and they were assigned a police escort. Soon, they were speeding through the streets, the escort car flashing its rotating blue lights to guide them.

Passing CleanSweep headquarters, they saw men in military uniforms surrounding the building.

"That was fast," Matt said in a whisper, as if he were still afraid to speak his thoughts out loud. They were waved through the next check-point. "It helps to have a police escort, eh?"

"We need to get to work, Remy—tired or not." Susan tapped him on the shoulder. "Pull over here."

He honked and flashed his lights to signal the escort. He slowed until the escort car braked as well. The back-up car pulled alongside.

"Do you think you're good from here?" the escort driver asked.

Remy gave a thumbs-up.

"Good luck." The window of the trailing escort car went up, and the cars drove off.

Remy stopped at the curb. The others watched as he walked to the trunk and retrieved a case, placing it on the hood of the car. He pulled out a camera.

"A gift. The guys in Kitchener gave me this," he told them. "Let's get to work, Susan."

"So, you're the boss now?" she asked, laughing, but Remy was already pointing the lens. He had his shot.

He tucked a phone under his chin, and began a slow pan to the right. "I'm sending B-roll now, live."

Susan turned to the camera as she walked, Remy keeping pace. The two were soon far enough away that Matt lost the sound of her voice.

Carling took the wheel. "What do these guys want?"

He held up his police badge when two men with stern looks and cam-ouflage uniforms approached the car. The taller one leaned in to examine his identification, his stern-looking expression turning to a grin. "They're OK, Sarge," he said, and they walked away.

Carling turned to Matt. "Where do you want me to drop you?"

"I can't face home, wherever that is," Matt said. "Not yet. We've been driving all night. I don't care what time it is; I could use a drink."

"The Ten-Eight it is," Carling said.

"The barkeep almost lost his business after the riots. A bunch of old-timey cops are sure to be there," he said.

Walking into the bar, Matt looked around. It was packed with men and women in police uniforms, with undercover officers in civilian dress mixed in. Matt and Carling stood in the doorway, silhouetted by strong sunlight. They appeared as dark shadows until they stepped in and closed the door. Everyone in the bar stopped talking. It was their custom to freeze out any unwelcome visitors.

"Carling, you old degenerate!" Scotty yelled from the back of the room.

A wave of recognition swept through the bar, followed by cheering. It was long, loud, and heartfelt—until Carling held up his hand.

"Enough!" he tried to yell. But his protest only made the others cheer even louder.

Matt watched Carling's face slowly blossom into a dark red, then purple.

"Hey, Carling!" someone shouted. "Who's that with you? You brought a civilian to the Ten-Eight?"

It was Matt's turn to feel embarrassed. He felt like turning to leave. In fact, he started to do just that.

Carling stopped him. "This," he yelled over the noise, "is the freakin' blogger that started it all!" He held up Matt's arm. "Matt Tremain, the guy we were all supposed to be chasing. He's my guest, and I expect him to get the same respect you give me." He ducked as napkins and straws were hurled at them.

"That means he picks up the next round," a woman yelled, and everyone laughed.

Carling looked over at the barkeep. "I thought you were out of stock."

"Look around," the man answered back. "They all brought in cases of beer to donate to the cause. Some brought liquor, and Sarah even brought a bottle of white wine—which, by the way, is still unopened."

That was met with jeers and booing.

"Shut up. Listen," someone said. A radio blared out news, everyone quiet.

"Until the TV's back to broadcasting from the main studio, we're following everything on the radio," a woman whispered over her shoulder to Matt and Carling.

"But look—they're back on the air now," someone said as if on cue.

The screen displayed a stock photo of Overstreet.

The volume was turned down, and everyone yelled for the barkeep to turn it up.

"Toronto Police caught Winston Overstreet packing a suitcase. He never made it to his car." That was met with a chorus of booing and hissing.

The screen showed a scene from Winston's upscale condominium; it was like something out of a television cop show. The camera panned to the right as two military trucks pulled under the porte-cochere at a high rate of speed, braking to a sudden stop.

Men and women in uniform jumped out and adopted combat stances, holding weapons at the ready. Suits poured out of a black SUV parked behind them, one obviously in charge issuing orders, as the uniforms dispersed to their posts. It was all being covered live by Action 21 News, Susan Payne providing the voice-over.

Matt and Carling looked at each other, knowing Remy was behind the lens.

On the screen, the building's concierge jumped around as if she were barefoot and stepping on hot coals. Trying to speak, she was clearly overwhelmed by the uniformed presence—and had no clue what was unfolding.

"Hand me the master entry card, now!" a deep voice demanded.

She trembled as she complied. "It's the master—key card," she barely got the words out before the man grabbed it from her and raced to the elevator. "The Overstreet suite is on the third floor," he said, ordering people in uniforms right and left through each stairwell.

An over-the-shoulder camera shot followed the team leader, who nodded as the door to Overstreet's unit was smashed in. Everyone rushed inside to see the occupant leaning over a suitcase. Susan Payne's voice could be heard as Remy got a great camera angle—his money shot. Everyone in the bar watched Overstreet straighten then turn to face the onslaught. He had a resigned look on his face and slowly raised his hands to show he wasn't armed.

As they left the building, the concierge could be seen holding her smartphone to take her own souvenir video, apparently recovered from her earlier shock.

Remy's next shot was destined to become video of the day, the high-and-mighty, secretive billionaire Winston Overstreet escorted through the overly ornate lobby of his condominium building at gunpoint.

• • •

"Faster, damn you, faster," Spencer shouted, the skyline of Miami fading behind them. Spencer stood alongside the captain of the bridge of his yacht, *Mockyachta*. Spreading his feet apart to steady himself, he grabbed a handrail to counteract the pitching motion of the ship. "Hurry, damn it. Don't stop."

The captain started to put his hand on the speed control panel. "It's no use—we have to stop. We can't outrun the coast guard."

"You stop when I tell you to stop," Spencer said, pushing the captain's hand away from the throttle. He ran to the starboard and looked up. A red-orange plane with a stripe and a twin-engine turboprop CN-235 maritime-patrol aircraft was circling overhead, just above stalling speed. Spencer shook his fist at the plane, feeling the *Mockyachta* slowing in the water. The yacht came to a stop amid rolling swells, the yacht yawing and pitching.

Evans, Spencer's chief of security, rushed the bridge. Spencer barked an order. Evans pulled out a pistol, holding it to the captain's head.

"You're both crazy," the captain said, pushing the throttle to full speed.

The copilot of the plane looked down, and seeing a growing wake, radioed the vessel wasn't stopping. "They're underway again."

• • •

Mockyachta's captain increased the speed, but carefully adjusted the controls for three-quarter power—a move that went unnoticed by Spencer. As the other two men went to the side to watch the plane, the captain made another adjustment, slowing the yacht even more, careful to escape notice. The captain was no fool. He trained binoculars on growing specks on the horizon. He knew the coast guard or navy was sending fast ships to intercept them. He also turned the wheel a bit at a time, until *Mockyachta* was heading directly toward the pursuers.

When Spencer realized what his captain had done, he yelled in a panic, "Idiot. Turn this thing around—now."

A loud boom sounded—a warning shot across the bow put an end to the pursuit.

"You're not paying me enough to die for this," the captain said, shutting the power down.

Evans holstered his weapon as Spencer looked at the approaching coast guard cutter. He was looking beyond, however, seeing far beyond the horizon. He was picturing his prison cell.

• • •

"Sir."

Richard Waverly was sleeping deeply. Ignoring his doctor's advice, Waverly took three doses of his prescribed sleeping pills instead of one. His wife was furious when she found out, but Waverly needed sleep.

Earlier, his wife watched him clutch his chest as he watched Susan Payne report the arrest of Winston Overstreet. He threw the remote against the wall, and shards of plastic scattered across the plush carpeting.

"Damn bitch!" he'd said, struggling for breath.

His wife wanted to call 911.

"It's too late for that. It would be merciful if it was a heart attack. Call our lawyer," he said, storming out of the living room.

He gulped down sleep aids and was soon snoring away in a medicated sleep.

"You can't go in there." He barely heard his wife's voice through his medicated haze. "He's an important man. He has the ear of prominent—"

"Shut up, lady."

The sound of splintering wood dimly registered. Richard was trying to make sense of being picked up by rough hands. He was dragged without ceremony to a waiting van. Richard Waverly wondered vaguely why his wrists were restrained. He hadn't taken enough of an overdose for it to be fatal, but it was sufficient to grant a feeling of peace as he was arrested.

Later, when the tablets wore off, he heard the charges against him, read by a stone-faced prosecutor.

• • •

Charles Claussen sat in his office, his flagship empire and Clean-Sweep crashing around him, and looked at the phone. *I can't order this to go away.*

"Angela, I told you this would happen if you didn't—" There was no reason to finish, an exercise in futility, and they both knew it.

Angela looked past her boss, gazing at the lake, knowing she wouldn't see it for a long time. She fingered the police badge in her pocket. She may have resigned from the force, but it was still her touchstone, reminding her of an oath. Standing there, it felt like an accusatory reminder of how far she'd fallen from grace. She hated to apologize and decided this wasn't a good time to start.

They heard approaching sirens.

"It won't be long now, boss."

Claussen looked back at her and shook his head. She couldn't tell what the head shake meant. Her cell phone rang. Angela still had a friend on the police force. It was her cop friend, Cindy, calling from the Ten-Eight. She heard excitement in her voice and the cheering in the background. Angela's face was expressionless as she closed the phone mid-call. *I didn't tell Cindy the cheering cops were about to see arresting officers handcuffing me,* she thought. Tears welling, *I used to be one of them, one of those cheering cops at the Ten-Eight.*

She looked at the phone in her hand when she heard a drawer open. Claussen placed his pistol case on the desk. Angela knew it was his prized Luger.

"Get out," he said. The steely quiet of his words was heard even over the sound of sirens.

She raced for help, on the phone at her desk. "You have to hurry," she said to the person called. She sat at her desk, trying to figure out her next move when she heard the shot. She ran to Claussen's office to see blood, bone, and gristle splattered on the window behind his body.

A .9mm Luger can do a lot of damage, she realized.

She was staring at the gory mess when the door shattered behind her. Officers rushed in with weapons at the ready. She raised her hands, then felt them roughly pulled behind her, cuffs snapping around her wrists.

"Damn, those old guns are loud," she told the arresting officers. "You need to know about Camp Free Eagle," she said, as she was led away. One of the officers whispered to a woman who appeared to be in charge. Vaughn was led to a special operations trailer parked in front of the building. She hurriedly told the lead investigator about Brunner's role in the riots—about Camp Free Eagle.

Charles Claussen heard the exchange between his former head of security and the police. He hid behind the wall, a narrow panel closed with a remote control he held.

When it happened today, he executed his plan. He knew he didn't have much time, but he acted with a deliberate haste.

As soon as Vaughn left his office, he opened the panel in the wall. A man stood in the secret compartment, Claussen's size, and wearing identical clothing. The man looked confused and upset.

"What did someone say about the police?"

Claussen waved the Luger, and with a reassuring gesture, invited the man to sit in the desk chair. He gave the unwitting victim an envelope. "Open it," he told him, watching the man's eyes widen when he saw the stack of money.

That chump is so captivated by the cash, he'll never see what's coming, Claussen thought. Too late, the man looked up. Indeed, he didn't anticipate Claussen's next move. Holding a towel to shield himself from blood spatter, Claussen stepped quickly, placing the barrel of the Luger under the man's chin. He pulled the trigger, then fitted the Luger into the victim's hand. Folding the towel, Claussen calmly removed the envelope and money from the dead man's grip. With a last look, he stepped through the secret door. The panel slid closed as Vaughn opened the door. Claussen edged along a secret hallway, leading to a prearranged exit.

He'd hoped the gruesome scene would prove a distraction. It worked. Excited voices and shouted commands faded as he followed the narrow corridor until he came to a service elevator. He'd arranged to have a locker installed next to the elevator. It held a of clothes. When the elevator reached the parking-garage level, he permitted himself a smile.

I'm not going to miss that fat slug, he thought about his wife. *It was supposed to be Angela. When it's safe, I'll have her join me and arrange for the children to join the two of us. They need their father.*

• • •

A fleet of helicopters ferried an elite team of special forces, members drawn from all branches of the military. The usual rivalry and teasing was set aside for this mission; each man and woman sat with hard, unsmiling faces.

Brunner's militia might have been good attacking unarmed civilians, but they were no match for the special ops units they now faced. Most quickly realized the hopelessness and put their arms down, surrendering without firing a shot.

"This ain't worth dying for," one said.

Even with little resistance from Brunner's militia, a rumor circulated afterward about several thugs "accidentally" killed during the raid. There was no follow-up investigation to confirm or deny the rumor.

• • •

Toronto returned to whatever was currently normal. Agents and employees of CleanSweep were interrogated. Those in management and top levels were arrested and detained. Some were charged and were issued orders to appear for further questioning. Others were interviewed and cleared, all weapons and identification confiscated. CleanSweep headquarters, offices, and satellite facilities were placed on lockdown, armed military guards stationed at all entrances.

• • •

"Is it really over?"

The 10-8 was subdued. Cheering faded as the full impact of what they'd been through set in.

Matt and Carling looked at each other, aware of the bond, despite the initial reservations each had about the other.

They started to say something at the same time.

"We've got unfinished business," Matt finally managed to say. He pulled his phone from his pocket and dialed a number.

"Susan?" It sounded like a question, but it wasn't.

CHAPTER 43

DEAR READERS

Matt looked around as he stood at the entrance. The sidewalk teemed with window shoppers and other walkers, traffic sounds providing a pleasant soundtrack. Little by little, Toronto was returning to normal, the reopening of Bistro 350 one signpost of recovery. He smiled and opened the door.

"May I help you, sir?" a young man said.

"I'm meeting friends," Matt said, looking around.

He saw them waiting. Carling sat across from Susan and Remy. They waved, and he squeezed past tables. Matt grinned, pleased they had a window table where they could relish the spectacle. Gerrard Street showed signs of healing. There was street lighting, and road traffic and pedestrians strolled by; this one of the hardest-hit areas during the riot.

Matt thought about Stinky and Gigantis, ushering him through the same streets. He'd made inquiries, but came up with nothing, whereabouts unknown. Matt began to wonder if it'd all been a bad dream.

Susan hugged him. "I know the owners, a hard-working husband and wife team. They're rebuilding and need help."

They all nodded agreement.

Matt felt a sudden surge of melancholy, swamped by painful memories. "I had to walk past the conservatory. I hate it, the awful reminder of what happened there."

"Sit...eat...enjoy," Carling said, slurring his words. He wore a broad smile. The detective sported jeans, a graphic T-shirt, with an open leather jacket—no fedora in sight.

Matt approved of the look. "Going for urban chic?"

The server arrived with a bottle of wine as Matt sat down. Carling snorted, reaching past Matt to grab it.

"My treat, and I'm pouring." He filled their glasses with a steady hand, a surprise to Matt. There was a small amount left, and Carling emptied it into his own glass. "Cops don't have class anyway," he said, laughing.

"To us." Susan raised her glass, her voice subdued. "To us, because we did it—together. Come on, guys. Clink."

No one spoke. Each sat with their own memories.

Susan broke the ice in typical reporter fashion—asking a question. "You first, Brick. What now?"

"The chief invited me to the sixth floor—a royal command. He sat behind his humongous desk, three deputy chiefs standing like trained poodles. A small man from human resources sat on a side in the corner. For some reason I noticed he was bald. Anyway, I guessed with him there, my career was toast.

"You should have seen it," he continued. "The chief tore strips up one side and down the other. He pointed out all the police procedures and laws I violated. I think his exact words were that I'd broken just about every rule in the book. Funny thing—he smiled the entire time.

"Then he said I'd provided the best publicity they'd had in years. He growled at me to get back to work. Everyone in the room was grinning."

Matt, Remy, and Susan looked at each other. "That's the longest speech I've ever heard you make," Matt said.

"What about you two?" Carling asked, looking at Remy and then at Susan. "Are you two going to make it official and get married?"

Susan started to laugh, resting her hand on Remy's arm. "No way. But we just signed documents making our relationship official. It's a new company called *Hotwire Creativities*. We've started a film production venture."

"Why not capitalize on our newfound fame," Remy said. "It's almost the same as getting married, right?" He paused. "Why spoil a good relationship doing something crazy like getting married?"

Susan looked at Matt. "What about you?"

"I'm lost," he said. "I'm taking a break. This morning I bought a ticket and decided to spend time in Paris. I haven't been able to clear my mind, to erase all the images. I start thinking about Tanner, Clifford, Stinky, and…"

The other three didn't prod. They sipped wine and waited. They knew he was thinking about Mattie.

The moment was broken when the waiter brought appetizers, and they turned their attention to the food.

Matt's mood improved with food and good companions. He regaled them with a vivid description of Stinky.

"What's that?" Remy said. He pointed outside.

It was like a parade, a procession of people slowly walking behind a large glass-delivery truck. The street was bursting with people. Matt heard singing. The four of them walked to the door, followed by the other patrons.

A parade stretched blocks to the west. Marchers held candles, singing *Amazing Grace*, the music growing in volume. When the song ended, the crowd continued walking, humming the melody.

Matt had to grab Carling's arm to steady himself. The sign on the truck nearly brought Matt to his knees. "The Mattie Project: Restore the Conservatory." Marchers wore bright orange shirts with a drawing of a dancing lady.

They watched until the last of the parade moved east. Matt, Carling, Remy, and Susan said their final good-byes, promising to meet again soon. Each secretly knew it was an unlikely vow.

Matt watched Carl and Susan walked away. "I've never seen two people more in love," he said to Carling.

"Want to go for a drink? You're an official member of the Ten-Eight now."

"No, but I appreciate the offer and your friendship more than I can ever say."

The two men embraced and parted. Carling started to walk when Matt yelled, "Stop."

Carling was standing by his car, parked in a no-parking zone in front of the restaurant. Carling fixed him with a 'who me' look and took his Official Police Business card from the dashboard, tossing it onto the seat.

"What?" He asked.

"What the heck does KBO mean?" Matt said. "You always signed your notes with it."

"Keep buggering on. During World War II, it was Winston Churchill's way to end phone calls, letters and notes. He did it to encourage people when everything looked hopeless, grim."

Matt grinned. "That's what he'd needed to do when things looked so desperate."

Driving away, the detective gave Matt a quick siren *whoop* in farewell.

Matt walked toward Alan Gardens and the conservatory. The parade crowd had gathered in front of the greenhouse. *I can't join them, not yet. The memory of her death is too fresh.* Matt still had visions of Mattie's body tumbling like a rag doll. He knew he'd never erase feeling partly to blame for her death dance.

Four weeks later, Matt's smile returned—almost. He read an e-mail from Clifford. "We're planning a dedication ceremony at the conservatory. They're renaming a section. It will be The Dancing Lady Wing, honoring Mattie. A lot of volunteers made it happen."

Matt read the e-mail again, knowing he wouldn't attend—he couldn't. He'd always feel responsible for her death. Most of all, he didn't want to share his memories of her with a crowd.

• • •

A week later, Matt staggered to the door of the Dancing Lady Wing. He looked around the conservatory, holding an expensive bottle of single-malt Scotch whiskey. He was unapologetically drunk. Matt started out, intent on getting drunk. He'd succeeded beyond expectations. He was glad nobody was there to see his tears.

He walked back to where he'd spent that night crouched under a workbench, hiding from CleanSweep agents. He took swallows of whiskey and thought of Cliff and Mattie, remembering how they'd roused him with their warning. He replayed Mattie's death dance in his mind as if it were a videotape. Tears streaming and the taste of whiskey on his lips, Mattie's odd way of talking echoed in his memory.

Matt knew he must live with that memory, somehow.

Matt didn't consider himself religious, but decided the moment called for some gesture. He poured some whiskey on his fingers, sprinkling it to anoint the ground, making it sacred. Borrowing from his Catholic friends, Matt made the sign of the cross, turned and left.

When he got back to his apartment, he thought he still wasn't drunk enough, disappointed to find only a can of refrigerated light beer.

He didn't bother undressing. Falling back onto his bed, his mind filled with mental images, flash cards, each with a name: *Tanner, Claussen, Brick, CleanSweep, Susan, Remy, Clifford, Tanner...Tanner...and...Mattie. Especially Mattie.*

The names began to fade.

Gigantis...Stinky.

• • •

Coffee was not match for the hangover. The next morning Matt sat, attempting to rub his headache away before he could face the keyboard. Considering the right words, he began typing, his fingers flying from key to key.

> Toronto, May 20
>
> Dear Readers,
>
> This is Matt Tremain, and I'm back. More than ever, I'm on a quest, a pilgrimage even. I'm in search of the truth. Perhaps, like Diogenes, we all need to seek out honest men and women.
>
> Let me tell you about a story. This one from Arkansas, in the United States. A reader wrote and asked me to consider a story about a suicide, a young girl, eleven years of age, bullied at school.
>
> I think you'll agree with me—"

Matt stopped typing when his phone chirped. He frowned at the intrusion and didn't recognize the number.

"This is Matt." He tried to sound as irritated as he felt.

"I knew something wasn't right." Carling was almost shouting into his ear. "I kept looking to see what was off about it."

"Good morning to you, too."

"Yeah, yeah," Carling sputtered. "Listen. It bothered me from the get-go. I sensed something wrong but couldn't put my finger on it. It hit me last night. Nobody's bothering to match the body with Claussen's prints or DNA. I got crime-scene pictures enlarged. Then I saw it."

Matt's hand tightened on the phone.

"I saw what bothered me. It's the watch. I looked carefully. It wasn't Claussen's watch. He always wore a watch costing more than a new Lexus or Jaguar. I don't know how he arranged it, but that so-called suicide wasn't him. The bastard's pulled a smooth one, I tell you. He's not dead!"

When Matt disconnected the call, he sat, gazing. He felt like he was staring into a dystopian future.

Finally, he typed a message to Cyberia.

# # #

If you enjoyed The CleanSweep Conspiracy, check out other novels by Chuck Waldron

Tears in the Dust.

"I was a party to two murders; therefore, I do not particularly trust in fate...I have given you, my last and only friend, my confession."

So, begins this gripping historical suspense novel set against the backdrop of the Spanish Civil War in 1937. It is with a heavy pen that a reporter, Michael, fulfills his promise to tell the complicated story of his departed friend Alec, who volunteered to fight in the International Brigade, but didn't realize the true price he would pay for his patriotism. Returning from Spain to his home in Vermont, Alec seeks healing but is instead accosted by Samuel T. Harrison, a dark, twisted investigator with a deep hatred of communism. Confronted with the unspeakable, Alec flees and assumes a false identity. But no matter how far Alec goes, he cannot outrun Harrison, who pursues him through the years and across countries only to catch up with him in a stunning conclusion.

Remington and the Mysterious Fedora

In this supernatural mystery, we meet Josh Cody—a smart, young, aspiring author who has challenged himself to write a complete novel in one month. Looking for inspiration, Josh stumbles into a run-down thrift shop and buys a classic Remington manual typewriter and a dusty old fedora. When inexplicable coincidences start to occur and the story of a frightened young woman begins pouring out of him, Josh wonders if the typewriter and fedora are somehow channeling an unsolved mystery from the past. Thus begins Josh's story within a story, and the journey of a lifetime. For readers...and writers... looking for a unique, fast-paced read, *Remington and the Mysterious Fedora* is an entertaining choice.

Served Cold

"An absorbing, taut thriller that keeps you turning the pages as the story shifts from one generation to another.... the action never stops."

~ five-star Amazon Reader Review.

"I have a terrible truth to tell you..." With those disturbing words, Sean Marshall Parker's world is turned upside down. The twenty-seven-year-old must now try to make sense of the fact that the man he has always called dad, sits before him confessing on his deathbed that he is not, in fact, Sean's father. His real parents, Sean learns, were entangled in a violent feud between two warring families. Sean was the casualty of their involvement in a brutal power play that involved deceit, murder and ultimately the need for a new identity and childhood spent in hiding.

Hearing the incredible story of his past, a conflicted Sean seeks atonement for the parents he never knew. As he delves deeper into the horrifying facts of his real life, he must choose whether to succumb to the fate of his brutal heritage or forego the desire for vengeance pulsing in his veins. As the Sicilians say, revenge is a dish best *Served Cold*. More ancient philosophers advise, "Before you embark on a journey of revenge, dig two graves." Walking a tightrope between life and death, Sean struggles to write the next, and perhaps final, chapter of his story.

Visit Chuck's site at Amazon Central
click on Chuck Waldron @ Amazon Central

Waiting for more about the adventures of Matt Tremain, his friends, and what really happened to Charles Claussen?

For reorders email chuck@chuckwaldronauthor.com*. Put preorder in subject line.*

THE CLEANSWEEP COUNTERSTRIKE
A Matt Tremain Novel

CHAPTER 1

BULLSEYE

Matt Tremain trained his eyes on the gun barrel, waiting for the shot. Charles Claussen smirked, aiming the silver 9mm Luger. Matt watched Claussen's finger slowly increase pressure on the trigger and braced himself for the blast.

•••

Jolted awake, Matt struggled to untangle the sweat-soaked sheets. *Another panic attack, the same nightmare. Charles Claussen with that weapon,* he thought. Matt tried to hold on to details, but the images floated away as soon as he opened his eyes. The acrid taste of stale alcohol was a reminder of self-medicating, desperate to stop the recurring night-time terrors.

He cringed, throwing off the sheets as a siren penetrated the quietness. *An ambulance?* he wondered. The city sounds of pre-dawn Toronto replaced the fading siren's wail.

Matt stumbled to the bathroom to rinse the fuzz from his mouth and was alarmed to see the water glass quivering in his hand.

Returning to his bed, Matt tried to rub away the hammering pain, but it didn't help. He tried to ignore the clock display as he drifted between awake and sleep. *It's no use,* he thought.

Matt walked back into the bathroom. He didn't recognize the face in the mirror. Murky bloodshot eyes looked back at him. Matt splashed his face with cold water. It didn't help. *Time to face the world. It's the best I can do.*

Matt had a world-class hangover, like someone tapping on his skull with a hammer. He'd hoped for a free day, no appointments nor commitments. Matt wanted to be left alone with his panic as he opened the door at the Beanery. He needed his go-to hangover cure, a robust Sumatra blend and three extra-strength pain tablets. *At least I'm not puking.*

The crowded coffeehouse was noisy, the aroma thick and curative. The barista handed Matt his coffee. He noticed a couple leaving and walked to the empty table then powered on his laptop. He took a deep breath as he faced the blank screen. Matt felt his skull throbbing. He lowered his chin, rotating his head to ease the pain.

"That's him." Matt heard a young woman at the next table whisper to her companion.

Shit, Matt thought. He wanted privacy. He looked at them until they turned back their conversation.

Matt looked at his computer screen. *It's no use. Who can focus on writing with a hangover like this?* He wanted to go back to the way it was, hiding behind his computer. He knew the clock couldn't be turned back. Matt's life changed forever when he helped blow the whistle on Operation CleanSweep.

Why am I afraid? Matt thought. *Charles Claussen, the man behind CleanSweep, somehow eluded capture. Claussen's a coiled snake, ready to strike without the warning rattle.*

Matt knew it wasn't his imagination. *With Claussen on the loose, I'm not safe. He's after revenge. He has the resources to carry out his threat.*

His phone vibrated and skidded toward the edge of the table. He grabbed it before it dropped to the floor. Matt opened the message and stifled a scream as he examined at the photo. *"My face. A sniper's target superimposed, the bullseye centered on my nose, between the eyes.*

Matt shuddered at the words. "I'm coming for you."

"Damn!" He slammed his phone onto the table. Coffee sloshed over the rim of the cup, covering the table and the back of his computer.

Customers turned. The barista rushed around the counter with a large towel in hand. "Matt, what's wrong? You look like you've seen a ghost."

"I have." He looked at the table. "Sorry for all this, Marsha."

"Claussen?" she asked, using the towel to soak up the coffee, first on the table, then the floor. "People are always claiming to have seen him. There's more sightings of Claussen than Elvis. I had the radio on yesterday. A woman called in, claiming Claussen's living in some rinky-dink town in Florida. Another nutty caller."

Matt didn't reply, keeping his phone display hidden.

"How can it be Claussen? The police said he killed himself—" Marsha was cut short.

It's too much. Matt felt the walls closing in. His face blossomed dark burgundy. "Sorry, Marsha. Sorry, I have to get the hell out of here." He stuffed his computer into his backpack, grabbed his phone, and ran to the door, unsure where to go.

Outside, he punched some numbers and held the phone to his ear. *Voicemail, damn,* he thought. "Carling. It's Matt. Call me. It's urgent."

Matt read the text one more time. "I'm coming for you." *This arriving today. After I had that nightmare.* He didn't welcome the coincidence. *It's Charles Claussen. He's alive.*

Matt was on edge—gripped by fear, paranoia, and sense of doom.

Two young men around nineteen walked toward him. One had a ball cap pulled down to cover his eyes from view. His companion pulled something from his pocket, swinging it upward. They had a 'gangsta' strut, twisting their hands and flashing what could be gang signs. They walked directly toward Matt.

Claussen. You bastard!

The two approached quickly, then brushed past, nudging him, staking a claim to alpha male status.

He wouldn't send punks, Matt thought, trying to shake off his intensifying sense of alarm.

The streetcar approached, clattering to a stop. Instead of getting on immediately, Matt spotted a park across the street. It was a small, grassy area flanked by two apartment buildings that stretched from the road to the lake. He changed his mind, motioning the streetcar driver on.

A bench faced the water. Matt leaned back and tried to relax. A shaft of light sliced through spring-fresh leaves, and he felt like an actor captured in the spotlight. He tilted his head back, wanting to absorb the warmth, but his body couldn't shake off the dread.

Matt removed his laptop from the backpack. His anger grew as he scrolled through the files. He felt something else: a wave of sadness. He located a blog post. Matt started rereading the blog he wrote after Charles Claussen and CleanSweep were exposed.

•••

The Evil of CleanSweep, by Matt Tremain

Looking back over the past months, I keep asking myself one question, a single word. How? How does evil like this grow and fester among us? The evil of CleanSweep wasn't imported. It grew on the inside like cancer.

We are distracted by speeches and tweets about terrorism, losing sleep, thinking hooded men are standing poised, ready to behead us. We've been shown the launder list of people to keep out, immigrants who don't speak our language, people who worship differently. We want to build walls, physical and virtual. What about the hate creating domestic terrorism?

Now, we have a poster boy for hate—the face of Charles Claussen.

Norman Rockwell created four paintings representing what our country stands for: Freedom of Speech, Freedom of Worship, Freedom from Want, and Freedom from Fear.

Claussen's versions are a perversion.

Speech? The first to go was Freedom of Speech. Anyone not agreeing with him would be heckled, threatened, or worse.

Religion? Sanctioned churches only. No Jews, Muslims, nor new age meditators need to apply.

Want? He claimed hard work and determination would free people from want. Those left behind needed to be gradually eliminated. Costly social programs will no longer suck the budget dry, thanks to a CleanSweep administration.

Fear. What about Freedom from Fear? Claussen's manifesto stated that people with nothing to hide from the government have no reason to fear.

I wonder how Norman Rockwell would paint Claussen's CleanSweep vision. A friendly janitor CleanSweeping away grit and grime, along with the great unwashed.

A text ringtone interrupted his reading and his gaze shifted on the screen of his cell phone. "In court now Got UR message We need 2 meet 10-8 @ 3."

Matt smiled and tried to relax. Talking to his best friend would help.

Matt looked at the glass-like surface of the water as the wind vacuumed waves away. He watched as a fish broke the surface and disappeared as quickly, spreading rippling concentric rings. Matt shuddered.

•••

Hidden in the shadows of a nearby building, a young man pulled back his hood, raising a phone to his ear.

Matt couldn't shake the feeling of rising panic as he walked back to the streetcar stop.